HellBound Books'

ANTHOLOGY of CAMPFIRE STORIES

Curated by Xtina Marie

A HellBound Books LLC Publication
Copyright © 2025 by HellBound Books Publishing LLC
All Rights Reserved

Cover and art design by Tee Arts
for
HellBound Books Publishing LLC

No part of this book may be reproduced, stored in a retrieval system, or transmitted by any means, electronic, mechanical, photocopying, recording or otherwise without written permission from the author
This book is a work of fiction. Names, characters, places and incidents are entirely fictitious or are used fictitiously and any resemblance to actual persons, living or dead, events or locales is purely coincidental.

www.hellboundbookspublishing.com

Contents:

t

This is How You'll Die Tonight

John Schlimm

<u>Note to the Reader:</u>

Dear Aspiring Slasher—

The following scripted activities, which you should refer to as "stories," just "silly-little-harmless stories is all"— categorized as "Option 1: Outdoors" and "Option 2: Indoors" to offer versatility—work best if a few pieces of seasoned advice are followed:

1. *This concept works the absolute best around a cozy, roaring campfire—see Option 1—while toasting marshmallows and before everyone retires to their sleeping bags (Please just avoid going rogue, and cliché, by wearing a hockey mask for it.). But it can also be executed—pun intended—indoors—see Option 2—at a friendly sleepover between pillow fights, gossip, and snackies*

2. *Choose one person to focus the story on. In fact, an audience of only one is preferred, and easiest*

for all the obvious reasons. Though if a group is gathered, then this story can simply be considered foreshadowing for another time—consider then the said "another time" as a sneak attack to come—rather than for the imminent future.

3. *Both options below work best if all cell phones are confiscated or the overnight shenanigans take place somewhere that is out of range for cell service.*

4. *Begin by suggesting that the other person tell a scary story first. It's the polite thing to do. After their story nearly bores you to death, it's game time. Then begin yours.*

5. *Finally, above all, HAVE FUN! This is the moment you've been waiting for!*

READY, SET, MORE GORE!

X

P.S. Bonus Tip: If at any point or points, and it will unfortunately happen because people are candy-asses, your audience grows frightened or freaked out while you're telling the story, simply smile, chuckle, brush it all off, and reassure them that this is all in good fun—just a silly-little-harmless story. After all, isn't this part of the sleepover experience? Then continue on from where you left off.

***

Option 1: Outdoors

YOU: "Okay, so have you ever heard the story called 'This is How You'll Die Tonight'?... I didn't think so, since I created it!

This is how it's going to happen: I'm going to start by tickling you. That's right. I'm going to get right up there in your armpits and tickle away, until your resistance turns to uncontrollable giggling. At which point, I'll slip the razor blade that's currently in my pocket into my right hand. While my left hand continues to tickle your right pit, my right hand will proceed to rapidly slice into your left pit.

At first you won't notice how I'm shredding your capillaries, lymph nodes, and sweat glands, unleashing a soupy blend of blood and body odor.

But when you finally do notice, your giddy laughter will turn to disbelief, but then you'll realize that I actually did tell you step-by-step how this was going to go down tonight. Once the realization and panic set in, I'll step back and simply instruct you with a single word: 'RUN!'

You may forget me saying this now, which I'm counting on: I've spent several days exploring this outdoor area, so I know the surrounding terrain like the back of my hand. Unlike you. In fact, I picked this very spot on purpose. And yesterday, I was here setting hidden traps in all directions to insure you'll never escape.

So, when you finally do turn and run, it will ninety-nine percent be in the exact direction I'm counting on.

I plan to give you to the count of ten. It's only fair since I will have sprung this on you out of nowhere.

In fact, by the count of ten, I should hear you scream, followed by a swishing, crackling, clomping down series of noises.

I'll smile.

I'll know I can take my time, because you're not going anywhere.

When I catch up to you and shine my flashlight on you, this is what I'll see: three strands of barbed wire deeply embedded—thanks to the sheer force of your hysterical running—in your ankles, your thighs, and your neck. These heights were specifically tailored for your size. This is very much a bespoke slashing. You should feel honored that someone is going to all this trouble just for you!

I'll tell you to calm down— 'CALM THE FUCK DOWN!,' if necessary. Then I'll proceed to rip the strands of barbed wire from your body—barb by beautifully-sculpted barb, each one's small spikes tearing and shredding your flesh as it's roughly yanked out.

Once done, I'll give you to the count of ten again. But I'll let you in on a little secret: I'll actually count to fifteen since you'll be slightly incapacitated now with all those small, gushing gashes. HA! *Gushing gashes*, now that's poetic!

Okay, then I'll start walking in pursuit of my prey— YOU! The trees and brush here are particularly thick, so, unfortunately for you, you'll more or less have to stay on the path I tricked you into taking from the start.

Soon I'll hear the loudest screams of pain yet, but hopefully not before I hear the metallic *SNAP!* Even—and this is best-case scenario, for me—the *SNAP! SNAP! SNAP!*

I'll start jogging towards you, the excitement and adrenaline rush getting the best of me. In fact, I can already feel those electric juices rising inside of me, just telling you all this.

What I hope to see when I arrive and shine my flashlight up and down the length of your body—and again this is best-case scenario, but with room for human error, as in your error in fucking it up—is you on the ground *CHOMPED! CHOMPED! CHOMPED!* by the metal jaws of the bear traps in three places: an upper arm, a love handle, and an ankle. I staged them carefully so you'd run into one that would ideally grab your ankle, causing you to scrunch and fall into the other two in quick succession, before you realize what's happening.

What I hope to not find is your head in mid bite down, because then it will be game over way too early.

There's no soft way to put this, so I'll give it to you straight: this is going to hurt like *fuuucking* hell, but it's not meant to kill you.

Once again, I'll calm you down, and pry open each of the razor-sharp traps long enough for you to pull out your hashed flesh. Your ankle and upper arm bones will be broken, possibly even protruding through your fileted skin. Your love handle will more or less have something akin to a shark bite taken out of it—I'm talking a sand shark, not Jaws here, so no worries.

This time, I'll give you to the count of thirty, but really forty, to get your head start. Heck, I'll even help stand you up before I announce, 'READY, SET, MORE GORE!' You know what, maybe I'll give you to the count of forty-five to drag your mashed-up body. I mean, it's not like you're going to get far.

Now by this time—knowing you like I do, and like any character running from the slasher in a horror film—I know that you're going to try to get off the path. In theory, wise move. But in reality, I saw this coming at this point, so the long stretch of path you're on is a solid wall of wild rose bushes on either side. Meaning long, sharp thorns.

Sorry, but when I hear the thrashing in the bushes and screams this time, I'll be rolling my eyes. I mean, SOOO PREDICTABLE! The real badass move would be to stay on the path. No one ever stays on the path, which becomes one of their final, dumbass, fatal mistakes.

Okay, so by the time I get to you and shine my flashlight on you, I'll find a human pincushion right here in the wilds. Please forgive me now—ahead of time—for laughing, but I won't be able to help myself.

Just like with the barbed wire, there's no subtle way to do this—the band-aide just needs to be ripped right the fuck off—fast and furiously! So, I'll get the best grip I can on you, and yank and pull your mangled ass free.

And keep in mind, the only weapon I'll have on me is the small razor blade. Which I will then use again when I swipe it across your one eyeball.

Since you'll be rendered a human cyclops, you'll get to the count of sixty to haul ass . . . well, hobble anyway . . . this time, which will bore me out of my mind. I may even stop counting and just wing it, which will be to your advantage.

Except, about a hundred yards down the path—which you will now reliably stay on—you'll come to a wide, rocky creek that is pretty much always full and raging.

You'll stop at the creek's edge. Your upper arm will be shattered, your ankle bones—Did you know there are fourteen of them? —will be crushed, there will be a big old bite out of your love handle, your one eye will be slit open, and your entire body will be oozing blood, sweat, and probably by this time some serious piss and shit.

You'll never see or hear me coming up behind you. If I squint, you'll appear hunched over in silhouette, much like a saintly figure drawn to the water for meditative purposes. No doubt you probably will be meditating on the mindfuck quandary of WHAT THE FUCK IS HAPPENING?

I'll pause to enjoy this moment, too. After all, we need to stop every once in a while, and just embrace and appreciate the moment we're in. You've got to smell the roses, right?

But then, I will shove you so fucking hard that you'll be airborne for the second or two before your rag doll body splashes into the rapids, bangs around on and off the rocks like you're in a pinball machine, and is then carried down the creek, over a small, dammed waterfall, and is eventually caught in the net I strung across it yesterday.

My plan—but then you know what they say about plans: 'We make plans, and God laughs!'—my plan is to get to you and drag you out of the water before you drown. Because there will still be one final activity on our schedule for tonight . . . well, actually two.

But don't worry, I'll be doing all the heavy lifting from here on out, since you'll hardly be able to move anymore.

Okay, so after I remove you from the water like the drenched log you'll be, I'll pull you to these incredible, sandy mounds of fire ants I discovered, which was such a bonus gift. Before I found them, this all was going to wrap up at the creek and then back at our campsite.

Did you know that a single mound can house between 100,000 to 500,000 fire ants?

Careful not to get any of those nasty little fuckers on myself, I'll toss your body onto the crawling colonies so the residents can have a feast unlike any they've ever had before.

Then I plan to return to camp to get some much-deserved shut-eye.

About an hour before dawn, I'll return to the fire ant mounds. Certainly you don't think I'd just leave you there? I wouldn't be much of a friend if I did that, would I?

I'll be bringing enough spray back along to kill all the ants munching on you and around you, mainly so I can then get a good, ant-free grip on you.

I'll pry you loose from the ant colonies and drag you back here to our campsite.

You can rest a bit while I build up the fire.

Finally, just before the first sunlight passes above the tree line, I'll toss your body on the fire. You should be good and dry by then. If there's one thing I can't stand, it's when wet shit is thrown on a fire and it becomes all smoky.

I'll be really interested to see if you have any fight or scream, or even a moan, left in you.

While you're cooking—pun so intended—I'll be whipping up some scrambled eggs, bacon, coffee, and maybe even a peanut butter and jelly mountain pie dessert over the coals, which should be red-hot and perfect by then.

Now to the best part; well . . . best part for me anyway, though you have a big role to play in it, too. Depending on how long you live, I've decided on First-, Second-, and Third-Place prizes for myself, just to make it more fun for all involved. I've always been the competitive type.

Okay, so here's how it'll work: if you die before you get to the creek, which would be *sooooo booorrring*, I get Third Place, which is a replica Chucky Good Guys doll. If you croak in the creek or on the fire ant hills, I get Second Place, which is a 1978 movie-worn Michael Myers mask I saw on eBay that's been signed by all the biggies—Jamie Lee Curtis, John Carpenter, Donald Pleasance, Kyle Richards, The Shadow himself, Nick Castle, P.J. Soles, Nancy Stephens, Sandy Johnson, Nancy Loomis, and John Michael Graham.

BUT, if you can make it—and please, *pretty-pretty-please* do your best to try—until I toss you on the campfire, then I will win First Place, which is . . . *drumroll please* . . . a ticket to see the kid, who's all grown up now, that played the original Jason Voorhees playing with his punk-and-heavy-metal band First Jason live in concert!

Just a heads-up before we proceed here: I REALLY want First Place!"

****

Option 2: Indoors
YOU: "Okay, so have you ever heard the story called 'This is How You'll Die Tonight'? . . . I didn't think so since I created it!

This is how it's going to happen: I'm going to start a pillow fight with you here on the floor in my bedroom. Playful, with our soft, down feather stuffed pillows, all *ha-*

ha and *he-he, until* . . . . I reach for the pillow that I constructed by wrapping a heavy living room pillow in razor blades fastened down by electrical tape and covering it all with a fresh white pillowcase. I considered using nails, but I realized the whole damn thing would get stuck in you and just make it clumsy and awkward to tear out so we could continue.

Once you realize the pillow is slicing you like pepperoni, you'll naturally freak out, scream at me, ask what's going on, *blah, blah, blah.* When my response to your predictable reaction is to laugh and keep swinging, I'm counting on you to finally take your fucking cue and start running. If you don't, I'll yell, 'RUN, BITCH!'

Even though there are several rooms upstairs here to run into, you'll predictably gun it for the staircase leading downstairs.

Did you know that when folks are scared and running, the bottoms of their feet hit the ground with more pressure per square inch than usual? Not to mention running down steps, allowing gravity to also play a part.

Okay, so as you bound dramatically down the steps—adrenaline, confusion, and blood pumping from the razor-thin slit marks all over your body—your bare feet will eventually pound down on one—hopefully more—of the several steps on which I placed strips of nails pointing up.

AHA! I got to use the nails after all. And I picked the rustiest ones I could find.

You won't know what happened at first as you feel dozens of stabbing, stinging sensations penetrate your heels, arches, soles, and toes. I'm banking on them sinking in there really good and tight, so you twist, tumble, and fall the rest of the way down, hopefully getting stuck and lacerated elsewhere along the way. I mean, how cool would it be if this is how you first lose an eye?

Numbly, I tried to pick Isaac up by his feet, but admittedly I wasn't much help, and I knew it. I let the man with the rifle take the lead, mainly because he seemed like he knew where he was going. As if he was reading my mind, a few minutes later, he finally said, "The cabin is just up ahead."

True to his word, a short while later, the shape of a small log cabin came into view through the trees. Once we'd made it onto the porch, the man with the rifle sat Isaac down and unlocked the front door. "Hurry up, help me get him on the bed."

I did as told, then stood back, watching as the man tore open a cabinet in the kitchen. He rushed back over to Isaac with bottles and some kind of gauze, and all I could do was stare. I think I was in shock. Maybe I should have said something to Isaac during that time—I don't know. Things happened so quickly that I was still taking time to catch up. I finally said, "Is—is he going to be all right?"

The man didn't immediately respond.

"Please," I continued, "be honest with me."

"I don't know."

There was a terrible sinking feeling in the pit of my stomach. "If anything happens—"

The man poured something around the gaping wound in Isaac's stomach, and there was the sound of something hissing. "To kill infection," he said.

"If anything happens, Christ, I'll have to tell his parents..."

"Look, I'm sorry this happened to you and your friend. Will you just give me a moment in silence to finish what I'm doing?"

I stopped pacing immediately. "I'm sorry."

What bothered me was the absolute lack of reaction on Isaac's part. His response was almost catatonic. When the man was done, he stood back, as if to survey his work. "It'll have to do," he said. "For now."

He crossed the room, again to the kitchen, and began washing the blood from his hands in the sink. I said, "I'm sorry. For talking so much. I was just worried."

"You're fine." He switched the water off and wiped his hands dry on his trousers. "I ought to be the one apologizing. I know what it's like to be in that sort of situation for the first time."

We stood, for a moment, without speaking. Finally, I asked, "Back there—you said there's nobody around for miles. We'd just walked from the main road. It isn't that far. Couldn't we call for a hospital or something?"

"I'm afraid you're mistaken." He exhaled as he sat down in a chair adjacent the bed, then gestured for me to do the same. "When I said we're in the middle of nowhere, I meant it. Your friend; what's his name?"

"Isaac."

"Isaac wouldn't be able to wait that long." He glanced up from the floor to look at me, as if he were actually looking at me for the first time. "And you?"

"Oh, I'm Tabitha."

"I'm Saul."

"I wish I could say it was nice to meet you, Saul." I glanced to the one small window sat high in the western wall. It was getting dark out, and beyond the constraints of that window, I heard the sound of howling. "Those things. What are they?"

"*Chiens de L'enfer*. The hounds of Hell."

"Those stories are true." It wasn't a question so much as it was a statement. I glanced at Isaac again.

Saul reached for a pipe and lit it. It was an old-fashioned thing, the kind that produced rings of blue smoke. Like something one might have seen their grandfather smoking. It only occurred to me, then, how old everything about him seemed to look. He wasn't physically old, maybe middle-aged at best, but his clothing, and even the rifle he'd placed by the front door, looked like something out of one of Isaac's studies.

"How do you keep them away?" I said.

"Like anything of that ilk. Salt."

I nodded, but I had no idea what he was talking about. "How long have you been out here by yourself?"

"You're awfully inquisitive."

I probably went red. "Sorry."

"You're fine. It's just that I am not particularly used to having company these days."

"That… makes sense."

"What does Isaac do?"

"I'm sorry?"

"What kind of work?"

"Oh. He just graduated from college. He's been studying history." I glanced at him again. It didn't seem fair. "He was really excited about it."

Saul didn't say anything, but he didn't have to. I knew Isaac's chances weren't good. Again, however, as if he was reading my mind, Saul said, "If he pulls through the night, he might make it."

"Those dogs… Those hounds of Hell, or whatever you called them, they damn near ripped him apart. Do you really think he'll be all right?"

"I can't say for sure. But I do know I'm going to do my best to make sure you get out of this mess." He glanced in the direction of the window at the sound of something outside and rose from his seat at once. "Infernal beasts. They must have tracked us here from the scent of blood."

"Are we still safe here?"

He reached for the rifle by the door. I didn't like how he hesitated when he spoke. "Should be. But… I'm going outside to check the perimeter. Stay here. And Tabitha?"

I turned to face him. "Yeah?"

"Whatever happens, don't look them in the eyes."

I watched him leave, then returned to the chair by Isaac's bedside. From beyond the cabin walls, I heard muffled grunting, varied barks and short, sharp bursts of howls. Each sound was another nail in the coffin, I thought. There was no way we were getting out of this one. I huddled in the chair, pulling my legs to my chest, and glanced at Isaac. Thought of the time we'd spent together, all those years—not knowing what awaited us at the end of it all, during our celebratory trip to the French countryside. We had visited the cathedrals and cemeteries and sacred sites all around that area of the country, satiating Isaac's thirst for all things historical. It was only natural, I thought. Yet it was only then when I remembered the camera.

If we did manage to make it out, would anybody believe us? At that point, would it even matter? I turned and reached for his backpack, when I finally heard the sound of my own name.

"Tabby."

He was awake. I released my grip on the backpack, for the moment the camera forgotten. I said, "Isaac. Oh, honey, don't try to talk. You're hurt."

He made a noise, a grunt that would have been laughter under any other circumstance. "I noticed." His gaze, made glassy and distant from pain, coasted around the room. "Where are we?"

"Saul's cabin." I could tell he had no idea what I was talking about, and rightly so. I added, "Don't worry about it. For right now, you're safe."

For a moment, neither of us spoke. I wasn't sure what I could do for him, if anything. It took me a moment afterward to realize he was trying to push himself upright. "Hey, hey. You don't want to do that."

He winced as he said, "Don't tell me what to do."

Again, had the circumstances been different, he would have been grinning as he said it, but there were no reasons to pretend otherwise now. "Isaac, will you just tell me what you're trying to do so I can help?"

"My watch."

I hadn't even thought about it. It had been a graduation gift from his father—a linked silver band, its face reading not only the time but the date, and doubtlessly expensive, at that. I reached for the sleeve of his jacket, the fabric stiffening with drying blood. At first, the wristwatch seemed intact, untouched—but then I turned it and saw the glass portion was starred. I wasn't sure what to say to him, but it turned out that I didn't need to.

"It's broken, isn't it?"

"I'm sorry."

He cursed as he exhaled. After a pause, I continued, "Well, maybe we can get it repaired…"

"When, Tabby?"

It wasn't a sarcastic remark. I could see exactly what he meant, but I didn't yet want to admit defeat. There was a sound at the door then, and for a moment I was certain it was death waiting on the other side. Saul stepped in and closed the door firmly behind him, saying, "It should hold for now."

Neither of us immediately responded. Saul moved around the cabin with some purpose I didn't yet understand, and it wasn't until he'd procured a candle and a match that I realized what he was doing. "Your friend," he said, setting the lit candle on the table in the center of the room. "How is he doing?"

He hadn't noticed. I said, "Isaac's awake."

Saul's expression was almost startled. He crossed the room to join us. The light made it a little easier to see, but the flickering of the shadows against the walls felt almost claustrophobic. He took the chair at the foot of the bed.

"Isaac," he said, his voice quiet in the silence otherwise. "I'm Saul. Your friend, Tabitha, tells me you studied history."

Isaac started to respond, but his voice caught. Saul continued, "You don't have to talk. But I'm going to take a look at the bandages, all right?"

I turned away as Saul lifted the tattered remains of Isaac's shirt. I didn't want to have to look at it. Saul finally said, "They seem to be holding up, so far. You've stopped bleeding."

"It really hurts."

"I know." Saul pulled away. "I have whiskey, but if you were to start bleeding again, it would only make things worse."

None of us said anything for what felt like a long time. If it wasn't already clear, I was certain it was going to be a long night. At some point, however, Isaac fell asleep, and I turned to Saul and asked if it was safe to go outside, on the front porch. "I haven't heard any noises in a long time."

He seemed to think about it for a moment. "I'll join you."

Outside, the sky was black and starless. I pulled my jacket tighter around myself and glanced out, through the sea of trees and fallen leaves. He must have been right about one thing, I thought: There didn't seem to be anyone or anything else around for miles. I said, "How did you end up out here, Saul? All by yourself. Barricaded against those… things."

"My brother and I, we traveled here from England. It was just supposed to be a hunting trip. How long ago it's been, I couldn't tell you." He reached for the pipe I didn't realize he'd brought out with him. The amber glow from the light was a warmth in the darkness. "When we were in town, we heard the stories, of course, but we didn't believe them. Wild dogs were one thing. But some mystical beast, a 'hound of Hell'? Who would ever think such a thing was real?"

I thought of the reactions the two of us had garnered in the local pub when we'd mentioned wanting to explore the woodland. Suddenly it didn't seem so funny.Saul continued.

"We went, regardless. My brother noticed something was wrong before I did. We made it close to three miles in before we got lost. And then we found the cave."

I glanced at him. "Cave?"

"One of the entrances to Hell. There's supposed to be several, all around the world. I don't know about that, but I *do* know there's one here. In these very woods."

It took a moment for me to process. Finally, I said, "What happened to your brother?"

He didn't say anything, for a while. Then, simply, he said, "The dogs."

It suddenly made sense why he'd seemed so determined to get us out of this. A distant howl rose from the silence, followed by several more echoing cries. Saul and I looked at each other. "It's time to go in," he said. "Even if they can't breach the salt circle, you don't want to be out here with them around."

Wordlessly, I followed him back into the cabin, but my mind was flurried with all the information I'd absorbed over the course of the day. Isaac was knowledgeable when it came to mythology; par for the course with studying ancient history—but still, the situation begged the question: What was reality, and what was fantasy?

The night dragged on restlessly.

It was just after dawn when I noticed Isaac beginning to stir. His breathing was labored. I tried to quell the rising panic in my chest, and said, "Isaac, what's wrong?"

He didn't immediately respond. Finally, he said, "It hurts."

I reached for his hand. "It's going to be all right, yeah? Saul is going to get us out of this."

"Tabby, it *really* hurts."

"I know, honey." I gripped his hand tighter. "You've just got to hang on a little longer. We'll be out of here soon."

He said my name again, the nickname he'd called me by almost from day one of our friendship—and then shifted, grew still.

"Isaac?" I said.

There was no response.

"Isaac," I repeated, then rose to my feet. "Isaac, honey." I turned to Saul and started to scream for him. "Saul, it's Isaac. He's—he's… Oh, Christ…"

Saul was up and standing at the sound of his own name. The frenzied look in his eye only softened once he glanced from me, to Isaac, and back again. For a long time, as the sun rose over the frostbitten landscape, neither of us spoke. I gripped Isaac's hand and wept. Eventually Saul drew to my side and placed his hand on my shoulder. He said, "I'm sorry, Tabitha."

"I really thought—he was going to make it."

Saul was silent, contemplating. "The dogs. When they get a taste of blood, they're uncontrollable. They roam the woods every night in search of prey. The same thing happened to my brother." He was quiet for a moment longer, then repeated his condolences. "I really am sorry about your friend."

Where was I supposed to go from there, I wondered. If I made it out of there myself—and that was, indeed, a big *if*—I would have to relay the news to Isaac's parents. The thought of it destroyed me.

"Tabitha," Saul said, at last. I don't know how long I'd sat there by Isaac's side without speaking. He nudged my shoulder lightly. "I am not trying to be insensitive to your pain, but I ought to bury him before too long."

"Wait." I swiped at the tears gathering in the corners of my eyes, but it ultimately did little to dispel them. I worked at the silver link which clasped the watch to his wrist, managed to free it. Even though the face of the clock was broken, I wanted to keep it with me, in memory of him. Then I finally let go of his hand, placed it at his side. "Saul, if there's anything I can do to help…"

He shook his head. "I'll take care of it."

For a moment, I watched as he fetched a shovel from the closet in the corner of the kitchen, and the shocking reality of the situation struck me, suddenly and wholly, all at once. I looked away as he opened the door and stepped outside. The room was silent in his absence.

At first, I tried to escape the thought of Isaac. I didn't want to accept the truth of what had happened—my dearest friend in the world was dead. It was not a reality which I had any desire to participate in; not any further. I said, "I'm so sorry, Isaac."

Sometime later—I don't know how much time had passed—Saul appeared in the doorway. I'd sat there by Isaac's side the entire time he'd been outside, the morning lost in the slipstream of time. "If you're ready," he said.

I didn't think I'd ever be ready, not really—but there was no other choice. I nodded and drew away from Isaac's side for the last time.

The skies beyond the treetops were endless, dusky and blue. I glanced up through the tangle of branches to its vaulted heights. The sun was shining. Fallen leaves crunched beneath Saul's heavy boots as he carried out the task of laying Isaac to rest. I stood without speaking. Nor did I move, nor even think. All I did was feel the weight of his wristwatch, turning it in my hands.

"I'm going to kill them," I said.

Saul glanced up at me but didn't say anything. I continued. "If nothing else, I'll send them back to Hell. So this won't happen to anyone else. His death, I'll make sure it wasn't in vain."

Saul dropped another shovelful of dirt into the makeshift grave. "I said the same thing."

The sound of his voice snapped me out of my trance. I think I was still in shock. "What is it?"

"When my brother died, I swore vengeance on those beasts. Or, at the very least, I swore I'd prevent the same thing from happening to anybody else." He wiped at his brow. "I guess I didn't do a very good job of it, after all."

"How long have you been out here, Saul?"

"I told you; I have no idea. The days and nights, they blend together and become one out in these woods. I have looked for the road," he added, "but I've never been able to find it again."

"The cave. Would you be able to take me there?"

He frowned. "Look, girl. I know how you feel. Believe me, I do. But I don't think that would be in your best interest."

I looked to the broken glass of Isaac's wristwatch, saw the date frozen behind its reflective surface—10/29. Had it really only been a single day? I thought about it for a moment, then clasped the watch around my own wrist. "Saul, please. I don't care what happens from here on out, as long as I know I tried to do the right thing."

He paused, squinted against the sunlight. "You're serious about this, aren't you?"

I didn't say anything. I didn't have to.

"Their patterns are pretty unpredictable, but they are more likely to travel in packs at night. In the daytime, if they're out at all, it's likely to only be one or two." He stood back at long last, surveying his work. The damp earth rose into a small mound before us, marking Isaac's grave. For a moment, neither of us spoke. Then he looked to me and said, "Do you know how to shoot a gun?"

"I took fencing in high school."

"Close enough. Come along."

He led me into the cabin, opened the closet in the kitchen where the shovel had been stored. "This," he said, handing me a hunting rifle, "was my brother's. You don't point it at something unless you intend to fire, all right? Just aim and squeeze the trigger right here. You got that?"

It was a lot to take in at once, but I thought I could handle it. I nodded.

"All right. These things, the hounds of Hell, you can't kill them permanently, I don't think. But you *can* stave them off."

"That isn't good enough. I want them dead."

He stopped and stared at me.

I thought back to what he'd said about salt being a repellent for them. "Isn't there some way we can pack the barrels with salt, or something?"

"I hadn't thought of that," he admitted. "You're good. There isn't much left, but…"

I made a point of adding as much salt to the barrel as possible. If my plan was going to work out even remotely close to what I had in mind, Saul wouldn't be needing much more supplies. He would be coming back to civilization, I thought. With me.

Before we started out, I made a point to fetch Isaac's camera from his backpack and placed it securely in my own bag. I didn't want to leave the memories behind. I'd lost too much already.

We finally left for the cave later that afternoon. The world seemed quiet as we trekked forward; impossibly so. I kept thinking of Isaac.

"I think we're getting close," Saul said, at last.

It was almost dusk now, and it seemed like we'd been walking for hours. Still, we probably didn't have much time to work with. If we caught them just as they left the cave, it might have been enough to destroy the entire pack. If we missed that chance, well…

He was walking a few paces ahead of me when he suddenly came to a halt and crouched down. "Tabitha," he whispered, motioning me forward, "we're here."

I lowered my rifle, its weight awkward and unfamiliar in my hands, and knelt next to him among the dried leaves and foliage. "What do we do now?"

His eyes scanned the woods ahead, presumably for any sign of the beasts. "We ought to wait until we see them leave. Take them out, one-by-one, for as long as we can."

"We fire at one, they're all bound to go completely batshit on us."

He glanced at me, and for a moment didn't say anything. "That's the risk we're going to have to take," he said, at last. He reached for his own rifle, then turned to face me. "Do you remember what I told you, last night at the cabin?"

I blinked at him, uncertain.

"Whatever you do, don't look them directly in the eye."

I nodded, attempting to appear braver than I actually felt. It was easy to say one thing about the beasts—during Isaac's burial, I was determined to take them out. I still wanted revenge, but it was something entirely different to be crouching outside the cave that the creatures called home. Indeed, it was easy to feel vulnerable, exposed, in that moment.

The air was growing colder, the skies darker. A sliver of moon rose against the horizon as the sun began its steady descent. I readjusted my grip on the rifle, tried to steady my hands. I had no idea if this was going to work—if it didn't, it doubtlessly meant death in the jaws of the dogs.

"Do you feel that?" Saul said. I'd been totally lost in my own world, until his voice jarred me back to reality. "The heat."

It didn't make sense—at least, not for the time being. For a moment, the wind that shifted through the bare branches was frigid. The next second, the temperature seemed to soar. By the time we heard the echo of claws on stone, the woods around felt like a blazing inferno. It was an entrance, I remembered, to Hell.

The first among them materialized all at once from the darkness of the cave's mouth. It was enormous; taut muscles rippling beneath tufts of coarse, black hair. There was an almost ethereal quality to it, I thought. Like trying to fix your eyes on a moving target, it appeared to be constantly shifting, immaterial. The acrid stench of sulfur filled the air as a second beast appeared from the shadows, then another.

Saul cursed and fired at once. It occurred to me that we'd waited too long—the chance to take them down one-by-one as they'd left the cave was gone. Both of us had been frozen to the spot and acted far too late. In spite of my trembling hands, I did my best to aim at one of them and squeezed the trigger. There was an eruption of salt and gunpowder—the beast yelped and skittered backward, as if wounded. I couldn't believe I'd actually managed to hit it. I tried to aim and fire a second time, but nothing happened. The rifle was jammed.

There wasn't much time to dwell, for Saul was suddenly on his feet. "Tabitha," he said, "there's too many of them. I didn't account for this."

The clearing below was swarming with the hideous things, and the chief amongst them had taken notice of us.

"I'm going to distract them. I want you to make a run for it."

"What?"

"Remember what I said—don't look them in the eye."

It was black as pitch now. I could hardly make out my surroundings, save for the scarce light of the moon from above. All I could do was watch as Saul fired into the air, then began running in the opposite direction.

It wasn't supposed to happen this way, I thought. None of this should have happened.

I took off in the direction of the cabin—or at least what I could distinguish of it. In the darkness, the trees all looked the same. Panic rose into a sharp sting inside my chest. Was I supposed to wait for him at the cabin? Was I supposed to make a run for the road? I didn't know what to do, and I couldn't think. The only thing I could do was to keep running.

The sounds of tearing, howling, frenzied barking carried on the wind. It almost sounded like laughter.

I thought of Saul, hoped and prayed he'd made it out of there. Somehow, I thought, somehow…

I thought of Isaac, my best and dearest friend, lying in a makeshift grave somewhere amongst the woodland, and of how he'd deserved so much better than he'd gotten.

They were closer, now. I could hear them. Tearing through the underbrush. Destroying all that stood in their path. They wanted me, I thought. I could feel the heat, smell the reek of sulfur and blood as they drew near. Up ahead, I saw lights piercing the darkness. I was certain they'd finally caught up with me, that the eyes of the dogs were the very eyes of death…

…And then I crashed out of the line of trees and collapsed to my knees on the gravel that lay beyond it. The lights were not the harbingers of doom that I'd thought they were—it was merely, bafflingly, the light of day. I glanced around, dazed, as a truck slowed to a halt nearby. A moment later, the doors to the truck flew open, and a man and woman dressed in farm clothes came running over to me. They spoke in French, and I understood very little of it in that moment, but I could hear the worry in their voices.

I tried to slow down, tried to think. Looked to the lush, dark thicket from which I'd somehow just escaped. The woodland beyond was quiet and still, as if nothing bad had ever happened there.

"Mademoiselle," the woman said, her English imperfect but relatively clear, "are you hurt? Please, talk to us."

I couldn't help myself. I burst into tears. How had I made it out, when Isaac hadn't? Where was Saul?

The man said something to the woman in French. It was something akin to, "I think she's in shock."

He gave me his overcoat, and the two of them walked me to their truck and sat me down. The woman said, "We are taking you to town, yes? We will call for an ambulance for you."

Numbly, I nodded, then felt for Isaac's wristwatch like it was my own personal buoy in the middle of a raging sea. I glanced down at it, and for a moment I thought it was only a trick of the light from beyond the window: The clock-face was no longer broken, but instead a smooth panel of unblemished glass. The ticking hands revealed the time to be a little before twelve o'clock in the afternoon, mere moments after the two of us had stepped foot into the thicket. The display behind it also read the same date that Isaac and I had set out for the woodland, our fated final adventure before returning home to the United States.

"The day," I said, looking up at the woman sitting next to me. "What day is it?"

She stared at me as if she were uncertain. The road opened up to the familiar hamlet of Havre de la Rose.

Lights glowed in the distance, promising warmth and comfort, but it was a reality to which I knew I'd never be able to return. At long last, she responded, her features etched with obvious concern as she spoke.

"It's October 29th, Mademoiselle. A Saturday."

***

"Did you hear about that American woman?"

Elise glanced up from her notebook as her boyfriend Don slid into the adjacent seat. It was a quiet evening in the local tavern; a pleasant hum of conversation suspended in the air. She sat upright, the notes she'd been taking forgotten in the moment, and said, "No. What about it?"

"This couple found her on the road just outside the Havre de la Rose. She was all bloodied and crying. Hysterical."

"What happened to her?"

Don reached into the pocket of his jacket and withdrew a cigarette. He was quiet as he lit it, the amber glow of its end looking something like a tiny orb of fire in the dim light. He finally said, "Outside of that town, there's a stretch of woodland that goes for miles. If local legend is to be believed, those woods are inhabited by some type of demonic beasts. Enormous dogs, ravenous things—hounds of Hell."

Elise thought about it. "What does that have to do with the woman they found?"

"Well, that's just it. For a while, nobody could make sense of what she was saying. They took her to the closest hospital, where she finally calmed down long enough to explain. She said the dogs were real, that they had killed her friend. That there was some kind of time loop, out there in the woods." He exhaled smoke. "Madness."

"That's crazy."

"Yes. I imagine there were drugs involved."

"The woman," Elise said, "where is she now?"

"Last I heard, she was still in the hospital. I assume there's going to be an investigation, and all that. Since there was a murder involved."

It was strange for her to think about how something so horrible could happen in such a peaceful place. The quiet serenity of the countryside in autumn—what had really taken place out in those woods, she thought.

"Word is the local police are going to put up trespassing signs. To keep anyone else from wandering in." Don puffed on his cigarette, and for a moment the two of them didn't say anything further. After a pause, he added, "The Havre de la Rose, it isn't far, you know?"

The sound of his voice broke her train of thought. She glanced up at him. "Sorry?"

"Would you want to do a little exploring of our own? Before it becomes completely illegal." He gave her a little smirk, the sort of mischievous gesture which meant he surely had something in mind for the evening ahead.

She frowned. "I don't know, Don…"

"Come on, it's all in good fun."

He finished the cigarette and rose from his seat in the corner booth of the tavern. Beyond the paneled window, the skies were growing darker, turning hues of deep purple with the onset of dusk. It wouldn't be long before nightfall, she thought. Not long at all.

"And anyway, they're just stories," he added, his smile broadening into a grin. "What's the worst that could happen?"

Before the Streetlights Come On
S. J. Krandall

*I*t was that moment, in the evening, when the sun was low on the horizon and the moon was just visible in the light. I was about to tell a story. Before beginning, I looked up at the sky, gazing at the clouds, gathering my thoughts. A slight throb pierced the right side of my head. I closed my eyes and rubbed my temple in a circular motion with two fingers. It was time.

I sprung open my eyes, took a deep breath and leaned forward. Then I spoke, "There was a time when kids would rule this town. They would be outside exploring from morning to night. But not anymore. Something happened that changed all of that. I'm sure you heard the story about the missing kids during the Summer of 1985."

Everyone nodded as they sat in the middle of the wilderness with their bottoms pressed against the cold ground. They formed a circle around me. A faded orange hue highlighted the world just above their heads as their gaze focused, anticipating my next words.

"It was a long time ago, but ever since then the town officials began to enforce curfews and parents started to keep their kids indoors a lot more."

I paused and took another glance up at the sky, falling silent for a moment. I felt the throb persist in my head as I checked for what remaining daylight we had left. Then, scanning their waiting faces, I recounted, 'That was the summer that started it all...''

***

It began on the day a boy named Colin got on his bike and road as fast as he could peddle, picking up his friends Jimmy and Susan along the way. All three of them drifted side by side, taking over the road, blocking cars as they spread out. They leaned into the turns, and at the corner of Main Street they rode up onto the grass of the neighborhood lawns and stopped at the fourth house in. Then they dropped their bikes and raced through the front door, leaving it wide open behind them. Laughing, and out of breath, they were calling one at a time, "Hi, Mrs. Baker!" as they sprinted past with a wave, flying down the steps to the basement of Mark Baker's house.

The music was blasting, the T.V. was on, and there was Mark lying on his stomach on the couch reading a book, his crew socks and converse sticking up in the air.

"Mark, put it on! Hurry!" Colin ordered, running to the television set and flipping the channel. Jimmy lowered the sound on the boombox, Dire Straits singing "Money for Nothing" in the background.

"Hey, I was listening to that!" Mark yelled, jumping up. He was staring at them in disbelief. "And I was watching that too," he said pointing to the television. He threw his book down on the table beside him. Walking off, he mumbled, throwing his hands up in the air.

They ignored him, making themselves comfortable on the sofa as they did every day that summer. They were happy to make it just in time for the opening pitch of the Mets vs. Astros game.

"Come on Col, baseball again?" moaned Mark, returning to sit in the chair next to them.

"You love baseball; what's your deal today?" Colin was asking, more aware of his friend's reaction this time. Mark, shrugging his shoulders, looked down. "Whatever man, I'm watchin' it, Colin said." He glued his eyes to the game. Susan and Jimmy were high fiving each other after the first hit. Mark sat quietly, staring at his shoes.

Mark's basement was the hangout of all hangouts. A place where you could spread out on soft bean bag chairs to talk about the latest gossip or sprawl across the sofa to play "Donkey Kong." The wood panel walls surrounding the green shag carpet kept it cozy and dark. A musty odor lingered in the space. There was not much light coming in from the ground floor windows and half of the overheads were flickering, but for years these four friends played in this basement together. Mark had the biggest basement out of all of them. They had birthday parties and sleepovers there. They played board games till all hours of the night. Some of them had even had their first kiss down there. In fact, it was earlier that summer during a game of spin the bottle that Susan kissed Jimmy. It was their home away from home, their clubhouse, their hideout when they were not in school, playing sports, or riding bikes.

Upstairs Mrs. Baker was trying her best to go about her day. She did not feel well. As she let herself into the house, she closed the door behind her, rubbing her temples at the sharp stabbing pain in her head, hoping for some relief. Then she made her way to the kitchen, mixed some iced tea in a pitcher, and carefully carried it down the stairs offering it to the kids, as she often did. She placed a few paper cups on a card table set up in the corner of the room, then turned to go back up. Reaching the top, she had to raise her arm to shield her eyes. The sun was setting, beaming through the kitchen window and blinding her at the angle she stood. It made her head throb even more. An uneasy feeling crawled up through her gut. Turning around slow and squatting down to glance through the wood railings above the stairs, she called to the kids, "It's going to get dark soon." Hesitating, she added, "If you're going out on your bikes you better get going." She waited for a reply. When no one answered she tried again, "Mark? Kids? Do you hear me? It is going to be dark soon." Her voice sounded rushed as she called their names. "Mark, Colin, Jim…"

"Ok, Mom!" Mark interrupted, still sulking.

She stood, about to leave, then squatted again. "And be home before it gets dark, before the streetlights are on." Again no one was answering. She sat on the landing, stomping one foot on the next step further down and pointed her finger at them. "I mean it! You kids get home before the streetlights come on! Don't make me worry. Do you understand?" She was firm this time.

"Yes, Mrs. Baker," they sang in unison. Satisfied, walking back up the stairs through the sun's rays towards the kitchen, she pressed her palms hard against her temple.

"What's up with the streetlights? It's like the new thing around here," Susan was asking as she poured the first cup of iced tea. "So, it gets dark; big deal," she added.

"My parents have been on my back about it too. I don't get it," replied Jimmy, reaching for the pitcher next.

"Beats me," Colin added to the conversation, half paying attention, half watching the game.

Then, as if on impulse, Mark jumped up and said, "Let's go, I want to show you guys something," never lifting his eyes from the floor as he left the room in a hurry. Jimmy and Susan glanced at each other with curiosity. They downed their drinks, slammed down their cups and began following Mark. Jimmy patted Colin on the shoulder as he was passing by the sofa, motioning for him to come.

"Come on man!" Colin whined, "the game's on! I raced all the way here to see this. It's a big game." He stood up to argue but they were already gone. "I'm talking to myself; that's just great!" he shouted up the stairs, hearing their footsteps and mumbled goodbyes on the floor above him. Knowing he was outnumbered, he ran up the stairs after them, calling out, "Bye, Mrs. Baker!" on his way out the door.

Mrs. Baker only grunted, leaning against the kitchen counter holding her head in her hands.

Outside, the sun was low. The rays reached out over the quiet neighborhood from in between the homes. Mark lived on the east side of town, where residential homes with lush green lawns stretched out to the sidewalks. Squinting, as the setting sun glared in their eyes, they peddled. They were following Mark in single file through the busier streets in town, allowing cars to pass this time. Then, turning off Main Street, they coasted down a hill towards the park. Mark said nothing as he led the way. Colin studied him. He seemed more reserved than usual, more unsure…scared even.

What could he be scared of? Colin wondered. A pit in his stomach was growing as they rode in silence. The air felt cooler as the sun continued to descend. The wind blowing through their hair felt good after sweating from the heat of the day.

Jimmy and Susan were lagging behind. They giggled, closing their eyes and letting go of their handlebars. They were flying for a brief moment before getting snapped out of flight.

"This way!" Mark was calling from up ahead.

They grabbed their handles, swerving a bit to avoid crashing. Laughing and peddling harder, they followed Mark and Colin onto the grass past the baseball field and into the deeper part of the park. It was gloomy here, more wooded and secluded. The sun peaking in from between the trees. When they reached the end of the wooded trail, where the railroad intersected the town, they stopped and got off their bikes. Laying them down alongside the tracks, Mark waved them in closer to him. They huddled, creating a circle with their clammy arms linking around each other's shoulders, all breathing heavy. Colin's headband stopped a small trickle of sweat from dripping into his eyes.

As they leaned in, Mark began to explain, "Guys, I was here yesterday." He paused to catch his breath, then continued," I was late coming home from practice, and I cut through the tracks so my mom wouldn't have my head. But I saw something. As I passed, I saw something. I didn't know what it was at first but I…I…" another pause; this time it was apparent his nerves were getting the better of him. He kept swallowing hard in between words, speaking faster. "I couldn't sleep; I kept thinking about it… so I snuck back out early this morning and…and you're not gonna believe this." Mark broke the huddle and ran across the tracks. Looking back at his friends, he shouted, "Come on. It's better if I show you." They all nodded.

Reluctantly following Mark to the other side of the tracks, they kept looking back and forth at each other. They were shrugging and gesturing with their hands in an *I don't know* way. Colin, wanting to say something, shook it off, feeling the timing was wrong. He thought it better to wait and let Mark show them first. He must have something that would make all this fuss worth it.

They stopped at the bottom of the slope curving off the track. Mark was standing with his back toward them, staring at a concrete wall. It had markings with graffiti covering its entire width. Mostly black and white in color, images of tall streetlights were stretching high in the background. It was messy and random, as if whoever created this art was rushing to do so. Words were written using white paint, covering the streetlight images. There were layers of letters upon letters. The same words repeating across the length of the wall.

Go Home.

Their eyes followed the words to the very end where the final letter cut off. A white letter *M* squiggling towards the ground changing to red along the way. The only red in the sea of black and white. It was dry like the rest of the art. It splattered across the word, dripping down towards the earth and pooled.

Mark picked up a spray can resting near the wall. Dark red covered the outside of the can. He was holding it out for them to see. Then, with a paling face, he pointed to the ground. Lying there was a half torn high-top sneaker, a matching deep red soaked where the white laces once crossed. Colin shivered while Jimmy's jaw dropped. Susan began stepping away from the scene.

"Wha…what is it; is it paint?" stuttered Susan, now moving slowly behind Mark to get a better look. "I don't think it is. I don't know. That looks like blood, Mark. But wh…why would that be blood?"

"I don't know." Mark was shaking his head.

Susan jerked away, catching her leg on a branch and falling. Jimmy was running to help her up when she started screaming and pushing her body backwards with her hands to try to stand.

"What the hell is that?!" she was screaming at Mark, pointing at something on the ground. Regaining her footing, she ran over to him. Hitting him, she asked, "Is this some kind of a sick joke, Mark? This isn't funny!"

"No! W-w-what is it?" he asked Susan, looking more shocked than she expected.

"Look!" She pointed.

Seeing it made him tremble.

"You planted these! You're crazy!" Susan was still screaming. She continued badgering him as he just stood there, wide-eyed. When she had nothing left to say, she walked away. "Screw this. I'm leaving. It's almost dark out now anyway. You guys can stay here all night for all I care! You coming, Jimmy?"

Jimmy began following her.

"Wait!" Colin said, observing Mark's face. "I don't think this is a joke."

Jimmy, debating, watched Susan let out a frustrated sigh. She climbed on her bike and swore at them, riding away.

Colin crept closer to where Susan fell. He was kneeling while taking in his surroundings. *She's right, It's almost night.* Noting it was harder to see, he picked up a stick and poked at the object. It rolled. Colin jumped.

"It's a freakin' foot!" Colin was yelling as he rolled back into Jimmy, who began to hurl.

"Why is there a foot, Mark?" Choked Jimmy, regaining himself.

"I didn't see the foot Jimmy; I don't know why," Mark insisted.

Colin was staring at the foot while the bickering continued, their voices growing louder. He reached out, poking it again in disbelief. *It looks so real.*

The foot was still intact, toes and all. Milky white bone stuck out from the center. Turning it over he saw maggots feasting on the raw flesh. The tendons oozing a bit where it tore near the ankle. Blood tarnished shreds of skin peeled down, touching the ground. It was in fact real.

Just then Colin heard a noise. It was faint and hard to hear over the yelling behind him, but the hairs on his arms were standing. He looked around, concentrating on the sound. Darkness was creeping in. A soft buzzing in the distance occurred when the first streetlight turned on.

"We gotta get outta here," Colin said.

He slowly backed up towards the tracks, eyes darting between the streetlight and the scene before him. His heart quickening. Mark put his hand up, stopping him, oblivious to the descending danger his friend was sensing in the night.

"Hold up, we need to go to the police with this. I didn't do this. Whether you believe me or not, this isn't a joke." He paced from the bloody foot to the graffiti-filled building and back again.

Jimmy shook his head. "Whatever. I'm out. Let's go."

Jimmy grabbed Colin's arm, pulling him along. The second streetlight buzzing on, closer this time. A quick movement in the distance catching his eye caused his throat to constrict.

"We gotta go," Colin whispered, wanting to run. Jimmy was frozen, still holding Colin's arm.

Mark, pacing the scene, began collecting the evidence on the ground. Colin, more urgently this time, yelled, "Mark, leave it, we gotta go. We're not alone here." Jimmy stiffened, panic welling within him. Colin, pulling from Jimmy's grasp, turned away from both of them while Mark walked over to the mangled foot.

"Mark!" Jimmy screamed.

Mark looked up, meeting his eyes, a shadow appearing behind him. Jimmy screamed, pointing and shouting, "Mark, something's behind you! Look out!"

The shape snatched Mark's body, lifting it into the thin, dark air above him. Before he could turn to scream, he was gone. Jimmy ran.

"Shit, what the hell was that, Col!" Jimmy screamed.

Buzz, another streetlight. The sound getting louder with the light turning on behind them.

"Don't stop Jimmy, keep running," Colin urged, running to his bike. His hands were shaking; he struggled to stand it upright. Jumping on, he peddled as fast as he could without looking back.

Jimmy was doing as told. It was all he could muster while his mind was racing. He was running through the park, leaving his bike behind. He was scared and unable to comprehend what was happening. He fled all the way to the baseball field. Then, scurrying under the set of bleachers alongside the first base line, he crouched down and hid. He was checking to see if anything was following him, but he couldn't see. He crawled back and forth, looking out into the distance. Searching through darkness.

Buzz! The light above the field turned on, making him jump.

Jimmy hit his head on the metal seat above him. Rubbing the tender spot, he let out a cry. Then he heard creaking followed by metal screeching and clanking around him. The bleachers began rocking, and he was afraid they were collapsing. Jimmy, grabbing the bars nearest him as if bracing for impact, squeezed his eyes shut, his breathing erratic.

This is not real. He pleaded with himself, trying to wake from this nightmare. *Stop, please stop.*

The bleachers stilled as if hearing his plea. Opening his eyes, sick with nerves, Jimmy gasped for air. Taking a long breath in, he slowly released the bars and ran his shaking fingers through his hair and along his face before letting it out.

I gotta get outta here, he thought.

He waited a few minutes, breathing hard. Then, convincing himself it was over, he crawled from under the bleachers. A sudden crunch on the metal above stopped him from going far. He let out a faint cry. Covering his mouth, he looked up. It was moving above him. Tears were rolling down his cheeks. He peered through the cracks between the seats. It was there that he met the blank eyes of something dark, a shadowy figure in the backdrop of the night sky, a shape of something inhuman yet familiar. It lurched at him.

Jimmy quickly got on all fours. He was crawling out from under the bleachers chanting, "Oh God, oh God, oh God."

In an instant, the shadowy figure was on him, grabbing at his feet. Jimmy was screaming as it yanked him back through the spaces between the bars, dragging him twisting across the dirt. Then, banging Jimmy's body hard against the metal bars like a rag doll, his body went limp. When all was quiet, the figure tore through his flesh without a fight.

Colin rode through the park, fighting the hill to get back up to Main Street. He was glancing over his shoulder, looking for Jimmy. Noticing he wasn't following, he began to worry. He found himself wondering where he was and wishing Susan made it home safe. Then, there was Mark. He never saw what happened to him. He only heard Jimmy scream and by the time he looked, Mark was gone. He was shivering, thinking he had no idea what he was running from. It scared him more because even though he did not see it, he could feel it. Out here, in the open, he was feeling as if he wasn't alone and that he was being watched. He tried catching his breath, but he was only struggling against it with the push of each peddle as he was moving.

Panicking, he willed himself to slow down and think clearer. He coasted for a bit.

In the still of the darkness, the streetlights made their debut… *buzzing* one at a time… following him.

Colin, flinching at each sound, thought *I'm not gonna make it home in time. I need to get inside. I need to go somewhere; where, where?*

Colin looked left, then right. *There! Mark's house! Yes!*

His gut sank. *Mark,* he remembered suddenly, feeling ill.

He needed to move quickly. He began peddling harder. His foot slipping in haste as he turned the corner. The bike was falling out from under him. Colin flew off to the side, rolling into the curb, scraping his arm along the way. He began cursing under his breath, lying there winded from the fall, or maybe it was the events that led him there.

Resting… panting.

Buzz, turning to see. The streetlights were closer.

Buzz… faster.

With his heart pounding through his chest, he stumbled to the bike. Ignoring the blood trickling down his arm, he picked it up from the ground and mounted the seat. He was shaking and trying to hold the handlebars straight, pushing down the peddle with his right foot. The bike wobbled, straining to move. He glanced down at the tire; the rim bent from the crash. He punched the handlebars, pounding his fists against the frame.

Buzz.

A block away, another streetlight. *It's coming.*

Dropping his bike, he ran.

Up ahead he could see the silhouette of Mark's house. The only light on inside was coming from upstairs. It was shining through the window where the bedrooms were.

Mrs. Baker! He was racing to her, passing by the neighbor's homes. He was almost there. His hair, now soaking through the headband from sweat and panic, was dripping into his eyes, making it difficult to see through the stinging wetness.

Buzz.

Shrieking, he glanced over his shoulder. The streetlight now on at the corner. Gaining speed, he pumped his arms with wild force, cringing at the pain from the forgotten scrape. He held it, willing his feet to move faster. Sweating and shaking, he was trying not to fall.

One more house, he was coaxing himself.

He was thinking he should call for help but he was too breathless to speak, let alone scream. Somehow, he knew getting inside was his safest bet.

Buzz.

The streetlight popped on in front of him. *It skipped one? That can't be!* Questioning his mind, his sneakers began skidding on the asphalt.

The light was shining bright, taunting him, lighting the edge of the driveway leading to Mark's front door.

Puzzling thoughts ran through his head, and he cried, "But how? Why?"

He was too close to give up. *I can make it.*

He released his arm, throwing himself into a turn and sprinted across the front lawn. He hurdled over small hedges blocking the railing to the front stairs. Taking two steps at a time, he made it to the door.

"Come on, come on, come on! Open!" he was begging, fumbling with the doorknob.

It gave and he pushed through the door with all his weight, falling face first onto the foyer floor. He was gasping for air. *Oh, thank you, Mrs. Baker, for never locking the door.*

"Mark, is that you?"

Mrs. Baker. It's me. The words never left his mouth.

He dragged himself forward to the thick carpeting at the bottom of the stairs, hoping she could see him. Colin heard her heavy footsteps.

She was scolding him from somewhere on the second floor, "You're late, Mark. The streetlights are on."

He was lying there out of breath, facing the floor, his body heaving. He reached out his hand, waving towards the empty space to the direction of her voice.

"The streetlights are on," he heard Mrs. Baker seethe. "They're on," then sounding more animal than human, "and you weren't home!"

This time her voice did not come from the top of the stairs. Mrs. Baker's sweet voice was changing…growling. Her words now echoing deeply from behind him. Colin stiffened.

"No!" he whimpered, lifting his head.

He felt her claws tear at his legs. He screamed, arching his back and dug his nails into the carpet for more grip. He tried crawling, but she continued ripping through his skin, making it harder to move. He felt the warmth of blood pouring out from the gashes as the pain seared through him. Then, as quickly as it began it stopped. He squirmed to get away, twisting to break free of nothing. He could feel her in the darkness behind him. A faint musty odor lingering. He felt her hot breath on his neck, then a whisper in his ear.

She was growling deeply, all evidence of Mrs. Baker's sweet voice disappearing. "I was worried about you."

Colin's screaming was cut off as she sank her claws into his side, tearing his body in two.

***

I finished talking. The pain in my head persisted, and I sat back with exhaustion. I opened my arms. "Well, what do you think?" I asked.

"Wait! That's it?"

"What happened to the girl, the one that left?"

"And Mrs. Baker…was it her?"

"Did they ever find out what she was?"

They all shouted at once. Their voices too loud.

Trying hard not to show my agitation, I responded. "More and more kids did go missing that year. Parents became strict and police patrolled the streets, but it remains unsolved to this day." Then added, "Mrs. Baker? Oh, she was eventually found dead. Old age they said, but there were rumors about that, too. Including talk of her whereabouts and her appearance when they found her. I can go on and on, but we'll save that story for another night." I squeezed my eyes shut and rubbed my temples. My head ached. "It's time for all of you to go in. It's dark now." A low grumble came from within as I said, "you better run." I stood and quickly walked away. I could hear the mumbles of questions and theories from my audience off in the distance. Without looking back I hollered, "Goodnight, everyone."

One by one they yelled back, "Goodnight, Susan!"

The Atheling Girls

DJ Tyrer

Nobody knows for certain what happened to the Atheling girls, not even us, but there are plenty of theories, you know? Most of them are dark and nasty and an insult to those of us who were there. We did our best to help, but I've had folks spit at me in the street, call me all kinds of names. It's horrible. Which is why I'm penning this to explain what happened, as best I can, although I doubt any of you will believe me. I'm not even sure I do.

Dan, Billy and I were squeezed into Dan's pickup truck, taking the back road up past the creek to Jimbo's for the evening. It was dark, and the wind was blowing in across the empty countryside, sending the odd tumbleweed bouncing across the road. I remember one ricocheting off the hood and the pickup swerving from side to side as Dan looked around, startled.

"Relax, it's not a hobo." I don't think Dan appreciated my joke.

Then, he swerved again and swore.

Billy and I hadn't seen a thing; I guess we were still yucking it up over his near-miss with the 'weed.

"Dammit, careful!" Billy yelled, as Dan slammed on the brakes and the pickup skidded dustily to a halt.

"It was a woman – I hit a woman!"

Dan was adamant, despite our doubts.

"You didn't hit a thing. Not a woman, not a deer, not a frickin' tumbleweed. Nothing." Billy wasn't having it.

"There was a woman! I hit her."

"Dude," I said, "You didn't. If you hit someone, she'd've bounced up on the hood or we'd've bumped over her, I'm sure. There's no way we wouldn't have noticed."

But he insisted we get out and take a look.

The pickup was untouched: No dents, no dings, no scratches, except for those that were there when we set out. The road was dry and crudely tarred, so there'd be no footprints. There were no marks other than the stains of black rubber where we'd squealed to a halt, and no blood. There was no indication at all that a woman had been there.

"Hey," shouted Dan, "anybody there? You okay?"

"Anybody?" I called, too, wanting to be certain.

"There was someone," Dan was still insisting, but he didn't sound quite so sure of himself. Still, he managed to persuade us to check the scrub to either side of the road, so I got out a flashlight from the toolbox in the back and they used their phones and we traipsed back and forth, shining lights across the bushes for any hint someone had been there. I got a couple of frights from ghostly shadows and startled a jackrabbit or something that spat itself out of a clump of tall grass and bounced a zigzag between rocks and bushes, vanishing before I could get a good look at it.

I was certain no one was out there, and the others traipsed back to the pickup with the same conclusion.

"I was so certain." Dan was shaking his head, as if the night had played a trick on him that he was still trying to figure out.

"Probably just another tumbleweed," was my conclusion. I remember kicking one off the road that might've been the culprit.

Of course, Billy couldn't let it rest and said, "Or, maybe it was La Llorona." I guess it was because we weren't too far from the creek. He had a thing about that piece of folklore, had read a book about her. It was interesting I guess, but right then, it was damn irritating as it got Dan thinking he'd seen someone, even a ghost, rather than letting it go. Very unhelpful.

Still, we'd wasted enough time, and I managed to persuade him we'd best get going if we were to reach Jimbo's before closing time.

I did ask if he wanted me to drive, but Dan shook his head and said, "No, I'm good."

We all got back into the pickup, and he put it in gear and we set off once more.

We didn't get far. About a mile, mile-and-a-half down the road was the turnoff to the Atheling house and that's where we got our third fright of the evening.

Dan had seemed okay, but he gave a sudden shriek and the truck swerved as the brakes squealed and we came to another sudden stop. This time, we all saw the white apparition that had startled him.

Of course, it wasn't a ghost: It was Mrs. Atheling in her nightdress, dark hair fanning behind her as she waved wildly at us, arms in the air, to flag us down.

It took us a moment to register that. In the darkness, with a hint of moonlight from a sliver not hidden by clouds, she looked like an awful spirit. She could easily have been La Llorona, an identification not hindered by the fact she was screaming, "My babies! My babies!" Obviously, she meant her missing daughters but could easily have been that old ghost wailing for her drowned offspring.

Still, as terrifying as she was, the fact Dan had braked meant we got a good look at her without being able to act on our immediate impulse to flee. I think Dan might have been about to mash his foot down on the accelerator, but then realisation struck and we saw this was no terrifying apparition but a flesh-and-blood woman in need of our attention.

We tumbled out of the pickup and ran over to offer her our aid. It was then that, disjointedly and with quite a bit of repetition, necessitating prompts for clarity, we learnt of the disappearance of her daughters and offered to help.

Perhaps it was only natural, but, despite Billy and I having satisfied ourselves there had been no person earlier, Dan immediately suggested that what he was still inclined to think was a near-miss must have involved one of her daughters.

Mrs. Atheling, of course, seized on it for the hope that her daughters might not be too far away. Not that the sighting, if sighting it was, offered any useful clue as to where they might be now. Nor did she or he care to ask why the girl would have run heedlessly into the path of the only vehicle on the road that night, nor why only one girl was seen and not two.

As I say, I don't think it was either of the girls, but if Cassie or Cammie had run out in front of us, it suggested this was more than a pair of runaways or the case of sleepwalking she seemed to be suggesting it was. Not that the latter claim made any sense, and I don't think anyone has offered a plausible reason for the two girls to run away together; if they had, we might not be the target of so many cruel rumours.

"Look; we'll help you, if we can." I was really thinking we could give her a ride into town to the sheriff's station, but she said her son had already gone, while her husband was out searching. She'd wandered out, calling for her kids, saw our headlights and decided to wave us down and ask if we'd seen them; but now, decided to enlist our aid in the search. So, we drove her the mile down the rutted track, back to her home, parked up, deposited her inside and, having made sure the girls hadn't returned home, took the flashlight, along with another from her kitchen drawer, and began searching.

Billy and I took a flashlight each and Dan walked between us, using the light of his cellphone. We swung our beams from side to side, so Dan had their light to assist him. We were maybe ten feet from him, moving slowly in a more-or-less steady line. The terrain was rough, but not excessively so. Every so often, we would shout the girls' names, but there was no reply. Not even an owl.

"Just how far do we go?" It was Billy who asked it.

"How far could two teenage girls go in a few hours?" If I'm honest, I reckoned it was most likely they'd pitched out of bed to meet dates or drink liquor, like so many kids their age. For all we knew, not only could they have gone in any direction, but some older boys could've picked them up in a car and driven them off for some fun. The whole search was feeling more and more like a waste of time. Overhead, the clouds grew ragged, and stars twinkled mockingly down at us.

Then, Dan yelped again, like he had in the car, the light from his cell phone flickering about as he waved it before him, yelling that he'd seen someone.

He seemed pretty spooked by this point and may have been seeing things. I know my nerves were all a-jangle. We shone our flashlight beams in the general direction he was gesturing, but while we stopped and searched for a while, we still found nothing.

Not there.

Something made us move on, despite the feeling that we were chasing shadows to no good purpose. I'd like to say it was altruism on our part, concern for the missing girls or the tears of their mother, or even a pigheaded refusal to give and go back without doing our darnedest to find them. I could say that, but it wouldn't be true. There was a compulsion. I can't say what exactly, but something, somehow, was making us go on. I know I wanted to turn back, but just couldn't force myself, and I think the others felt the same.

There was that sort of gallows humour, especially from Billy – *"We'll be at this till dawn, if we don't fall in a ditch and break our necks first"* – *"I wish I could see a point to all this; hell, I wish I could see"* – *"Every bush looks like a girl and every girl looks like a bush out here at night"* – the sort you get when you know you're headed for disaster and can see no earthly way out of the mess you're in. The sort that tries to bolster a morale that's long since given up hope and abandoned you.

Problem was, while we could all sense it, we couldn't pinpoint it or describe it, and we didn't dare speak of it for fear of being thought a fool.

So, we stumbled on through the darkness, unable to force our feet to turn from their course and take us back to the truck.

"I saw something," Dan exclaimed suddenly, halting. I would've said he was seeing things again, only this time, I saw it, too.

"There!" I swung the beam of my flashlight and Billy did likewise. While we didn't quite fix on them, there was enough light to see it was a woman, or maybe a teenage girl, in a white or pale nightdress and with light-coloured hair flying back from her head. We didn't get a good look at her, but it was enough to convince us we'd found one of the Atheling girls and, while the sense that something wasn't right remained, it was overlaid with a misplaced sense of hope that allowed us to ignore, or suppress, our niggling doubts and fears and give chase, hoping to bring the night's sorry escapade to an end.

Instead, it brought us to a farmhouse. An abandoned property that had belonged to a family called Castaigne, I'm told, years ago.

We'd lost sight of the white spectre we'd been following, but the house loomed out of the night, dark and dreadful before the starry sky, blotting out their light. The twin beams of our flashlights played over it, and it looked every inch as ghastly as its silhouette had. I don't know what colour it once had been, but it was now scoured to an off-white, blotched with dark stains, the paint flaking in patches like the curling petals of some ugly, pallid nocturnal flower. Tumbleweed had bundled up on the front porch, blocking it with a tangle like a dense barrier of razor wire, and a creosote bush appeared to be growing from between the slats of the left-hand wall. Not a pane of glass remained unbroken, and some of the boards that comprised the building's wall hung loose from the frame or had fallen to the dusty ground. It was the very image of a haunted house, and the soft night wind seemed to blow a low mournful tune through the gaps in its fabric.

I think we all stood pressed together in awe before it, much as we might have had we found some ancient monument from a primordial age, before Dan spoke.

"She must be inside."

Such simple words. It was true, after a cursory and rather nervous circumnavigation of the old farmhouse showed no indication of the pale figure in the vicinity, that she must have been. Sometimes logic does us no favours.

"How do we get in?"

That was Dan's next contribution. It was the obvious question. The front door and neighbouring windows were hidden behind the barrier of tumbleweed and we'd neither seen a backdoor nor stumbled over a cellar entrance. Our options were to risk the jags of glass and climb through a window or pull away some of the loose boards. We opted for the latter, tearing some down and kicking out the interior plasterboard to create a gap.

With a little bit of effort, choking somewhat on the dust we'd stirred up, we pushed our way through and found ourselves standing in a lounge.

The room could have been vacated just five minutes before, if it wasn't for a little dirt and a few twigs and leaves blown in through the broken windows. Other than that, there was nothing to hint it had lain empty for – years? decades? The furniture had the slightly faded look you expect to see in a farmhouse like this: poor, but proud. Except for the dirt that had blown in a little plaster that had fallen from the ceiling and the dust and detritus that had accompanied our entrance, there was no appreciable layer of dust on the low table, nor on the chairs or floor. There was even a coffee mug and a rolled-up television guide on the floor beside one chair, only a touch of brittleness hinting that they hadn't been laid aside by someone who'd just stepped out for a moment.

The beam of Billy's flashlight rested on the bare floorboards to reveal a series of marks like unshod footprints left by damp feet on the dry wood.

Damp feet. Here in the dry scrubland. It took no great leap of the imagination to reach just one conclusion.

"La Llorona." Billy said the words slowly and without his earlier teasing tone.

"It has to be a prank." I said it, but I didn't wholly believe it. Was someone playing a trick on us? It seemed too unlikely that some prankster happened to be here at such a deserted spot at the same time as us, waiting to have their fun, and the idea that Mrs. Atheling had concocted the ruse to get us here, not even knowing we'd come in this exact direction or walk so far, seemed even wilder than the notion that a spectre out of folklore had apparently taken up home here.

"It can't be…" Dan shook his head, as unwilling as we were to believe it and yet unable to quite envisage an alternative.

The fact was that there was a certain logic to the mad thought. Having been cursed to wander the world as punishment for drowning her offspring, La Llorona was a threat to other women's children, and there was no reason to suppose teenage girls were necessarily immune. The thought that the spirit could be here fitted perfectly with events. It was impossible, yet plausible.

We exchanged glances, quizzical looks with raised eyebrows and twisted lips, as we dared one another to voice the concept: hoping that one of us might be brave enough to do so. But we weren't, and we looked away, embarrassed. We coughed a little, as if the dust from the plasterboard lingered yet in our throats and attempted to work up enough bravery to break the spell and run away.

Instead, Billy suggested we search the rest of the house, "Just to be certain."

"Okay," I said, "but watch out for rotten floorboards." Of course, what I really meant was… look out for ghosts.

We stepped out of the lounge into the entrance hall. Behind a door that didn't seem to sit quite straight, looking as if it leaned to the left at times, and at others, to the right. Behind it, we knew, were the tumbleweeds. The footprints seemed to lead round to the dining room. We followed them.

Dan screamed. I might've, too. I think Billy just stared.

The dining room was like a scene out of a nightmare, or a tableau from a waxworks museum: Two teenage girls were seated either side of the table, not in nightdresses or pyjamas or whatever they went to bed in, but yellow summer dresses. They could almost have been alive, except for their pallid, waxy faces and fixed expressions. At the head of the table was a tall figure in a yellow gown. But our attention was drawn most of all to what was laid out upon the table as if a meal.

I vomited.

Laid out on the table was, I think, a woman. It was difficult to tell. Viscera was piled up, purple and shiny in our flashlight beams. I couldn't look at it, but it made me think of the ghostly figure we'd seen: La Llorona. I didn't *want* to look at it.

We turned away, looked at each other, the ceiling, the floor – anything but that ghastly scene.

"What do we do?" I'm not sure which of us said it. We were all thinking the same thing. Maybe none of us spoke; maybe we just understood our shared conundrum.

Dan tried his phone. There was no signal.

"Should I take a photograph? For the police?"

We had no answer. He hesitated, then turned and we heard a click.

Then, there was another sound, a scraping sound, and Dan swore.

We turned to look. I know you won't believe me, but I swear it's true: It's what I saw and maybe I was hallucinating or mad or something, but I saw it, and so did Dan and Billy.

The figure at the head of the table had eased back its seat. We stared for a moment in dumb horror, as it stood, taking in the scene. Suddenly, the gory heap atop the table was no longer the worst thing in the room.

The figure that I'd taken for a woman in a gown when I gave it a cursory glance was actually, as far as I could tell, a tall man, over six-feet tall; in my memory, he seems to loom eight or nine feet in height. I don't know. I'm not even certain it *was* a man; it just didn't seem to move like a woman. Then again, it didn't really seem to move like a man, either. As it began to step around the table towards us, it put me more in mind of some predatory insect or spider.

And its face… I don't think it was a face. It seemed more like a mask, yet it had the same pallid, waxy complexion as the dead girls. I can't really picture it now, I don't want to, but it was almost as if someone had taken the face of another and placed it over their own. Yet, that wasn't quite it.

I turned away, nausea rising up within me. I felt weak, yet I knew I needed to move. The man, yes, it was a man, I'm certain of it, was coming round the table towards us. I didn't know what he intended, but I knew it was bound to be terrible; we had the example of the eviscerated corpse before us.

Billy was shouting something about the man wearing a mask, or not wearing a mask, I'm not sure, but I grabbed him and began to pull him away. Dan was already running out ahead of us.

Billy was stumbling after me. He seemed to be in a state of confusion, but I dragged him along and, a moment later, we were back outside. I'm not quite sure how. He'd dropped his flashlight (not that I'd noticed at the time), but we managed to run away from the house by the light of mine.

Somewhere ahead of us, I heard a cry. It was Dan. He'd ran into a low-level bush and gone sprawling into a shallow ditch. I managed to locate him by his moans and shone my beam over him. His jeans were dark with blood where a snapped bone had broken through the skin.

I paused to look back towards the house – I couldn't help myself – and saw the figure standing there, somehow, on the porch, as if the tumbleweed that had clogged it had all blown away. It, he, was gazing towards us, but I was too far away to make out an expression. If there was one. Not that I looked for more than a moment, before turning back to my friend.

Billy still seemed stunned but did as I told him and helped me lift Dan from the ditch. We held him between us and hustled him away through the scrub. There was a vague hint of a path from the house, barely any easier to walk upon than the surrounding country, but a guide back towards the road.

It shouldn't have taken so long, or maybe I was wrong about just how long we'd been walking before reaching the house, but the red blush of dawn was already on the horizon when we finally reached the road.

I took out my phone but could get no signal.

We knew, at least, the direction in which the pickup waited. We reached it in about half an hour. That too didn't seem to mesh with the time we'd spent walking. None of it made much sense in the daylight. It was almost as if we'd spent the night in some awful nightmare. Yet, I was certain, am still certain, it was real. Somehow. In some sense.

We drove into town and found the sheriff. He and his deputies had been out all night, searching for the girls. Two of his men swore they'd searched the vicinity of the Castaigne house but had neither seen nor heard any indication of our presence. I would've assumed we'd reached a different farmhouse, but it was the only one in the area where we'd been and, when I went there with the sheriff after the others had been taken off to hospital, I recognised it, right down to the hole we'd made in the wall to get in. It was the same place and, seeing that hole, I knew we hadn't just imagined being there.

We went inside. The footprints, if ever they were there, were gone. Perhaps dried up, and there was a little disturbance to the dirt and leaves that showed we'd been there. But nothing else.

The dining table was there, but no gruesome corpse was laid upon it, nor were the Atheling girls seated at it. Nor was there any blood or vomit. It was almost as if we'd been in the room without actually being in it.

I might've assumed we'd hallucinated it all, but Billy had dropped his flashlight in the house and Dan had lost his cellphone, either in the house or during his flight. But while the deputies searched inside and out, they never found them.

They did find the girls. Apparently, they were laid out on the beds upstairs. There was never anything to link us to them, but we'd admitted being in the farmhouse, so the sheriff questioned Dan and I. I guess he also spoke to Billy once the doctors decided he was up to it. (Billy still isn't quite right.) I guess he could see how shaken up we were and, regardless of how ridiculous our account must've sounded, still sounds, knew we weren't the ones responsible for the girls' deaths.

No account of how they died has been made publicly, nor to us in private. That's why there are so many awful rumours; a mystery always invites speculation. I'd like to think my explanation of what we experienced would put an end to the accusations levelled at us, but I've provided no answers, and ghoulish supposition will continue to be proffered to fill the void.

I don't know what happened that night, nor why it happened to us and not to the deputies who came to the area of the house. Did it begin when Dan thought he'd hit someone, or did he imagine that? I honestly don't know; I can't explain any of it.

What I do know, now, is that the Athelings were related to their neighbours and that the Castaignes had vanished from their home in equally mysterious circumstances. We've all heard the story, but the names and details blur and vanish like they did.

Last week, that house went up in flames. I admit I did it. Something happened in that house. Something was badly wrong there. And, while I don't understand it, I pray that I've brought it to an end; cleansed it with fire.

I just wish I could have my life back. I wish I could blot out all memory of that night. But it haunts my dreams, and I know I'll never quite be free. No matter what you all think.

The Wasp
Ryan Wu

Jamison first felt the wasp's sting on the small of his back as he bent down to pick up a coke bottle on the side of the trail. The instinct was ingrained in him at a young age — his parents were hippie collectivists who introduced him to weed before any of his peers could — and though age and disappointment had injected its customary load of cynicism, he still found this one humanitarian gesture hard to shake. A thought gestated inside him — *"This is what I get for being a hero"* — and it made him chuckle as he crushed the wasp with the back of his palm.

It was small, the size of a jewel wasp, with a light lavender carapace streaked with bands of gold. The insides were unusually viscous, and a prominent gland poked out of its smashed hindgut.

"Venomous," thought Jamison, more out of bemused observation than anything. *"Will have to pick up some antihistamines."* Indeed, he already felt a burning sensation spreading under his skin.

Jackie was still standing by the car when Jamison got back to the road.

"Any luck?"

Jamison shook his head. "No reception."

"Dang. You went all the way to the clearing?"

A flash of annoyance shot through him. He quickly tamped it down. "I told you, there wasn't a clearing."

Jackie held up her hands. "Alright, no need to get mad. The sign said clearing, that's all."

"I'm not mad. And the sign's 40 years old, it's probably out of date."

"Okay, Jami. We'll just keep driving, then. Maybe there'll be a rest stop."

"Sure. Hey, by the way."

Jackie stopped just as she was entering the driver's seat. Jamison had been driving. Another flash of annoyance, another quick tamping down.

"Got stung by a wasp."

"Oh no! Are you okay, honey?"

"Stings a little, but I'm fine. Check it out, though."

He pulled out the empty cigarette box he'd stashed the remains in.

"What do you think? *Chrysididae?*"

Jackie shook her head. "At this time of year?"

She took out a pen and nudged the wing.

"Helluva wingspan."

"Right?"

Jackie grinned.

"Maybe you found a new species."

"That'd be something."

***

The Cascadia Sciences Conference, where Jackie and Jamison first met, disbanded amid funding concerns a few years back, so they couldn't follow through with their cutesy idea of going back for their ten year anniversary, but a couple of the old organizers had started a new conference at Corvallis, which they figured was close enough. Jackie didn't expect very much from life anyway. Early dreams of changing the world — perhaps through the discovery of some insect-based miracle medicine — were quickly dashed, so she chose to pride herself on her modesty. Even if they weren't the most attractive (Jamison had narrow-set eyes and a wide face; Jackie had a beak nose and a small chin) or the wealthiest (they were academics), they could at least be the most contented in their relationship. Their friends from college took their outwardly meek demeanors as permission to offload all of their latest relationship dramas on them — cheating, scandals, petty snipes. They responded by acting less like conversation partners and more like sounding boards, validating and echoing their concerns back at them like they were speaking into a well. Satisfied, their friends would go home happy to have someone who understood, while Jackie and Jamison would go home and talk shit.

Otherwise, they passed easily through the years. Jackie, having the more naturally forceful personality of the two, regularly planned dinners and conference visits and international trips to keep them occupied, which Jamison tagged along on and politely enjoyed. Then one day, an offer came for Jamison to take on a departmental position at Berkeley. The couple toasted it with some leftover champagne that they had in the freezer (Jamison had suggested they buy a fresh bottle, but Jackie thought it would be gauche), but two months before the move, Jackie's father was stricken with Lewy Body Dementia. Treatment was expensive, constant vigil a necessity, so even though Jamison protested, saying that they could move her father to Oakland, or he could otherwise accept the more lucrative position across the state and send money home to help with treatments, in his heart, he knew he had to listen to his wife. The Berkeley position went to David Roberts, a previously obscure academic who once spilled his wine on Jamison's suit jacket at a function before saying that his latest research paper was "lacking in rigour or insight." Jackie's father died three months later. He never got another offer, although Jackie, through force of personality and an insightful paper on cyanide-resistant beetles, was able to secure tenure at Loyola Marymount.

"We're happy, aren't we?" asked Jackie one night, with a nervous tinge in her voice.

"What do you mean? Of course we are, honey."

***

"Oh man, that's pretty bad."

After a short drive, they had managed to find a room at the West Oregon Holiday Inn. The motel light was weak, their supplies were limited, and their next-door neighbors were a group of obnoxiously loud frat boys from U of O who played bass-heavy Trap music through the walls despite repeat visits from the manager. Still, she did her best to inspect the sting, as Jamison leaned as far as his gut would allow him.

What she saw puzzled her. It wasn't just the swelling, although the welt had grown to the size of a walnut in the space of an afternoon; it was more so the pus. Most of it had dried into a shimmering snail trail running down to Jamison's waist, but even four hours later, there was still a thin trickle of discharge coming from the sting.

"Doesn't feel too bad."

"It doesn't hurt?"

"No."

"Not even when I do this?" She pressed her thumb against the sting.

"Ow!"

"See?"

"Okay, what do you want me to do, Jackie?"

She shrugged. "Probably just disinfect and bandage it for now."

"Any other way you want to hurt me?"

Jackie chuckled, which pissed Jamison off.

"Are you sure?"

"...Yeah?"

"That's good. I just had to confirm because it's *all you seem to do lately.*"

He said it loudly, the growl of a cornered animal. He was angry like he'd rarely been in his life, but just as quickly as it came on, it went away. Instead, he just felt embarrassed. He'd been annoyed with Jackie before — what couple hasn't? — but this felt different. As though an alien voice, tiny but sharp, had infiltrated his brain.

Jackie stared at him, frowning.

"What the hell does that mean?"

Jamison flushed red.

"Nothing."

"Jamison, what's going on?"

He paused, scrambling for an excuse.

"David is gonna be there."

"David?"

"David Roberts–"

"Oh Christ, you're still mad about that?"

Jamison didn't answer.

"Jamie, that was *seven years ago.* You need to fucking let this go, man."

Jamison stared at her, struggling to respond.

"I'm sorry."

He paused.

"You're right."

Jackie nodded.

"It's just the sting, you know?" he added, quickly. "It's itchy."

"Don't scratch it, Jamie. I'm serious. You don't want an infection."

Jackie shut off the lights and slept on her side, facing away from Jamison. A short moment later, the music from the other room started up again. Jackie sighed and got up to ineffectually complain, once again, to the manager, giving Jamison ample time to scratch at the now fiercely itchy sting.

***

Jamison awoke to find his bandage sopping wet with pus. In the bathroom mirror, he saw that the sting had worsened from a minor welt to an angry sore, rimmed with black like the mold spot on a rotting orange. The clear discharge from yesterday had thickened into a yellow, custard-like substance, and an itchy rash that looked like a bad case of hives had now spread across his entire lower back. The pain had also worsened since the previous night, transforming from a sharp prick into a deep, throbbing pain, as though someone had planted a hot coal in his torso. He thought of calling Jackie, but residual embarrassment from last night stopped him at the last minute.

At breakfast, he found his mind taken off the pain by another curious sensation: a sudden, gnawing hunger. He found himself devouring second and even third helpings of the sliced fruit and crappy pastries the motel provided, and yet when they got to the conference, he still found himself repeatedly heading for the endless buffet.

"You trying to bulk?" asked Jackie with a conciliatory smile as Jamison piled his plate high with fingerling potatoes.

"Hmm?"

She nodded at his plate. "Are the potatoes good?"

"I guess."

By the time they got to the conference hall, the itching had spread past his stomach and into his chest and legs, wriggling like a strange creature under the folds of his skin. His afternoon was fully booked with lectures and presentations, but he could barely pay attention as he tried to scratch himself without drawing notice. He tried to pay attention as David Roberts, his old nemesis, discussed new findings in the genus of *Chrysididae*, the parasitoid wasp:

"We know now that when the wasp lays its eggs inside its host, the resultant larva has the remarkable ability to influence its prey's behavior, inducing tranquility, increased appetite to better provide the parasitic larvae with food, and aggressive behavior towards others. It almost acts like an alien voice within its mind, telling it that things are okay when it's slowly eaten alive from the inside out..."

…But he couldn't focus. All he could think about was the itch.

It was driving him crazy.

Finally, he nodded at Jackie.

"Excuse me."

Then popped to the bathroom.

Safely inside the bathroom, he pulled down his pants and finally began scratching at the angry rash that now covered much of his inner thighs. His frantic attack eventually started drawing blood, but he hardly cared amid the relief he felt–

"GAH!" Jamison swore. Amid his assault, he accidentally scratched off a piece of skin. The scrape was shallow but bled a surprising amount. He swore again.

Later, as he sat on the toilet and pressed a wad of paper towels against his wound, he finally became aware of a strange sensation around his gums. Not an itching, but a *wriggling*, as though something were caught inside the roots of his teeth. Confused, he ambled to the bathroom mirror and tried to see what was happening.

He tilted his head up, but the angle of the overhead light made it impossible to see inside his mouth. Finally, he took out his phone and shined the flashlight inside to get a better look.

…Nothing. Just ordinary gums. Just an ordinary mouth.

But when he tested his front incisor with his finger, he found that it *wiggled*, like a baby tooth about to fall out.

And soon, he realized that something else was *wiggling* underneath it, too. Something in his gums.

Jamison stared, apprehensive. Something was wrong. Something was *very* wrong.

But then the itching returned, and soon enough that was all he could think about.

***

That night, Jamison snapped at Jackie while they were driving back from the hotel. She kept asking if Jamison was alright, which annoyed him for reasons he couldn't quite articulate. Then she said that he should see a doctor, and that he was "looking like shit."

Jamison felt the foreign anger return. Ever since the incident in the lecture, she'd been prodding him about his health, but his reactions were always oddly calm. Somewhere inside, a rationalizing voice was telling him everything was okay. *"Jamison, you're rational. A smart man. This is just a strange case of pollen sickness or hay fever. Things will be okay. Your children will be okay."*

Children?

Jackie and Jamison had no children. Jackie was too focused on her career and didn't want kids, while Jamison...

Jamison was worried they'd be bad parents. Jackie, he thought, would become overbearing and neurotic, fretting over every aspect of their lives, while Jamison wouldn't be able to push back.

"Because you're weak," came another voice, dripping with venom. *"You won't be able to protect them."*

So, they never had kids.

This latest indignity, however, caused the anger to return, and all the weird, unconvincing deflections were replaced with something sharper and angrier: *"She ruined your life, you know. She's the reason why you're stuck without tenure at a third string college. If she had simply let her father, who she resents, as she has confided in you multiple times, who insulted her and neglected her and eventually terrorized her as he got sicker and more confused, die alone in that nursing room in Bedford, then you wouldn't be here."*

He turned to her and snapped, "Jackie, shut up. There's nothing wrong. I just need *rest*. I'll rest *better* when you stop *bitching* at me."

Jackie turned to him. Jamison watched shock and anger play out over her expression. She opened her mouth to speak and then closed it and said nothing.

Immediately, he felt ashamed, but soon enough, the anger wrestled those feelings back down. By dinner time, he had assumed a silent and haughty posture, and although Jackie still didn't say anything, he could tell that his new demeanor puzzled and bothered her, which gave him no small amount of satisfaction.

That night, at around 3:00 AM, Jamison awoke to a tickle in his throat and a strange buzzing in his ear. When he staggered to the bathroom, he found that he couldn't turn on the light without recoiling at its sudden brightness, forcing him to instead inspect himself in the thin light of the not-quite-morning. What he saw were pinpricks covering the entirety of his body, from his lips to the bags under his eyes, lining the entire inside of his mouth as well as his tongue and — he was dismayed to see — pockmarking his genitals, around where he had scratched himself. It was like his entire body had sprouted gooseflesh. A strange film, like a caul, covered his left eye.

He stood transfixed by the thing in the mirror. Then he suddenly felt the wriggling in his gums again. He opened his mouth and tried to see, but that was impossible in the dim light of the morning. Finally, he was forced to turn on the lights to see inside his mouth. When he did, he nearly screamed.

All inside his mouth were little abscesses, almost like large pimples or cysts. They were clustered in a honeycomb pattern all along his gums. Jamison ran his tongue over them — they felt hard, like little bullets in his mouth. And they were moving.

He stood there frozen for nearly ten minutes, cycling between panic and a strange, alien calm, until the rapidly rising sun forced him to retreat to the closet. Then, safe for a moment in the cocoon of dark, he finally felt it: a strange, sharp wriggling under his left eyelid, as though a thumbtack had wedged itself into the jelly of his eye. Rubbing it only worsened the pain, so instead, he picked at it like it was an itinerant blackhead. There was an odd little nodule on the top, almost like the head of a pin, and he thought that if he could just pull it out—-

Suddenly, there was a wet squelch, and everything started to leak. Jamison's vision went blurry… his head swam as he lurched forward… he felt a pop in his ear… the closet began to spin… vomit bubbled up in his throat… he held it in his mouth for a futile second before letting it dribble past his lips… He felt his eye drip from his socket and onto his lap, like the inside of a rotten grape.

When he recovered long enough to sit up, he felt the wriggling again, but even stronger. No longer was it just a spasm or twitch– the thing that was moving was muscular and determined to tunnel out of him. More curious than anything, Jamison pinched the end of the struggling thing and pulled. It resisted at first — Jamison felt it tug against the remaining meat of his eye — but then it came out with a wet *pop!*

He opened the closet door just a crack and held the thing that he'd pulled out of his eye to the light. What he saw pinched between his fingers was a long, white, maggoty thing, many-segmented and plump, with a black, nub-like head studded with visible teeth. A papery chunk of retina still clung to the bottom, where two large, needle-like legs wiggled for purchase.

Jamison stared, fascinated. The part of him that might've been alarmed was oddly mute, as though smothered by laughing gas. His intellectual side took hold; it was clearly some kind of parasite, something that had gestated inside of him and had now eaten its way out in preparation for the final stages of metamorphosis. Already, he could see wispy strings of silk emerging from the black, nubl-like spinnerets lining its side, no doubt the start of some kind of cocoon. He'd gotten this one while it was still a little immature, but the others that were emerging from his teeth were still molting, still gorging themselves on his body, still preparing to spin their silk prisons and, after a short while, become beautiful, bejeweled wasps.

He briefly considered the possibility of announcing a remarkable new discovery at the next conference, a new species unlike any before seen. *Chrysididae Edohomulus.* The Man-eating Chrysalis Wasp. Surely such a discovery would come with some prestigious prize. Maybe a Nobel? At least a Vannevar Bush Award. But suddenly, his stomach growled. The larvae inside of him were hungry. Absently, he scooped a handful of vomit off of his lap and into his mouth. Sour, tangy, warm…

It helped, but even after licking his palm clean, he was still hungry. He turned his attention to the squirming thing in his fingers. It was fat, like a cashew. He popped it in his mouth and chewed.

***

Sometime later, he heard the thumping bass of his next-door neighbor's music. *Are they fucking serious?* A flare of aggression swept away his apathy. They were disturbing him. They were disturbing his *wife*. They were disturbing his *children*. A caveman instinct took hold, and he staggered out of the closet. A bizarre, squirming lump — no doubt a large cluster of parasitic larvae — had found its way behind his left kneecap, making him groan with pain with each step, but he still managed to shuffle awkwardly to the door and put on a visor to shield his ruined eyes from the sun.

Behind him, he heard Jackie stirring.

"Jamie?"

"Go back to sleep." His voice was low, choked with phlegm. A clock on the stand read 8 o'clock.

Rave music at 8 o'clock. What the fuck were they thinking?

He went outside and knocked on the neighbor's door. A young man in a varsity jacket answered the door. He had a crew cut and a rash of pimples running down the side of his face. Behind him, a few girls smoked weed from a crusty bong.

"Hey, what's up–"

Then he got a better look at Jamison and stopped.

Jamison sneered, his abscessed gums visible from under his visor.

"Listen, you fucking asshole–"

The words died before he could speak them. Something was shifting in his mouth– He felt with his tongue a mass of silk pushing through a hole in his gums–

Before he knew it, he was spitting something pearly, smooth and white into the palm of his hands. When he looked, he saw that there was a thread of meat clinging to the bottom.

His tooth.

But there was something else now, too. Something that fluttered angrily in his hand.

It was a new jewel wasp, small but shiny. It was using its mandibles to clean Jamison's saliva off of its antenna.

This one had come out of his gums. This one was early. It must've matured long before the rest of the brood.

Jamison smiled at it.

Hey there, little guy.

Then he looked up at the young man in the varsity jacket. His eyes were wide with terror, staring at the thing that just came out of him.

Then more started to come from Jamison's mouth.

***

Jackie drove with a hushed urgency. Her mind cycled between paralyzing terror and eerie blankness, like a TV caught between channels.

She'd always had an analytical mind, even when she was ten. Growing up, her greatest joy was coming up with her own scientific classifications for the various trees, ferns and shrubs that populated the woods behind her home, grouping them based on the shape of the leaves, their arrangements on the stem, the color of the stem and the color of the trunk. It was a skill that she soon applied to the people in her life, starting with her friends at school before moving onto her parents as their divorce made them increasingly distant.

In Jamison, she found a refreshing lightness. A man who took his work seriously but not himself (when she met him, he was already drunk; he struggled for twenty minutes to come up with a pun combining *Lepidoptera* with Long Island Iced Tea before giving up and buying her a gin and tonic). After they got married, however, Jackie became unnerved by some things she noticed about Jamison's behavior. He had a tendency to get snippy, and he often found a way to turn minor setbacks — a flat tire, a slow waiter — into a melodramatic conspiracy against him. In general, there was a stink of resentment coming off of him, which Jackie could sense despite all her attempts to assure herself that they were fine after the Berkeley debacle.

That awareness limned even her happiest moments, but still, she consoled herself that compared to the issues that other couples faced, it wasn't that bad, and besides, she was strong enough to get through it. There was still joy, spontaneity, occasional moments of surprising thoughtfulness. On top of that, though, her childhood had instilled in her a strong sense of independence, the feeling that she needed to make her own way, and a little part of her couldn't give up that she'd *chosen* Jamison, and that he was hers. She never forgot her father's look of trepidation when she finally told them that she planned to get married, nor the look in his eyes when he said, "Jacks, you're making a mistake." The insult of that, from the man whose marriage she had seen dissolve up close, kept her going longer than she cared to really admit.

Only now, she was scared. She had vaguely heard the music from the other room stop after Jamison confronted them, but that was hours before she awoke in earnest. When that happened, she heard a low moaning coming from the closet. Inside, she found a grey, fleshy mass that had curled into a ball like a Guanajuato Mummy. Its skin was glossy and thin looking, like the pages of a magazine, and covered in angry bumps tipped with white crowns. A cluster of tubes covered in thin, off-white filaments sprouted out of its lower back, where a small wasp sting had grown to the size of a crater. Jackie stared for a second, mesmerized, as the growths (she thought of spools of threads, cotton candy) wafted to-and-fro, to-and-fro, to-and-fro like seaweed in a tank…

"Baby…" said the thing in the closet. *"Can you close the door? It's kinda bright."*

***

A crowd had gathered outside of their room by the time they got back to the motel. A mix of housekeeping, other guests, and the motel manager, a perpetually irate man with a shiny bald spot who suddenly looked very, very ill. Jackie pushed her way to the front along with David Roberts, who was thankfully staying just a short distance away.

She grabbed the manager by the shoulders. "Is he okay? What did you see?"

He could only stammer. She looked down and saw that he'd wet his pants.

David led the way into the room, an industrial smell wafting off of him. When Jackie told him what was happening — showing him the dried remains of the wasp all the while — he immediately began covering himself in wasp repellent and ordered her to do the same. He saw the size of the ovipositor sheathed in the wasp's hindgut and knew that it wouldn't be long before its larvae finished gestating.

"Will this work?" asked Jackie, as she applied a second layer of repellent to her forearms.

"Yes," said David, although he couldn't say for sure, since the can was old and the success rate for that brand of repellent was spotty even with regular, non-maneating wasps.

The room was dark and humid when they entered. Jackie immediately noticed that someone had drawn the curtains. A rank smell, like rotten eggs, permeated the air, causing David to dry heave into the bandana covering his face. Somewhere in the room, they heard a wasp's wings beating. The large cans of hornet killing foam that they brought with them suddenly felt inadequate.

Jackie flipped the light switch but shut it off immediately. A cluster of wasps, purple and gold and shimmering, covered the plastic dome of the ceiling light like writhing Christmas ornaments. They broke apart and batted angrily against each other but regrouped as soon as the light was off. The hum in the room grew louder.

Jackie squinted and saw that many of them were pressing their backsides against each other, and many more were crawling over the ball looking for a partner. "They're mating," she whispered to David. He nodded back, grimacing.

Suddenly, there was a *thump* against the wall. It was coming from the neighbor's room. Jackie looked at David.

"The other room."

"What?"

"This morning, Jamison went to the room next door to talk to them."

David swore under his breath and left the room.

Alone, Jackie approached the closet, whose door was open like a waiting mouth. She walked in utter terror, worried that a creaky floorboard would alert whatever was inside, worried that something would lurch out, something vaguely human but wrong, twisted, pockmarked, diseased, collapsing, oily, corrupted–

She burst past the threshold and saw that the closet was empty. Only a few shreds of silk were left on the floor. Jackie sighed, nearly crying with relief.

Then she listened and realized that the hum they were hearing wasn't just coming from the ceiling; a separate sound, a more lyrical sound, a more *human* sound, emanated from behind the closed bathroom door.

 She walked over and opened it.

The bathroom was normal.

But the sound was louder now.

It was coming from behind the closed shower curtain.

Jackie could see something poking out the top. But she couldn't see what it was.

"Jamison?"

The humming stopped.

"Is that you?"

No response.

Slowly, Jackie reached her arm out.

She opened the shower curtain.

A thing was sitting curled in the corner.

It stood up, unfurling to its full height.

***

A tall thing. Taller than her husband was, Jackie thought, by at least a foot.

A thin thing. Thinner than the shower rod that she saw peeking through the dark.

A leg that had swollen to triple its original size with pus and organic debris. Jackie thought of her college epidemiology courses, the ones that taught her she didn't have the stomach to become a doctor - *Elephantiasis.*

Skin that had gone gray and papery.

Clusters of holes, like lotus roots, like the craters on the moon. All over the body, in little clusters of nine, ten, twelve, twenty.

A face that drooped, as though it were melting.

Silk cocoons sprouting in clusters like branches of coral.

More wasps, still more, more of them worming their way to freedom, worming their way to their siblings, worming their way to their mating partners…

"Hey babe," said the thing. It was smiling.

***

In his mind, he was at a wedding reception. He was at the state fair. He was at a baby shower. He was at *their* baby shower. They were having a boy…

"Jamison."

"Hi, Jackie." His voice was a rocky growl, like a rock singer's. He liked it.

"How are you doing?"

"Pretty good."

"What's happened to you?"

"Nothing's happened."

"Have you seen yourself?"

Suddenly, he was in the ballroom at his wedding. In the mirrored wall, he saw his plump skin; his chiseled jaw; his coiffed hair, no longer thinned out with age.

"I look great, babe."

"Jamison."

"Jackie?"

"What have you done to yourself?"

Suddenly, he was in the bathroom. He was toweling himself off. They had just started talking about a kid. No specifics were discussed, but they both had agreed: they would not sign their kid up for swimming. Both of their parents had signed them up for it, and they both hated it.

"Just got a little messy, babe."

"Jamison."

"Jackie?"

"..."

"What is it, babe?"

"..."

"You know, I know we've been mad at each other."

"Yeah?"

"Yeah."

He saw a can in her hand. Whipped cream? He remembered that after watching *8 ½ Weeks*, they tried recreating the fridge scene with a bottle of honey and Reddi-whip. It was a disaster; the cream got into the grout between the kitchen tiles and was stinking and curdled by the time summer rolled around. But maybe this time it'll all be different, he thought; maybe they could put some towels down and it'd be fine.

"I forget that we tried that."

"What?"

"What were you thinking, babe?"

"..."

"Jackie, I just wanted to say…"

"Yeah?"

"We'll get through it. Whatever it is."

He took a step forward.

"I know I haven't been the… easiest to get along with. I know I haven't always been open about myself, but it's only because…"

He took another step forward.

"I think if I said what I was thinking, it would become the only thing we shared. And I didn't want it to become real. I should've talked about it with someone, I know that…"

"…"

"And that was unfair. And I'm sorry."

He took a step forward. She took a step back.

"What is it, babe?"

"…"

He glanced at the can again. He grinned.

"You wanna try again?"

He reached for it.

She backed away.

He frowned.

"What's wrong?"

He reached for it again.

Anger flashed through him.

"Jackie? Why are you running? *Why are you running from me?*"

He reached for it again.

A voice called out.

"She's trying to hurt you she's trying to hurt you she's trying to hurt your babies–"

***

The seven-foot-tall Jamison-thing howled and stretched his arms out and lunged for the can of foam. New wasps emerged from the holes lining the left side of his torso, crawling out of Jackie's husband like ants from a hill.

She backed up and sprayed the hornet foam at him. It traveled in a lazy arc and landed on his chest, expanding and filling the many holes dotting it. Jamison roared in pain and doubled over, exposing a massive, tumorous mound of cocoons on his back, even bigger than it was in the morning.

Jackie doubled back, trying to flee.

Then she slipped– the can went flying–

She looked back with horror to see Jamison ambling towards her.

It awkwardly swung its swollen leg over the edge of the tub, trying to pursue her.

Out of instinct, she kicked the bloated limb. It made a sickening *squelch* and wobbled as all the fluid sloshed inside of his ruined skin, before suddenly *peeling* open, spilling blood and pus all over the floor. . .

Jamison went down, screaming like a wounded animal. His bones cracked upon contact with the floor. Jamison looked up at her, eyes full of pain. He opened his mouth again to scream. The inside of his mouth was completely covered with little holes, like a honeycomb. The holes reached past his tongue and the lining of his mouth and down into his esophagus. Dozens upon dozens of new wasps crawled along his tongue, seeking freedom.

Jackie could only stare in horror. Then suddenly, she felt a pair of hands grab her shoulders. Jackie screamed. . .

***

David pulled her out, away from the Jamison-thing, and slammed the door, wedging a chair under the doorknob for good measure. The thing inside began banging on the door and screaming, but David ignored him and began spraying the cluster of wasps on the ceiling, covering it completely until it resembled a massive, twitching snowball.

Jackie looked up at David, baffled, struggling to even think of a question to ask.

David answered for her. "The kids next door are alright."

Turns out that they locked themselves in the bathroom as soon as they saw Jamison vomit out the wasps. Stuart was able to find all seven of the brood clustered on a tabletop and dispatched them with foam before they could finish mating.

Jackie got up and dusted herself off as Stuart scanned the room for stragglers. There was a distressing amount of them: in the folds of the bedsheets, in the closet corner, in the grooves of the cheap polyester carpet…

"What do we do now?"

"We gotta destroy the building."

He nodded towards the front door. Jackie saw that he brought in a can of campfire starter.

"It's the only way."

"But–"

He grabbed her shoulders.

"Listen, Jackie. Chrysididae follow a strict schedule for their life. They are born across a wide expanse of territory, they gather in one spot to mate, and then they disperse. If we don't burn down the nest *right now*, then the entire brood will escape, and they'll be free to turn the entirety of central Oregon into a breeding ground."

Jackie stared, searching for words.

David shook her.

"Jackie. *Thousands* could die."

Finally, she croaked out one word. . .

"Jamison."

David paused, pursing his lips.

"Jackie, Jamison is doomed."

"I know. I just. . . I gotta talk to him."

As if on cue, there was a banging on the bathroom door. *"Jackie?"* came a voice.

***

"Hey, Jamie."
"Babe, it's dark right now."
"I know."
"What's going on?"
Jackie paused. Inside the bathroom, she could hear the angry beating of wasp wings.
"I'm sorry we couldn't start again."
"What do you mean, babe?"
She opened the door.
The entire bathroom was covered in wasps. They crawled over the shower curtain, they crowded on the mirror, they crawled over the closed bathroom mirror.
Jamison was covered in holes.
He looked up at her, wheezing like a dying animal.
"Baby."
"Jamison." Jackie clutched the bottle of campfire starter to her chest.
The wasps filling the room kept mating, beating their wings angrily, ignoring the two.
For the moment, at least.
Jamison croaked.
"It hurts, baby."
"I know."
A few of the wasps started finishing up. They pulled away from each other.
A few of the wasps were buzzing around the room now. A few of the wasps were full of eggs.
The thing that was her husband croaked.
"Can we start again?"
Jackie struck a match.

***

At first, the fire that consumed the West Oregon Holiday Inn was investigated as potential arson, but a short conversation between the local sheriff and state officials changed the verdict to an accident. The story was now that a spark from the electrical outlet lit up an unusually high quantity of flammable aerosol in the air. Miraculously, there was only one casualty.

To the police, the press, and eventually to the mourners at her husband's wake, Jackie struck a conciliatory tone. She told a story that she used to tease him with at casual gatherings. They were white water rafting in San Diego, and her husband — who sat at the front — bore the brunt of each splash. At the restaurant afterwards, Jamison wondered aloud why the hostess was giving him odd looks, and it was only after Jackie pointed it out that he realized that the particular way that the water soaked in his pants made it look like he'd peed himself.

Jamison sighed, "that's what happens when you don't pay attention." The two cut their meal short; Jamison changed his pants at the hotel and the two went out for ice cream.

"That was Jamison," said Jackie at the funeral. "He rolled with the punches. We didn't have everything. At his worst, he'd remind you of what you didn't have; that you were stranded on a rock, looking up at the people who reached the stars. But at his best, he'd remind you that was all you needed. *This is what happens when you don't pay attention.* You forget about the beauty of the rock."

A team of biologists with the ODFW recovered samples of the wasps from the remains of the motel. Their conclusion was essentially an unsettled shrug of the shoulders: the wasp had no clear genetic lineage, no known biological origin, no known natural habitat. All they could do was warn travelers away from the Klamath County State Forest where Jamison was stung that fateful day. A few weeks later, Jackie joined David on an expedition into the woods to learn more about the origins of the wasp. The team was outfitted with beekeeper suits in order to protect themselves from any errant stings. Jackie additionally brought a can of hornet foam for herself, just in case.

Meanwhile, Mr. Ernest Halloway, the bald clerk that Jackie interrogated on the night her husband died, sweated like a pig in his one-bedroom apartment in Salem, Oregon (population 177,400), not far from where the motel burned down. His skin prickled with a rash, and at night, his eyes quaked in their sockets as though they'd been hit with a tuning fork. He had an odd fever he couldn't seem to shake even after three tablets of aspirin. The sting on his left thigh was rapidly worsening into a sore.

Maybe some fresh air could help?

He opened the window.

The Red Man

Kevin LeCompte

One of the most perplexing things I contemplate anytime I relive this story, is the fact that just before my friends and I entered the woods, I took a good, long look around. I took in the paint crumbling barn that my father had all but relinquished to nature years ago, the old play set beside it and the overrun field of mint and onion chives that had taken over the empty lot behind us. There was the house I grew up in of course, resting about a hundred feet away from the barn, a nightlight vibing up a ghostly ambiance that radiated from my parents' bathroom up on the second floor, the home otherwise dark and quiet being that it was after ten o'clock. Memories of growing up spilled out over the flood gates as I recalled some of the most significant moments of my life, good and bad alike. It was strange, because I hadn't ever been that kind of person before then, the type that dwells on things that happened and the nostalgia that gravitates from the homes we grew up in. It's strange too because it was as if I were saying goodbye, and yet how could I have known? How could I have known that by the time I'd step back out of the woods and look upon my home again, my life would be changed forever?

Not knowing, of course, I'd turned along with my two friends and disappeared into the forest. We were excited about the expedition we'd be going on that particular night. We'd been planning it for months and it took a pretend campout in my parent's yard to bring it all together. My good friend Lawrence insisted it had to be on that specific night at that specific location, because that's how we'd be able to find the red man.

We'd all heard the stories about the red man, or Far Darrig as my grandparents had referred to him. Folklore ran rampant in that part of Wisconsin back then and I grew up listening to stories about the red man as we leaned in close to autumn bonfires or drank hot chocolate next to the fireplace in my grandparents' living room as winter whistled and roared its stormy voice outside.

"I always heard he's more of a hairy rat who stands up on two feet," Chelsea said as we began treading through the hilly forest near my parent's house. "More of a creature than a man. Might as well call him the red rat. It sounds better. Alliteration, right?"

"I heard he can change and make himself look like whoever or whatever he wants, even look like people you know," Lawrence added. "But who cares what he looks like? It's the money that matters. That's why you wanna find him, no?"

They were both right, I considered as I trudged along behind them through the not so quiet forest, taking in the sound of an owl hooting near where we were zigzagging our way through trees. A coyote howled somewhere off in the distance and a couple others howled back. Dead leaves crunched beneath my boots while live ones rustled in the wind as Lawrence worked his way back beside me.

He grasped my shoulder, then pulled me in for a quick man hug before letting go of me completely. "This is awesome, man." He took a cigarette out of his pocket, then glanced my way as he reached out to offer it to me.

I hadn't been much of a smoker, and he knew that. But that night was meant to be special, memorable, and it felt right to take that smoke and light it up, to embrace our rebellious moment in more ways than one.

I pinched the filter with my fingers, brought it up to my lips and inhaled. Then I coughed. He laughed as we walked on together.

Lawrence took his walkie-talkie out of his bag to test it out, play with the switches for a second before holding down the send button and saying, "You decide what you wanna do after high school yet?" He'd asked.

Mine was already powered on and latched onto a belt loop on my jeans. I grabbed it, lifted it up to my mouth and said, "Not yet." I stuttered in between coughs before asking, "you?"

"Yeah, man." He nodded, smiled a bit even. "I think I did."

I grabbed the smoke back and toked it, didn't cough at all as I handed it back to him. "Oh yeah? What'd you decide?"

He took a drag, and smoke surrounded his face as he said, "I think I wanna be a physical therapist."

"No shit," I responded because he hadn't ever mentioned that as being an option in the past. "Seriously? That sounds awesome, man."

He nodded as he smoked again, then handed it back my way. "Thanks, man. I think it's the right choice."

I smoked, trying not to cough as Lawrence skipped on ahead towards Chelsea, singing about how he was about to stare down at the red man then go on to live a wealthy and prosperous life.

I put the cigarette out and ran to catch up with the two of them.

"I won't have to work at all after I see that reddish little man in his pimped out little cave," he'd said to Chelsea.

She turned towards him, waving a finger as she said, "don't forget you have to live to tell about it."

"Yeah, yeah," he'd said, as we all continued through the thicket. There was a strangely sweet scent of burning wood somewhere out there suddenly.

"It's about a lot more than wealth and prosperity," Chelsea said, as she took her phone out and began recording the three of us working our way deeper into the forest. "Tonight is about history, it's about culture and folklore and it's about us facing the fears of our childhoods."

Lawrence jumped in front of her phone then, waving rock'n'roll fingers with both his hands, his tongue hanging out before he yelled, "It's about the money, baby!" He proceeded to pull her into his arms then and nibble on her lips for a moment before she laughed and shoved him away.

"You're messing up my video," she said as she smiled.

I smiled too. It was entertaining to see their back-and-forth banter, third wheel jealousy boiling in my bowels or not. And again, they were both right. The story always changed of course, I mean, that's the nature of folklore, right? But most iterations included a mysterious cave that rarely appeared and when it did, it was never in the same place twice. Supposedly. But if the cave did appear, and if you were to come across it and if you were brave enough to venture in all by yourself (being by yourself was key or the red man would not show), you might be rewarded. The word was that if you saw the red man and lived to tell about it, you'd be wealthy and prosperous for the rest of your days. Problem was, most versions didn't have a happy ending, and the person was killed, went mad, or simply vanished all together before they had a chance to live that wealthy and prosperous life. Though a few versions generously granted such happy endings, they were usually told by drunken Irishmen who'd been at the bottle for a few hours by then.

And so, heading into the forest around our parts became a rite of passage for high school seniors before heading off to college in hopes of finding the red man, living to tell about it (hopefully…), then going off into the world to enjoy their wealth and prosperity. Nothing official of course. No, I didn't grow up in some crazy cult where people had to follow the yellow brick road towards some fantasy land made up sort of graduation ceremony. It was just something most teenagers did at some point. Every town has their rituals like that, no? I remember hearing all about Bachelor's Grove Cemetery when I visited my uncle out in the suburbs of Chicago. Jokingly (I think…), he'd said he'd take me there to check the place out if it weren't for the fact that one of us would have to stay there forever afterwards, pay the tax and all.

You have to understand that the myths surrounding the red man had evolved as we'd grown up in the sense that the folklore we'd hear grew more serious, more graphic, more consequential. I still remember the versions I'd heard when I was little, the stories that ended with kids getting candy or even hugging the red man as they thanked him. Then in middle school, the red man held kids captive in tiny, bamboo barred prison cells that kids easily crawled their way out of before racing home to tell their parents, at which point villagers gathered arms to search the area but couldn't find any evidence of a cave where the children claimed to have been held. Hell, by the time we were teenagers, we'd heard versions where the red man ate kids alive then spit their bones out onto the forest floor before taking his magical cave and moving further up the river to prey upon the next little town. I mean, in one version I'd heard, an entire damn river of blood flowed through a cavern, kids went in on a raft, the raft came out empty, and the bloody river rose an inch or so.

Chelsea had just put her camera away when I stopped dead in my tracks, reached into my pocket to see if I had my inhaler, then swore several times. Ya see, it was a major problem that I'd forgotten my inhaler. Allergies had been bad that year and air quality in Wisconsin was worse than it had been in decades in part because of wildfires up in Canada that summer.

I sat down on the sideways trunk of a fallen tree and laid my head in my hands, feeling the frustration turning and screwing the tension in my chest tighter and tighter.

"So what?" Lawrence asked, his frustration flung up into the air with his arms. "We have to go all the way back over this? Hell, we're a mile in. Might as well call it a night then and head on home."

"Chill," Chelsea said as she sat down beside me. "You know he's got bad asthma. Don't be an asshole."

I sighed as I shook my head, then stood abruptly. "It's fine. I'm fine. Let's just keep going."

Nobody said anything so eventually I just kept moving, walked on past them both and continued our journey towards the area where we'd heard the cave had been spotted.

We walked in silence there for a minute or so and it made me feel bad. I certainly hadn't wanted to be *that* guy, the one who popped the balloon, brought the fun back down to earth and ruined everyone's good time. It just made me nervous for a second, that's all. I'd truly needed my inhaler several times already that summer and it just made me uncomfortable to not have it within arm's reach.

"Look there!" Lawrence shouted as he pointed up towards a hill off to the east. "What is that?"

I turned to look where he was pointing and I thought I did see something, but just for a sliver of a second as it disappeared, retreating back down the hill and out of view. "What was it?" I asked as I turned back towards Lawrence, who had placed his hands on the back of his head as if in awe of what he'd just seen.

"Had to be the red man," he said. "Had to be. I'm sure of it. Let's go." He took off running and he was a fast runner, faster than either of us.

Chelsea hollered after him, telling him to wait as we tried our best to keep up. He'd shouted back, telling us to hurry just as he reached the top of the hill then vanished onto the other side, his voice growing more and more muted.

Chelsea and I found ourselves leaning on our knees panting as we reached the top of the hill. We could see Lawrence down below maybe one hundred feet or so away. And though the slope down wasn't too steep, I had to stop and take a break in fear that my asthma would go spinning off the rails after that uphill run. Chelsea rubbed my back and asked if I was ok. I told her I was but that I didn't feel great and had to catch my breath. I told her to go on after him, that I'd catch up in just a couple of minutes. Then she was gone. And I was alone.

I could see them down there together now, though I couldn't make out much else of what was going on. Their flashlights illuminated what seemed to be an argument between them. Chelsea was pacing back and forth, flinging her arms into the air. Then a brighter light made its presence known as it seemed Lawrence had fired up his camping lantern. That's when I was able to make out more of the scene down there and that they quite clearly were standing outside of an entrance to a cave.

I stood up slowly as I stared at the opening, which was dimly lit up with what looked to be a flickering candle or two. I felt like I was floating weightless, as if someone had just released me from my anchor of disbelief, allowing me to hover there and take in this impossible sight. We'd found a cave. Had we found *the* cave? I wasn't aware of any others in the area, and I'd lived there my entire life.

My wonder and excitement turned quickly to concern as I watched Lawrence shake his hand back towards Chelsea as if waving her off before he headed towards the entrance of the cave. Maybe my emotions have manipulated my memory as I think back, but I swear he stopped just before entering, turned to look up towards me and nodded. I saw the gleam in his eyes then, the mole on his cheek, the excited smile on his face but then the light down there grew dimmer as he crossed the threshold and disappeared from view. I took off jogging down the hill then, no longer thinking about my asthma at all.

Lawrence was gone. He'd entered the cave alone and Chelsea was spouting hysterics by the time I reached her. "He insisted on going in there alone," she said as she paced back and forth, clearly trying to gather herself. "I'm not his mother. I'm not his babysitter." She kicked a pile of stones just then, sent them tumbling down further towards the base of the hill which seemed rather dramatic to me, though I supposed I hadn't been there to hear the argument take place.

Besides, I'd had my own problems again by then as I could feel a full-blown attack coming over me. I sat down slowly, didn't say anything to Chelsea as I prepared to save as much oxygen as I could. I forced slower but deeper breaths, felt my stomach rise, my lungs fill the best they could as I prepared for the downward spiral I knew was coming.

"What's wrong?" Chelsea asked, as she knelt beside me.

I waved her off but not in a mean way, at least not meaning to. But I knew I had to focus on myself just then if I wanted to get through this terrible situation alive. I mean, we were far away from my home by then. Lawrence was gone. Chelsea was super upset. I had to focus, had to hold myself together.

Lawrence's screams from within the cave were sudden and guttural. They dragged on for a long time, so long in fact that I thought he must be messing with us. Then he stopped screaming. And an even more painful silence followed. Complete and utter silence. We stared at the cave, and I heard Chelsea whispering something I couldn't quite make out. My chest burned and I felt dizzy. I was able to breathe, just not very well, and it was starting to affect my vision as everything around me seemed suddenly blurry.

To be honest, when Lawrence screamed it made my asthma attack worse because then I felt I had to jump up and do something. I wanted to dash off into the cave and save my friend from whatever danger he'd encountered, but I grew so dizzy when I stood. I felt so lightheaded from a lack of oxygen that I immediately collapsed back onto the forest floor and watched helplessly as Chelsea moved slowly into the cave, her flashlight illuminating a dark, hollow hole, and for a moment I saw her inching forward, her arms wrapped around herself, clearly shelled up in fear but moving into the cave, nonetheless.

She'd screamed minutes later, over and over again, wrenching out high pitched eruptions of terror before silence swallowed everything just as the darkness had swallowed her. I'd assumed she was gone too, and that I'd probably be next. But she emerged shortly after, whispering something over and over, something I couldn't make out, her hair a sort of gray now and spread out and up as if she'd been electrically charged or something.

By shock or by some other means, my attack slowly passed, and I was able to help Chelsea work her way back through the woods towards my home. I recall looking back towards the cave as we reached the top of the hill just above it and I could swear I saw someone standing just outside of it; a little person, a child maybe. When I glanced back one more time a few seconds later, I saw nothing; no creature, no man, no cave for that matter.

Years passed since the newspapers told our story. Headlines ranging from "Northern Woods Mystery" to "Unexplained Disappearance" to "Suspect Questioned." There was of course "Friend of Missing Teen Lawyers up" to "Case dismissed; Questions Remain." Years passed since I'd entered any wooded area whatsoever. Years passed since the last time I'd visited Chelsea in the institution, not because I didn't want to see her, but because of what would happen when I did.

She'd glance around at random things, not seeming to focus on anything at all, whispering something repeatedly, something I couldn't make out. But eventually, she'd spot me, make eye contact, take me in and seem to understand who I was. Her eyes would blow up, stretch impossibly wide as her face. Her cheeks and even her throat followed suit, and that same guttural scream came with it all. Again and again, screaming as she stared at me as if I were the devil himself, while orderlies held her down and security pulled me out of the room. After the third time, I stopped visiting. For her sake. At least that's what I always told myself. One of her doctors had tried to explain to me that I just woke up dark memories when she saw me, that it had nothing to do with me per se and that I shouldn't take it personally.

Years passed. Years since I'd read the news stories claiming that no body had ever been found, no cave either for that matter, stories that questioned my version of what happened. Years passed where I had no close friends nor wanted any.

Years passed where I tried not to think about Lawrence.

Where he was, if his bones had been spat out by some mythical monster or his blood had been donated to a river that ran through a cave.

But it was impossible; impossible not to think about him, to wonder if he was somehow still out there somewhere. I liked to imagine that he'd skipped town, gone to college somehow, become a physical therapist. And occasionally, once or twice a year it seemed, I'd put fresh batteries into that old walkie-talkie, fire it up, then spend a few minutes calling out to him, asking him to come in, to give me a sign, anything. Asking if I could help him, if he needed anything out there. By then I was usually sitting down against the wall, telling him what had been going on with my life, telling him how Chelsea was a mess and that it would probably do her good to see him again. I'd reflect on how my father had passed, and my mother had moved into her sister's house out in Tennessee and how it was just me there now though I'd moved away, far away from any wooded area. Then, after a while, I'd sit there in silence and wait, wait for someone to come in, for some sound, some explanation, some purpose to present itself. It never did.

Years passed.

Looking back, I'd spend the years that followed slowly preparing to return to where it had all gone down. But it was more of a subconscious thing. I'm not sure I even realized that was what I was doing but my actions spoke for themselves. You would have questioned my choices, found them strange. For starters, you might have wondered why I even kept the walkie-talkie, why I charged it back up so often. You might ask why I spent so many hours researching the red man when all I wanted to do was forget about him, to forget about what had happened to my friends. You may have wondered why I spent hours in libraries, on chat pages, staring at the stars deep in thought. But if you're asking those questions, then I'm guessing you've never lost a friend to a mythical cave in the woods.

The planning was something I did bit by bit, piece by piece over many years. I put together a scrapbook of information that might be helpful were I ever to actually go looking for my old friend. It would be a quiet Sunday afternoon, one where I'd just finished watching a film that involved a cave or a curse or anything that reminded me of what had happened that night so many years ago, and I'd research a bit, print out a screenshot of an article, an image I came across, and I'd throw it into this binder rather quickly as I immediately regretted pursuing the issue at all.

But perhaps the most powerful tool I'd picked up during those years was my own memories, memories not just of the incident itself but of things I'd heard and seen when I was younger. Those early morning half awake, half asleep moments where I'd recall my grandparents referring to the red man as Far Darrig, or the fact that my grandparents always kept salt in every room of their house, that my grandma in particular would always keep salt on her, in some container or small bag in her pocket just in case, just in case she had to fend off some sort of evil spirit.

Far Darrig. I began researching it instead of doing "red man" searches and I came across different information. One entry in particular that stuck with me was to be polite, despite its sinister games, that this sent it off balance and gave one a chance to protect themself. Another piece of information surprised me as I hadn't come across it before, that Far Darrig would try to trick you and that you must keep your guard up. I swallowed the lump in my throat as I read that entry.

So it was that years of information wound up stuffed in this binder, and that one morning after a particularly bad breakup with some girl who'd been racing with me towards the inevitable dead end that all my relationships raced towards, I'd wound up turning on the walkie-talkie again for the first time in a solid year or so.

I'd said my piece, even took a few minutes to complain about my most recent ex when the impossible happened; a response, an immediate response. "Kevin? Come in, Kevin. Are you there? It's Lawrence. I need you. I need your help to get out. Look for me where you lost me. I'm still there. I'm still there buddy, and I need your help."

"Hello? Lawrence? Is that really you? It can't be." I'd whispered that last bit to myself, though if he'd really been there, if he'd actually been alive and listening, he would've heard me whisper it.

He didn't respond again. I tried every channel and frequency over and over again hoping to get him back but to no avail. Had I imagined it all? I wondered.

Still, feeling that I had nothing to lose, and probably feeling self-destructive as well, I grabbed the binder and threw it into a backpack along with some flashlights and other essentials, then prepared to head out to my car to drive the 30 miles back to the town I'd grown up in.

I stopped while backing out of my driveway. I sat there with my foot on the brake for a moment before shifting into drive and pulling back up into my garage. I ran inside and grabbed all the salt I could find before getting back in my car and heading out to face the red man.

I pulled up to my childhood home which had long been abandoned, heard the gravel growling under my tires before the brakes screeched and silence followed.

As I neared the woods, treading the land in black boots now, feeling more prepared than I had those many years ago, I took a moment to turn and glance back towards my childhood home. The plague that had destroyed the barn had spread to the old house and it was a wonder that either structure still stood at all.

I followed the path the best I could remember. It was dusk now and I hurried along hoping to reach the hill before it was completely dark, but the sun must have set just as I reached it. I'd need flashlights from there on out and I swear I saw something at the top of the hill when I first switched one on and pointed it up that way. If there had been something, it was gone. And the grey skyline, shadowed by trees, seemed to call me back up to the top of the hill to face this demon that had defined what felt like my entire life.

So that's what I did, headed up the hill, my inhaler in hand this time just in case, and a bag of other resources. I took the binder out as I walked, pointed my flashlight down upon it, trying to take in all the information I could as I prepared myself for what I might find over that hill.

There, I came across an incredible row of large boulders that simply shouldn't have been there. They formed a wall, and I walked along it until I found a cave, an opening in the wall, much different than what I remembered and not quite in the exact spot it had been in but almost. I gathered the most important supplies at that point, the flashlights and the weapons and the salt, then made my way inside, no longer all that scared as I felt I had nothing to lose.

I heard Lawrence's voice as soon as I entered the cave, though it was quiet, muffled, distant. I could still make out the words as I'd heard them just an hour earlier. "Kevin? Come in, Kevin. Are you there? It's Lawrence. I need you. I need your help to get out. Look for me where you lost me. I'm still there. I'm still there, buddy and I need your help."

It hit me right away, that it wasn't just the words that were the same as I'd heard earlier, but the voice, the tone, the way the words were spoken, as if it were a recording. I heard them again as I worked my way further into the cave. There was a light up ahead and it clearly wasn't coming from my flashlight, so I switched it off and continued slowly ahead.

Then I saw my friend, or at least his shadow as I came

around a curve and a flickering candle sort of light rose up before me. My heart grew warm then. I felt excitement, life, energy in my very bones as I considered the possibility that my story still could have a happy ending, that I'd find my old friend, that he'd somehow be ok and that together we'd gallop in on white horses to save Chelsea from the madness that took her.

But then I turned the corner and grabbed at my chest, gasped as my old friend stood before me, his face the same as it had been back when I'd seen him last, mole on his cheek and all. He was right there before me, my old friend, except that he'd grown smaller, half his size I'd say, maybe three feet tall at best.

He looked up towards me, walkie in hand as he spoke into it, "Kevin? Come in, Kevin. Are you there?" I could see that his face seemed heavy, weighted, that his eyes had sunk so far into his face that I could barely make them out.

"It's Lawrence," he spoke into the walkie, now clearly looking up towards me though I still couldn't make out his eyes nor could I make sense of the fact that he was about three feet tall. "I need you. I need your help to get out."

He walked toward me then and I realized his face hadn't changed at all, hadn't formed any expression whatsoever as he reached up and dug his nails into the front of his scalp, then peeled his face off and held it there in his hand, a red man's face revealing itself in his place. The candlelight roared an angrier light in the room suddenly and I could see the walls around the cave more clearly now, the faces that hung there, hundreds and hundreds of them, men and women, children too, and they all frowned in my direction as they draped hanging down all around me. Then the red man, who held my old friend's face in one hand, raised his other arm, walkie in hand, up to his mouth before hitting the button and speaking into it. "Look for me where you lost me. I'm still there." He smiled then, and his teeth were rotten, his tongue black, and the red man changed again, his nose growing long and hairy, a rotten smell emanating. A rat wearing clothes standing on two feet stood there before me and he spoke into the walkie one last time. "I'm still there, buddy and I need your help."

I stared down at this creature before me, swallowed the fear into my throat, and tried to remain focused on my preparation; on the notes I'd read as I walked up the hill. "Thank you so much for thinking of me." Silly response, I know, but polite and unexpected. "It was very nice of you to remember how much I cared for my friend and to give me this opportunity to say goodbye."

The little creature grew angry at my polite response, began dashing around his little living quarters and kicking over objects, throwing a tantrum of sorts. It bought me just enough time to pull my bag off my shoulders and dump everything out on the ground before he turned back and zeroed in on me again. At which point he lowered his sights and grinned, looked like a little devil ready to eat me all up and spit out my bones, and then he dashed towards me.

I didn't hesitate. I started with the salt, just sprinkling it all around me, and the screeching anger the little creature emitted sounded so satisfying, as clearly the salt did something. Then I grabbed weapons: daggers, lighters, anything I could and attacked in all directions, crying and screaming and laughing all at once it seemed, before I eventually realized I was laying down and that the ground felt soft and the air smelled fresh, and it all felt safe.

I gathered myself, looked around, realized it was daytime now and I was laying on the grass. There were weapons strewn about, and salt was spread around me like a light winter snow. But there was no red man, no Far Darrig, no cave for that matter.

Things changed quickly after that. I felt better, to be honest, and was ready to grow up and move on. I got my shit together, opened a business and made smart investments. Then things took off fast, so fast I couldn't even explain to you except to say that I'm a known figure in most circles now. What I say and do matters. When I move, others notice and wanna move with me. And I like it. I mean, I worked hard to get here. This wasn't luck.

But that's a lie and I know it. And that's the problem. I feel like I'm still trapped in that cave, not literally, but rather that anytime something good happens to me I just assume it was good luck, the fortune I'd earned paying off, though it feels more like a curse. I went on a date just last night, ordered surf and turf and fake-smiled my way through a margarita. The steak might as well have been sandpaper and the lobster playdoh, the lime margarita cyanide on the rocks for all I cared because that was the price, right? All the money in the world and I can't enjoy any of it because all I see is my friend's face, picture it hanging on the red man's wall, mole and all, wondering why mine wasn't up there beside it.

People come up to me all the time, get all worked up, ask me the most boring, unoriginal questions. Some friendly gentleman might ask if the owner was ever around, to which I'd come out and introduce myself if I had been within earshot. Or I'd run into a regular customer outside of work, at a restaurant, or a concert, or maybe just at a grocery store. Or I'd find myself cornered at a barbecue by some couple or group of sports fans or a hen party of single ladies. "What's your secret?" They'd ask. "How'd you do it?" "How's it feel to be so successful, so wealthy, so prosperous?" They'd ask. But that's never what I hear, not thanks to the guilty, finger-pointing voice in my head. They might as well just say, "I heard you saw the red man, and that you lived to tell about it."

Hodags Eat Bullies, Not Bulldogs

Rachel M. Martens

I ron Heart Lake recognized the arrival of spring in 1973 slowly and regretfully, as if the last thing it wanted was to open its waters to the spring fishermen. The ice did not break until the last week of April, and when the tourists from southeastern Wisconsin and Illinois descended upon the town of Newswich for opening weekend that year, flat icebergs still bobbed on the dark surface of the lake and a northern wind whipped flurries of snow like tiny razorblades at the reddened cheeks of the fishermen. Arrowsmith's Sporting Goods sold out of their end-of-season stock of cold weather wear on Friday, and by happy hour on Saturday, Cindy Carver's Dreamcatcher Boutique sold out of outerwear too, even though most of her stock had been floral-patterned housecoats. True to form, the weather unexpectedly turned on Sunday evening, and the town's bars and restaurants found themselves in possession of dozens of abandoned pink and lavender coats when they opened on Monday morning.

"Alright, I've had it with this fucking place," Paul Gamble growled, throwing his fishing pole with its busted line into the lake. His friends went silent, and he ground his teeth and ignored their slack-jawed stares as he fought his way out of the confining embrace of his sweaty rose-print coat, his face on fire from the sunburn on top of the windburn. This damn trip had been his idea; he and the guys had needed a getaway after the shitshow work had been since the stock market took a nosedive in January, but the only thing that had been good about the weekend was how cheap the booze was compared to Chicago. Even then you had to make allowances for none of these backwoods bartenders knowing how to mix a decent martini. "Kevin, pull up the anchor; I can't do it anymore."

"What?" Kevin asked from the front of the rental boat. "What do you mean?"

"What do you think I mean?" Paul snapped. "I need a fucking drink; I'm done with this stupid lake. Pull up the anchor, we're going in."

"Calm down, Paul. I think you're catching big toothy bastards with those flashy lures; do you want some worms?"

"Fuck the worms, I want a drink." Paul glared at George, who held up both hands in apology. "If you chuckleheads want to come back out here and lose more baits, be my guest, but drop me at the damn dock."

If he wasn't getting exactly what he wanted, Paul might have been miffed by how eager the guys suddenly became to raise anchor and deliver him to the resort's dock. All he cared about right then, though, was the shortest path between him and a goddamn martini.

The dock was empty when they arrived; everyone else was either already back to work for the week or out on the lake, and the resort grounds with their manicured pathways and cutesy cabins were vacant. The sun was still beating down hot, glinting off the whitecaps on the windy lake like blades bared at Paul's eyes. He waved off the guys and quick marched it up the dock and into the cover of the tall pine trees around the resort. *Finally, some damn shade.* He thought about going back to the cabin to use the facilities and get the car, but that sounded like an unnecessary detour between himself and the much-needed martini. Carver's Club where they'd had dinner and drinks last night was right over by the dam, and there were hiking paths from the resort that carved through the woods to said dam. He'd walk it and let the guys find him there later.

All weekend, the lake had been buzzing with the rattling hum of boat motors, and the town had been alive with honking cars. But the forest was quiet and almost pretty with the hot sunlight cutting through the evergreens and the bare branches of deciduous trees Paul couldn't begin to name. The ground was soft and squishy, covered with a wet blanket of half-rotten leaves and, on the hiking trail, hastily laid fresh bark mulch, all of it muddy and moist from the sudden snowmelt over the weekend. Paul curled his lip at the mud he was getting on his shoes, but he'd come this far, and he really only cared about that martini.

It was still a break from Chicago; a much-needed break. But damn if he wasn't sick of this place, of the Main Street USA atmosphere and the insane weather and all the damn nature. The air was crisp and clean, that was nice and all, but he was going to hear loon calls in his nightmares for years, and he was ready to get home to his perfectly pressed suits and a decent cup of coffee.

The wind kicked up and rustled through the woods, making the trees creak and sway. Paul cast a distrusting eye at a big beast that was weaving like a drunk. When the wind eased and the quiet returned, he remembered how long it had been since he'd pissed off the side of the fishing boat this morning and figured he might as well water a tree, the better to get his martini efficiently when he got to Carver's. All these wood ticks pissed in the woods anyway, right? When in Rome, as they say. He wandered a few paces off the hiking trail and chose a birch that lay fallen against a pine at an angle, unzipped, and got down to business.

It must've been the exposed sensation that came with having his dick out in the freaking woods that clued him in to how weirdly quiet it was. Paul tilted his head to listen, but the forest seemed to be completely silent aside from the splash of piss striking nature. Shouldn't there be birds? Or squirrels bouncing through the trees? He thought he was almost to the supper club, but he couldn't hear the rush of the water over the dam or any traffic noises. His skin began to creep and crawl, and he gave things a shake and hurried to zip up. "Stupid, creepy place," he grumbled out loud.

Crack! It was a branch snapping, surely, not a bone breaking like such a loud, sharp sound suggested, but it sent Paul's heart into his damn throat, and he jumped a foot in the air. At least he didn't scream; just shook his head in bewilderment and turned to look…

…his jaw dropped, and cold terror turned his veins to ice.

The bartenders had been telling them stories all weekend about the area, about the ghosts and the monsters and the lore. Carver's Club had supposedly been the site of a shootout between bootleggers, and the FBI and Iron Heart Lake had been an iron ore mine until the river suddenly rerouted and transformed it into an underwater tomb. One of the favorite tall tales had been about the hodag of Rhinelander, some big, hairy, horned monster that prowled the woods looking for white bulldogs to eat or some shit. The locals readily admitted that the hodag some guy had been trucking around to the county fairs was debunked as a hoax, but they also seemed to believe and love the stories about their local cryptid. Paul thought it was a clever marketing scheme but hadn't given the stories any more consideration than that.

Now, though...now he was staring at gleaming yellow eyes looking hungrily into his own. Now he was marveling at how damn long those fangs were, at least as long as his hand and protruding out over a mouth of razor-sharp teeth like a sabertooth tiger. Now he was seeing how easily a fallen tree trunk as thick around as his bicep had apparently snapped beneath the weight of one four-clawed foot.

No one had said that a hodag slunk over the forest floor on its short legs like a creeping, grinning cat, that it would match his pace to pursue him as he back stepped and damn near tripped himself over brush. No one had said that it would *chuckle* like some old black-and-white movie monster that just crawled out of a lake or a crypt or a lake that happened to also be a crypt. No one had said that it salivated over the smell of human flesh or piss or whatever was drawing it so quietly nearer, but it *was* salivating, viscous drool dripping from its massive fangs as its nostrils flared. The mouth opened wider, and a great pink tongue lolled forward like it was a dog begging for a bone and not a seven-foot-long prehistoric beast covered in moss-green fur and white spikes that gleamed in the sunlight.

The hodag reached the fallen birch that Paul had pissed on, perhaps ten feet away now, and the creature paused there. For just a moment, it broke the staring match they'd been in to glare down at the yellow-stained birch bark. It snorted and sniffed at his piss.

This was his chance. *Should I run? Fight? What the hell do I do?*

The hodag lifted its hideous face again and grinned ear-to-ear at Paul, forty or fifty sharklike teeth bared. Then, it lifted one front foot, closed its three claws around the piss-stained birch, and it snapped the tree trunk in its grasp with an eardrum-splitting *CRACK.*

Oh shit...

Paul Gamble didn't have time to run. One instant he was staring into the wild yellow eyes of a beast whose forest he had unwittingly pissed on and the next he was on his back, pinned beneath the crushing pain of a massive weight in the center of his chest with those yellow eyes inches from his own. A lump of hot drool dripped off the hodag's right fang onto Paul's left cheek and oozed slowly towards his ear. A wail of utter terror so very much louder than he could have ever guessed his lungs were capable of making ripped itself from Paul's lips and echoed strangely through the northwoods, dancing in the air like his fear was being mocked by a forest of ghosts.

The hodag chuckled down at him, *"Gr, gr, grrf,"* and the last thing Paul saw was those awful teeth flashing down at him and the flood of red that filled his wide-open eyes as the flesh was ripped from his face.

***

"School's out for summer!" Alice Cooper snarled gleefully from the speakers of The Dragon's Den. The radio wasn't usually turned up so loud in the bookworm side of the combined book and record store, but the celebratory change got Bobby Arrowsmith to smile for the first time all day. *"School's out forever!"* No, not forever, unfortunately, but it was 3:15 on the last day of the school year and Bobby would gladly take that with the sigh of relief it was due.

He was in the bookstore out of habit mostly, and to steal a few minutes of peace before he finished the walk to the Arrowsmith Motel & Campground and got to work. He didn't have the cash to buy anything today, hadn't had cash to spare in months and wouldn't for months unless his big brother Joe flipped him a few bucks. They never really had much money to go around, but things had been especially tight with the news of dead fishermen in the woods driving tourist traffic down. Bobby would eat his own shoe before he'd ask Mom for a quarter to buy another Lovecraft volume right now. But he could have these five precious minutes to listen to the radio and look at the grotesque covers of the new horror books The Dragon's Den had on display.

There was a new Robert Bloch book. Bobby's fingers itched with the temptation, but then his stomach growled and reminded him that that asshole Billy Edricson had stolen the precious bologna sandwich Mom packed for his lunch and eaten it in front of him while his goons laughed. He was so hungry, and if Mom was wringing her hands comparing the prices of bologna and peanut butter then Bobby was not going to get a new Robert Bloch book to escape into. He'd feel bad enough snitching a snack when he got home.

Bobby sighed and ran a longing finger over the gleaming cover art, then turned on his heel and retreated from the bookstore. He was needed at the motel and if he got his work there done efficiently, he could escape into the woods until dinnertime. Hunting for cool bugs and animal tracks didn't cost money. Maybe he'd even dig up some worms and do a bit of fishing off Grandpa Eugene's dock.

The little bell above the door jingled to wish him farewell as he left The Dragon's Den, then the busy hub of Main Street Newswich in mid-afternoon greeted him. Cars rumbled past and drivers honked and waved at people they knew on the sidewalks. A shiny red Ford screeched to a stop and honked at a band of reckless kids who darted across the road in front of it. Music hummed from the radios of a few cars and out the open windows of businesses. Newswich's one radio station was playing "Smoke on the Water" and the song made Bobby think fondly of the way the mist drifted across the lake some mornings. That was one of the very few benefits of living right next door to the motel. From the breakfast table and from Bobby's bedroom window, there were clear views across the road to the boat launch and Iron Heart Lake. As much as he hated Newswich Junior High, Bobby loved that lake and the northwoods that surrounded it. He wasn't sure he'd ever fit in in town, but he could never leave this place.

Bobby jogged across Main Street and followed the sidewalk to the corner. He waved at his older brother Joe through the wide glass windows of Arrowsmith's Sporting Goods, but he was in too big a hurry to get to the motel and didn't stop to talk; just took his usual route north on Oak Street to follow the sloping terrain downhill towards the lake. He could catch up with Joe tonight after work.

He hadn't gone far along Oak Street, when he saw something that made him stop in his tracks. Half a block up and across the road, Billy Edricson and his goons, Tank Mitchell, George Carver, Nathan Klein and Johnny Larson, were gathered around a little white dog. They'd managed to get a rope around its neck, though it obviously was not happy about being leashed, and they were trying to push and pull the little dog along without getting close enough to risk a bite.

Bobby loved animals and hated seeing one mistreated. He'd been known to rescue injured wildlife from the side of the road and bring all sorts of creatures to the vet for treatment, had even nursed a raccoon back to health in his closet last summer, though his mom screamed like a banshee when she found out. He knew better than to mess with Billy Edricson's crew, had a very vivid reminder not to mess with them in the form of his rumbling stomach and missing lunch. But he couldn't turn his back on the dog.

The poor thing was whining and thrashing around now, and it was hard to tell for sure from this distance, but those goofy wobbly legs and big feet screamed 'puppy' and Bobby just couldn't walk away knowing that jerk Billy Edricson might hurt a puppy. He walked on, staying on his side of the street but approaching cautiously.

"Billy, you sure this is a good idea?" Johnny asked.

"Shut up!" Billy snapped at him. "It's the best idea. If we kill the hodag, we'll be heroes. The tourists will come in droves, and the town will be saved, and the girls will swoon over us, which is the only way you're ever gonna get a girl, Johnny. But if we want to kill the thing, we need bait. Now quit being a pussy and help me out here."

It wasn't a terrible plan, actually. Bobby had heard the rumors floating around school that it was a hodag that had killed the ill-fated out-of-towners, a savage forest monster that folks of this area and the nearby city of Rhinelander had been spinning stories about since the loggers started it in the 1800's with their campfire tales. A guy named Gene Shepard had even claimed to have captured a hodag seventy-some years ago and raked in a ton of cash selling tickets to folks who wanted to see the beast at the local fairs. That hodag had turned out to be a hoax, but the stories persisted, including a bizarre claim that a hodag's favorite meal was white bulldogs. And that white puppy did actually have the squashed face of some kind of bulldog relation.

If the rumors were true and it was a hodag that was murdering tourists, then that jerk Billy was probably right that whoever slayed it would save the town and become a local hero overnight. Bobby put in enough hours helping his mom run the motel to know. The motel's eight rooms and the campground's twelve sites were normally fully booked every weekend from Memorial Day through Labor Day, May too if the weather was good enough for camping, but as the number of bodies found in the woods around Iron Heart Lake piled up, business had been dwindling. They'd been getting phone calls from regulars canceling their reservations for the first time in years and the walk-up customers had trickled to half what they were used to. Last weekend they'd been at less than fifty percent capacity, which was unheard of for the first weekend of June and meant dire things for the motel's bottom line. And the thing was, people had a short memory, especially out-of-towners who didn't keep close tabs on the town gossip. If people just stopped dying this would all blow over and things would be fine, but every weekend another tourist went missing and another search party went out, and another corpse got trundled off to Skelton Funeral Home missing its face and internal organs. Everyone in town was feeling the squeeze of the thinning tourist business as word got out about the deaths. And yeah, if whatever was responsible for the killings was hunted down and killed, the town would be saved overnight.

But that wasn't the kind of thing that was worth sacrificing an innocent puppy for. In Bobby's book, nothing was worth that. What was the point of slaying monsters if you became one yourself?

Ah, hell, he thought to himself. *I'm about to get myself killed for a dog.*

"Hey!" he yelled across the street. Billy and his goons all spun to look at him, and Bobby set his jaw, determined not to flinch or back down. "What are you doing with that dog?"

"None of your business, pipsqueak!" Billy yelled back. The dog, definitely a puppy, whined and tried to weasel out of the noose around its neck. Billy jerked at the rope and the puppy yipped. "Hey! I've had enough out of you!" the bully snapped at the pup.

Fuck it, then. Bobby stalked across the street, red staining his vision and fists tight at his sides. "I've had enough out of you!" he echoed. Then he took a swing and punched Billy Edricson right in the jaw.

The next few moments were a blur of movement, shouted curse words, and pain. Bobby definitely saw the dog take off running, so that was good, but nothing else was going well here. He'd just taken on a kid a year older and eight inches taller than him who had four friends at his side and yeah, he only got that one punch in. In seconds, he'd taken two hits to the face and was on the ground curled inward on himself as kick after kick rained down on him. "I'm going to kill you, you little shit!" Billy screamed down at him.

"What are you boys doing?"

It was a woman's voice that had spoken, but the boys all recognized it instantly and turned to stone, as if Medusa herself had caught them red-handed. The comparison wasn't far off. That voice with its slightly low tone and its slow, haunting syllables, that voice that made its owner's words behave like softly spoken utterances carried to all nearby ears on a northern wind, *that voice* belonged to Mrs. Hawthorne, the town witch. And they were currently fighting on the sidewalk directly in front of her flower shop.

"Go stir your cauldron, witch!" Billy said, the brave and stupid words only wavering a little. "This ain't none of your business."

Bobby looked up from the armadillo ball he'd become with wide eyes, wondering if he was about to witness Billy Edricson being turned into a toad. There on the stoop of her flower shop stood Mrs. Hawthorne, her eyebrows raised at Billy in a way that very clearly said, *excuse me?* She was a strangely beautiful ageless woman, her skin wrinkle-free and her dark blue eyes as sharp and dangerous as the lake on a stormy August day. Her long black hair that was very quickly fading into grey and streaked with white was the only indication that she was older than twenty-five; much older. There were rumors around Newswich Junior High that she kept her skin so young by bathing in the blood of children, that she was over a hundred years old, and that she was the one who had rerouted the river to turn the mine into Iron Heart Lake and kill all the miners in 1892. She hadn't exactly done anything to dispel these rumors, either. She ran a flower shop and greenhouse that turned out supernaturally beautiful flowers, sold herbal remedies out of the back room, and her only living family since her husband died mysteriously a few years ago was a black cat named Jinx. All she was missing was green skin and a wart on her nose, but honestly the ethereal beauty she wore instead was scarier.

"'Witch,' is it?" Mrs. Hawthorne asked, her meandering syllables twirling around them like tendrils of dark magic. She floated slowly from the stoop down to the sidewalk and with each of her steps, Billy Edricson and his crew took a faltering step backwards. "You say 'witch' like an insult, but I don't believe you understand what it is you mock, William Edricson."

Billy took another clumsy step back and tripped over the curb. With a cry, he stumbled backwards, arms flailing and finding nothing to catch his fall. It was only a sudden gust of wind whipping down the street and hitting his back that kept him from hitting the pavement. Just as he caught his balance, a loud truck horn blared, *BEEEEP*, and a delivery van barreled down the road, ripping past and missing Billy by mere inches. A rush of wind off the draft from the van sent Billy's hair into a whirlwind and he stumbled forward now, tripping over the curb again and this time being caught by George Carver and Nathan Klein.

A beat of horrified silence fell heavy over the group, and everyone very slowly processed what had just happened; what had *almost* happened. When each of the boys looked up to Mrs. Hawthorne, they found her smirking.

"Holy shit," George breathed.

The words broke the spell. Half a second later, Billy was shoving past his friends and tearing down the sidewalk. "Let's get out of here!" he yelled back. The others were already running after him, though; hadn't needed to be told, and a moment later they had all vanished around the corner.

Bobby stared after them, still sprawled on the sidewalk. He was just starting to realize he should probably run too when Mrs. Hawthorne glided closer, her shadow stretching over him like the wings of a massive raven. He cringed and looked up, expecting the worst. What he found instead was the witch smiling down at him, one open hand outstretched in invitation. "Let me help you, Bobby," she said. "If you're not too frightened of an old witch, that is."

Maybe it was a spell, or maybe it was just the musical laughter behind her words, but when he thought about it, Bobby really wasn't afraid of her anymore. He was certain he'd just seen her purposely cause Billy Edricson to *almost* get hit by a truck. That was pretty intimidating, but he got the very strong impression that as dangerous as the witch may be, she was on his side, and it would be poor manners to refuse her help now after she'd just saved him from a serious beatdown. He took her hand and let her help him to his feet. Once he was upright, the sting of swelling bruises and wind on open wounds hit him and he cringed, looking down at himself and assessing the damage. His hand was all kinds of messed up from the one punch he'd gotten in, his knuckles all bruised and bloodied. His shirt was stained grey and brown in patches where the bullies had kicked him with their dirty shoes. And he was pretty sure there was blood running down his face from a split on his bruising eye socket in addition to his nose that was gushing blood.

"You are a mess, aren't you?" Mrs. Hawthorne mused. "Come on inside and I'll patch you up."

Bobby let the witch guide him into her flower shop. She latched the front door and flipped the sign to *Closed*, then led him to the back room. He'd never been in there, had avoided it like the plague everyone said it was. His heart raced in trepidation as they walked through the shop, and when she opened the door marked *Employees Only,* he was braced for a witch's lair. Big cauldron in the middle of the room, bats hanging from the ceiling, jars of disgusting dead things lining the walls, rats scurrying around. The workroom she revealed was almost disappointing, though. One big open window above a workbench filled the room with brilliant sunlight and a fresh breeze. Drying flowers hung upside-down from the ceiling in place of the bats he'd pictured and there were shelves overflowing with jars, but the jars appeared to be filled with dried cut plants of a variety of colors, each one neatly labeled by a bit of masking tape marked with careful writing. Plants were everywhere, too. Flats of young seedlings sunbathed under grow lights, sickly plants in individual pots recuperated in a place of honor on the window ledge, and hanging plants stretched long limbs out around the room, scouting for more sunlight and soil. A boombox in the corner was playing the opening riff of that new song "Simple Man" that seemed to be on the radio all the time, and though Bobby never would have guessed Mrs. Hawthorne was a rock radio listener, the song somehow fit perfectly here.

Mrs. Hawthorne pulled a stool out from the workbench and directed him to it, so he sat obediently and tried not to stare too obviously as he watched her rustle through her cupboards. She clearly knew exactly what she was after and where to find it. Only a minute later, she set on the workbench a first aid kit, an amber dropper bottle, a jar of dried flowers, and a squat little mason jar filled with some kind of yellow ointment. She poured a bit of the dried flowers into a square of gauze, wet it at the sink, and wrapped it up tight, then placed it in his hand and brought the hand up to his bleeding nose. "This will help that clot, hold it just so." He did without question and watched quietly as she wiped his open wounds with a bit of gauze dampened with whatever alcoholic something was in the amber bottle, then dabbed at his bruises with the ointment. "You're usually the sort to steer clear of trouble," Mrs. Hawthorne mused. "What got you mixed up with those boys?"

"There was this dog," Bobby answered quietly. "I guess he was a stray or maybe a puppy from somebody's litter that they didn't want to keep. He was little like a puppy, all white with this squashed face like a bulldog. He was crying and howling, trying to get away from them...they had a rope around his neck, and they were dragging him." Mrs. Hawthorne frowned deeply, and Bobby hesitated, but at her serious, expectant look, he decided to tell her all of it. "I heard them say they were going to kill the hodag and be heroes. And I don't want anyone else to get hurt, but I didn't think it was right, them using a puppy as bait. Do hodags even eat white bulldogs? They're not supposed to kill people and this one does, so maybe it wouldn't have even wanted the puppy and when their plan didn't work, they'd have hurt him. That seems like the kind of thing that creep Billy would do. And besides, maybe the hodag isn't so bad that anyone should kill it. I met the guys it killed when they were coming and going at the boat launch; they were all dicks. Maybe they messed with the hodag and shouldn't have. It hasn't hurt any locals or anyone decent; it's not like it's stealing babies out of windows or some shit."

Mrs. Hawthorne nodded slowly, her brow deeply creased. "I see."

Bobby sighed and looked away, shy now at these words that tumbled off his tongue so easily in the witch's presence. He wasn't good at talking to people, really only ever said more than three words at a time to Joe and Mom, nobody else. But Mrs. Hawthorne was so easy to talk to and was listening so intently. No one ever listened to him like that, not even Joe. "I wish we could just move away," he admitted very quietly, like his mom might somehow hear the whispered betrayal from all the way at the motel. "I don't fit in here. I don't have friends, everyone at school makes fun of me because I'm short and quiet and poor. They say terrible things about my mom. Everyone knows my dad offed himself and they whisper about it. I always know they're talking about it by these pitying looks they give me."

"You can't move away, though," Mrs. Hawthorne said very simply. "You're an Arrowsmith. Your ancestors helped found this town, and folks with blood in this land never really leave it. Besides…" At her pause, Bobby met her dark blue eyes and his breath caught at her knowing smile. "You may not fit in with your classmates, Bobby, but the forest and the lake know you and love you. This place is your home."

"I won't be in the forest or the lake much if I have to work my ass off helping my mom put food on the table," Bobby said bitterly. "Or if we have to move away because the motel goes under. If there's no tourists, there's no guests at the motel or campground, and if there are no guests we can't make money. Maybe Mr. Barinov would let me help out at the bookstore and I can make some more money that way, but even that won't be enough."

Mrs. Hawthorne nodded and pursed her lips, thinking for a moment. Lynyrd Skynyrd sang the final chorus from the radio, *"So be a simple kind of man..."* Then, one side of the witch's mouth turned upward in a knowing smile. "So, you're telling me you need some friends. And you don't want to kill the hodag, you just wish it wouldn't cause such problems for your mom's business?"

"I don't want to kill anyone," Bobby insisted automatically. "I don't like bullies, but I couldn't kill anyone, not even the hodag."

"Mm-hmm." Mrs. Hawthorne gestured to his hand and the gauze-wrapped flowers in it. He lowered the bloody bundle and was shocked to realize his nose was no longer bleeding. The witch smirked and began to wipe the sticky blood from his face. "Maybe the hodag doesn't like bullies, either."

***

Bobby left the flower shop in a daze. He was very confused by everything he'd seen and been told there, especially by how casually Mrs. Hawthorne had talked about the hodag, which most grown-ups said wasn't real. At the same time, though, he felt lighter; like he didn't really know or understand what was coming but he knew *something* was coming and that when it came, he would know exactly what he was meant to do.

Mrs. Hawthorne had insisted on giving him a jar of the ointment to keep putting on his bruises and beat-up ribs, as well as half a watermelon she'd gotten at the grocery store and said she couldn't possibly eat all on her own. As he walked down the slope of Oak Street towards the lake and home, Bobby packed the ointment and the carefully wrapped watermelon into his backpack for safekeeping. He was tempted to dig into the watermelon right now he was so hungry, but he had a half-baked plan to share it with his mother and tell her the story about Billy and the dog and Mrs. Hawthorne. Mom worked hard and never treated herself to anything. He hoped the watermelon might brighten her day and distract her from the canceled motel rooms and the mounting bills. It wasn't a solution to their problems, wasn't a hodag pelt and a tour bus full of fishermen, but he hoped it would make her smile.

As Bobby followed Oak Street downward, the houses on either side disappeared and the woods crept in close, the sidewalk running out and dumping him onto scrubby grass. The campground at the bottom of the hill was almost totally unoccupied today and when he got close enough, Bobby could see Iron Heart Lake between the bare trunks of the tall pine trees. The lake was as dark as ever and strangely still, like it was waiting for something.

He was almost to the motel, could even hear the radio in the lobby spewing a surprisingly heavy rock song out through the windows, when a terrible yelp echoed through the woods. Instantly, Bobby thought of that white puppy and, praying that Billy Edricson hadn't found the poor thing and decided to take out some impotent rage on it, he sprinted into the woods towards the source of the yelp. It hadn't sounded too far off. He wasn't any better equipped to defend the puppy or himself than he'd been before, not unless Mrs. Hawthorne's watermelon had some magical properties he was unaware of, but he had to try.

He ran deeper and deeper into the woods, always westward; ran on and on listening for signs of life. *Am I too late? What if he killed it?* But then he heard the terrified whine of the puppy and changed course slightly, heading southwest. *Hang on, buddy. I'm coming for you.*

Bobby broke into a clearing and there was the little white dog, tied by the neck to a tree branch stabbed into the ground like a stake. Bobby rushed forward and scrambled to untie the squirming puppy. "Shh, shh, you're okay, buddy," he said to the puppy, "Don't worry, I've got you."

"You little bastard!"

Bobby yanked the rope out of its knot and the puppy leapt into his arms as he looked up...and found himself staring down the barrel of a rifle. *Oh shit.* Cold terror froze him on the spot, and his heart began to pound inside his skull so loud he was sure Billy Edricson could hear it from where he was glaring down at Bobby four feet away. Beyond, Bobby could hear more footsteps, Billy's goons, but he couldn't really see a single fucking thing except the dark pit he was staring into, the black hole that at the tiniest touch of Billy's malicious finger would send a bullet tearing straight through Bobby's face.

"What the fuck do you think you're doing?" Billy snarled. His eyes were wild with crazed rage, and when he yelled, spit flew from his lips like he was a rabid animal. "You stupid little shitstain, you fucked up our hunt! There're fresh tracks all around here, this was our shot, and you fucked it up! Maybe now I'll fuck *you* up!"

Bobby wrapped his arms tighter around the puppy, which was trying to burrow inside his ribcage and hide there. He was about to die, he was sure of it; Billy was out of his fucking mind right now and had a fucking gun on him, but with that certainty came a strange sort of calm. Nothing he said or did right now was going to change what Billy did to him, so there was no point to fear or anything else. Instead, there was a strange sort of peace and a rush of confidence that Bobby had never in his life expcrienced. As all the fear washed out of him, Bobby lifted his gaze from the mouth of the rifle and focused on Billy's wild eyes. "Yeah, maybe you will," he said, "But at least I'm not an asshole bully like you, and that's a hill I don't mind dying on."

Billy's face twisted into a hideous scowl, and he hefted the rifle more securely into his arms. A mechanical *click* cut into Bobby's soul and he braced for the bullet.

Crack!

Billy, George, Nathan, Johnny, and Tank all spun at the sound of a tree branch snapping, Billy whipping the rifle around so fast he smacked Tank with it. Tank barely flinched, though; was too busy gawking at the wood edge. Something quiet and foreboding hummed under Bobby's skin, something that whispered *this is it*, and he very carefully wrapped the puppy more securely in his embrace.

"Holy shit…" George breathed.

"Dude," Tank whimpered, "Billy, it's…it's really big. It's not supposed to be that big."

"*Gr, gr, grrrf.*" The sound was very distinctly a *chuckle*, but it was all wrong, like the laugh of a massive swamp creature rising out of a Universal monster movie. Nathan shuddered and took three clumsy steps away from the source of the sound and then, in the space between the boys the bully had created, Bobby got his first look at a real live hodag.

It was *exactly* what Bobby had grown up expecting a hodag to look like: gleaming yellow eyes peering out of a massive head framed by great white horns; a wide demonic grin showcasing dozens and dozens of sharp teeth, including two huge fangs that stabbed down over its jaw like a saber-toothed tiger; a big, muscular body rippling with fur that camouflaged terrifyingly well with the forest undergrowth; big, clawed feet like a dragon's that stepped silently over the brush and into the clearing; an impossibly long tail unfurling behind it and stirring the tall woodland flowers, but never quite dragging on the ground; dozens of shimmering white spikes in a row along the hodag's spine from the top of its head to the tip of its tail like a very dangerous mohawk; and yes, unlike Tank, Bobby had always sort of expected hodags to be this big, at least seven feet long and as tall as the Larsons' St. Bernard. This was not the little bulldog-sized hoax that Gene Shepard had fooled fairgoers with seventy years ago. This was not just real, it was clearly, indisputably, the result of a nasty mix of an angry, abused, dead ox and some extremely weird forest magic.

The bullies all began to stumble backwards as the hodag stalked forward, chuckling again. *"Gr, gr, grrf."* It was laughing at their fear. Billy Edricson fumbled his rifle and, when the hodag took a lurching step forward, damn near dropped it. George caught it and wrenched it from Billy's quivering hands as the hodag laughed. "Give me that, you dumbass!" George snapped. Then, he raised the rifle and fired. *BANG!*

The hodag made a terrible shrieking sound, and Billy was the first to turn on his heel and make a break for it. Bobby cringed and curled himself into a protective ball around the puppy, still on his knees and not liking his odds for outrunning the hodag or the bullies. Tank was running too, and Nathan and Johnny were grabbing at George and the gun, trying to get him to bail with them. George was chambering another round, though, stars still shining in his eyes as he thought of the glory they'd come here for.

But there would be no glory for George.

The hodag went suddenly still, its searing yellow eyes glaring balefully at George and his rifle as red blood seeped from a wound in its shoulder. A low, hateful growl rattled from the base of its ribcage, maybe from the bottom of Hell itself, and then the hodag launched itself across the clearing in a flash of green fur and white teeth and claws. The boys screamed, and Bobby's breath died in his lungs as he watched the hodag rip the rifle from George's hands and cleave it into three pieces in its massive mouth. It spat out the pieces of the gun in an instant and swiped out with one clawed foot at Nathan, who'd turned and only made it two steps. The hodag's claws tore into Nathan's back and crushed him down into a sobbing heap on the ground, ripped downward and tore canyons of blood and gore from the kid's shoulder blades to his hips. Johnny was scrambling backwards too, but the hodag whipped a full 360 degrees around, and with the momentum buried the spikes of its tail in Johnny's belly, throwing him to the forest floor with the force of the blow. Johnny screamed, and the tail was gone and then back again, slamming down on him and knocking the air from his lungs with a huge *"OOomph."*

Then only George stood there, staring at the hodag with wide, terrified eyes. He walked slowly backwards, hands up as if to claim he meant no harm, and the hodag watched his retreat with greedy eyes. *It's not done.*

Apparently, George came to the same conclusion. Suddenly, he spun to Bobby and grabbed at his arms. Bobby realized instantly he was after the puppy, now whimpering in fear and squirming again, and he held on tight and shoved at George with his shoulder. "Fuck off!" he said to the older boy. "You wanted it here, you fucking got it; now *you* deal with the consequences!"

The hodag chuckled, *"Gr, gr, grf."* Both boys looked up to see it grinning at them, blood dripping from its claws and its spikes as Nathan and Johnny moaned and died slowly on the ground. Then, the hodag leapt into the air and George screamed.

Bobby rolled sideways over the grass as the hodag pounced on George. George was screaming bloody murder and there were awful, wet ripping sounds happening amidst the boy's garbled cries and the hodag's happy grumbles. Bobby didn't look, though; only crawled across the ground to Nathan, who was wheezing wetly and oozing endless bubbling blood from his back. The hodag had torn into the boy's lungs, amongst other parts, and as Bobby watched, tears in his eyes and a terrified puppy in his arms, Nathan suffocated and fell limp. Johnny was groaning weakly, so Bobby crawled to him next. He at least looked like he might live if Bobby could get him out of the woods or bring help here, but neither of those options felt very plausible right now, not when George had just stopped screaming and not in a good way.

Thunk. A severed hand, *George's hand*, hit the ground a foot away from Bobby's knee. For a moment, he could only stare at the hand, watching the crimson blood seep from the torn veins, the fingers just lying there so very lifelessly. Then, Bobby looked up.

The hodag stood right there, crouched only three feet away and staring into his eyes, grinning with a mouth full of sharp teeth dripping blood and gore. A torn strip of human skin hung from between two razor-sharp canines, just barely twitching from the silent movement that had brought the hodag so close.

And in that moment, even as death grinned monstrously at him, that sense of calm fell once more over Bobby. Softly, he said to the hodag, "I won't let you have the puppy. But if you spare us, I have something else I could give you."

The hodag blinked, and Bobby took advantage of its momentary confusion, taking care to remove his backpack without startling the hodag or losing his grip on the shaking puppy the beast was eyeing. He tugged open the zipper with one hand and withdrew Mrs. Hawthorne's gift of watermelon.

The hodag's greedy, yellow eyes locked on the watermelon like a homing beacon. For a moment, it froze completely still, as did Bobby and the puppy. Then, the hodag's mouth curled into a wide grin and its pink tongue lolled over its sharp teeth.

"You want this?" Bobby asked the hodag. The yellow eyes never left the watermelon, but the creature licked its teeth and thick, bloodstained drool oozed from its mouth. It absolutely wanted the watermelon. "Okay," Bobby said. He lowered the watermelon to his left hand so he could tear open the wrapping without letting go of the dog, then he tossed the fruit into the air. The hodag pounced at the watermelon like a huge cat, and caught it in its mouth with a wet *crunch*. The creature stilled, then hummed happily and shut its eyes as if in bliss, slowly gnawing at the watermelon. Bobby raised an eyebrow at the sight and watched, bewildered. The hodag savored its treat for several minutes, then finally swallowed the watermelon and looked to Bobby once more. "We good?" Bobby asked.

The hodag grunted. It was as close to a 'yes' as Bobby could expect. The beast shot another baleful look at George's torn-apart corpse, then shook its head and began to lumber off towards the woods it had emerged from. Bobby watched it in shock, still stunned that the absurd watermelon bribe had actually worked. He'd have to thank Mrs. Hawthorne somehow.

Then, a moment of inspiration struck, or maybe it was insanity. "Wait!" Bobby called after the hodag. The creature did wait, stopping right at the wood edge and turning to look back at Bobby. "I don't like bullies either," Bobby said to the hodag, "But if you keep hurting tourists, it's going to kill the town. My mom's motel will close and so will the resort. All the businesses will be gone. People will move away. I don't fit in with regular folks either...people tease me or ignore me mostly; I don't have friends. But this is my home, and I don't want to lose it. What if you and I were friends? If I brought you more watermelon and we hung out in the woods together sometimes and you weren't so hungry and grouchy, would you stop hurting the tourists?"

For a long time, long enough that Bobby began to feel ridiculous, the hodag only stared at him. *God, I'm dumb. Now it's going to kill me after all.*

The hodag did not kill Bobby Arrowsmith, though. Instead, the beast smiled its toothy grin and, slowly, it nodded its head. *Deal.*

Elephant's Graveyard

Barend Nieuwstraten III

"Holy crap, this thing's off the chart," Kevin said, standing at the front door of the boarding house. Looking through his thick glasses at one of his gadgets, he turned a dial at the side of it, making it squeak in a slightly different way. Catherine never truly understood his odd little gizmos, but the sudden change seemed to blow Kevin's mind.

"Try and be a bit more subtle with that thing," Catherine insisted, already twisting her face with embarrassment before she'd even knocked on the door. "Your subharmonic spectrometer or whatever it's called is going to have them thinking we're kooks."

"Kooks?" Kevin pulled his head back, offended. "I'm bringing science to this venture. *You're* the mystical one." He wriggled his fingers in the air.

She put her hand on his wrist and pushed his gadget-wielding hand down. "At least wait till after we've introduced ourselves before you start waving that thing around."

Kevin grumbled under his breath, then made a bunch of mumbling sounds, as if he was consoling and reassuring his home-made contraption.

It was, in all fairness, an impressive tool that had served them well, but she despised the nineteen sixties science fiction aesthetic her husband chose when building it.

Catherine knocked on the door. There was the sound of shuffling slippers on the other side, and soon the door was opened by a man whose age was hard to gauge.Maybe thirty, maybe forty. It did not look like he'd slept in a long time.

"Hi," he said, squinting at the light from outside. "You here about the uh…" he swiped a finger around, pointing up.

"If you mean the ceiling, no," Catherine said, hoping to break the gloomy atmosphere. It was so immediately rife with misery, it practically poured out the door with the stale air. "If you mean the unknown, then yes. Catherine and Kevin Clements, supernatural investigators at your service. May we come in?"

The man nodded and pulled the door properly open, leading them down a few stairs into a corridor stained yellow and beige by decades of cigarette smoke. It smelled of cheap aftershave, air-fresheners, and ash. It smelled like the nineteen seventies. Catherine flashed back to her early childhood and wondered where the whitewashed half-tire hanging over the water meter, lawn flamingo, plastic lobsters, and orange bead curtains were. She took a second to compose herself and prevent her nose from twitching in protest before following the man in.

Catherine looked the man up and down, once she'd adjusted to the lower light of the dank corridor. He was yawning, unshaven, messy haired, and in an open dressing gown over his faded red and white tee-shirt and shorts, dragging his slippers on the floor in a miserable shuffle.

"So, you're Michael?" she asked.

The man shook his head, seemingly oblivious to Kevin scanning the walls with his device and humming in fascination like a young child at an aquarium. "Stephen, room E," the resident flippantly introduced himself, before turning around and knocking on one of the many doors.

"Michael," he called through the door. "Those people are here."

When the door opened, they were greeted by a man in jeans and a blue shirt, who at least looked showered and shaved in his smart casual apparel. He exchanged a nod with the man who'd let them in and shook hands with the pair who'd answered his call. "Hi, I'm Michael," he said. He too looked tired and worn out but at least presented like a human with purpose. He stepped aside and ushered them in as Stephen skidded his slippers down the corridor.

Catherine and Kevin stepped into a room that was more like a prison cell, with an attached bathroom and built in wardrobe. A single bed, bedside table, lamp, and laptop. That was it. There was a high window, at street level.

"It's not much, but it's home," he said, seemingly responding to their sympathetic looks of pity. "Once you get used to all the sobbing, ranting, and screaming, at least."

"The manifestations have come through as upset voices ranging from sad through to angry?" Kevin confirmed. "That's fascinating; such emanations are typically so mono-emotional. A complex range like you've described is abso-"

"No," Michael said, waving his hands at them. "That's just the other tenants. This is *not* a happy place. Those are the *day* sounds."

"What exactly is this? A half-way house for parolees?" Catherine asked.

"More of an elephant's graveyard for divorced men."

"You make it sound like a place they come to die, rather than a place to stay while they get their life in order."

"Talk to the others who live here and stay the night to hear the voices of those who once did, and I think you'll agree, this is very much a place where we *do* come to die. Very few get their life back in order. Courts see to that. This is a desperate place. You should see the emergency numbers list in the kitchen. Every man here has lost *everything*. Then, on top of that, there's the 'night crew', as we call them. Generations of men fed through the meatgrinder of our family courts. You see, all these men *do* have their lives in order. At least what's left of them. They all work, paying off houses they've been kicked out of, sacrificing up to eighty percent of their pay to help raise children they're barely able to see, if at all. They have just enough left over to cover the cost of scraping by and paying rent to live in a single room like this. All just to be kept up all night… by the dead."

"Why would anyone stay here?" Catherine asked.

"Well, the other options are homelessness or suicide. And if the former doesn't find them first, enough choose the latter, eventually. In fact, people don't typically move out of this place. Even *after* they die, as you'll see tonight. Everyone who stays here leaves something behind. If not their corpse, their spirit… if that's what you want to call it, and compounded misery. You can feel it. Like I said, this is an elephant's graveyard. There isn't a room in this place someone hasn't ended it all in."

Both Catherine and Michael were suddenly drawn to Kevin's device, beeping and alerting with flashing lights. "Whatever's in this place, there's a lot of it," he said. "To get a dormant reading that's already bumping the red, is…

terrifying." He raised his eyebrows. "This is going to be an interesting night."

Catherine and Kevin set up their own foam pad and double sleeping bag on the floor, near the door. They set up recording equipment around the room. Michael heated a couple of frozen pizzas in the shared kitchen, and they sat around like a small slumber party waiting for the sun to go down.

"So, are the hauntings, sightings, or manifestations limited to the rooms where former tenants have died?" Kevin asked, sucking and blowing air between words to cool the hot piece of hard-base pizza he'd bitten off, burning his cheeks.

"Well, there's never been anything in the shared bathroom as far as I know," Michael said. "Unless ghosts just have boundaries of decency, I say that's weird because someone definitely killed himself in there. Cooper, his name was. A few years ago. No one knows what his first name was, because the stack of posthumous mail all just said, Mister Cooper." He looked to the high window contemplatively. "Everyone said it was so selfish of him to do it there. There, in a shared space. One in high demand."

"Isn't that a bathroom in there?" Catherine asked, pointing to a different door than the one through which they entered.

"Basically, identical to an airplane toilet, with an awkwardly narrow shower recess jammed into it. The one down the hall, past the kitchen, is a *proper* bathroom. Something that was built when this was once probably an actual house before it became an animal shelter for discarded dads. It's got space. It's got a bath. I'm not sure why people slit their wrists in a warm bath. I mean baths are nice sure, but why make a warm human soup that someone has to reach into to unplug?"

"I think in most cases, suicide is a selfish act," Catherine said, adjusting settings on her tablet that connected the more conventional devices set up around the room.

"That's a pretty rough assessment," Michael said with a grimace. "A lot of desperate souls come here. When you meet them, you can tell *them* what you think. See what *they* have to say about that."

"Do we have to keep noise down to a respectable level considering the shared nature of the building?" Kevin asked, seemingly unaware of the conversation. "The walls seem pretty thin."

"To get through the nights in here, most of my neighbours are big believers in sedation through self-medication," Michael explained.

"And that works?" Kevin asked, in disbelief. "They can just sleep through being haunted?"

"They have terrible dreams. They do not escape the torment, and by their sedation they can't escape whatever they're put through in their sleep. In some ways, it's worse than staying present for it, because they can't wake from it, but one way or another it's coming for them and at least *that* way, their body gets a full night's rest. Even if they wake up more disturbed than they were the day before." Michael looked up to the high window. "It's getting dark. Our other guests will be arriving soon," he said, ominously. Sitting on his bed with his legs crossed, he leaned over to switch on his lamp.

Catherine looked between it and the ceiling light that was already on. The lamplight added nothing to the brightness of the room. She cocked an eyebrow, looking back to Kevin sitting on the floor beside her as she heard sniffing from another room through the wall. It turned into groaning and when she looked back to Michael, he shut his eyes and sank his head.

"That'll go on for a little while," Michael said, pointing to the wall, then back to the opposite one behind him. "Then *he'll* start for a bit. I'd join in myself, but the schedule seems pretty full." He gave a half-smile of resignation.

Catherine couldn't help but appreciate the joke and gave him a mildly amused grin back.

Kevin shuddered in the middle of adjusting one of his devices and quickly grabbed another, pointing it around the room with purpose. Catherine wrinkled her brow at him but felt all the hairs stand up on the back of her neck and forearms.

"Baseline's rising," Kevin said, as little LED graphs started pushing up on their tiny display screens.

The room grew darker as both the lamp and ceiling light receded in brightness, reducing their light to dull, glowing filaments within their bulbs. Behind the diffuser of the ceiling light, the glowing orange lines could be seen, but Michael had to flip the cover of the desk lamp on his side table to expose the room to its diminished but direct remnant of light.

Soon, the number of voices they could hear crying through the walls multiplied, coming from more discernible directions than there were rooms from which they could possibly originate. More and more, pleading voices, obscured by the walls and ceiling and even the floor. They created a muffled cacophony of desperation. Sad voices, angry voices, defeated whimpering, and infuriated yelling.

Catherine was close to putting her hands over her ears, but her professional curiosity kept her listening. She checked to make sure the recording devices were working. The displays indicated they were picking up a great deal of noise, much to her excitement. Though, it would be a hell of a time separating it all out from each other later.

Voices emerged from the chaotic chorus.

"Just let me see the boys," one said.

Another cried, "we were supposed to grow old together; you threw it all away for *him*?"

"Don't do this. Please God, don't do this to me."

"She needs a father. What you are doing is wrong."

"Why?" so many voices asked. "Why?"

"Do these sound like the voices of men who were hiding from responsibility?" Michael asked. "Men who had somewhere else to be?"

Catherine held up a palm to protect the recording and Michael nodded apologetically, refraining from speaking further.

The minimally luminescent light globes soon began to flicker, occasionally flashing brighter. Each time they did, they caught the contours of a human shape. A man standing in the middle of the room that startled Catherine and Kevin, though he disappeared as quickly as he had appeared. Another manifested, sitting on the edge of the bed in a flash. One appeared with his head buried in his hands, sitting upon a chair that was no longer there. Another laid on the floor with his head between Catherine and Kevin, startling them again for the brief moment in which the apparition stayed with them.

Kevin stood up with his device, excitedly moving it about to point it at all the figures briefly flickering into existence, struggling to keep up with them. Catherine rested a hand on his leg, staying connected to him. She had seen spectres passing through the bowels of old homes, faces in mirrors, and all manner of odd and unsettling apparitions, but it was still just as confronting every time. Here, the way these figures were revealing glimpses of their miserable existence, was like a city crossing or shopping mall of the afterlife. There were so many of them and they began to overlap, sitting here or there, leaning, pacing, doing push-ups and sit-ups, drinking alone, smoking, getting dressed, reading letters. What united them was a clear physical display of fear, anxiety, and morbid depression. It *was* a jail cell. A prison without bars or guards that had housed a great deal of inmates who never completely left.

It was a window into so many lives that fell into ruin and found the same isolated patterns and routines. A voyeuristic window into the empty repetitiveness of hollow existences. Catherine straightened up, angry at herself. She had seen ghosts before and been moved to tears by the cruelty of their lingering spirits. Old places where women and girls had been murdered by some cruel man that kept them, tortured them, and snuffed out their bright light, leaving them to haunt the rooms and corridors of the place of their final trauma. They carried these horrors well beyond their years when their tragic deaths provided no release for them. They had stories to tell. Stories where wrongs needed to be made right. These, on the other hand, were simply sad pathetic men who failed to make their marriages work or get back up on their feet afterwards. She felt insulted that they had the audacity to try and haunt sympathy out of her and resented herself for almost giving it to them.

Catherine looked back to Michael, sitting cross-legged upon his bed. He was watching her and, by the look on his face, knew precisely what her assessment was. He slowly nodded.

"I've read your book, you know," he said, as the flashing apparitions began to dissipate. The diminished light of the two sources began to slowly restore to brightness.

Catherine looked around the room as the glimpses of misery went away. "Is that it?"

"Merely the first wave," Michael said. "We've some time for now. A short reprieve."

"This is amazing," Kevin said, looking to the equipment readings. "Just amazing. I've never seen so many competing visitations. All confined to such a small space."

"More than that serial killer's basement from eleven years ago?" Michael asked. "What was that again, seven?"

"Yes, seven victims."

"What did you count here?"

Kevin shrugged. "I'll have to review all the data later, but it was dozens."

"Dozens," Michael said, still looking at Catherine. "And that's just *this* room."

"They're all like this?" Kevin asked. "The other rooms here?"

Michael nodded. "In your book you call it 'un-haunting,' when you observe ghosts over a period of time to assess what their message is. Finding out what they're trying to say, what injustice their haunting is screaming to the living. Mysteries and crimes to solve. Leading you to their hidden bodies and evidence that will see those who wronged them brought to justice."

"Or at least the names of those who lived some time back and wronged them. Exposed for what they truly were when they were still alive," Catherine boasted. "I can't bring the dead to justice. But having it known to the public what monsters they were, appropriately tarnishing their revered legacies, in some cases, seems to bring peace to their long-passed victims. It gives them the closure they need to move on."

"I think it's good work that you do, for what it's worth," Michael said, sincerely. "I wouldn't have even looked at a book like that before coming to *this* place. But now that I know this is actually a thing, having seen it, lived with it, first-hand… well, I have to admire the pair of you. You found justice for voices most people don't even believe exist. Will you give *these* apparitions a voice? Or do you condemn them as society does, without knowing their stories? Considering them to be right where they deserve to be, as if those who took everything from them are owed it all? Because if so, I don't think there'll be any un-haunting of this terrible place. But to be honest, I think it's impossible. It's far too great an undertaking and no one's going to bring the callousness of society itself to justice. Nor the selfish cheating hearts of lovers turned mercenaries when it came to try something new, simply on a whim. Not the lawyers working for a percentage of a destroyed life, run through a wringer. No, these spirits will *never* move on. No one will bring their killers to justice. These men, on the surface look like they died at their own hands, but they were *indeed* murdered. Murdered by far too many who'll never be questioned. You can't bring the justice system to justice. There's no justice for judges and lawyers nor oath breakers and homewreckers."

Catherine shook her head. She couldn't believe she'd signed on to spend the whole night in this room with *him*. But what they were observing was too important a find to walk away from. She just hoped he'd finished his surprisingly calm tirade.

"Every room in here is like this, you know," Michael continued. "Except the bathroom. Old Cooper… leaving a horror for others to find, but then somehow finding peace. I've wondered about that for some time. And I think…" he stopped talking as the lights began to diminish again, recoiling to filament glow alone. Michael closed his eyes. "These visions are a little harder to watch for me."

Again, flickering from the lights, flashed partial reflections of the past. A chair appeared in the middle of the room alone. A figure of a man only appeared as it stepped up onto the chair and fed his head through a noose. Whatever fixture the rope had been tied to existed no longer, but it had at some point and when the man kicked out the chair from under himself, he fell. Dressed in a suit, the man stopped inches from the floor and jolted. Even in making his choice, his feet instinctively searched for purchase to save him. A spectre of dust and fragments of plaster fell as the long since removed fitting gave way, but by the time his feet hit the ground and slid out, he'd already had the life choked out of him.

Another began to fade in and out of view as he moved about the room, bent over. Flattening out some tarp before he finally sat down naked and picked up a large sharp knife. He turned it around and took several deep breaths before driving it into his chest. The pain on his face was beyond anything Catherine had ever seen before. It completely changed shape under the shock before he pulled it out and collapsed on the floor, pouring blood from the wound.

Another sat on the bed overlapping Michael, who shuddered. Even with his eyes closed, seemingly feeling its presence. The apparition of a man pulled a plastic bag over his head and sealed it by unrolling adhesive tape around his neck repeatedly, until he eventually lay down on the bed and rustled the bag with the inflating and deflating of it, sticking to his face with each inhalation. His breathing laboured and faded and he slowly vanished.

Another man began breathing heavily on another chair. He fed the barrel of an old revolver into his mouth. A loud bang echoed about the near walls in a deafening assault on everyone's ears and the recording equipment. He blasted a hole through the top of his head and soon slipped off the front of the chair, onto the floor, pushing it against the wall with his slumping body. Blood poured like a pair of waterfalls out of his nostrils until he too faded away.

As it was before, the appearances began to overlap instead of taking turns. They watched men empty bottles of pills into their mouths, drink a bottle of bleach, and all try a variety of methods of ending their existence in this one cursed room.

Whatever Catherine believed about these men; it didn't make the sight of their gruesome deaths by their own hands any less harrowing to witness. She had seen so many dark things and learned of so many horrible truths in the places she had investigated. But this frank display of misery claiming so many souls was more than she could bear. Murders were at least emotionally barricaded by the anger they would elicit. This desperate display provided no such luxury. She wrapped her hands around Kevin's upper arm as he continued to read as much data as he could on his equipment. Even *his* face was wearing a sour grimace. He too was barely able to take it.

"They all killed themselves," she said, sliding into a panic of discomfort and disbelief. "There's no mystery to solve here. There's no justice to find. Why do these spirits persist? What do they want?"

"What do the spirits want?" Michael scoffed. "What they want can't be given. They want to be loved. They want to know what happened to the love they had. How their children are. They want to know that their children understand what happened and why they never got to see them. That they aren't just these so-called 'deadbeat dads' who gave up. They fought hard for them and lost. They worked hard for them and lost. They want to know that all the poison their mothers poured into their ears about them wasn't believed. Can you give them that? You can't rid this place of the dead who plague it. They're practically the mortar that holds this place together. This place was built on misery. It's all it knows. This place just is what it is and there's no turning back."

The shocking visions dissipated again, and the lights slowly returned to perhaps a third of what they should be.

"Now I know why Cooper killed himself in the main bathroom," Michael said, sounding exhausted. "Not for the convenience or serenity of the warm bath but just to be found. The world had discarded him like a hamburger wrapper on a freeway and forgot that he ever existed. At least dying there, where someone would have to find him, meant that someone would know. Someone would know that he was gone. Because his wife and kids wouldn't. They took everything he had and asked no questions. Just like *my* family. My wife found someone new, and despite the hours I work and everything I gave up and sacrificed for them, my kid is just going to believe whatever his mother tells him about me. Why wouldn't he? She made sure I couldn't see him, then told him I didn't *want* to see him. He doesn't care about me because he doesn't know *I* care about him. I'm already dead to him; I'm dead to the world. I lost contact with all my friends to focus on my family, and it threw me away as a reward. No one will know that I'm gone unless I do something like Cooper to make sure someone will see me off. A semblance of peace these poor souls that appear here never found because it was far too long before they were missing to anyone. Even then, it was just people chasing rent and utilities. No one who actually knew them. No one that had even ever spoken to them or met them before. But Cooper was a talkative man. A socialite of this emotional hospice. I think telling your story to anyone who'll listen, even if with cynicism in their heart, makes a difference. At least, I hope it's enough not to join the others who dwell here forever."

It was then that Catherine pushed herself up and looked to Michael's hands resting on his folded lap. Blood was pouring out of his wrists. He was pale and his quilt was growing a red stain beneath him.

"Kevin!" she yelled.

When Kevin looked, he dropped his equipment and went to Michael. "God damnit, the kit."

Catherine quickly grabbed their small first aid kit and popped it open, handing bandages to Kevin. He quickly began wrapping them around one of Michael's wrists. "Call an ambulance."

"At least they can rent out my room sooner with someone to tell them it's available, instead of finding out weeks later," Michael said, sounding weaker as he stretched his words.

"Why would you stay in this horrible place?" Catherine asked, as she entered the number in her phone and listened. "Why wouldn't you leave?"

"These ghosts aren't here to haunt, I don't think," Michael said, fading and slurring his speech.

Kevin lightly slapped his cheeks with his bloody hands. "Stay with us," he said, before quickly making to bandage the other wrist.

"I think they're here to show us we're not alone."

"Why wouldn't you leave?" Catherine repeated, as a recorded message played in her ear.

"I just did," Michael said, too weak to smile before slumping over.

By the time an operator asked what the emergency was, Kevin was shaking his head, feeling Michael's neck for any sign of life.

Michael left the building on a gurney with a sheet over his head. Catherine was sat to one side with a blanket placed around her while a policewoman questioned her. The other tenants of the boarding house had defeated looks on their exhausted, groggy faces. This was all routine to them. Though Michael was probably the freshest corpse to leave the building in a while.

Another policeman approached with Kevin, holding a note in a clear plastic envelope. "He left a note," Kevin said. "Do you want to hear it?"

Catherine pondered a moment before she finally nodded.

"Dear Catherine and Kevin, thank you for coming. I don't know how much I'll have managed to say that needed to be said, because I'm writing this before you arrive. Firstly, I suppose I should apologise. It's a hell of a burden I'm planning to inflict upon the pair of you. Especially as events have led me to become quite a fan of your work. I would hope that given what else you would have seen this night, hopefully my exit won't be as shocking as it might otherwise have been. Still, I can only apologise for dragging you into it. I hope you share my story and continue investigating. I've paid rent for the next few weeks, up till the end of the month, so you may use my room as you wish to record what you can. I only hope that anything you might publish on this place, will provide the only closure you might help bring to the spirits that linger here. For myself, my only hope is that by doing things the way I did, I'll end up wherever Cooper went instead of stuck in this damned place forever." Kevin took a breath and looked away for a moment before he continued reading. "I didn't leave a letter for my son. Anything I might have to say to him or wish for him to know would only contradict whatever his mother has taught him to believe. I think it's better that he grows up taking her side if she's to raise him. I still believe in a united front when it comes to parenting, so this is the best way to back her up. No contradiction or argument. Just a straight line to follow. He'll grow up better that way. I suspect those stuck in this boarding house as apparitions are probably the fellows who left this world hoping to defend their name, while I'm hoping that making peace with being hated by those I loved the most will actually free me. So, if you wish to tell the stories of this place, it will mean a lot to me. But leave my name out of it. Sincerely, Michael."

Kevin handed the letter back to the policeman and sat beside Catherine, wrapping his arm around her as they watched the ambulance leave.

The Collector of Eyes

Dana Gricken

Thunder boomed, then lightning lit up the dark sky a second later. I jumped from where I was sitting on the log around the fire. Rain poured from the sky, but the large tree we were beneath kept our campfire dry and blazing.

"Uh, shouldn't we go inside our tents?" one of the girls at our camp asked. Tessa Harvey, the outdoorsy girl, and complete know-it-all. "It's dangerous to be out in a bad storm with all these trees—"

"Relax, will you?" Logan Hughs, our school jock spat. He poked the fire to keep it burning. "We'll be fine. Besides, we have a chaperone."

He pointed at our camp counsellor, Mrs. Lisa Kimball. She was asleep and loudly snoring on the log next to mine. Tessa furrowed her eyebrows but didn't say anything else.

There were only nine of us on this little camp excursion, sent on a field trip by our school to learn more about nature. And all I learned was that I hated bugs and sleeping on the ground.

Our class clown, Carter Stewart, reached out and poked another kid with a stick. The boy, Jack Lewinsky, jumped so high in the air that his round glasses fell off his face and hit the ground. Carter and some of the other kids found it hilarious, but I wasn't laughing.

"Here," I said, picking up the glasses and handing them to Jack. "Sorry about that."

Carter frowned. "You're no fun, Rachel. Sitting here is boring. Can someone tell a scary story already?"

The group looked around at each other. My best friend, Matthew Parker, leaned forward and cleared his throat. He loved the spotlight and wanted to grow up to either be an actor or a performer. "Yeah, sure. How about Bloody Mary?"

"Boring!" Carter cried. "I've heard it all before. Doesn't anyone have anything original?"

Watching Jack clean off his glasses and then put them back on his face gave me an idea. I glanced around at my classmates, the glow of the campfire bouncing off my cheeks. "I think I do. How about…the Collector of Eyes?"

Murmurs broke out. Carter leaned forward. "Now you're talking—that sounds sick. What's it about?"

I closed my eyes. "There's this girl…we'll call her Jane. Anyway, she came to this very camp for a good time, but she tripped and fell onto a tree branch. It plucked both of her eyes out."

To make my point, I picked up a nearby branch, then crackled it. Some of the kids shivered.

"Gross," Jessica Payne said, the class mean girl. "And painful."

"Oh, very." I brought the branch up to my eyes. "It should've killed her, but some dark force in the forest kept her alive. And now? Now she haunts this place, searching for eyeballs to pluck out. None of them are quite right for her face, but she keeps trying. Kinda like a morbid

Goldilocks. And rumor has it she's going to appear tonight…boo!"

When I jumped up, everyone screamed. Mrs. Kimball shot up from the log and wiped the drool from her mouth. "Huh? What's going on?"

As some of the kids murmured in fear, I just laughed. "Nothing, Mrs. Kimball. Just telling scary stories."

"Oh." She clutched her heart. "I thought someone was in trouble."

"Nah, there's no trouble at all. The camp's been pretty boring, actually. Sorry to scare you."

"That story is so unbelievable," Tessa hissed. "Dark forces don't exist. I've never heard of a haunting around here—"

"That's because Rachel made it up. Duh." Matthew patted my shoulder. "Don't listen to Ms. Smarty-Pants. Your story was really cool. I freaking loved it."

As Tessa rolled her eyes, another crackle of thunder went off. It started to pour harder before Mrs. Kimball rose to her feet. "All right, kids, it's getting late. Time to head back to the tents. I'll come get you all at six a.m. tomorrow morning. All right?"

We grumbled but nodded anyway, heading to our row of tents. As far as I knew, except for a small family of four, we were the only ones at the campground. I unzipped my tent that I shared with Shana O'Leary, the artsy girl in our class, and crawled into my sleeping bag. She did the same before pulling out a small sketchpad.

"Whatcha drawing?" I asked, when I heard her scribbling.

"Oh, just your story. The Collector of Eyes girl." She held up the drawing. "I did it kinda fast, but I like it. What do you think?"

I gasped when I saw the rough sketch. It was terrifying—a young girl in a long, black gown, her eyes missing. Her skin was all scratched and torn and her hair was matted and dark.

I nodded. "Yeah, that was exactly the kinda vibe I was going for. Nice job."

"Thanks." Shana beamed, tucking the sketchpad away. "I'll probably work on it some more, but I'm happy for now. Anyway, goodnight, Rachel."

After saying goodnight, I drifted into dreamland, one that was a black and empty sleep. Until a feminine scream in the distance startled me awake. I sprang up in my sleeping bag and reached out to jostle Shana awake.

"Hey, did you hear that?" I whispered.

Silence. Reaching into my backpack, I pulled out my flashlight, then shone it around the tent. Shana was gone. Only her sketchbook remained, the girl with no eyes giving me the creeps.

I unzipped my tent, then stepped out with my flashlight. The other kids were already outside. I looked up, watching as it rained even harder. I could barely see two feet in front of me.

"Hey, Rachel, you okay?" Matthew asked, rushing to my side. His pajamas were soaked from the rain. "That scream wasn't you, was it?"

"No, I think it was Shana. Everyone else accounted for?"

"Yeah, even Mrs. Kimball. Come on, let's go find out what's going on."

"Kids, wait!" Mrs. Kimball cried, standing by her own tent with the rest of our classmates. Everyone was there except for Shana. "We shouldn't split up, especially in a bad storm like this."

Matthew shrugged, keeping his back to her. "A kid's missing. I'm not just gonna sit around, no matter how dangerous it is. Come on."

I nodded, following Matthew as Mrs. Kimball continued to scream at us to come back. We headed past a swarm of trees in the direction of the scream. Besides the rain, I heard nothing as I swung my flashlight around.

"Shana?" I called out, rain bouncing off my skin. Matthew stuck to my side like glue. "Are you there? You all right?"

Silence. When I turned my flashlight to the left, investigating a nearby clearing, I gasped. A body was lying on the ground.

I ran over, bending down. It was Shana. She was face down, her back to us. Pressing a finger against her neck, I searched for a pulse, not finding one. I turned her over and let out a scream.

She was missing both of her eyes. They had been plucked out, leaving only the empty sockets behind in a bloody mess. Matthew gasped as he stood over me.

"Oh my God," he muttered. "What the fuck?"

I rose to my feet. "Shana, she's…she's dead. And in the same way that the girl in the story I made up killed people."

Neither Matthew nor I said anything for a minute. What could we say?

"But…how?" he asked. "How is that possible? Your story wasn't true, was it?"

"Of course not! I saw Jack's glasses and got the idea. It was just a stupid scary story to tell around the campfire."

We continued to stare down at Shana's dead body. She had no scratches or scrapes anywhere, suggesting she hadn't fought anyone off. Maybe she knew the attacker. But what was she doing out here?

"Maybe…maybe it was an accident," Matthew whispered. Another crackle of thunder echoed across the sky. "Maybe she had to go to the bathroom or something, then tripped and fell."

"In the same way as my story? I just don't think—"

A scream bellowed behind us. Jumping, I spun around and shone my flashlight on Mrs. Kimball. Her eyes were wide, her clothes soaked, her hand over her mouth as she stared down at Shana's body. She then rushed over and started doing CPR. She did chest compressions first before starting mouth-to-mouth.

"It's no use," Matthew said as we watched. "I think she's gone, Mrs. Kimball."

"How did this happen? Where are her eyes?" Mrs. Kimball screeched. "No, no, no. My teaching career is already on the line because of how often I fall asleep. When the school board finds out a student under my care died on this camping trip, I'll be fired for sure."

I scoffed. "Is that all you care about? Your job?"

"Of course not!" She rose to her feet, glaring at me. "I'm also concerned for poor Shana. Did you see her enter the forest? Was anyone after her?"

I shook my head, having no idea.

"Come on, back to the tents," Mrs. Kimball said, reaching for our arms. "I only came to make sure you kids were okay. If this…if this is indeed a murder, we should get back to the others. We'll be safer in numbers."

I nodded, my throat dry. Who could do such a thing? Murder an innocent teenager? The campgrounds were mostly empty.

Mrs. Kimball dragged us back to our tents, keeping a hand on me and Matthew's arms the entire way. I glanced back into the dark forest where we had found Shana's body. My hands shook around my flashlight.

The other students were still by the tents when we returned. They were whispering and murmuring, then looked up when they heard our sticky shoes approaching through the rain and mud. They must've known something was wrong by the looks on our faces because their eyebrows raised.

"What's going on?" Jack asked, wiping the rain off his glasses. "Mrs. Kimball went to find you two, then we heard her scream."

"You're all here, right?" Mrs. Kimball took attendance, then sighed in relief. "Good, good. I don't know how to say this, kids, but…Shana is dead."

Everyone's faces froze in shock.

"Dead?" Tessa clutched her mouth. "Oh my God. I'm going to be sick…"

And then she turned, throwing up the hamburgers we'd grilled for dinner onto the ground. The other students winced in disgust.

"Ew," Jessica hissed. "But…how did it happen? Did she, like, fall into the lake and drown or something?"

"Not exactly," Matthew said to my right. "We don't know why she was out there, but it looked like she tripped and—"

Mrs. Kimball cleared her throat. "And I'm sure you can guess the rest. Did anyone see anything suspicious tonight? Or hear anything? Did anyone follow Shana out there?"

I hadn't noticed anything—and Shana had slept right next to me. But it had been too dark and rainy.

"Why?" Carter raised an eyebrow. "If she tripped, why would there have been anything suspicious?"

Mrs. Kimball didn't respond to that.

"I, uh, might've seen something," Logan said, turning to our other classmate. A kid in overalls and slicked back hair. "I heard Patrick sneak out of our tent not that long ago."

Everyone turned to stare at him. He stuffed his hands in his pockets, then shrugged. "What? What are you all staring at me for?"

I glanced at Matthew, finding him already looking at me. He must've been thinking the same thing. Patrick Vaughn was a weird kid—always keeping to himself, sometimes muttering and disappearing. He'd even brought a knife to school once and got suspended for a few days. Could he have done something to Shana?

"Well, Mr. Vaughn?" Mrs. Kimball asked. "What were you doing out of your tent? I made it clear that I wanted everyone to go to sleep."

"Well, I couldn't. I went for a walk around the campgrounds to clear my head. That's it."

"And you didn't see anything?" I asked. "Like Shana? Or anyone who might've…"

I trailed off, but everyone seemed to understand what I meant.

"Nah, can't say that I did." Patrick glanced over at the forest. "Too bad, though. Shana was a nice girl."

Tessa wiped her mouth, looking up at the sky. "I have a really bad feeling about all this…"

Mrs. Kimball pulled her smartphone out of her pocket, then lit up the screen. She scowled when she stared at it. "Darn! No signal out here in the woods."

"No duh," Carter spat. "We're out in the middle of nowhere. Perfect for a serial killer."

"Don't say that!" Mrs. Kimball hissed as the students began to murmur.

"What? I'm just thinking out loud. You ever see a scary movie? This is how it starts."

I hated to admit it, but Carter was right. And somehow, this possible serial killer was using my story to murder people. Had they been listening when I told it earlier?

"Shouldn't we, like, get the hell out of here?" Jessica asked. "Let's drive back into town, then call the police."

She pointed at the yellow school bus; the one Mrs. Kimball had driven to take us here. But our teacher shook her head. "No, it's too dangerous to travel in the storm. We'll have to take shelter until the morning."

"I just hope we're not all dead by then," Matthew whispered in my ear, making me shiver.

A flash of lightning lit up the sky again. Mrs. Kimball glanced up, then gestured at the tents. "Please, just get back inside and lie down. We'll deal with this in the morning when it's safer to be outside. Nobody touch Shana's body, all right?"

We all nodded, then headed inside our tents. Mine was empty—and being alone made me nervous. I zipped it up behind me, lying down in my wet clothes. But I couldn't sleep after what I had seen.

Those eyes…torn out of their sockets. Just like the kind in my story. What monster could do something like that?

Ten minutes passed, then more as I laid there in my sleeping bag, thinking of Shana and her possible murderer. But then it happened again.

Another scream. This time, it wasn't Shana, but someone else I recognized. Jessica.

Ripping open my tent, I peered into the rain. It was still pretty heavy. "Hello? Did anyone hear that?"

The tents opened around me, then Mrs. Kimball stepped out with her flashlight. "I did. Stay here, kids. I'll go investigate."

Mrs. Kimball headed into the forest, following the sound of the scream. The rest of us looked on in horror from inside our tents. When the minutes passed and our teacher hadn't returned, I got worried. I grabbed my own flashlight and stepped out.

"Hey, where are you going?" Matthew asked as he followed me. "She told us to stay here."

With my classmates peering at me, I shrugged. "She's been gone too long. I'm gonna go check it out."

Matthew sighed and whipped out his own flashlight from his pocket. "All right. But I'm coming with you."

I thanked him, then we left the tents behind us as we headed toward the woods. I entered the clearing with my flashlight as Matthew followed. Shana's body had vanished, but a new one had taken her place.

Jessica. The scream had come from her. She was lying on her back; her eyes ripped out just like Shana's. I couldn't find a pulse when I checked her neck. And that's when I knew we were in a shitload of trouble.

I turned to Matthew, tears welling in my eyes. "Another one, Matty. What the hell?"

He grabbed me, pulling me into a hug. He patted my hair as a few tears slipped out of my eyes. "It's okay, Rach. Everything will be okay. I promise."

I sniffled, pulling back, though I wasn't sure. "Okay. Okay, I hope so. But where did Mrs. Kimball go? Is she…do you think she's dead too?"

Matthew didn't answer. When I heard footsteps to my left, I raised my flashlight, finding the target. It was a middle-aged man dressed in jeans, a raincoat, and rubber boots.

"Stop!" I cried. "Who are you? What the hell are you doing out here?"

"Hey, calm down," the man said. "I don't mean you any harm. My family and I are camping nearby and our flashlight stopped working. I knew there was a class of kids on a camping trip here, so I was coming over to see if you had a spare. Sorry to scare you."

So, he was part of the family I'd seen arrive earlier. It made sense—until my eyes landed on the large blood stains he had all over his raincoat.

"What's up with that?" I demanded. "All the blood?"

"Oh, this?" He glanced down at his raincoat. "I hunted a bear and butchered it myself for my kids. They love bear meat. Guess I got more on me than I thought."

It sounded believable, but after everything I'd seen, I questioned his story. What if he had plucked out Shana and Jessica's eyes and the blood on his jacket was theirs?

He glanced over my shoulder, then his eyes went wide. He pointed at Jessica's body lying on the ground. "What the…is she okay?"

"No," I said, holding back tears. "She's dead, her eyes ripped out. And she isn't the only one."

The man gasped. "Jesus Christ. You're joking!"

"Does it look like we're fucking joking?" Matthew snapped, and I'd never seen him so angry. "Then we show up and find you, a stranger, poking around with blood on your jacket. How do we know you didn't kill our friends, huh? You bastard!"

He swung at the man, punching him in the jaw. I stepped back in shock. I'd never seen Matthew strike anyone in the ten years we had been friends, meeting in kindergarten. But then again, we'd never gone on a camping trip where our friends had been murdered.

"Oof!" the man cried, clutching his face. He put his arms up to surrender as Matthew continued to attack him. "I didn't do anything! I'd never hurt anyone—I swear it!"

"Lying murderer!" Matthew sneered, then pushed the man into a tree.

He caught himself before he could fall as I grabbed Matthew's arm, holding him back. "Matty, stop! We don't know he's the killer. We don't know anything."

Matthew's chest heaved from the fight. "It's him, Rach. I just know it is!"

The man was shaking his head, holding his hands up. "No…no, I didn't do this. Please, don't hurt me. I have a family!"

Matthew turned around to attack him again when we heard yelling. It was coming from the river that ran along the campgrounds. Turning on my heel, I rushed over to investigate, glancing over my shoulder to find Matthew chasing me. The man rose to his feet and took off in the opposite direction.

"I hope that guy really isn't the killer, Rach," Matthew said behind me. "Because if he is, we might've just let him escape."

I hoped so too. I wanted justice for Shana and Jessica—which meant catching the killer before we all ended up dead.

I ran through the forest, coming out on the other side to the lake. Mrs. Kimball stood near the water with her phone in her hand. She was yelling at it, pressing a bunch of buttons. "Work, you bastard! Come on!"

"Mrs. Kimball?" I asked, shining the flashlight on her. "Are you the one who screamed?"

She nodded, turning to us. Raindrops pelted off her body. "It was. When I found Jessica's body, I ran out here to see if I could get a signal to phone the police. But this damn phone still won't work!"

"It probably won't until we leave the campgrounds," Matthew said. "And I wonder if the killer thought of that."

I gulped. "Maybe they did. Maybe…maybe they wanted us isolated out here. Look, I think we should get on that school bus, Mrs. Kimball. Let's get back into town."

But she shook her head. "No, we can't, Rachel. The rain's too heavy—I won't be able to see to drive. We'll go as soon as it clears, okay?"

I wasn't thrilled about staying there—the scene of two grisly murders—but Mrs. Kimball wasn't taking no for an answer. As she walked back to the campground, I followed as Matthew told her all about the man we had seen.

"It's gotta be him. Our murderer," Matthew said. "Who else would do this?"

When we reached the campground again, all the students were outside, murmuring. They turned to face us when they saw us approaching. Carter was the first to surround me, then the others followed.

"I saw Jessica's body," Carter said. "I went to see it for myself, but you guys were already gone. Her eyes…where the fuck were her eyes?"

"We don't know," Matthew said. "But it's how Shana died, too."

The murmurs grew louder.

Patrick pointed at me. "It's just like your story, Rachel. The collector of eyes. Why are people dying in the way you described?"

With everyone staring at me, I could only shrug. "I don't know! I swear to God, I don't get it either."

"Yeah, right." Carter scoffed. "Maybe you're the one killing everyone. Maybe you planned this!"

"What?" My eyes widened. "Why would I do that? I liked Shana and Jessica. I didn't kill anyone!"

When all the students started screaming at me, accusing me of being a murderer, Matthew stepped forward. "Shut up! Shut up, all of you. I've known Rach forever. She couldn't have done this. She wouldn't."

"Then who?" Jack demanded. "Because it wasn't any of us."

Matthew opened his mouth, looking like he wanted to tell them about the man we saw, but Mrs. Kimball stepped forward. "Enough—all of you. This is stressful enough without pointing the finger at everyone. Let's head inside one tent and stay awake until the morning. The rain should clear by then and we can leave and get the police."

"Fine," Logan huffed, glaring at me. "But I'm keeping an eye on her."

Mrs. Kimball took us into Matthew's tent, then zipped it up behind us. It was cramped but it was a lot better than being alone. And this way, we could make sure no one else got killed. The minutes passed as we sat there in silence, staring at each other. The heavy rain bounced off the tent's roof.

I looked around, seeing only one sleeping bag in Matthew's tent. I frowned. "No roommate?"

"None," Matthew said as we broke the silence. "It was nice to have a tent all to myself."

Tessa cleared her throat. "Um…is this a bad time to say I have to use the bathroom?"

"Can you not hold it?" Mrs. Kimball asked. "I really think it's better if we all stay in here."

But Tessa shook her head, her leg trembling. "No, I really have to go. Can…can someone go with me? I don't want to go alone."

No one volunteered, not even Mrs. Kimball. None of us wanted to risk getting killed out there.

"I'll do it," Matthew said with a sigh. "Let's just be quick, okay?"

"Be careful," Mrs. Kimball urged. "I'll wait outside for you."

Tessa nodded, rising to her feet before she left the tent with Matthew. Mrs. Kimball followed and waited outside. In the tent, everything turned silent, with the others glaring at me.

"I'm sure they'll be fine," Carter muttered. "Because I'm pretty sure the killer's right here."

"Are you talking about me?" I shook my head. "You've got it all wrong. There's a guy with his family out there. It could be him. Or maybe even Patrick. He's the class weirdo, isn't he?"

"I'm weird. I'm not dangerous," Patrick hissed. "I didn't kill anyone! Maybe you're just trying to distract us from—"

The scream made us all jump. We rushed out of the tent, then I spotted Mrs. Kimball running toward the forest. I followed her and saw the outline of a body on the ground. When I got closer, it was Tessa, her eyes removed. Blood was everywhere. For a moment, I was just relieved it wasn't Matthew.

He stood by the nearby tree, covered in blood. "Holy shit!"

"Matthew, what happened?" I asked as the others caught up to me.

"Some guy…he ran up to us and stabbed Tessa in her eyes. Right as she was going to the bathroom!" he cried. "I turned around to give her some privacy, but when I looked back…she was dead, and he was running away."

"Which way did he go?" Carter asked.

Matthew pointed north. "That way. To the other row of tents."

When Carter took off, the other students followed. Mrs. Kimball chased after them. "Kids, stop—it's not safe!"

As they vanished, it left only me and Matthew with the dead body and the pouring rain. I reached down to touch Tessa's poor face. She hadn't deserved this. None of them had.

"Tragic, isn't it?" Matthew whispered. "Those young lives, taken too soon."

I continued staring down at Tessa's body. "Yeah. It's fucked up—"

"Watch out!"

When I looked up, the family man stood there, pointing at someone behind me. I dove out of the way just in time as Matthew held up a bloody knife. He must've been hiding it behind his back.

And that was when I realized my best friend, the boy I'd known for a decade, was the Collector of Eyes killer.

"Oops," he said with a little laugh. "Guess I should've killed you a lot quicker, huh?"

"What the…Matty!" My eyes widened as I rose to my feet. "How could you? Why?"

"Just to see what would happen, really." He stared at the body, his eyes hungry. "I took inspiration from your story. It was really good, you know. You should be a horror writer."

"Then…there was no man who ran up to you. You killed Tessa. And the others." I stepped back as Matthew took small steps toward me, the knife held out in his hands. "Look, Matty, I don't know what's gotten into you, but…please, don't kill me. I'm your friend!"

He laughed. "And? The others were too. But trust me, once everyone learns what I did here, I'll be famous, and your names will live on as victims of the Collector of Eyes killer. Maybe it'll even inspire other killers. Isn't that cool?"

It was anything *but* cool.

As he lunged at me, I screamed, tripping over Tessa's body behind me as I stepped back. I fell to the ground with a thud as Tessa's blood splashed onto me. Matthew stared down at me with a crazy look in his eyes and a smirk on his lips. Maybe he'd just lost his mind and done it all for fame—or maybe there really *was* something evil in this forest. I wasn't sure, but I knew one thing for certain.

I was about to die.

As I closed my eyes, thinking of my family, the man screamed. I opened my eyes as he flung himself at Matthew and wrestled him to the ground. They fought for the knife before the man grabbed it. Kicking Matthew in the shins, he rose to his feet.

"Do it!" Matthew cried. "Kill me! Because I won't stop. I'll kill everyone here, including your little family. It was good luck you happened to be here, you know. You made the perfect scapegoat—"

The man drove the knife into Matthew's chest, making him gurgle mid-sentence. And then he went still.

I panted. "Thank you. You…you saved my life. And I don't even know your name."

"Fred. Fred Hansen." The man helped me to my feet. "I couldn't let him hurt anyone else, especially my family. Are you all right?"

As I nodded, my classmates ran over with Mrs. Kimball. Carter pointed at the man. "It's him—he's the killer. And he just killed Matty!"

"No, no!" I cried before they could pounce on him. "You've got it all wrong. Matty…he was the killer all along. Having his own tent helped him slip out. And he was there alone with Tessa. When you guys left, Matty turned on me. Tried to make me a victim. It seems he was obsessed with becoming infamous or something." I glanced at his body, dead and still. "And I guess he got his wish."

Fortunately, the others believed me. We huddled together in one tent, along with Fred and his family, and waited for the rain to stop. By morning, it had cleared, casting a rainbow over the sky. I found everything in Matthew's pockets—more knives, the stolen eyeballs. He had hidden the other bodies in the bushes and probably would've killed us all if not for that nice family man. Now I really regretted accusing him of murder.

We boarded the school bus, then drove far enough to get service for our phones. The police arrived ten minutes later, took our statements, and dragged all the bodies away—including Matthew's. Fred and his family were given the clear to leave, along with us. Officers then put crime scene tape around the campgrounds and declared it off-limits until further notice.

I headed home to my parents, my hands shaking while vowing to never go on another camping trip again. I'd even had enough of scary stories.

The Day After the Sky Blushed

Alexander Vincent

The valley between the small, rounded mountains was quiet. Coniferous trees crowded the small pasture and swayed in a gentle breeze. An early morning sun cast loose shadows along the western slopes, promising mystery and the allure of a new day. Soft snow glared into the perfect blue sky while the brook, loath to be as frozen as everything else, babbled just enough to become a part of the silence. The water wormed its way along the eastern slope, swaddling the edges of the meadow with crystal clear melt off.

At the center of the valley, Tyler perched over the carcass of a deer he just shot. The beast had nosed its way from the safety of the trees into the open air. It might have caught his scent, but he was faster on the trigger than it was to run. He'd only needed one shot and his .270 did the rest of the work.

Tyler poked one dead eyeball with the barrel of his gun; better to check than catch an antler in the face or a hoof to the gut. He then knelt over the dead creature and fingered his way up the belly of the deer, searching for the soft vacancy just underneath the base of its sternum. The knife left its sheath with a soft *snick* and, recently sharpened, slid in with only a slight, satisfying pop.

He pushed the blade down to the creature's testicles, shoving them aside with his free hand. When he felt the bump of its anus, Tyler pulled the blade free and yanked open the body cavity. He then began about the gory business of severing the stomach, testicles, and anus from the deer. The blade slipped against the anus and poked the stomach. Tyler wrinkled his nose in anticipation of the feces but was glad to discover he'd only scratched the surface of the stomach. He'd have to be careful yanking the thing out, but he was probably safe from its contents. Once the purple-white-red intestines slid out, he rolled up the sleeves of his hunting jacket and reached in with both hands. Careful to preserve the tenderloin, his knife did gentle work in unlodging the rest of the organs. It didn't take him long before he had a pile of organs staining the snow red. He smirked to himself as he observed his work; some coyote was going to be really happy with Tyler's kill.

Other hunters liked to keep the heart or lungs in to inflate the weight of the deer, but not Tyler. He just wanted to eat the thing. Bragging rights didn't mean much to him; he preferred to kill his deer, check it in, then keep quiet. It also didn't help he was three miles from the nearest road. He'd driven in on a four-wheeler, but his back appreciated his efforts to lighten the load.

He took a moment to breathe and looked up at the clear sky. Thanking his lucky stars, he took a moment to send thanks to the heavens for an early snowfall and cold temperatures on opening day. Then, Tyler looked back at his hunting blind and gauged the distance. He didn't think anything would mess with the corpse while he was there.

The noise he made huffing through the freshly fallen snow would keep the wild at bay. So, he decided to make his way back to the wheeler. It was either that or he strapped up to the deer with his harness and dragged the thing a hundred yards. Again, his back appreciated his good decision making.

The short journey back was cold and quiet as Tyler's labored breaths filled the air with wispy steam. The soft scrunches his feet made seemed to echo, then die in the mountain air. It was peculiar to know silence surrounded him, but his ears were filled with the sound of his own heaving lungs and thumping heart.

The tarp he'd thrown over his wheeler was dusted with a light layer of snow. He'd driven in the previous night and slept in the small hutch he used as a hunting blind. That way he'd lose most of his human scent. He kept his sleeping bag in an airtight plastic wrap and his hunting gear hung from a tree most of the year, regardless of the weather. Tyler thought of himself as the consummate professional hunter. None of it was necessary, but he enjoyed the action, the ritual of it all. It wasn't about becoming one with nature; it was about violating it as quietly as possible.

He took a moment to brush off the tarp before he realized he should just take it off. The four-wheeler underneath was skinny and cheap, just good enough to get him where he needed to go.

Straddling the seat, he twisted the key still in the ignition. Nothing. Frowning, he tried again. Still nothing. "Fuckin' piece of shit," he cursed both at the vehicle and himself. He serviced the thing every year, but he knew it was just a matter of time till it died. He just wished it wasn't at that moment.

Opening the fuse box, he checked those first. They all seemed to be clean and intact. Then he went for the spark plugs, as those were next most likely to shit the bed. Sure enough, something seemed to have scorched the ends, rendering them useless. He took but a moment to thump the fender in frustration before he set about problem solving.

He glanced at his phone and confirmed what he already knew: no service. It was part of the reason he loved hunting so much. No fucking idiots to bother him. No wife up his ass, no whining kids, and certainly no bitch-ass coworkers. Tyler knew his way in and out of this meadow; that wasn't what bothered him. He was annoyed that he forgot to bring an extra set of plugs knowing he'd be so far out from his truck. Now he'd have to drag the deer two miles to his truck. The snow wouldn't help in the endeavor, nor would the frequent hills and dips along the path to the park and ride.

Squinting in the morning sun, he decided he shouldn't dally. He did a few half-hearted stretches, placed his rifle inside his hutch, locked the door, and made sure his pistol was still strapped to his thigh. The rifle would just weigh him down and no one human was going to mess with the valley or his hunting blind while he was gone.

Trudging back over to the deer, he couldn't help but notice the retreating sun. A thick, rippled blanket of clouds had intruded upon the sky. As he sniffed his disdain, he then noticed a small breeze echoing through the trees to the southeast, right where his truck was. He decided not to dwell on the potential weather; he'd be long gone before it would ever set in bad enough to bother him.

The buck's antlers provided the hold for his rope harness. He'd learned long ago that it was much easier to drag an animal behind him than it was to yank it along with an arm. After he was done fixing the harness around his shoulders and chest, he took another moment to put on his gloves. They were thick enough to protect from mild cold, but thin enough to operate his handgun without much issue.

He then peered to the corner of the meadow that was home to the trail he followed.

Despite his success, despite his joy at having succeeded in taking down his quarry, something didn't sit right in his stomach. He was forgetting something, and that bothered him. The edges of the meadow seemed to hedge themselves into darkness. Like they wanted to huddle together to spare themselves the building wind. They agreed: he'd forgotten something. But he wasn't one to dwell on the past. He had to get back to his truck; he'd get to worry about other things once he got the hell out of the meadow.

The walk to the tree line was longer than he remembered, but then again, he was dragging at least another hundred pounds behind him. The snow was stubborn too; instead of letting the dead creature glide along its surface, it bunched and piled against the buck's muscular shoulders. That meant that, every so often, he'd have to shrug the deer up and loose from the building pile of snow. Just another ache to add to the list when he got home.

As he approached the corner of the meadow, a peculiar sparkling caught his eye. Normally dull and brown, the trees had become partially opalescent. He blinked away the snow blindness and peered again at the trees; sure he was just seeing snow spots. But no, the trees seemed to shimmer in the dull grey light of the absconding sun. Frowning, he shuffled closer as he pulled his knife from its sheath. It only took a moment to pry a large chunk of bark from the pine tree. Using his body to shade the bark, he raised it closer to his face.

The dark brown ripples and roughshod valleys of the piece of wood had given way to a bizarre porcelain texture on his gloves. It shimmered as he tilted back and forth like a glowing oil slick, only he saw the colors purple, blue, and something deeper; almost black, but more inscrutable.

Held within those shimmering hues, he saw the thing that he forgot. The deep unknown, a mild feeling of discontent mixed with the fear of amnesia and unknown nostalgia. It was like he was staring deep into his childhood, the black mass of forgotten memories hidden just under the traumatic grind of reality and life.

"The fuck is this shit," he muttered just to hear his own voice, just to escape his thoughts. Reaching into his pocket, he grabbed one of the plastic bags that held a granola bar and deposited the bark therein. Tyler rubbed his gloves together, trying to work away the sap that had stuck there. It was then he noticed that the opalescence was a heavy film glossed across the surface of the bark. It oiled against the bag and left a thick residue, also bizarrely luminescent. He lifted his glove to his nose and gave a tentative sniff. It smelled like boiling mud. Petrichor assaulted his nostrils and almost made him sneeze.

Before glancing at the trees one last time, he checked to make sure none of the stuff had gotten on his nose. If it was just a tree disease he'd never heard of, he wanted to make sure he wasn't carrying that shit where he could easily ingest it.

With one last glance back at the meadow, Tyler took a moment to enjoy the pristine picture of nature he'd invaded. The deer leaked bits of bright red blood behind him, the fleeting evidence sure to dissolve within the day. Coyotes would lap up the pile of gore at the kill spot and carrion feeders would dab at the bits of blood spotted here and there. The bright snow would sublimate in the intense midday sun, invisibly dissolving with the passage of time. Then, within a day or two, all traces of his passage would disappear. Neither he nor the deer's absence would matter. It all kept spinning.

He turned, shouldered his dead burden, and quickly stepped through the pair of maddening trees. It might have been the deer, or the hidden dread implicit in a two-mile trek through familiar wilderness, but Tyler felt himself push through an inert barrier. A sticky, gelatinous film that pressed his face against a wall of arctic wind. He sniffed through a newly raw nose and leaned further into the weight of the deer. Two miles was nothing. Even with the dips and trees and small creeks cricks weaving their way through the slight mountains, two miles should go quick. Tyler wasn't as fit as he could have been, but he was strong, and the deer added weight he'd already lost. Two miles was nothing.

At first, the trip went quickly. He passed by familiar logs and folded saplings. Sometimes his foot would slip on mud hidden by fresh snow. Other times the deer would veer off trail, caught in grabbing pockets of pricker bush. As his feet followed the old divots cut into the earth by continued travel, both by four-wheelers and tractors, he kept his head moving. Tyler scanned the elevated wood line, a formidable ten-foot wall of stone and slate. He imagined bears and mountain lions. He mistook a dead tree trunk for a powerful wolf, stalking and fantasizing about clawing into his flesh. There were moments when the crackle of tickling branches made him imagine a hunting sasquatch, salivating over the kill slung on Tyler's shoulders.

Eventually, maybe half an hour in, the cloud cover dominated the sky in a perfect, smooth blanket of oppressive stuffing. The sun couldn't even peek through, and the canopy forced the forest into a dilapidated grey, both shadowed and shadowy. Somehow, the bits and patches of lingering darkness cast by the swaying trees became darker, sinister, and more pronounced. A slight shade became hazy pitch, and the light-thrown figure of a massive tree became rumbling, bubbling tar. The bits of trickled light let in by the forest cover became thin lines of barely visible silk. Light became bizarre. The forest came alive.

Tyler stopped to catch his breath. The dead deer behind him glared with dead glassy eyes, accusing him of murder. He thought briefly about turning its muscle into jerky. What recipe would he use? Red flake pepper, soy sauce, Worcestershire sauce, and ground black pepper maybe. Salty, tangy, and sweet.

Sparkles bit into the air. Leaves glittered with half-frozen dew. Everything that was still green seemed to lean in so they could watch his sojourn with death. And the deer still watched him. Its tongue lolled, purple and swollen. Rigor mortis took the body for itself and wrenched the limbs straight.

The blood ceased to leak from the agape body cavity. A faint crust of dried blood had settled on the edges of its fur, and its antlers left a distinct track behind him. He smiled at the beast. "Don't worry, I'm still gonna eat ya," he said, hoping the forest heard him. He wasn't superstitious, but he also didn't want to be accused of being wasteful. He'd eat this fucking deer, and he'd do it after dragging it two miles out of the forest. His friends would laugh and berate him and tell him he was dumb for forgetting back-up spark plugs. That he was even more stupid for spending the night in his hunting blind. That was the dirty secret most hunters never shared with non-hunters. You could be stinking drunk or skunky high, but if the deer was up wind, it never mattered.

That was when the second one snuck up on him.

He saw the beast before he heard it. It came snuffing up the tree line to his right, pawing at the detritus under the snow. The buck must have had twelve points and been well over two hundred pounds. He'd seen animals this size dead, but never in the wild. At first, he watched as it continued huffing at the ground, alternately raising its nose to the wind and hunching down to forage for food.

Tyler thumbed the handgun on his right thigh, gauging the distance of the shot. His outer range for accurate fire was about ten yards; much beyond that the spread widened and widened until it no longer made sense. The deer strapped to his back would interfere with his stance, making anything beyond the initial ten a definite crap shoot. Before he could mull the decision over any further, the buck on the ridgeline caught a scent of something it didn't like and took off.

Sighing his relief, Tyler relaxed and tossed the other buck from his mind. It was a shame he didn't have a shot at it, but realistically he wanted to get out of the woods. It was dark, dark, and clearly heading toward inclement weather. He didn't need another gut job on his hands.

The forest scarcely changed for the rest of his journey, and the pallid light only became heavier, thicker. Trees still loomed over him; they tunneled his vision into a peculiar place of intense focus buttressed by the fantasies of the creatures the forest held just out of sight. Tyler thought of the buck and imagined it stalking him, eager to avenge its fallen friend. But what if the two were rivals, he thought? What if they detested each other and mauled and locked horns with one another? Did they share females and eating spots? What if they were related? What if the opalescent slime spread across their antlers and infected their skin?

Would the antlers reflect the dim light and cascade it into a prism of a luminous oil slick? Would the skin peel back as the infection spread, yielding a healthy heart to a grotesque alien sickness? Tyler shook his head as he came upon his truck. The silver F350 was covered in snow but otherwise was left unmolested. Dragging the dead deer behind him, he moved to the back of his truck, fishing his keys out from his jacket's internal pocket. He clicked the unlock button once and was more than disappointed at his truck's lack of response. He clicked it again and again and again, until he angrily shoved the key into his tailgate. It unlocked with a satisfying pressure and click, but he was officially worried. It was odd that his four-wheeler's spark plugs went, sure, but it wasn't uncommon. But for both his truck and the Suzuki to be electrically dead? That was a coincidence he didn't believe in.

Once more he was overwhelmed by the feeling that he was forgetting something. That he'd witnessed an event, a breaching of the sky, a mutilation of reality, and forgot it. It wasn't the same as thinking he forgot to lock a door or turn off the oven, but he also didn't dread what he forgot. It was like tangling his brain within the tendrils of an immutable but evanescent dream.

He shook his head and muttered a few curse words under his breath as he unleashed the deer from his aching shoulders. He grabbed its horns and heaved it up and into the bed of his truck, fighting the rigor mortis of its stiff limbs. The tailgate closed and folded its head up so it could stare at the back of his truck and the toolbox latched behind his rear window.

Shuffling around to the driver's seat, Tyler took a moment to toss a prayer up to whomever might be listening. He'd really prefer it if his truck had just started. The key slid into the hole, and he watched the locks pop up with a turn of his wrist. Opening the door, he watched the overhead light with too much interest. When it failed to light, he let his head go to the worst places. It was at least another five miles to the nearest town and that was almost all uphill. The road was scarcely traveled, which meant he was unlikely to catch a helpful soul. And the forest kept creeping up on him. It was like the trees were vibrating with the enthusiasm of rupturing stars.

He tried the ignition. Nothing. The truck was dead. He popped the hood and grabbed his voltage meter out of the toolbox. The battery was dead, the spark plugs singed and destroyed just like his four-wheeler. He listened to his heart escalate his panic. It thumped through his ears and into his spine and reverberated through his soul. He wondered when the panic would come. He then took a breath and decided there was no need to get hysterical yet. Tyler would just have to walk the five miles uphill to get a tow. It was a simple solution, just a shitty one. The forest had different plans.

As Tyler turned to the exit road, he was surprised to find a thick barrier of trees instead. Swollen branches of several robust dead trees interlocked in a brambled wall. As he approached closer, something in the back of his head told him to keep ahold of his holstered pistol. The trees were impossibly overlapping and had needle-like growths peppering their limbs. Contemplating what sort of tree this was, the needles caught his eye. Each sparkled just at the tip like a shining dew drop.

Withdrawing his knife, he slid the blade against the nearest thorn. The tiny goblet was reminiscent of the slime he found on the trees back in the meadow. He shuddered to think what purpose the goop served.

Somewhere in the woods the wind blew, crackling and creaking the worshipping branches against one another. Ridiculous thoughts overwhelmed Tyler as he tried to make sense of the situation. Was that a squirrel or a massive beast? Perhaps it was the buck, just as confused as he was, lost in a nacreous labyrinth that leaked bits of sky. But what if it was something stalking him? What if that something was the thing he was forgetting? What if it was an alien shimmer constructed of the amnesiac shadows crowding Tyler's brain? Why couldn't he remember? What was wrong?

Tyler was starting to panic; he knew that. He turned from the barrier of brambles and counted to five while breathing deep of the chilled air. It was a plan he needed, something to keep him alive while others realized he was missing. His hunting shack held his backpack, which in turn held at least a day's worth of food. The deer in his truck could keep him alive for quite some time, but he'd need to close his tonneau cover and check on it at least twice a day. A four-mile hike seemed like a bit much, but he had no other way to protect the corpse from scavengers. "Fuck," he muttered as he took another breath. "I'm fine," he said to himself.

He shouldn't need that long, he realized. Both his wife and brother knew exactly where he hunted. If they came first thing in the morning, he should have plenty of food and water to keep healthy. Yeah, that was it. He just needed to go take shelter in his hunting blind until someone could find him. In fact, it could be fun. He'd been wanting to finish the book in his bag. The military sci-fi tickled some part of him that he'd buried long ago in high school. Even a redneck needed his vices.

But the trees haunted the voice in his mind, the one whispering sweet insanity in his ear. It wanted him to slurp the sap and snow, to dance naked and frolic freely in the forest. There was no bliss in that moment. Just a man hyperventilating as he clutched his chest. "Yeah, fine. I'm fine," he said to no one.

Taking another glance around the small clearing, Tyler made sure he wasn't being stupid. The exit road was indeed gone, and he no longer had a solid grasp of direction save for the path he dragged the deer down. Yeah, his hunting blind was the smart move. The tree's radiated a frightening madness. Their brambles stunk of mistakes made and knowledge spurned. If he tried to penetrate their thorns, he was afraid he'd just get lost and risk exposure. Without a real compass, a functioning phone, or even a shining sun, he was better off hedging his bets and taking this time to himself.

That was the beauty of nature, right? It hid solitude within itself. It only gave to those who drenched themselves in its milieu.

Swallowing his pride, he began walking back to his hunting blind. The trip went much faster than the first time. Though the walk felt lonelier than usual, he appreciated the flimsy beauty of the dead forest around him. Only a light cover of snow managed to fall to the ground, the rest finding a home in thin streaks on craning branches. The forest floor was visibly muddy underneath the pristine white. Sometimes bunches of pine needles and lone pine cones rested on in the cushion of snow, adding a dead texture that Tyler swore he could smell.

Sometimes the snow would fall to the ground in a puff, thumping and making Tyler jump. When his head spun around to address the sound, all he would see was a jiggling tree branch, mocking his nervous nature.

Then, other times, he would hear a faint scraping sound followed by a resonant growl or snort. His brain told him it was just the wind. His fluttering heart told him something was following him. It wanted his soul and his blood. It wanted to crash upon him after terrifying him with thunderous footfalls and slash into his throat and drink his blood. Tyler had to tell himself to keep walking, to not panic, to not run, that everything was fine. If he ran, he could slip, and if he slipped, he could hurt himself. No need to do that.

He was fine. He knew he was fine.

After only an hour or so he saw the encroaching meadow where he made his kill. The opalescent slime had spread to other trees, forming a visible wall of glowing rainbow shimmers along the snowed-over field. As much as he tried to ignore the peculiar virus aggressively infecting other trees, the shine was worse than snow blindness, even though the sun still retreated behind a stolid blanket of thick clouds. Tyler was forced to cover his eyes with one hand, and he shuffled back to his shack and dead four-wheeler.

With everything just as he had left it, Tyler made the decision to go into his shack to get away from the oppressive light shining in the meadow. He closed the camo blinds and settled into his sleeping nook, where he could snuggle into his sleeping bag and read his book in comfort.

It only took a few chapters before he felt himself nodding off, his eyelids heavy with the fatigue and stress of being lost in the woods. For a moment his brain stopped trying to make sense of the slime and the barbed trees and the persistent scraping. Instead, it lulled him to sleep.

Bleeeehhhhhhhhehehhehh. The deer outside bleated. *Bleeeeehhheheheheh.* Tyler's eyes snapped open, and he reflexively grabbed the rifle leaning in the corner next to him. Blinking his bleary eyes, it took him a moment to remember where he was and how he got there. He was dreaming of neon misted clouds in a pitch-black sky that contorted and writhed like a living ecosystem. Within his eyes he saw flashes of impossible creatures hanging within the mist like sleeping sperm whales. His brain buzzed with fascination and horror, and he knew there was more.

Bleeeeehhheheheheheh. The deer outside was in distress, searching for its calf or its herd. Tyler slowly peeled aside one of the blinds with a single finger. He was surprised to be greeted by the grey-blue pallor of late afternoon twilight.

The funny thing about twilight was its ability to add creatures and shapes that weren't there. Many a hunter had been fooled by a bush or a gap in the trees and became convinced that there was a deer just there, barely out of sight. Even the barrier of rainbow slime had quieted to the presence of twilight.

But Tyler knew exactly what he saw. The deer he'd shot in that same meadow was standing just feet away from his hunting shack, bleating at him. He could see its carved-out body, leaking bits of gore with each plaintive call. Blood had begun to dribble from its clouded eyes and even pooled and clogged its flaring nostrils. As he closed the blind and tried to still his racing heart, Tyler reached for his phone to take a photo.

He clicked the side button, but the damn thing didn't light up. Pressing so hard that the edges of his right thumb lost color, Tyler stifled the worried curses bubbling in his throat. Remembering then that his battery bank still had at least three-quarters of its storage left, he plugged in his phone. More panic welled when the battery bank indicated it too was empty.

The shack began to close about him. Claustrophobic panic bit his brain. Shadows hid behind the loose cobwebs that lurked within each corner. His sleeping bag was encrusted with dew from the heat of his own pulsating body.

Bleheheeeehhhhhheeh. The fucking thing was closer. Tyler's heart began to beat in his ears as he felt adrenaline pump into his veins. He knew he'd have to do something about the deer, but he had no clue what to do to an already dead corpse. How does one kill something that was already dead? Common sense told him to shoot it again, that more bullets would eventually fix a thing that wasn't supposed to move. But nothing made sense. Not the trees, the forest, his electronics, or the gap in his memory that was now burning through his skull. Something had been forgotten and right now Tyler would kill to remember.

The deer kept bleating, and Tyler resisted the urge to cover his eyes and cry in the corner. He was done pretending that everything was ok, but just because it wasn't ok didn't mean he could make it so. With renewed determination, he grabbed his rifle, slung it over his shoulder then drew his pistol. He figured he'd try to limb the thing with his pistol, shoot its legs so it couldn't move. Then he'd use the rifle to shoot out its throat; at the very least it wouldn't be able to bitch at him. Worst case scenario, he could probably find a way to render the creature helpless, then he could use his knife to his heart's content.

For a moment he found himself relishing his imagination as he saw flashes of blood spraying his face and the pristine snow. He hoped the grin spreading across his lips was induced madness, not a peek behind the curtain of his mind.

He took in a single breath and placed his back against the wall of the shack, as he opened the blinds so the creature couldn't see him. Then he carefully opened the glass window and hooked it so that it wouldn't fall open.

There was only a moment's warning before the creature's head crested the threshold of the window. Close up, Tyler could see that something was wrong with the corpse. Flecks of embedded purple-black crystals like small, studded diamonds ate away at the deer's head. Bits of desiccated flesh hung from strings of shrinking fur. Its retreating skin and hair left patches of black coagulated muscle and skin sinew along the edges of its eyes and horns. Even its tongue lolled out and seemed to be consumed by glittering crystals.

Tyler only took a split second to observe the impossible bust of the deer before he emptied his entire magazine into the side of the deer's head. His ears became clouded with ringing, and he flinched against the blood spattering his face. Brain and viscera splashed against the side of his shack as the deer trembled with the impact of the .45. Eventually it fell over, slapping its neck against the windowsill and lolling its tongue out one more time before it became quiet.

As he sat trembling in the corner of his shack, Tyler wondered what the hell just happened; what the hell he just saw. The thing looked like something he'd see in a low budget straight-to-streaming horror movie. Something he'd watch with his teenage son, like something they'd make fun of. For that moment he yearned to be home. To sit on his couch and drink a beer, talking to his wife about her day or his son about the cute girl on the cheerleading squad.

But he came back to reality quickly as he realized he now had to focus on surviving. Imagining better places and better times was for someone who was in a better place at a better time. The grumble that echoed through the woods and into his shack shook him. It was a buck snort only more vicious, more alien. Clacks and scrapes echoed through the hunting blind and Tyler forced himself to look. The only problem was the twilight. Like he knew it would, it morphed and formed to match the brief shadow of terror his brain brewed up. Against his will, he saw more bloodied deer carcasses, each staring at him with those greyed out eyes.

He blinked. It was just another dozen shadows hugging a doom threatened tree line. Craning his head to look at the deer he shot, he stifled the vomit roiling in his belly. There were no brains left to speak of. The twelve-shot magazine had cratered the side of its skull to reveal squirming bits of light sheltered in corrupted blood. A stiff stench like that of pancakes baked in bubbling oil wafted through his nostrils and cheered on his gag reflex.

Slamming the window shut and shuffling the blinds closed, he decided to huddle in his sleeping nook. He cradled his head in his arms and sniffled to himself. Everything was so wrong and yet he still forgot.

Tyler didn't even know he'd fallen asleep this time. The swirls of purple and black running wild behind his eyelids subsumed his consciousness to a deeper, darker place. It was only the persistent sounds of bark rubbing on bark that eventually brought him back to reality. The hunting blind held no light. The darkness was so black, he couldn't see his hands or his legs or anything else. His stomach rumbled in the dark, and he contemplated eating the sandwich he'd made the previous day, but he could still smell that dead deer. He'd have to move the fucking thing before he could eat.

The bark scraping had become a sort of lullaby to him, a reassurance that everything was still fucked up. That something still haunted the hollow nooks of his memory. But it seemed different this time. It was closer, louder, and more urgent. In fact, as he held his breath to listen closely, he realized it must be right behind him and the shack. Moving as slowly as he could, he kept track of the sound as much as he could, following the scrapes and clacks as it moved. Tyler reached for his pistol and checked the breech. He forgot to reload the thing. Gently prying out his backup mag from his backpack, he let the other fall into his sleeping bag. As he slid the new one home and gingerly racked the slide, he realized the clacking had moved from the front of his blind to the meadow.

As his night vision set in, he realized he could see the blinds. From behind, they were emanating a faint ethereal light, like someone had set a black light deep in perfectly transparent waters. Then he heard *shhhhhhck shhhhhck shhhhhhck* from just behind the window. Tyler froze.

Slopping flesh sounds were followed by a resonant, gushing swallow. Something was eating the corpse.

He breathed deeply before opening the blind and sent a prayer up to heaven. Maybe his luck was finally running out. Maybe what he'd forgotten was the sins of the past, something so sinister and evil he forced himself to forget.

When he saw it, he forgot about all that. The creature, the thing, was the second buck he'd seen that day… only it had changed. Its torso was held aloft by twelve ruptured, spiderlike limbs, six on each side. Its legs were velvety with fur like newly sprouted antlers, only the hair was faintly purple and glowed in the dark. Each individual hair seemed to twitch and sputter of its own accord, whipping around like a snake feeling about in the dark.

All four legs were gone, replaced by black, chitinous claws tipped with an ebony-dripped scorpion's stinger. Its body had shriveled and tightened around a sagging skeleton; dried bits of blood globbed where its new legs had sprouted. The head held its mouth agape, tongue lolling out with those same amethyst crystals burning holes in rapidly renewing flesh. Massive rows of teeth had erupted on the roof of its mouth and followed its throat until Tyler could only assume the teeth were a part of the throat as well. Its fur had turned rancid with a deep, sickly green emanating from the roots of its hair.

The thing was guzzling the deer that Tyler had killed twice. Slurping its loose skin like he would a tangy slushy. Then he noticed the sky.

It was blushing.

The northern lights twirled and danced in the sky. Purple and blue and green mist contorted and writhed along one another. The stars twinkled and the moon grinned as they consumed the implicit, raw energy of the interaction between the earth and the bombarding dangers of the universe. They watched the beautiful, horrific dance with silvered vigor and mythical personality.

Tyler remembered what he'd forgotten. He'd seen this once before. The lights, not the creature. The night before he shot the deer, the lights had come out to play. They'd whispered in his ear and danced up his skin, tickling a sticky mist up his body and the meadow and the trees. He'd bathed in radiant and cosmic light until he'd dipped a toe at the edge of the universe. He swallowed madness and loved himself for it. He'd forgotten the truth because he thought he had too. Tyler didn't want to live and still know what he knew. The cavity left behind was madness.

The beast born of Tyler's madness finished its meal and locked dead, grey eyes with his. Something spiked deep within Tyler's brain; a siren call to the abyss.

His limbs moved of their own accord. The door was open before he could tell his arm to raise the pistol and shoot the damn thing. Snow had crunched underneath his camo boots before he realized he stood in front of it.

Tyler didn't feel the bite of the scorpion stingers, didn't see his skin bubbling and boiling beneath his jacket, didn't feel it. Only the sky and its twirling lights were witness to the growing crystals replacing his skin, the mucus and purple pitch erupting from his nose and his mouth and his ears. Spouts of beautiful umbral vomit, let loose from Tyler's gaped mouth, rained from the canopy of the sky. Blood erupted from his eyes and his nostrils as his ribcage was torn apart, and the seeds of the cosmos planted within.

For his part, Tyler could only dream of swimming in the misted lights, floating with the slumbering creatures that hibernated deep within unknown corners of the night sky.

Rainbows Dancing on the Breeze
P.S. Traum

Taylor kicked at the ribcage with the tip of his white sneaker. The blood-stained skeleton rattled as some loose bones fell away.

"Gross. What was it? A dog?" Kori brushed his long blond bangs away from his eyes.

Taylor shook his head and put his fists on his hips. "Naw... Look at the skull, it's like a deer or something."

Kori stepped around the remains slowly, careful not to get any blood on his bare toes. He glanced at the soles of his soiled sandals and frowned. He almost tipped over holding his left foot up and grabbed Taylor's muscular arm for support. He squeezed it before he let go.

"That's a hell of a lot of blood. See where it soaked into the dirt? That 'mud' is made of blood." He poked at a bony leg with his shoe. "Look."

Kori giggled. "Oh yeah, duh, hooves. It *is* a deer. Hey, the grass is long, I couldn't tell..." He squatted down and was surprised the corpse didn't stink. "Jeez...there's nothing left. The animals really picked it clean."

Taylor stared, a frown forming on his face. "Yeah, but..." He turned away. "Fuck it."

Kori stood up straight, stretching and arching his back. He was conscious of his own exposed ribcage. He looked at Taylor. The sun felt warm on his skin, but they weren't sweating. Both boys were only wearing shorts, which highlighted their many differences. Taylor was more tanned, brunette, and certainly not skinny like Kori. *We're like night and day...*

"Fuck. I'm glad we skipped, dude." Taylor spread his arms wide. "Look at this place! Isn't this better than a damn classroom?"

Kori smiled. "Oh yeah. Three-day weekend..." He admired the view, soaking in the postcard-worthy vista. Kori faced the breeze and breathed it in. He loved the smell of the forest. The boys headed to the river.

The water was a deep blue and flowing rapidly. It was at the far end of the small canyon they had climbed down into. Most of the enclosed area was light forest, with patches of meadow grass. The surrounding short cliffs behind them were rocky and steep.

"Wow... it's so beautiful here! Look at that waterfall..."

"Yeah. Really badass..." Taylor pointed. "Think we can dive off that rock? We came to swim, right?"

Kori barely registered his words. "It's like a lost world... I keep expecting to see a Velociraptor or something!" He started to twirl, then stopped himself self-consciously. He glanced at Taylor, who was facing away.

"Think we're missing anything today? It's not like middle school; there's always some damn test or quiz or some bullshit... Plus there's always something going on, like a rally or a party or some shit. Not that the assholes would invite us..."

"Well... yeah... being a freshman really sucks."

"Dude, I used to be the best in… well, *any* sport... Now I'm nothing."

"Come on, Taylor, that's not true. Besides, you'll make it, eventually. And at least *you* don't get teased... I'm just a skinny blond kid who looks kind of girly." Kori darted a look at his friend. He was irritated Taylor wasn't offering any reassuring retort as he had.

"There's something bothering me about that deer..."

"What? Why?" Kori got nervous. He didn't like the tone.

"I don't know... Why was it just sitting there in a pool of blood? Animals would've torn it apart, or dragged some of it off, like, uh..."

"Yeah, you're right; it was intact, like it got stripped right there on the spot. Maybe a hunter?"

"Maybe," he mumbled unconvincingly. "But those bones were clean! You'd have to really hold each bone and scrape away to get all the meat off. My dad does that kind of shit."

"Oh God... what if it's like Ebola or something!" He noticed Taylor tilt his head at him questioningly. "You know, a flesh-eating virus or something!" Kori scanned the area for animals. Within minutes he had identified birds, rabbits, and other creatures moving about. "Well, maybe not... Why would all that fresh blood still be there?"

"Maybe it wasn't fresh, dude."

"I don't know. I think it was; it was bright red. Blood congeals and turns brown, plus –"

"Plus, the bugs would've ate it up, right? So, something *just* happened, and really fast? So..." Taylor was distracted, staring at Kori's hair.

"What?"

"Nothing."

"Tell me!" Kori lightly punched his best friend's chest.

"Your hair looks different in the sun. Sort of... like honey." They laughed.

Kori could feel his long hair whipping around in the wind. He wondered if it was time for a haircut. It was almost down to his shoulders, and his thick bangs covered his eyes. He combed his hair back, and gasped.

"Hey! Look!" Kori pointed to the riverbank.

Taylor followed his direction and saw two figures moving in the pale green grass. One was taller and carrying a basket or satchel.

"Damn! Damn! I thought no one knew about this place!" Taylor punched his palm. "Damn... I guess we couldn't keep it ours forever."

"Yeah... This sucks. We found it first! It's ours!"

"How did they get down here anyway? It seems like we would've seen them on our way down..."

Kori thought about how difficult it always was, struggling to climb down the steep cliff, crawling over sharp rocks, some of them loose. And all while wild heavy crosswinds were pushing them around.

"Let's see who these yahoos are..." Taylor started marching toward the new couple, who had moved to a clearing between a thick grove and the shore.

Kori followed silently. He could barely make out a canoe in the river, with a lengthy rope securing it to a tree. *So that's how they got here... Cheaters.* He gestured to his companion, who ignored him.

The boys moved in slowly, too annoyed to speak. Then Taylor reached out behind him to stop Kori, placing his hand on Kori's smooth chest, holding it there. It felt warm on his flesh. Kori smiled.

"Wait... check it out, dude..." Taylor said quietly. "Look."

The teenagers hid in the trees where the foliage was lush and green. Kori inhaled the scent of the leaves and oozing sap. He shuffled over to stand beside his friend, who was watching the intruders intently.

Kori could see them clearly now. A young couple embracing and kissing. The man was tall and casually dressed in what looked like a preppy jogging outfit. The curvaceous redheaded woman wore a short skirt and a loose, bright yellow blouse. They were standing barefoot on a layer of blankets. The woman suddenly tore off the man's shirt and laughed loudly. He joined in and unbuttoned her blouse.

Taylor was grinning, and smacked Kori's chest with the back of his hand. Kori nodded, smiling.

The girl shimmied out of her tight skirt and kissed the man, wrapping her arms around his neck. He ran his hands up her sides and cupped her ample breasts. She lowered her arms so he could slide her blouse off.

"Kori!" Taylor whispered excitedly.

"I know!" Kori couldn't hear the couple whenever they spoke, so he knew it was unlikely they'd hear the boys.

"They're huge!"

The man stripped down and laid back on the blankets. The woman stood over him and slowly peeled off her panties, dangling them and dropping them on his face. He sat up to kiss her between the legs, and after a few minutes she pushed him back down and slowly lowered herself onto him.

Taylor was entranced; his eyes looked as big as ping pong balls. Kori laughed. He glanced down. A familiar shape was straining against Taylor's swim trunks. Kori had observed it more than once that summer.

"This is really turning you on, isn't it?" he whispered into his friend's ear.

"I don't know..." the boy mumbled almost inaudibly, still staring intently.

Kori steeled himself and took a deep breath. He placed his hand on Taylor's trunks and took hold of him. Taylor froze but held his gaze. In the clearing the girl started to gyrate and grind.

"Damn! Look at that sweet ass... Fuck..."

When his friend didn't move or react to his hand, Kori slid it up to his lower abdomen. He slowly backed up so that his butt cheek pressed against Taylor's palm. He smiled when Taylor squeezed it. Kori slipped his hand down the swim trunks. Taylor gasped.

The woman started to sway and buck more intently as the man thrust upward. Kori realized Taylor had started to squeeze his butt in rhythm to the woman's gyrations, so he did the same with his hand.

Taylor moaned. He whispered to Kori. "You're... getting off on this... aren't you..."

"Um... maybe..." He stopped moving his hand. "You could find out..."

Taylor hesitated, then sighed and slipped his own hand down Kori's cutoff blue jeans. Kori squealed and resumed his gentle motions.

The woman slowed down and then stopped. She was distracted by something in the sky. Taylor followed her gaze. He slipped his hand out of Kori's underwear. The woman was mesmerized. The man started to knead her breasts and nipples vigorously as he continued to thrust.

"Hey... look." He pointed and pulled Kori's hand away reluctantly. "What the hell is that?"

A huge, ribbon-like object was swirling around in the wind high above them. The multicolored streak spun and twisted in the air currents. It unexpectedly spiraled and dove downward.

"How strange..."

"What the fuck is that, Kori?!"

The colorful phenomenon swooped down rapidly and continued to cut swiftly through the winds. It was a serpentine rainbow dancing through the sky in shimmering, graceful arcs.

"It's beautiful... I've never seen anything like it... Taylor... Have you?"

Taylor had turned his attention back to the young couple impatiently. They had interrupted their feral lovemaking to sit and watch the snake-like spectacle circling above them. It began to swell.

"Taylor! Do you see it?!"

Kori stared as the serpentine shape gradually enlarged and then dissipated as it revealed itself to be some kind of insect swarm. It tightened again and was flying down ever closer, spinning in long arcs as the unknown insects coalesced into a cleaner serpentine formation. It... they... were startling; a long, sparkly metallic cloud that performed complex aerial maneuvers like a flock of birds, iridescent and rainbow-hued like an oil slick...

The glittering serpent abruptly curved into a diving arc and aimed at the young couple, straightening as it gained speed.

"Oh no..." Kori felt rather than thought what was coming and trembled in revulsion and dread.

The condensed swarm struck the shocked man full force in the face, in a sudden onslaught of violence. A spray of blood showered the screaming woman.

Kori opened his mouth to scream, but Taylor clamped his hand over it.

The vicious swarm spun and swirled in rapid, relentless attacks upon the couple. They couldn't get their bearings and run or even stand. The man looked blinded, and when he faced the boys' direction Kori saw empty eye sockets and exposed bone. The swarm attacked repeatedly in a relentless onslaught, like machine gun fire. Everywhere they struck, a pile of flesh was torn away in a scarlet spray.

The mysterious insects were sandblasting the screaming young couple.

Kori and Taylor were frozen in place, terrified to move and unable to tear their eyes away from the grisly tableaux. Kori took his friend's hand and clutched it hard, shaking.

Blinded and staggering, the couple were helpless when the swarm attacked again. The insects were clearly targeting the victims' heads and groins and appeared to be entering the writhing bodies though every orifice, forcing their way in, a fresh splash of blood signaling every successful invasion.

Kori shook uncontrollably and tried not to vomit. The woman's face had become a grinning skull with blood-red hair. Blood and viscera gushed out of her pelvis as she toppled to the grass. The man's head fell off his body as he too collapsed.

Kori could see the nightmare very clearly; his eyes had focused on and absorbed every detail. Shiny skittering insects were squirming and burrowing into the flesh, chewing and consuming as they went. The vivacious, beautiful young lovers were being eviscerated within minutes; seconds even...

Taylor hugged Kori's trembling body. The thinner boy almost collapsed.

"We need to get out of here," Taylor whispered. "Don't make a sound."

"Wait..."

Once the couple's bodies were immobilized and had gone still, the voracious swarm plastered itself over them, encasing them in the gnawing death. The boys stared silently in horror. Those athletic, perfect physiques were being skeletonized before their very eyes.

"O… okay... I think they're... settled..."

The boys slowly backed away out of the grove, keeping their eyes on the swarm. Kori grasped Taylor's hand fearfully.

"Those fucking things are like flying piranhas..."

"Did you bring a phone?" Kori looked at Taylor and regretted asking. They were both practically nude. He dropped his head.

"And put it where? Besides... my little brother broke mine. You have pockets, why didn't you bring yours?"

"These?! Not really! We were going swimming, that phone's too expensive to bring out here... We –" Kori stopped and pointed to the sky. There were a couple of sparkly flashes whizzing by. "Are those –" he whispered.

"Maybe... A few rogues wandering, probably. We better lay low a minute." He pulled his friend towards a pile of boulders, and they sat down under a fallen tree trunk, obscured by the tangle of branches. Kori rested his head on his best friend's chest.

"I can't believe you... uh, you know..."

Kori blushed. "Yeah... um, I've been wanting to do that for a while..."

"For how long?!"

"Since summer began... when you started wearing... nothing." He giggled. "I think yours is a little bigger..."

Taylor shook his head. "No, don't... Uh, I don't really want to talk about it... you're making it weird."

"Oh. Do you regret it?"

"No… but..."

"We didn't get to fini–"

"Look, let's just try to get out of here, okay?" Taylor felt an itch and slapped his shoulder. When he pulled his hand away his palm was bloody. "What the fuck?" There was a tiny gouge in the flesh where he had hit it.

"Sshhh!" Kori was wide-eyed, a frightened expression on his face. "Hold still..." He reached up and jerked something off Taylor's forehead. A thick drop of blood rolled down his nose. "Oh my God... Look."

Kori held it up. He was grasping a small, cricket-sized insect. It squirmed in his fingertips, hissing. Taylor glanced down next to him at the bug he had just crushed. It was much larger and bloated, like a cicada. But they were the same creature. The living one was still chewing on a sliver of skin. *His* skin.

"Look at this thing!" Kori turned it over. He thought it looked like a coiled dragonfly, with large clear wings, and a long spiral abdomen. He poked at it; the head felt hard, with sharp edges and sharper "teeth." It didn't seem to have legs. "It looks like metallic plastic! I've never seen colors like this... see how it reflects the light? It's... iridescent or something."

"It's sick and fucked up. Fuck, dude... It's all mouth. Beady little eyes... What an ugly fucker. Look at those fucking jaws!" Taylor poked at its head. Then he pointed to the tail end, which was oozing waste. "This disgusting thing's shitting itself while it eats! Greedy fucker..."

Kori squeezed the insect tightly, avoiding its biting mouth. "See if you can stretch out its body. It looks soft... rubbery."

Taylor pinched the spiral abdomen near the end and pulled. Kori could see how the tubule of a body would engorge and unfurl as the creature fed, distending like a swelling condom full of blood and tissue.

"Sick, dude. And this one's small... How many are as big as *that* fucker?" He pointed to the squashed bug. "How do they even fly when they get that big?"

"Or when this thing gets full?" Kori held it against the stone and pushed another rock into it to smash its head. "Yuck."

Taylor stood up. "We can't stay here forever. I bet it's after six... What do we do when it gets dark? We won't even see them!"

"And they'll be able to zero right in on us like mosquitoes. Our body heat will glow like neon..." He shuddered. He looked down at his skinny body. He was basically naked, dangerously overexposed... and painfully vulnerable. "Oh God... We're in trouble, Taylor..." He felt his eyes watering.

Taylor ruffled his thick hair. "Not yet." He pulled Kori up.

The boys slowly made their way to the cliffs. The breeze carried a scent of rain. Kori wondered if rain would be good or bad.

The friends swatted the occasional rogue insects that landed on them. The creatures always struck face first and usually had already just taken a bite when they were noticed. The teen's bodies accumulated tiny red gouges all over.

"I'm glad they die pretty easy..."

"I'm glad these are just the little ones. Maybe they're the babies... larvae maybe?"

The wind picked up and started whipping Kori's hair around. When they reached the cliffs, they could see the familiar serpentine rainbows dancing over the river.

The boys started to climb... until Taylor suddenly stopped and grabbed Kori's arm. He pointed up. A different swarm was attacking a canine-shaped animal higher on the cliff. Kori thought it might be a coyote.

He whispered into Taylor's ear. "Now what?!"

"Shit dude... I think this valley is *full* of those fucking things!" He grasped Kori's shoulders and buried his face in his shoulder blades. "Fuck fuck fuck... *Fuck*! We're in trouble, Kori..."

"Sshhh! Even with this heavy wind, those things might still hear us, or sense us, or hell... I don't know!" He tried to hold back his tears.

"Okay... just, uh... Shit. Let's get back into the trees for now..."

As they moved away from the cliff, the boys could clearly observe several of the shimmering serpentine streaks racing through the sky.

"Why didn't we see them on the way down here? Where the hell were they?"

"I think we're damn lucky they didn't see us climbing down..."

Once they were under cover of the lower brush, they foraged for thick leafy branches they might use as a temporary shield or cover. Kori stared up at the cloudy sky, worried.

"It's getting dark soon! We need to do something."

"Yeah, no shit. Can we make a fire somehow? No, fire wouldn't help..."

"Hey... what about the river?"

"What, swim? Our heads would be perfect targets... No thanks..."

"Taylor, those people, they had a canoe."

"So that's how they got here... Same thing, dude, we'd be sitting ducks, right?"

Kori didn't want to give up his idea. He felt there was something about the river... "Oh! Okay...how about this, we tip the canoe and hide under it. We let the river sweep us away downstream..."

"Yeah... yeah... Okay, yeah, maybe... The river's deep though and flowing pretty fast. It might be rough."

"Better than those damn piranha bugs!" A wave of panic crossed his pale face. "Crap... assuming those things haven't invaded the whole county! What if they're like those giant locust clouds?! *Billions* of –"

"Dude! One problem at a time... I've never seen those damn things before. Have you ever heard of anyone seeing them anywhere?" Kori shook his head. "Okay then, let's go. Those things don't look like they can swim. Fingers crossed."

The teenagers headed for the river, holding their fan-like branches, staying low and moving slowly and quietly. Halfway there, one of the serpentine swarms dive-bombed the boys.

"*Fuck!!*"

"Taylor! I'm scared! What do we do!" Kori was crying, tears streaming down his face.

Taylor shoved Kori hard. The smaller boy fell into a mud puddle near a rotting log.

"Hide! I'll draw them off..." He ran parallel to the river, yelling and waving his arms. "Come get me, fuckers!"

"*Taylor*! Don't!"

"I have shoes! Get to the canoe! I'll circle back!"

Kori realized his friend was right; he'd never be fast enough in his loose flip-flop sandals, and barefoot he'd just slice his feet open on all the rocks and twigs and wouldn't even be able to walk. He looked up; there were no other swarms nearby. He hoped Taylor really could outrun a diving swarm, or dodge the thing. The rainbow snake was slicing through the air above the boy, apparently in no great hurry to shred him to ribbons. Kori started fast-walking towards the river.

The glittery streak suddenly dropped and blasted into Taylor full force, knocking him down. He held the branch up and covered his face with his free arm. The bugs tore a long chunk out of his bare thighs in a bright red splash. He could hear his friend's screams. The onslaught of the voracious storm of gnashing was horrendous to witness.

Kori kicked off his sandals and broke into a sprint. Soon he was only yards away from the riverbank, but far from the canoe. He paused when the swarm launched another attack against Taylor. The boy zigzagged and leaped just before the mass struck his torso. Another crimson spray followed by more screams.

Kori began yelling at the swarm. "Over here, assholes!" He jumped up and down, waving his arms to no avail. He could see the dead couple... skeletonized lovers. "*Taylor! The blankets!*"

His friend heard him and understood. He scanned the grass and saw the bodies. He ran for the blankets and dove into them when the swarm swooped down in another deadly descent.

Kori ran towards the canoe. Taylor grasped the blankets and ran. The decimated bodies spilled away in pieces. Both boys headed for the river, with the canoe just down the bank, beckoning. Kori smiled.

"Taylor!"

"Kori! Your legs! Your body!"

Kori looked down and was shocked to see dozens of tiny insects covering him. He started slapping at them, creating splashes of blood all over. He couldn't feel much pain. *The fuckers must be too small...*

The reunited friends hugged and started swatting insects off of each other. Taylor was getting chewed up; several of the larger, slower cicada types were gouging chunks of meat out of him.

"Oh God, Taylor..." Kori was sobbing. Taylor threw a blanket around the kid. Then he wrapped the other around himself. The heavy wind fluttered the blanket like a cape.

"Fuck it, we're here, dude!" Taylor took Kori's hand. "To hell with these fucking bugs!" The boys ran into the river's edge, splashing as they walked towards the canoe.

As they moved closer, an explosive force emerged from the river. The boys fell back in shock and terror as a massive swarm of the insects burst out of the water, filling the air around them with shimmering rainbows of death...

The Root of it All

Kevin Hollaway

"That is one ugly-ass tree."

Karen had never been this deep in the woods, but she wanted her final farewell to this stinking town to count. College beckoned, and she would never come back.

Strolling up to the twisted black trunk, she navigated around curling roots that wound their gnarled glory along the ground before diving down however deep they chose to go. Above, the few branches remaining stretched high and stopped just short of the canopy, never touched by the sun.

More than ugly, this was a rotting tree that had the appearance of a slow death that would never finish. Yet, it seemed to regard this new visitor, the first in a very long time to enter its lonely space.

Karen straddled the thickest root of the lot and held her palm up. She mumbled the spell with a grin. It was amazing what you could find in the occult section of the town library. She didn't think it would work, and never believed in that sort of thing, but she wanted a nice warm-up. Besides...

It was an ugly-ass tree.

She was never coming back.

So why not?

Hell, she wasn't even sure she had the spell memorized correctly. It was in some forgotten language, and the damn book was too thick to drag out here. Oh well, it was just a prep for the main course anyway, like spraying cooking oil on a pre-heated skillet.

Curling her hand into a fist, Karen moved on and began reciting a ritual so perfectly memorized and burned-in that life without it didn't exist. The short rhyme was the subject of all double and triple-dares from the elementary playground to junior high gym to high school prom. One she chickened out on each and every time. Just hearing the other kids mention the tree was enough to make her shake herself to sleep at night.

Now, she was finally here in person and realized all that fuss was for nothing.

Knock one – you're still not done.

She shut her eyes and knocked, hitting the bark just enough to knock some shavings off. They drifted down and were lifted by the wind, bringing on a different chill as it played with her hair.

For a second her logical mind stalled all rational thought. It was just the wind, but still a nice touch. A brisk crack came from behind the tree. She peered around and noticed a branch landing on the crest of a large deadfall containing countless others the tree had shed over the decades, centuries, eons...

Knock two – it all rings true.

Karen closed her eyes and rapped the trunk again.

A stronger gust of wind floated in, carrying not an actual ringing but more of a sharp tapping.

Wow, it's really working, she thought, as her mind's darkness gave way to a silhouette approaching. She gasped and opened her eyes, then scolded herself.

"Damn, girl; you're too old to be this gullible. Just one more and you're outta this hellhole."

A sharp pinch flared from her finger. She scratched it and continued, proving to everyone not watching how she could conquer her fears and never come back.

That's right girl, you're never coming back.

She proceeded with the final knock.

Knock three – come fly with me.

The backfire blew Karen back twenty feet. She blacked out briefly and was jolted back with dry heaves by her deflated lungs screaming for air. She stood too quickly, lost her equilibrium, and collapsed. Memories came of how she recovered from sprints at track meets, wrapping her arms around her knees with her head bowed.

Steady breathing returned with the calm wind, but her mind's eye gave birth to that silhouette again. It was a person approaching her, rubbing their hands together, reaching out. She screamed and tried to open her eyes, but they were sealed shut like all those mornings she would wake up to her crusty lids glued together.

What's the name for that? I'm going to be a doctor, dammit! What's that called?

She stood with her imposed blindness and turned to walk away from the ugly-ass-tree-that-could-not-die. Her finger flared again. She dug into the itch, drawing blood. Screaming for help was no good but she did it anyway, her voice dampened by the living trees, the good trees.

"Yeah... well... you did it didn't you, Karen? Proved them all wrong."

That attempt at humor made her laugh hysterically one last time when the silhouette filled her mind and her body. Karen collapsed against a tree and slid down as the hands clamped around her brain. Her ears filled with the sonic reverb of the tapping that came after she recited the second verse. It vibrated her skull, now clasped between her own hands trying to steady it.

Once gone, she welcomed the deafness left behind.

Yeah, you were going to leave it all behind.

Every tactile sense heightened as the man stretched within her, as if test-fitting a new suit. Karen's finger flared again, but she was calm now, scratching it lightly as she succumbed and faded into the man's embrace. Only the second verse of that playground rhyme could be heard, leaving her lips over and over and gaining speed.

"Knock two – it all rings true. Knocktwo it all ringstrue. Knocktwoitallringstrue."

Left behind, the black tree regarded the scene and shed another branch for the deadfall.

* * *

Despite all Blake had experienced, he never considered himself a religious person. At least not subscribing to any single set of beliefs. His cases had taken him to the end and back, seeing just everything that did – and some that shouldn't – exist.

Faith being what it was – the assurance of things hoped for and the conviction of those not seen – was a luxury Blake could not afford. Actually, he took more comfort in knowing what was there or what he may come up against, although that left little room for hope. He shied away from denominational religion, feeling it was a customized safety net humanity created to serve a particular mindset. Which was fine; most couldn't function if they knew what he knew.

Blake considered himself neutral and believed in all of it because it was all there.

Obviously, the faith represented in the room he now sat in couldn't do the job he was about to be presented with.

I guess the money helps, he thought. That's a nice desk.

He stood as Father Cruce entered the room and greeted him with a firm handshake.

"Mr. Graham, thanks so much for coming on short notice."

"No problem, Father."

"We can dispense with all that; first name is fine. Call me Ben."

That was a relief; the less formalities the better.

"Then you can call me Blake."

Blake chuckled at the memory of a Paul Simon song but couldn't remember the title. The tension eased completely when Father Ben opted for the chair next to him instead of his giant desk that looked like it belonged in Pottersville.

"I know I didn't give you much to go on over the phone. She shows some signs of possession but— "

"I don't do possessions."

"I know, we tried that."

"How so?"

"We brought in our best man."

For a second Blake felt he was in some top-secret briefing from his detective days.

Ben continued. "The exorcism really the attempted exorcism – lasted twelve hours. Nothing worked, no reaction and no further harm was done to the girl. Just a waste of time, really."

"Well, let's see her."

* * *

Karen stood in the middle of a side room adjacent to the main sanctuary. A cot and chair were nearby, but Ben pointed out they were of little use since she barely moved. Her clothes were filthy and torn. A steady trail of dirty footprints wound their way to the door and back.

"We wanted to make her as comfortable as possible, but she won't let us touch her long enough to clean her or change her clothes. I spotted her while I was out running an errand. She was walking across the field from the tree line at the edge of town. I couldn't get her in the car, but she followed me all the way here. It was hard getting her to enter the building; she acted like she wanted to go around it or through it instead, but then finally gave up and followed me in."

Blake approached Karen and stopped when she suddenly turned and headed to the door, explaining the dirty prints.

"She does that several times a day but doesn't attempt to leave."

As if on cue, she marched back to the center and stopped like an off switch had been flipped.

Blake slowly approached and stooped down. Through her matted hair he could see Karen's eyelids clenched shut, like she would burst out in tears any second. Her lips were moving, but Blake couldn't make out what she was mumbling.

"She won't open her eyes and has no reaction to sound," the priest frowned.

"Why is her finger bandaged?"

Like another switch was flipped, Karen started scratching her finger.

"Never mind."

"She barely let me get close long enough to wrap it. She does not want to be touched and won't open her eyes."

Blake sighed from the lack of information he had to work with and wondered if this was nothing more than a mentally disturbed girl.

"Any family?"

"Her parents are overseas traveling on business. We haven't contacted them yet. Karen had a flight booked, she's about – she was – about to head off for college."

"Friends?"

"Not now. They all scatter once school and graduation are over. No one stays behind; call it the town curse."

Blake's next question was his most important and would tell how much or how little room he had to work.

"Have you called the police or anyone else?"

"No, that's why we called you."

"Good, let's keep it that way."

"Blake, I'm afraid she'll be committed if we can't help her."

"Quiet, please."

Blake snapped his fingers next to each of her ears, bringing no response. Then he brought his hand up near the back of her head and inched it closer. She cringed, almost falling to her knees.

"PLEASE DON'T TOUCH ME!"

Blake backed away. As if nothing had happened, she started for the door again – paused – and went back to her spot, scratching her finger the whole way.

He waited for her to calm, then pulled his phone out and held it up as close as he could without touching her and started recording. The playback was low, but enough to hear as he increased the volume.

"itallringstrue-knocktwo-itallringstrue-knocktwo..."

"What does that mean?" Ben asked.

"I don't know; it sounds like a poem, but you're right," Blake surmised. "She's not possessed in the typical sense. No blasphemous language or speaking in tongues defiling God, no signs of scars or self-mutilation – except for that itch she has. She's doing the exact opposite; she's docile and shy."

Ben held his hands out in a hopeless gesture. "Then what?"

"I think she's haunted, for lack of a better word."

"Excuse me?"

"Demons possess; people haunt."

"I feel like I'm back on square one here."

Blake strolled to the door. "In a way, you are. Usually those haunting a person are somehow incomplete and need to be sent on their way."

"So, whoever it is has unfinished business."

"Yes. It's the who and why that makes it hard. An exorcism would be a cakewalk compared to this."

Father Ben took a breath and nodded. "Okay, I'm with you. I'll have Kev keep watch on her; he's my most trusted deacon. What's next?"

"You said you found her near the tree line? Let's have a look at those woods."

* * *

They drove to the woods and started the trek at the approximate location Karen was found wandering. Thankfully, the clear sky made it easy to navigate along a nature trail they found. Deeper in, the path abruptly disappeared into thicker foliage.

"I guess I should have dressed for this," Ben joked.

Blake offered to go the rest of the way alone, but Ben insisted on sticking together, either out of fear or stubbornness.

Further in, a cool breeze filtered through the trees and the natural sounds of insects and birds started to dial down. Something strong was near; Blake could feel it.

"The ground looks worn here," Ben said.

"Yep," Blake replied. "Let's stay on it."

As they progressed, the light dimmed as if prohibited to show them anymore. The wind picked up, and they heard a fluttering sound. Around the next tree was a torn piece of cloth caught in the bark. Trailing down to the ground was a thin line of dried blood. Blake studied the crushed weeds and branches at his feet. "She was here, maybe fell unconscious."

"God," Ben sighed, "who would attack — "

"No, think about it," Blake corrected, turning to the priest while keeping his pace. "Who would be hanging out this far in off the trails waiting to attack someone? It's even too far to drag a victim and do who knows what."

"Blake!" Ben gasped and pointed. Blake turned forward and almost walked into it. The black tree stood, stilling the wind and muting any remaining sounds of existence. Blake was on his feet before Ben could help, and was already walking around the trunk, taking it all in.

"This is one ugly-ass tree."

Ben's face squirmed with disgust. "Disgusting! How could something like this still be standing? It looks like it's been rotting forever!"

"Probably," Blake said from the other side, "with this deadfall I wouldn't doubt it."

"So... she's haunted by this tree?"

"No, but it helped. Like a focal point for transference, a channel to pass through."

Ben approached the pile of dead branches and kicked a few with his feet. Blake did the same and hit something solid. He bent down, pushing more limbs aside. Underneath were random chunks of cut wood, some smoothed out and finished.

"What the hell?" Ben asked.

"Language, Father," Blake joked, "but my thoughts exactly. Someone has a strange hobby."

Ben jumped at the sound of his phone.

"Kev? Yeah, speak up, we've got bad reception."

"Father Ben, she's just started speaking a lot louder. She keeps saying 'knock two – it all rings true.'"

"We know Kev; we'll be back soon."

"Wait, I know what it is. It's the Dead Tree Triple Dare!"

Static bled through the line, then cleared as they walked away from the tree.

"What's that?" Blake asked.

"Just one of those town legends kids joke about during recess. Find the black tree in the woods. Knock one – you're not done. Knock two – it all rings true. Knock three – come fly with me. I never tried it; I was always too scared to go in those woods."

"That's very smart of you," Ben said, glancing back at the deformed abomination of nature.

Blake leaned in. "Kev? I guess you don't know anyone that's ever tried the knocks?"

"No, I always thought it was just another stupid ghost story. She's going to the door again."

"Wait, don't hang up and don't let her out."

Blake started back toward the tree and was shocked to see Ben's arm raised to block him.

"Let me."

"You sure?"

"Damn straight."

He handed Blake the phone and found a large knot on the black trunk, perfect for knocking.

Ben doubled up his fist and rapped.

Shavings of bark fell through a chilled wind.

"Anything?" Blake yelled.

Kev's voice fought the static. *"No, she's back at the center of the room, but scratching her finger very hard."*

Ben rapped again.

A stronger gust flew in, starting a dance amongst the living tree branches, bending in waves along the canopy. Then the tapping came, each louder than the last.

"She just rushed to the door again. She really wants out. Did you hear that hollow ringing sound?"

Blake fought the wind to hear, "Yeah, you mean you heard it?"

"Yeah, it's coming from the east side of the building."

Blake cocked an eyebrow at Ben for an answer. The priest hopscotched around the massive roots back to solid ground. "That's the founder's cemetery."

Blake played the only card he had left.

"Let her out, Kev."

"You sure?"

Ben started to ask the same question when it dawned on him what Blake was thinking. He took the phone.

"Yes, Kev. That's why she acted lost and wanted to go around or through the building. Just lead her to the cemetery, we'll meet you there."

They headed back when Ben paused and said, "Shall I try knock three?"

Blake's eyes went wide. "Are you shitting me? Did you hear what knock three was?"

"Language!" Ben chided back.

* * *

They found Kev and Karen side-by-side at the edge of the cemetery amongst several empty plots. The girl rapidly scratching her finger, bringing fresh blood.

"I'm sorry, Father," Kev said. "I tried to put a fresh bandage on, but she won't let me."

"It's okay. So, this is where she stopped? There's nothing here; it's all vacant."

"We won't know until we dig." Blake said.

With shovels from the church utility shed, the three made it down six feet by dusk. Karen stood idly by, her scratching and mumbling slowing at a steady pace. Her face appeared peaceful – almost appreciative this was about to end for her.

Blake glanced up at her through dripping sweat. *Maybe you're still in there, Karen. Once we let whoever it is out of you. If they'll even leave. God, I hope so.*

Just then Ben's shovel made contact.

They cleared the dirt off a very unassuming box, just large enough for a body. It was nothing fancy, save for the four support posts at each corner.

The box was solid black.

Ben gasped as his hand exposed a crude plaque nailed to the lid.

"Oh God have mercy."

"Not on him," Kev said.

"Who?" Blake asked, climbing out of the grave to catch some fresh air.

"It's Bishop Franklin, the town's worst secret."

"Our worst sin," Ben continued.

Blake creased his brow in confusion, then he understood.

"Wow, even way out here in the middle of nowhere."

Ben's eyes welled up. "Excommunicated. So many boys, as the story goes. It was way before our time here. Such an abhorrent man. I feel ashamed."

"It wasn't your sin," Blake reassured him. "It was his."

"He killed himself in the sanctuary, one bullet in the head." Kev said. "He wasn't worthy to be buried here with the others, but I guess they had no choice. Cremation isn't allowed, so apparently an unmarked grave was suitable."

Blake and Ben both looked at the young Deacon, stunned at his wealth of knowledge. "I studied hard, Father," he said modestly.

Blake hopped back in the grave. "He's tethered for some reason — he can't move on."

"Like in limbo?" Ben asked.

Blake nodded. "Look at that lid. That's what those solid pieces are under the deadfall. He didn't deserve a normal coffin, so they took the wood from that tree to build it."

"It was probably a normal tree until they buried him," Ben suggested.

"Maybe. Then Bishop Franklin found a channel, passing through the wood and those leftovers they dumped out there, poisoning all he touched to slowly rot with his soul."

"So, what do we do?" Ben asked. "What's his unfinished business?"

"Open it."

Once the lid was off, Kev turned away, fearing the worst. He had never seen a corpse before, much less one this far gone. Maybe a skeletal hand would shoot up and drag him down with gnarled fingers. Ben rested a reassuring hand on his shoulder and he turned back, fighting his fear.

"God, it's like he was buried yesterday."

Karen was on her knees now, serene and relaxed.

"In some cultures, it's believed the excommunicated don't decompose when they die," Blake explained. "They have to be allowed to. We have to send him on his way."

Bishop Franklin rested in the black box as Ben searched for some sign of what was missing. The body looked normal, save for the bullet hole in the temple.

"I don't see anything Blake, I don't know what I'm looking for."

"His ring," Kev pointed. "Knock two – it all rings true."

Ben looked at the corpse's folded hands. "It's gone; there's no ring." He dug around the body — hoping the jewelry had fallen off somewhere – but came up empty.

"Dammit!" Blake yelled, throwing his shovel down. It clanged against a corner of the coffin, knocking off the cap from one of the corner posts. The sound that followed was the sweetest the three of them heard all day. A steady clang echoed from the hollow cylinder.

Blake jumped down and reached in. Empty. He went to the other corner. Nothing. Ben was already checking the posts on his end, holding his breath. Then he smiled.

From the last one he retrieved a gold-plated ecclesiastical ring. Ben held it up, shaking the dust off the amethyst. It shimmered in the setting sun.

"They removed it. I guess he wasn't worthy of that either," Kev said. Karen was breathing hard next to him, her shut eyes yearning.

"He's not," Ben said, "but we have to send him on his way and free Karen."

With that, he carefully slipped the ring onto the bishop's finger.

Rapid gusts encircled Karen. She shot upright, arching her head up, mouth wide open and arms splayed out. Her feet left the ground, floating on the wind. A dark vortex emerged on her chest. One final blast of wind lowered her back. Kev cradled her limp body. In her place was a black silhouette. It floated down to the grave and turned to Father Ben. He spit in the phantom's face.

"Back to your grave until Judgement Day and God have his way with you."

Bishop Franklin's dark spirit lowered and embraced his corpse. Ben and Blake stared as it reacted like an old film reel in fast motion. With a final death-rattle of air, the chest collapsed. Cheeks sunk in, exposing the skull. The eyes dried in their sockets. Flesh on each finger withered to dust, but the ring stayed on.

Before they had the lid secured, Franklin was mostly ash and bone. "Be thankful you didn't see that, Kev." Ben joked.

Kev chuckled and kept his arms around Karen, who was crying through open eyes. She pulled the bandage from her finger, the itch now gone with barely a wound in sight.

Against the setting sun, Ben and Blake started shoveling dirt back over the dark coffin of the banished bishop. The wood was starting to turn, gradually assuming a natural color.

"I hope to never see this bastard again," Ben said.

Blake shook a naughty finger at the priest.

"Language, Father."

Somewhere deep in the woods, a final branch fell from a once forsaken tree no longer poisoned. The last of its rotted bark was also shed, making way for something new.

Digger

Matt Martinek

We had done it before. Many times, in fact. The beginnings of it were much like the seeds of anything else... fertilized by chance. We had accidentally unearthed the remains of some poor kid's pet. From the looks of it, it was either a kind of hamster or small ferret. Its body was placed into a glass bottle, along with a note inscribed with its birth and death dates... and, of course, its name. "Edgar." The metal lid of the bottle was jutting out of the soil just the tiniest bit, and my buddy, Derrick, spotted it, instantly plucking it out of its burial spot without much thought or effort whatsoever. The bottle ended up broken, with glass shards spraying off of the filthy park bench it was thrown against. Edgar's sad little bones were strewn about. On a whim, I kept the skull. Drilled a tiny little hole into each side of it, too, and ran a chain through it to make a necklace. That was the start, I guess. It didn't seem significant at the time, but, oh... I suppose it was.

The years passed, as did the times of youth. Before we knew it, we were already young men. Or maybe not nearly men at all. We were diggers. It's all we knew how to be, and everything we needed. The tools consisted of flashlights, hammers, shovels, and crowbars. Our muscles pushed the tools about… made them do the work. Our morbid fascinations made the work possible to begin with. The seed had exploded, with its tendrils reaching every lobe… the synapses firing, ablaze with a sickness very few knew the symptoms of. It was a dirty little secret, kept amongst friends. Because diggers don't say… they only do.

"Damn it, John… put that smoke out and help us, for Christ's sake!" I always had to rein him in… get him back on task.

"Oh, Tommy! Would you chill out already! I'm just taking a tiny break. You don't wanna break union rules, do ya?" Johnny flicked his ash to the ground as Derrick and I toiled away in the dark, shovelful after shovelful, sweat dripping from our brows.

It was a typical dig. We had it down to a science by then… we usually chose older plots, preferably from around 1910-1930, as we found that the majority of those didn't have burial vaults installed. Our concern was speed, and busting open a concrete vault is more time-consuming and difficult than one may think. Anything earlier than 1910, though, was pointless… unless you wanted to go home with nothing but a pocketful of bone dust. Been there. Done that. We wanted somewhat intact skeletons, as that's where the money was. We could get about $800 for a few hours' work if the pieces were in good shape. Occasionally, though, we would break the rules and hit a newer plot. If flesh and clothing remained, we could hoist a generous two grand for our troubles. Not a bad hour-to-wage ratio for something that we would probably do for free. It was quite a worthwhile venture. Well, if you didn't have any hang-ups about the stink, or the risk involved. And the gelatinous flesh… that was always a little tricky. You always took some home with you, either stuck to your pant leg or dried to your shirt. Poor Derrick once got it in his ponytail, of all places. He was so paranoid about it that he tried to cut off all of his hair with a straight razor. His mom was pissed. It looked like hell.

"Alright, fellas, I think we hit pay dirt!" I heard the clank of the shovel hitting something hard as Derrick gave us the good news. John finally joined us back at the plot. His timing was impeccable. Bastard, I thought.

"Nice of you to join us, Johnny! Thanks for the help!" I flipped him off as I spoke. The gesture was captured as a shadow by the illumination of his flashlight.

We gathered around as we carefully removed the dirt from around the edges of the coffin, which looked in terrible shape and barely held together. This was by far the hardest part. If you weren't careful, the calcified treasures inside could easily be damaged, and the night completely wasted. Thankfully, as we removed handfuls of moistened, stinking, wooden fragments, we knew that we were in luck. Good thing, too… a year or so more and the coffin would've given way completely, with the earth claiming the treasure for itself. Nonetheless, there he was. Gerald Rainey, Loving Husband. 1852-1928. Pieces of the burial suit still remained, although tattered and hardened. Absolutely no visible flesh remained, so the only odor was from the mold itself, and whatever processes the bugs and worms had going on. The skull was in decent enough condition… the teeth had fallen out and were strewn about the casket floor, but that was nothing new. The left femur was worn completely through at the middle, but that was the only glaring defect that would affect our price point. Everything else was pretty much as expected. The three of us gently collected the blackened bones and placed them into the multiple canvas bags we had brought for the transport home. I pocketed the corpse's wedding ring to hopefully sell at a later date (who says crime doesn't pay?). Afterwards, we replaced the dirt of the burial plot as quickly as we could. That was of utmost importance. It would be easy to jet out of there as soon as we snagged the bones, but patience was required to ensure no one suspected a thing. The dirt needed to be level with the ground… nothing out of the ordinary. Any excess was shoveled into the weeds. After everything was as neat and tidy as we could get it, we jumped into the car and got the hell out of dodge. That was our 19th dig in two years, spaced out between the oldest and most out-of-the-way cemeteries in the tri-county area. Our record was intact. Never caught.

***

There aren't too many ghost stories about the tiny little shit town in which we reside, but the ones that do exist receive as much fanfare as possible. I mean, the town is boring. It's full of boring folks and boring activities. But Becky's Grave… that isn't boring at all. I had thought about it often but had never gone there myself. The story went that a woman named Rebecca Kring was burned alive in her home as the townsfolk suspected her of witchcraft and occult dealings. And, of course, her spirit was said to roam the grounds of Snavely Cemetery, the original place of her burial. It's kind of a cookie-cutter story, sure… and I didn't believe a word of it. That is, until the story gained a morbid update, of sorts. A local man, who just happened to be a self-proclaimed paranormal expert, wrote an article about Becky's Grave for his college newspaper. In it, he provided an interesting bit of information about the legend. He contended that Becky wasn't even buried in the cemetery at all, but she was instead interred further back in the forest, near some swampland, and that he had seen it for himself. A few months later, this man died under suspicious circumstances. The doctors said it was something with his heart, but his friends knew better. They said that he was never the same since he visited that grave. His health deteriorated steadily, day by day, from the moment he returned home from the cemetery that night. He was only 20 years old. As I was always into the darker side of life, this more than piqued my interest. So, I came up with this plan. I was going to find Becky's Grave myself. And rob that fucker. With a few friends, of course.

As it was kind of a passion project of mine, Derrick and John weren't really interested in helping me at first. The grave itself was most likely too old to provide anything of value. And who's to say it even existed at all? It could have very well been a gigantic waste of time. They thought I was nuts, but after a little prodding, I finally convinced them to join me in my little haunted expedition. Interestingly enough, on the very night after our high school graduation, we set out to find Becky's Grave. We were now men. But we were diggers, first. And diggers we would remain.

So, as it turned out, Snavely Cemetery was little more than a family plot… by far the smallest actual graveyard I had ever visited. If you weren't searching for it in particular, you wouldn't even realize it was there at all. The road was complete darkness, and the cemetery sign was tiny. But there we were, in the dead of night, entering the pathway, climbing the black hill by flashlight, carrying our tools and bags. Within 50 yards, we reached the plot itself, which was hidden to the left in a thicket of trees and bushes. It felt secretive… it felt off-limits. But we continued on, nonetheless. The stones were few, and all as old as sin. I sprayed the beam of light across the faces of some of the worn granite markers, and within no time I came upon the

Kring surname. I surveyed more than a dozen Kring plots, but Rebecca's was not amongst them, just as the article had stated. I did notice something interesting, however… there were two infant plots from the Kring family… one baby boy, one baby girl. Both died at one day old, at about five years apart. Brother and sister, connected not only by blood, but by fate itself. It seemed that this family was no stranger to pain on the grandest of scales. I paused for a moment, but Derrick and John nudged me on, past the cemetery, back into the trees. I became afraid.

Past the first few yards of forest, we entered a boggy ground of mud and wetness that seemed to bleed juicier with every step. We had prepared for this and had worn the oldest boots and pants that we owned. It was like the ground wanted to stop us from continuing… it seemed hungry enough to suck us into its bowels whole, so I urged the boys to pick up the pace a bit. Every hair on my arms and neck stood edgewise as we trudged forward. My heart was pumping fast as more than a bit of nervousness poked at my innards. And then, there came a moment in time when the party stopped moving at all. Derrick spoke up.

"Tommy… man, let's turn back. There's nothing back here but mud and shit. It doesn't feel right, anyways. Let's pack it in and go have some beers." John looked at him and nodded his head in agreement. They both looked kind of ill.

"Awww, come on, you two! Are you serious? Is it because of this ghost crap? It's the big two-zero! Twenty digs!" I was putting on a brave face, but deep down I wanted to join them in their retreat.

"Naw, Tommy, we're not scared of anything. You know that better than anybody! Something just feels off, bro. Best to trust your instincts, right?" John's lip quivered as he tilted his head at me like a puppy dog.

"Alright, pussies! Here's the deal. You guys go back to the car and wait for me. Take a nap or smoke a joint or some shit. I'll take the stuff and root around for a little longer, see what I can find. Can you do that for me, at least?" I wasn't leaving empty-handed, not by a long shot. Derrick shoved the two bags of tools into my chest and quickly began to make his way back through the mud pit. John wasn't far behind. I knew that they were pissed, but I wasn't giving up just yet.

About 20 minutes passed, and it seemed like I was no closer to my goal. The mud was nearly up to my knees at this point, and my feet were now freezing cold. The bags slung across my back seemed to grow heavier by the second. Maybe it wasn't worth it after all. Or maybe it was just some made-up bullshit from some crazy guy trying to drum up paranormal business. Regardless, I realized that it was time to pack it in. Like my comrades, I turned around, defeated, and began to trudge back. It was over. But then, as it sometimes tends to do in life, fate played its hand.

Within ten steps of my retreat, my flashlight shone upon something that barely caught my eye. It was a small gravestone, jutting out sideways a foot or two from the swampy mess off to the right of me. I approached slowly, unbelieving of what I had found. What else could it be? There was no inscription on the stone, but this did not stop me from quickly reaching for the shovel and plowing into the moist ground with reckless abandon. I worked and worked, as quickly as I could, with shovelfuls of mess flinging over my head into the blackness behind me. The growing stink of methane tickled my nostrils as I dug further into the swampy bog. I thought about going back to the car to get the boys to help me, but there was a part of me that wanted it all to myself. I deserved it. I stayed when no one else would. She was mine to have, and mine to take.

It could have been an hour, or it could have been three… I do not know. Time ceases during situations of true excitement, and I was never more excited than at that very moment when my ear caught the clunk of my shovel-tip hitting against the lid of Becky's Grave. At this point I was a rabid fool, down in the muddy depths of the plot-hole, groaning, clawing, and pulling at the edges of the coffin lid. I wanted it! I needed it! And, as I yanked with all my might and the lid finally let loose, I received my bride, in all her putrid glory! I grabbed my light and witnessed it all! Amongst the crumbled wood I beheld her rotting face… earthworms protruding from every orifice… her gray, stringy hair floating in the puddle of brown mess that had already entered the coffin. My hands caressed the translucent, soapy flesh of the corpse's cheeks… my fingers poked inside to the splintering bone underneath. The worms and maggots crawled onto me, just as they had with her, wanting to feast upon my living flesh. As we became one… it happened. I heard the creaking joints come alive and felt a cold, rotting hand grasp my arm. Rebecca Kring was a living being once again! And through her touch I saw, deep in the recesses of my mind, the fire itself! I breathed the smoke into my lungs! I saw the burial! I heard the whispers! Her crumbling jaws opened, and she spoke two words to her suitor as her teeth fell about… "I AM!"

According to John and Derrick, I returned to the car about three hours after they left me, stumbling about in a complete daze. I wouldn't say one word to them. As I stated before, diggers don't say… they only do.

***

It really didn't take long at all to notice the changes. Hell, I felt something from the moment I woke up the very next day. Either I lost something at Becky's Grave, or maybe I brought something back. Wasn't sure. All I knew was that I felt things less. A kind of constant inebriation, but without a drink or drug. Sounds were muffled… lights were dimmed. Nerve endings were no longer doing their normal work. I was floating, numb to the pains of the physical world. But, of course, I couldn't let anyone know... not even my fellow diggers. I played the game as best as I could, especially around my parents. I still lived at home, and I couldn't completely avoid interaction with them.

Beyond the physical issues I was experiencing, there was another problem I was concerned with. Some memory of the attempted exhumation eventually returned to me… it was a botched experiment… an unfinished one, at that. What did I do? Did I leave the open grave, just like that? With Becky's corpse left in the open for any onlookers or animals to do with as they pleased? And how did I even make it out of that mud pit on my own? I had broken my own rules, and I was just hoping that my errors wouldn't come back to haunt me. I attempted to gain enough bravery to return to the grave and finish the job, but the thought of coming face-to-face with the witch once again was too much for my weak little mind to handle. I couldn't even bring myself to ask Derrick or John to do it for me… I didn't want to introduce them to whatever forces were at play in that swamp. I was already doing a pretty good job of ignoring their calls. They were looking for another pay day, I was sure, but I was afraid that my days as a digger were most likely over, at least temporarily.

At the end of the first week, a new symptom came upon me. My breath… it began to stink. Even my dulled sense of smell could pick it up. It was like that of a rotting tooth, ripe with infection. I began to keep a secret stock of mouthwash in my closet, but it was barely enough to get by. My mother insisted on getting me to the dentist as soon as possible, but I skirted the situation. I simply stopped speaking as much, to try to hide it as much as possible. Soon after, I noticed that I was losing weight, as well, and that my skin was becoming pale and itchy. There wasn't much that I could hide with this… it was just a matter of time before some intervention was needed, or even worse… forced upon me. I thought back to the ghost hunter, and what his friends said about his last months on earth. And I had gone so much further than he! I had not only found the grave, but I went inside! A line was crossed, but at what price?

In the midst of my body falling apart, I did attempt to keep some semblance of normalcy in my life. I had just graduated, and I already had an interview scheduled at a local warehouse. Now that the digging was on hold, I needed to make as much money as I could. My parents knew that I wasn't feeling well, so they urged me to cancel, but I wouldn't have it. And so, I put on the best clothes I had, covered my neck in cologne, doused my throat and mouth with antiseptic rinse, and went on my interview. Unfortunately, I should've listened to my parents.

I will never forget the man's face… the absolute horror and disgust. Everything was going fine at first. I was acing all of the interviewer's questions, and I was closing in on sealing the deal. We were going over whatever meager wage was going to be offered to me, and then, all of a sudden, I sneezed! A spray of bright red blood covered the man's desk and paperwork, and I heard a clicking sound as something rolled over the desk and onto his lap. He picked it up, aghast with the horror show that the interview had turned into. A tooth! He held it out in the palm of his hand, offering it back to me, as his other hand covered his mouth as he dry-heaved into it. Appalled, I busted out of the office as fast as I could, embarrassed and covered in blood. The interviewer followed me into the parking lot to see if I was okay, but I was already shifted into gear and speeding home. Obviously, things were getting much, much worse.

Thankfully, when I returned home, my parents were off running errands, which allowed me to clean myself up without any questions or concerns on their part. Eventually, the bleeding from my nose stopped altogether, and when I checked out the tooth situation, I realized that all of my teeth were loosening, and my gums were starting to recede down to the roots. The stink was that of a dead animal by this point. As I looked into the mirror at the absolute creature I was becoming, I winced at the patches of red that were now forming upon my pallid, sunken face. Whatever curse that I had brought upon myself was progressing. But what was the endgame?

More days passed, with myself hiding in my room, door locked. Any sporadic appearances into the living room or kitchen were quick. I always wore a hooded sweatshirt, to hide my concerning form. My hair had begun to fall out. I could not eat. I could not sleep. I was like a ghost. Avoidance was key. Limited speaking, mainly consisting of "yes" or "no." I knew that I was running out of time… my parents would surely act soon. I began to scratch at the red splotches on my ravaged face as they became unbearably itchy, but when I did the skin broke open and I bled… but not red. It was black, and thick. I was becoming necrotic. The flesh was fucking dying! I tried so very hard to deny it. I tried to take my mind somewhere else, to a place where I was healthy, to a time when I wasn't a digger… a damned ghoul. It became undeniable, however, when I relieved myself into the toilet and saw the thick, dark brown fluid that was left behind. It reminded me of old motor oil. It was no longer just my outer shell rotting, but my insides, as well. Who could help me? Who would believe me? Rebecca Kring did this! She lives, as I die!

And so, I am. Just as the words that Becky spoke to me on that very night. But soon, hopefully, I will cease to be. I sit here, on my bathroom floor, amongst a pile of flesh, fingernails, teeth, and hair. I've fallen apart, yet I am still here. I hold the razor blade in my rotten fingertips, though I can't feel anything at all. As the skin of my wrists spread open and the black flows, will the curse finally leave me? Will I finally die? Or will I be left to contend with a living death, until there is simply nothing left of me? I prepare myself for the end… my black heart beats faster, the soiled breath quickens. A deathly panic comes over me. But it must be done. Diggers don't say, they only do.

"Honey? Are you okay in there? Your father and I want to talk to you…"

Stillwater

Dylan T. Bosworth

Swamp don't give nothin' back. You know this. Her words bang around inside my head like thunder as I follow my brother's soggy footprints down the stairs and out the front door. I see him there ahead, waiting for me at the edge of the trees.

My skin is damp as soon as it touches the outdoors, and I'm assaulted by the brightness of the night and the things croaking beyond the reeds. The night swells with chittering things, branches snapping like cracked bones filched for their marrow, and despite the sheen mimicking the warmth of the blood moon, I shiver. My brother raises a hand, a gesture, *it is me—I am home,* and he waves me forth and turns.

The mossy earth squelches under my boots, and before this moment, I was sure that I was in a dream. After a brief pause, I step forward and hesitate. My brother turns and beckons me on again. This time, his eyes glow like they've been replaced with pieces of the night sky. Pinpricks of light scatter as he catches my gaze, and my toes sink into the moist ground again.

I cannot help but think what Miss Boudreaux would say if she saw me on this night. The vacant hollow of her empty silence—I can hear it even now. The way she clicks her tongue before she is about to speak her many wisdoms; it echoes around me in the night, bouncing off the water like dollops of rain spiking in the swamp.

The cypress trees calling out to me in such a manner is as though they are warning me to heed my own thoughts. The rain, like that admonishing tongue, *turn back.*

"Turn back."

Something brushes against my neck as the words dance down the funnel of my ear to my clawing mind.

"Who's there?" I say, and then, "Gabriel?"

Because whatever whispered to me, supplanting the Sheriff's words in my head, the voice did not belong to her.

Nothing answers.

I know the mistakes of this night are many and may yet serve to stall my progress, but I am hopeful I can proceed without the aid of Miss Boudreaux.

There is a part of me that turns cold before I can stop it, and it goes cold with the thought that Miss Boudreaux would not aim to prevent me from searching for my brother at all. I stutter in my very steps. It is clear to me how the night plays at my perceptions, and this is the second moment my skin has prickled this night, worse than being startled awake by my brother's sopping form.

Is it possible the sheriff, my—*our*—old nemesis, and even caretaker at the soggier points in our parents' path, could have enticed us all these years in order to wander? Deep inside, I know this is a lie of the musk spiral. I know what she would say if I were to drag her from her bed on this night, but I also know that she is wrong.

She is wrong because here is my brother now before me, and the fresh dots of crimson poking through the slices in my forearms from the barred fortress of the Yucca hedge make this night as real as any other. I am tempted to call her out to my land again, so that she may see.

Sometimes, the swamp does return.

***

"He jus' gone off, yeah?"

"That's what I am saying, yes." When she had first appeared in the drive two nights before, Officer Boudreaux sat in her car for far too long to be considered natural. I had watched her through the window as she stared at the edge of the clearing, out into the swamp.

She was still staring that way as she took down my words, the bright spinning reflection of her flashing light on her vehicle silhouetting her, obscuring her features like I was speaking with a shadow.

"Hmm." Her lips went tight over her teeth like they hid something behind them, but she shook the thought from her mind. "How long?"

"Last night sometime. When I woke, he was… gone. Never returned."

"He been actin' kinda strange, yeah?"

"I—strange how?"

She shuffled her feet, kicking stones down the drive before swallowing hard and stopping to peer out over the reeds.

"Prayin'. Prayin' to somethin'. Out here in the trees, yeah? Mumblin' quiet, eyes gone far. You seen that, non?"

***

There is no church in these swamps, no matter what the locals say. What Miss Boudreaux says. No missing congregation, swallowed by the twining maze of the mire paths. Only loons and herons splashing behind the curtain of the fog that clings like a mosquito net. American alligators and various types of slithering things, but if you pay them no mind, they tend to go on about their business, alone.

There are these things, and there is my brother.

The ground squelches beneath my feet, and the soft earth is like molding clay. I wish to lay in it, as if the ground and all its living things—warm and inviting—they wish for me to stay. To dig a small den for myself and curl up with the worms.

My brother's moonlit eyes, corpse-glow in the shadows of the Cyprus canopies, burrow into me and tug like long fingers, poking through and curling up to grip the inside of my skull. I'm led along like a bull by the nose.

Something gargles, a deep bellowing hitching, roiling in the chest of some empty creature, and I cannot keep from shaking; so much so, that I rest my palm against a stout tree to steady my legs.

The blue rays that filter in through the scattered heights of the cypress trees—these errant slices of moon—only serve to illumine the leeches that streak my legs by the dozens. Frantic, I peer ahead on the path, *what path,* and see that my fair brother has moved deeper among the trees to a place I cannot see.

The soggy earth and moss have given way to wetter land. I shiver despite the warmth, and I can't help but think of Miss Boudreaux, her warnings all those years ago when my family had first acquired the home, at odd times then on, and more, the full story just two nights ago now.

Fondness seemed to shine on her face briefly, but only briefly—her recollection of her grandmother and her legends, and all the ones that came before, fading into something else. The wrinkles that had pinched the corner of her eyes, had come and gone like a smile turned sour by a tragedy and made me promise not to follow my brother— that he was lost to the swamp for good.

I am sure now that she was right that I should not follow, but she is wrong about the rest. He is here, he has come back for me, and I intend to return him to our home. Ahead, there is no trail, only black muck, and the only way for me to know what direction to follow is to peer closely at the ground below.

There, my brother's bare footprints are swallowed in the silt, leaving only trace remains that guide my path. Somewhere out in the trees, with their limbs hanging low with strange bends, a bell tolls and my blood freezes under my flesh.

The church.

It isn't — it can't... be. I wait for another sign, something to join alongside the spectral clangor, but nothing follows. I've stopped for too long; my brother's prints are now lost to the mud, and I'm turned around and frantic.

"Gabriel!"

My voice is answered by its own echo and the sudden silence of the swamp. My brother's name carries on the empty wind like gun smoke, lingering long enough for second thoughts to ring louder than before.

An egret screams in the distance, and I lurch, pulling my foot out of my boot, leaving it stuck behind in the muck. My socked foot comes down next to me as I stumble, landing on some piercing debris hidden beneath the black mud, a full needle of fire injected from my foot to my hip. I fall backward, landing on my seat, clutching my foot in the air so I can peer at the damage.

I was never one for blood. The sight alone had caused me to faint a time or two and now is no exception. I peel off my sock—thick and dripping black—to expose my bare foot to the air. A line of blood snakes from a small hole in the center of my sole, slithering down to drip with quiet taps against the viscous murk in which I lay.

I attempt to avert my eyes, but already…

My vision—

grows

dark.

***

When I wake, the night is a deeper sort of dark. Out in these ancient places, so undisturbed, the trees may have lived and died without feeling the shadow of a plane, the fear of an axe, or the ache of unwanted intrusions.

The stars are in the millions, and I feel a comfort in the glow. More, the music of the trees swells over the grating chucks of the gallinules, and the throated bellows of the frogs. For some moments, the breeze is cool against my skin, the rumble beneath my bones deep under my pulsing bed of muck, soothing like being lulled back into a dreamless sleep; *where had I been?*

The ache returns to my foot first, then the fire of a stab wound. I sit with a start, remembering…

The ground rumbles again and I spring to my feet, hole in my foot be damned, and I'm sprinting across the patchy, pitted slough of land toward the only place that looks like solid ground. I feel heavy, my legs pumping but full of acid, slow, like they've only tested their weight now, after a thousand years interred.

Over the sound of my panting, there is singing. I hadn't *imagined* the singing, and I cannot yet decide if that's a good thing, or a bad thing, that I hear it now. At least I'm mostly sure I'm not mad.

Although, the case could be made to throw me away and lock me up, I suppose to myself as I run, as I jump through the tree line onto sturdier clay. I cannot help but consider the fact, oddly, suddenly, that my brother has been missing for two days, and tonight, appeared at my bedside and motioned for me to follow. It feels like days, months of dreaming.

How long had it been? I wish I had taken my watch from the nightstand, but even then, I'm not sure what good it would do. The trees are so dark under the hanging limbs, intertwined, weblike, like I'm walking into something I will not escape. I am coldly aware, this feeling blooming in my heart like I had always known, that even if the day were ever to come, I'd never see the sun.

I walk on like that for some time, morose, wishing then regretting that some ill thing would swing down from the trees and pluck me from my other shoe. Each noise quiets at the squelch of my feet, as the mud gives way to the ochre splash of the intruding miasma, mixing like oil as it swirls around my ankles, and my face is soaking, dripping, sweat or tears; I no longer know.

I think I see faces in the water, but they shift and change under my spilling eyes until they are other things I cannot speak. Things that I do not have names for, if ever one had existed. My heart is a frozen knot in my throat, and despite my efforts, I cannot cough it free. Vines, hanging things twist into nooses, lowering, lowering to swing toward the soft plane of my eager neck.

Spanish moss hangs like burial shrouds, and the trees bend low with something far heavier than time. Over the rash howls that rip through the trees, my teeth chatter like sparking rocks.

Where is my brother? Losing him once was enough to paint my pillow in clear lacquer, spilled over from my gored heart. God, how I swore I could not live, and on the night I smiled, and finalized the idea in my head, that yes, I would follow too. Only that resignation was for my own death, my diversion from the path and subsequent disappearance. But this full moon has seen fit to return my other to me—this better part.

"Gabriel!" I yell, again. The echo is snuffed out by some large crack or splash—the fever-pitch haze of clouds of gnats and other, worse, biting things. The cacophony swells like static until my ears ring, ring high and loud and unbearable and I am forced to my knees again.

When the ringing fades, the singing fills its place. I feel my chest heaving, but I cannot hear the whistle of my ragged lungs or the sticky pull of my cotton-tongue. Only the music, linear, floating as if on a tendril of fog, sweetly enters at my ear.

Many voices gently carol some lilting chorus, and the ease over which fell muscles threaten me with slumber beg at my eyelids like they've been pierced with hooks and are slowly being cranked toward my cheeks. I force myself to stand—to place my shoulders high and back, despite the pain, like Gabriel would have me do, and I trod on blinking horrid depths of intrusive things away.

Webs and the crawling, hateful little hunters that had built them, weaponized them against the flying things of the dark, are in ruins in my hair—scrambling, biting, infecting me with venoms unknown to humankind. Things hiss, whether snakes, over or under me—alligators somewhere bellowing just below their quiet ripples, there is no way to know.

I can barely see.

A scream slices out in the dark, violent and high, and is cut off just as soon as its echo could sound. I stop in my tracks as a coil of fear nestles gently in my chest. It wasn't my brother; I have to tell myself. It wasn't him; it could not have been. It was too shrill, too—

Another scream digs its claws through the fabric of the night, tearing it open, freezing me in a deeper tremble. I can't move, each command to my muscles is denied: they can only shake and shiver.

Gabriel...

The night stills after a lifetime of me quaking where I stood—if any foul thing had walked upon me in that state I would have been no game at all. Would I have screamed like those that hastened my search? Forcing me to run despite this gnawing hole, filled with pieces of swamp and meat?

"CALEB!" The call, my own name, is so clear, so very *him,* upon hearing it I immediately vomit. I wonder if he heard the other screams. I wonder if those were people, animals, or something else, and then I wonder if I had heard anything at all.

"Brother?" I yell, my throat burning like it is filled with broken glass, ground down by pestle and mortar. "Follow my voice."

The fog burns my eyes like smoke. I can feel it smothering my pores, drowning me in my own boiling blood. My sweat, my stink, now blending indecipherable from the fumes of decay, rising like immolated creatures still burning in their graves. I feel my very breath curdle on the wind. My lungs are becoming jellied preserves as my air sacs cling to the blighted mist. Spores ride through my veins, mycelium clings to my pants as the silken sheen of water fades to murky sludge again.

"Gabriel!" I feel my voice grate against my throat. Blood clings to the back of my tongue, hot like cast iron, but I can't hear myself over the spectral choral swell. It swoops in again out of nowhere, drowning out the sounds of the bog—even the sticking black sludge that pulls up and clings to my bleeding foot with each step. I can't hear it.

But it feels like fingers tempting me down.

I part through a copse of trees into a clearing, tinged with reeds, cattails, and moldering yucca. The slices on my arms burn and I am glad to watch the leaves of the swamp wilt.

It's real.

The chanting, rhythmic words of the choir climax over the hidden valley as grouse and other sleeping birds explode from the surrounding weeds. I am not as shocked as I expected, if indeed I expected anything at all. Still, mesmerized and tugged along by the ghostly draw of my brother's passing, entranced, intrigued, I gasp when I look upon the church's walls.

The clearing beyond the reads and thistle is a black pool of still water. I wade into it up to my knees, carefully, feeling along with my one bare foot. There are things I cannot name under the water, and my forehead breaks out in a cool sweat as I question whether this is water at all. I am only thankful the singing has stopped.

The building, if you could call it that, is only a remnant of its former being. One thin, black wall tilts at a harsh angle, separating it from the rest of the frame, and the bell tower with the ornate, ebon spire, is impaled deeply in the ground. The face is cracked open like a porcelain doll, an entire corner, gone, lying steaming in the mire.

They take their seats, the choir. Their tattered robes drip black water that looks like molten gold as it reflects the braziers placed burning bright around the single room. My hands are wrinkled from the moisture, and I try not to rub at the pads of my fingertips as I stare. The congregation turns, their faces, the faces of the choir, drip—melt off in waterlogged gobs of rotting flesh. Their eyes are swollen, white, with flakes of translucent film trickling down their wrinkled cheeks.

Bugs enter my mouth, but I am unable to close it. I scream as flies crawl across my eyes and the black murk I wade through begins to bubble against my skin, opening wounds. Each sore adorning my shrinking flesh is now home to nestling things that burrow in and out, taking their fill as I collapse to my knees.

"Caleb, my sweet, you've made it."

My brother holds out a hand, but he is too far for me to save myself. I'm melting in this water tomb, no longer able to support my own weight. I wish to collapse. I want only to drown in this scant depth of water.

When my arms give out, my face bounces off the hard planks of the church floor, and suddenly, I am before the pulpit where my brother stands.

"Ga—Gabriel." Eternity pours from my guts, spewing from my innards, pooling on the floor in an oil-slick, night sky of refuse and swamp matter. Tiny things squirm and squirm in the murk of my putrescent gorge. "Gabriel," I say again, clearer this time. My nose makes bubbles against the slime coating the floor and my face. "Are we no longer living?"

He laughs. The black cassock he wears is thick and crisp, and to my surprise, it is dry. It swishes against the pulpit as he rounds it and comes to his knees to hold my head upon his lap.

"Dear brother, you know we never belong there." He makes a vague gesture behind where I lay. Toward the path that just claimed my life. "We have never belonged with *them.*"

I hear Miss Boudreaux, and my mind will not allow me to consider if I care. Her words merely pass through me, reminding me we never should have come to this place.

As if he can read my thoughts, my brother—whose gaze is still somewhere behind— looks back to me with wild eyes, and I can see the sheen of his gaze has already faded to near gray.

"I am scared," I tell him, and the choir chants low, some Gregorian thing. The ground rumbles again, so hard I can hear the pool of reflected night bubble at my back. I'm forced to roll over so I can see what is making my brother's eyes knit with longing, the film of them wetting like grasping a lover, returned from war.

The black pool churns, sloshing with violent acceleration. White bubbles hiss to the surface and steam in the air. The chanting of the choir grows and grows, some thunderous, repetitive, tolling things, like a human bell made of flesh.

I'm on my feet, stepping into a run. Pain explodes through my foot, shutting off all the function in my leg, and I'm left, scurrying across the ademic, disintegrating wood like a rat fleeing a twisting knot of gnashing snakes.

The thing that splits the surface of the water rises up, twisting, towering over the broken church, dripping black globs of sediment onto the skeletal and mushy congregation. At first, as my eyes follow, I can only think of some ancient snake. Some lost mythical beast, but that is quickly bound up and thrashed against the insides of my skull as the twisting thing is followed by another, and another, and another, all reaching toward the pallid mood, arcing like tentacle spires, ready to twist around my feet and drag me to whatever hungers below the surface.

My brother, the leader of this drowned flock of worshippers, looks back to me and the smile that shines on his face is one of elation. He holds his hand in front of him, cupping it, like holding some essence only he can feel.

"Brother," he says. "I heard the whispers slither through the reeds, twisting around the trees, the truth about the world. I listened, and I prayed as the words in the wind had ordered done. I listened, sweet Caleb. And it spoke."

I watch my brother hold his hand in the air as the intensity of the choral verse ramps up. As his hand reaches the sky, palm open to the limbs of the creature, they stop their thrashing, and the choir holds a discordant note.

"This is where we belong, Caleb. It is where we have always belonged."

The black pool bubbles violently, as if the pressure of this starless void, the ghostly clearing, brought it to a boil. Upon its waves, washing forth gouts of bubbling black and red, bits of flesh and bone, rises my brother's corpse, still in the clothes he wore the other night.

His papal ghost can only smile. "This is where the whole world belongs."

The water explodes, washing forth body after body, their decimated beings rolling and bouncing off of pews and other drowned debris. Over it all, the choir holds their note, high, dissonant, vibrating the strands of the connective tissue of my soul.

My voice gives out as I belt a scream to shatter stained glass as I watch my body, beaten, bloodied, and newly drowned bob to the surface of the oblivion pool. With hands clasped in prayer, it floats gently across the hardwood floor on a thin black wave.

The Wendigo's Whisper

Martyn Lawrence

Sitting in the driver's seat of the black SUV, Sarah zipped up her thick coat as her breath plumed in the crisp mountain air. She pulled her hat over her auburn hair and took in the sight before her; Blackpine National Forest – two million unforgiving acres of trees, mountains, and lakes. Sarah wasn't a stranger to search-and-rescues in Blackpine and knew better than anyone that straying just a few feet from the track could leave even the most experienced hikers completely lost. And with knee-high snow, winter searches were the worst.

"We've not got all day, Sarah," Mya called from outside the SUV, her voice light as the snow.

A wry smirk crept over Sarah's face as she considered the countless times she'd said those exact words to Mya. "Yeah," Sarah muttered to herself, before joining her team out in the bitter cold.

Mya, biting back a smile, put her multi-tool in her pocket and tossed her huge backpack onto her back; John, the rugged 6-foot-4 tracker, methodically checked his tracking equipment – infrared camera, and maps of every part of the forest, a compass hung from his pocket like a pocket watch; and Ben, the new guy with the thick brown beard, fumbled with the straps on his backpack.

"Alright, y'all," Sarah said, her husky southern accent carrying across the empty parking lot. "One last check. We've got ourselves a missing hiker out there, and a nasty storm system moving in. We've just had one pass already, and time's not on our side 'til the next one."

Ben glanced up at the looming grey clouds drifting ominously over the trees. "How long before that hits?" he asked.

"Weather service says 48 hours, tops," Sarah replied, her eyes scanning the dense tree line. The forest had a habit of swallowing light, creating a wall of darkness beyond the first few rows of pines. "Let's hope our fella just got himself turned 'round and is holed up somewhere waiting for rescue."

"Only a damn fool hikes in a storm," John said, his words trailing off to a mutter as he swung on his backpack.

"Well, fool or not, this guy did, and you're here to help, so let's get stepping, shall we?" Mya said, before trudging towards the trees.

John rolled his eyes and followed, Ben sharp on his heels, while Sarah made sure the car was locked before catching up.

***

Sarah led the team through a forest that seemed to close in around them – becoming almost claustrophobically tight. The occasional rustling of snow-laden pines and spruces gave the creeping sense that the trees were watching their every move.

"Raynor Ridge was his last known whereabouts. Bless his heart, there ain't much around there 'cept from a mighty big fall and a hecka lotta trees," Sarah said, raising her voice to be heard over the increasing wind and the crunch of snow beneath their feet. "Bout 5 more miles, give or take."

"'Bout 10 miles it'll feel like in this snow," John added, brow furrowed, as he waded through the snow that reached halfway to his knees.

Mya snorted at the tall man's woes. "Yeah, for you, but about twenty miles for those of us you got a foot on," she said, voice muffled through her red scarf. With the snow almost at her knees, each step was a battle against nature itself. Her black hat was completely white with snow, and her short black hair frosted at the tips.

The weather turned vicious, releasing snow in thick waves, as if the entire season had decided to fall in a single hour. The deeper they went, the colder it became, like every crunch of the white blanket released more cold into the air. It felt as if the forest itself was trying to freeze them in their tracks.

Sarah looked up at the canopy, where the towering trees sagged under the weight of thickening snow. "Don't matter none, we're closer to there than back anyway. There should be an old cabin up ahead soon, though. If we don't find anything, we can set up there for the night, and hope this snow settles down a bit," she said.

The group trudged on in silence, the eerie quiet of the forest broken only by their heavy breathing and the occasional snap of a branch. Not a single bird called in the trees. Nor was there any rustling or scurrying of animals. The forest was listening, and it wanted them to hear themselves.

Ben stopped abruptly mid-step. "What's that?" he asked, his hand rising slowly, finger trembling as it pointed to their right.

The team turned and followed his finger, straight to a large black mass, a few hundred feet away. For a moment, none of them moved. They all stood frozen, eyes narrowed, heads cocked forward, trying to focus on the shape that was partially obscured by the swirling snow.

"What the fuck," John muttered to himself, as he shrugged off his backpack and pulled out a small spotting scope.

"You see anything?" Sarah asked, her heart racing as she watched John struggling to focus through the deteriorating conditions.

"Well, I see something. It's big, it's black, and it ain't moving. Too much forage around it to make anything out." He lowered the scope and glanced around, hoping for some sort of clue before they went any closer.

Sarah led them forward, the snow crunching underfoot, her stomach tight with dread. She'd found bodies before. That thought didn't help. If anything, it made the anticipation worse because now she knew how it looked, how it smelled. She took a deep breath and offered a silent prayer that it wasn't their guy – or anyone else, for that matter.

The others followed in her footsteps, all experiencing those same fears as Sarah. Vomit loomed in the back of Ben's throat; the rest of the group were experienced, they'd seen it all, but him? He'd seen nothing, he'd never even seen snow this deep before.

A minute later, the group walked up on the remains of a black bear. Its belly was torn wide open, guts steaming in the cold, blood soaked deep into the snow. The thick fur was slick and red, yet completely untouched by the snow.

"What the fuck?" Ben breathed, wide-eyed, heart galloping. He looked around, frantically scanning the trees for the killer. "What the fuck kills a bear?"

It wasn't the biggest of bears. Sarah guessed at a slightly smaller than average female. "A bigger bear," she replied to Ben, eyes never leaving the bloody beast. "But that ain't the whole question. What wakes a bear from its hibernation, kills it, and did it recent enough so she doesn't get a flake of snow on her?"

The colour drained from Ben's face, mind racing with thoughts he hadn't even considered.

"I don't see much in the way of tracks, neither," John added.

The four of them looked around, straining their eyes and ears for sights and sounds that never came. Around them was nothing but wind-whipped snow and uncaring trees.

"Maybe our guy shot it?" Mya offered. "Spooked her, scared himself and shot her? Don't need to be close for that?"

"Maybe," Sarah mused, her thoughts turning like gears. Then, with a glance at the others, "or maybe it's the Wendigo." Her eyes wide in mock alarm, a hint of gallows humour was all she could manage.

Like every other national park, there were stories. Spirits in the trees. Wendigos in the darkness. Serial killers lurking on the trail. But no one had ever seen anything. No one who was taken seriously, anyway.

"I reckon we'd have heard a gunshot though, don't you? Then again, I reckon we'd have heard the poor girl fighting as well," Sarah continued. She had been tracking and exploring Blackpine for more than half her 40 years alive, but she'd never encountered anything like this. But there was always a reason, always a trail that led to the answer.

The team stood in tense silence, eyes darting through the white blur of trees, nerves frayed.

"You know, if he's out here killing bears," Ben said, voice trembling, "maybe we ought to turn back? The wind's picking up something bad." He didn't mention the blood. He couldn't look at it. The sheer volume, and the thick stench of death made him want to throw up.

Sarah didn't flinch. Her jaw tightened, and her eyes stayed locked ahead, as she battled her own nerves. "No, we need to find our guy. The weather's as good as it's gonna get, so we best make the most of it."

As if in response to her defiance, the temperature dropped further and the wind rose, as a sudden gust of sharp, icy air slammed into them. Its howl pierced through the trees with a shrill, sharp scream.

Sarah turned away, shielding her face from the bone-chilling cold. As she wiped frost from her lashes, something carried on the wind – a murmur, almost too soft to be real.

"…Sarah…"

Her heart slammed against her ribs, almost daring them to keep it inside. Her blood ran colder than the air around her. Frozen in place, she strained her ears.

Nothing. Only the relentless howl of the wind.

It was the wind. The wind in the branches. But she knew what she'd heard, no matter how much she tried to convince herself otherwise. *The wind can't talk, can it? Silly girl.*

"…Sarah…" The sound brushed past her ear again, softer this time, just a whisper on the breeze.

Her eyes darted wildly around the tree line, searching for something, anything, to explain the voice that was neither male nor female, old nor young. But the forest just stared back.

It's only the wind. Just your mind playing tricks on you.

Her stomach twisted with doubt as a cold dread rippled through her.

"Sarah!" Mya's sharp voice snapped Sarah back to reality with a flinch.

Sarah blinked rapidly, brushing snow from her eyes, and focused through the blur. John and Ben stood ahead, their eyes locked onto her. Waiting for her to catch up. She grabbed Mya's hand, as much for her own comfort as to stay grounded, and together they crunched forward to rejoin the group.

"Look at this," Ben said as they reached him, his voice unsteady.

He led them to a towering sugar maple tree; its red and orange leaves jarring against the backdrop of the pine and snow surrounding it. With a trembling hand, part cold but mostly fear, he pointed to the trunk.

Deep claw marks slashed through the bark, nearly six feet from the ground.

"Something ain't right," John said, face twisted in frustration as he shook the satellite phone he'd taken from his bag. "The phone's not working. That, and I don't know where the fuck we are anymore, on account of you wandering off," he said, glaring at Sarah.

Sarah's brow furrowed, bewildered. She hadn't wandered anywhere – had she?

Patience frayed, John didn't wait for a response; instead he spun on his heel and marched off. "We need to get back on track and find this fucking cabin," he barked, eyes locked on his GPS. He checked it against his compass, gave a sharp nod, and pressed forward – completely uninterested in the claw marks or anything Sarah might want to add.

The others hurried after him. Sticking together wasn't optional in that sort of weather. No wandering. No detours. Just follow the path that John's GPS laid out like law.

As they followed his lead, Sarah couldn't shake the feeling that something was watching them from behind the trees. Waiting.

***

Darkness came early at this time of year, especially in the dense forest, and it was close to nightfall by the time they found the cabin. This, after John's GPS had led them in a circle back to the slashed tree.

Ben stared at it, uneasy. He could've sworn the claw mark had been at *his* head height earlier. Now, it lined up with *John's*.

"That's a different tree," Ben insisted. "We can't have gone in a circle."

But John didn't even glance his way. He had no time for the new guy's opinions on direction.

Sarah had said nothing for the last hour. She was too afraid to speak, too afraid that if she did, it wouldn't be her friends who answered, but the trees instead.

"…Sa…rah…"

She'd flinched at every drawn-out syllable. Her whole-body tensed; her pulse thumped in her ears.

It's the wind, dang it. It's the wind, it's the wind, it's the wind, it's him, it's the wind. The hiker shot the bear, a bigger bear killed the bear, he killed the bear, I killed the bear.

"…Sa…rah…"

Her stomach was rumbling. It felt like days since she'd last eaten, but she could've sworn she'd had some jerky not long ago. *You've lost track of time. Focus, you silly girl.*

Mya had been the glue holding them together, trying to keep the focus on the hiker. Keeping Ben from turning around and running home, keeping Sarah from vanishing into the trees, and keeping John from storming off to the cabin alone.

When they finally reached it, the cabin was little more than a shack in the middle of a small clearing. Barely a cabin at all. Sarah forced open the door, spilling in the snow that was packed against its base.

The place was empty, except for the deer.

It lay in the centre of the cabin's only room, mutilated. Its belly had been slit open like the bear's, entrails spilling over the warped wooden floor, blood dried into the grains.

Mya slapped a hand over her mouth and turned away, gagging. The stench of rot and death was thick, sour, clinging to the walls, overwhelming in the small space.

Ben held his arm over his mouth and looked to Sarah for guidance, hoping for the leader to be some kind of anchor. But her face was twisted in disgust, frozen as the deer's glassy black eyes stared straight into her. Dead. Watching.

"No gun did that," John muttered, stepping forward. "The sooner this thing's outside, the sooner we can set up for the night. I'm done with today. Something's fucking with us, and if it's that fucking hiker, I'll bury him in the snow myself."

Sarah dropped her bag and slumped against the wall. She pulled out a couple of protein bars and devoured them like they were nothing. Her stomach rumbled again, calling for more. She felt like she could eat a horse.

She looked at the deer. *You could eat that*; after all, it was just meat now. Her mouth watered. *Cook it. Don't cook it. You'd be full either way.* Her thoughts were so intently locked on the creature that she completely missed John saying he was taking it outside.

"…Sa…rah…" The whisper came again, floating through the cabin with the cold.

John grunted as he dragged the carcass, its blood smearing a thick, red trail across the floor. Mya winced at the slither of its organs dragging like a tail behind it. Ben opened the door without a word, eyes wide and unblinking.

The weather had worsened further. Gale-force winds howled through the clearing outside, slamming against the cabin walls. The snow was so heavy that John could barely see the deer he was dragging. They were supposed to have had 48 hours before the storm hit. *What the fuck.* But at that point in time, he really didn't care. He just wanted the dead animal gone.

The trees weren't far, maybe twenty feet, but as John trudged toward them, squinting into the wind, the cabin behind him already looked like a dream. A shadow in the white.

Inside, Ben shoved the door closed, bracing against it to keep the storm at bay. "Surely we need to turn back in the morning?" he asked, looking at Sarah. She was still sitting against the wall with her eyes locked on the bloodstained floor.

"No," Sarah snapped. "We'll be fine, but that poor hiker might not be." She reached into her pack and pulled out another strip of jerky, eating it like she was starving to death.

Ben turned to Mya, silently pleading for backup. But she avoided his gaze.

She knew he was right. The storm had obviously come early, but she trusted Sarah with her life. She always had. After a long pause, she finally spoke, "He's right."

Ben pressed his lips together and gave her a small nod of thanks, while Sarah just sat eating her jerky.

The door blew open, a violent gust of wind slamming it against the wall with a deafening crack. All three rescuers almost jump out of their skin. For a split second, it felt like the storm itself had broken in, hunting them.

"…Sa…rah…"

It took a second for the bang to register. When it became clear it wasn't John pushing the door open, Ben hurried over, shoving against the wind to force it closed again.

He leaned out into the blizzard, one arm raised to shield his eyes as snow whipped across his face like needles.

"John?" he shouted into the blinding white. It was a shout that the screaming wind barely allowed to cross the threshold of the doorway.

Mya rushed to Ben's side; afraid he might disappear into the white abyss after John.

Sarah didn't move. She sat cross-legged on the floor, eyes unfocused, lightheaded, hungry, thirsty, like the storm was raging in her head.

"You know what I like?" Sarah murmured to herself. "Honey. What a wonderful thing bees do. And folks just kill 'em. Stomp on 'em 'til they're dead."

Unaware of Sarah's rambling, Ben pointed at something outside. "He's fallen," he shouted over the shrieking wind.

Although Mya stood only a few feet away, the storm sucked his words into its wind. She strained to see what he was pointing at, but the swirling snow blurred everything beyond the doorway.

Sarah vaguely made out the word fallen and pulled herself to her feet. She took a step towards them, stumbling against the wall, unnoticed by the others, who's eyes were locked onto whatever they were seeing in the snow. She stepped up beside them, brow furrowed, trying to focus through the blizzard.

A body. Still. Crumpled. Less than five feet from the door.

Her breath caught. In the next heartbeat, she was outside, plunging into the cold, Mya and Ben at her heels. Together, they grabbed John's arms—Sarah and Mya on one side, Ben on the other—and dragged him, inch by inch, back toward the cabin.

Thirty seconds passed by before there was a slight break in the snow, just enough to glimpse the shape.

A motionless body barely five feet from the door.

Sarah's eyes popped open, as she sucked in a gasp. Without a word, she bolted into the storm, Ben and Mya right behind her.

They reached John in seconds. Sarah and Mya together grabbed one arm, while Ben took the other. Together, they began the slow, grueling drag back toward the cabin, boots sinking into the deep snow.

"…Sa…rah…"

The calling was the loudest it had been, no longer a whisper in the wind, now nearer a shout in the wind.

Sarah's head snapped around. Left. Right. Behind. She didn't know where it came from, only that it *was*.

What do you want? What do you want from me?

"You."

Her body went rigid.

"…Sa…rah…"

"What?!" she screamed, turning toward the trees, eyes wild. Her fingers slipped from John's arm as her name echoed again.

The wind carried her words, replacing them with its own shriek, and Ben and Mya didn't hear her. As far as they knew, she'd only cried out a warning, that her grip on John was slipping. Not her grip of reality. Not of her mind.

No voice answered her. Only the white roar of the blizzard. Jaw clenched, she grabbed hold of John again, and thirty seconds later, they hauled him back into the relative safety of the cabin.

Mya used all the strength her hundred-pound frame could muster to try and force the door closed against the wild winds that fought against her.

As Mya shoved at the door, Ben rolled John onto his back.

Except it wasn't John.

It was a stranger. A man with icy blue skin, wide eyes, and a mouth frozen mid-scream. A face twisted in a look of sheer terror.

Ben staggered back, slamming against the wall as if the corpse had physically attacked him. His breath came fast and shallow, on the verge of hyperventilation. He couldn't blink, but nor could he look away. It was like staring at a car crash – he didn't want to look, he knew he shouldn't, but he just couldn't stop himself.

The man was well-equipped for the cold: thick coat, sturdy boots, a heavy backpack, and a red wool hat pulled low over his ears. There wasn't a scratch on him. No blood. No guts like with the bear or the deer. No claw marks like those on the tree. Just that face. Eyes and mouth stretched wide, like he'd died from pure, unbridled terror.

Mya turned from the door, letting it slam back open. Her body tensed at the sight. She knew that face from the missing person's photo.

The hiker. Wearing John's coat. Or one identical to it.

She looked to Sarah, who stood motionless, gloved hand clamped over her mouth.

"Why is he in John's coat?" Ben said. "Where the fuck did he come from? And where the fuck is John?" The question flew like rapid fire from his tongue. His whole body shook, now more through fear than the bone-chilling cold. "Why does he look like that?"

He turned back toward the storm and screamed into it, "John!"

"Ben?" Came John's response from somewhere out in the storm. Faint, distorted, but unmistakably calling his name.

Ben snapped his head to Sarah. "You hear that? He's out there!"

But Sarah and Mya stood oblivious. Nothing had reached their ears but the screaming wind hammering through the rickety wood of the cabin that was trembling around them.

Ben didn't wait. He didn't hesitate. Drawn by the voice, he bolted through the doorway and vanished into the swirling white, as if the storm itself had swallowed him.

Mya's body jerked in alarm. "Ben," she shouted, rushing to the door. She got only as far as the threshold before the wind hit her like a wall.

He was already gone.

Clinging to the doorframe, Mya leaned out, eyes squinting against the driving snow, lungs burning with every shout as she screamed his name again and again.

Inside, Sarah stood beside the hiker's corpse, her eyes locked on the frozen face. "They're gone," she said flatly.

Mya couldn't hear her over the storm, and kept yelling for Ben, desperate, frantic.

"They're gone!" Sarah screamed, this time loud enough to be heard through the wind.

Mya whipped her head around, glaring. "What do you mean 'they're gone'? They're not gone! They're out there!"

"They're gone."

The wind howled through the cabin as Mya stepped forward, her heart pounding with a fury she didn't know she possessed. "That's your team out there. You're in charge, you're the senior, and you couldn't care less?"

Sarah's eyes went glassy. Then, without warning, she raised her hand and cracked it across Mya's face. The sharp slap echoed off the shaking walls. "You need to simmer down now, ya hear?" Sarah said coldly.

"…Sa…rah…"

"Shut up!" Sarah screamed, wrapping her arms over her head, trying to squeeze out the voice in the wind. The voice in her mind.

Mya staggered a step back, hand to her cheek, brow tight, jaw clenched. "What the hell is wrong with you?"

The cabin shook harder. The wood groaned and creaked. A loud crack split the wood above them, like bones breaking. Mya glanced up, eyes wide, then snatched her backpack off the ground.

"We gotta go," she said, urgency rising in her voice.

Like a striking snake, Sarah lunged forward. She slammed Mya against the buckling wall, hand clamped tight around her throat. "We can't. Don't you hear it?"

"…Sa…rah…"

Sarah raised her free hand and held it up like an antenna, head tilted, wild-eyed. "Listen."

"…Si…ster…"

Mya froze. Her mind blank. She didn't know what to say. She shook her head slowly, fear overtaking her anger. Scared by her friend's breakdown, terrified of the impeding collapse of their shelter. Worried about their colleagues, worried about being buried alive.

Another loud crack, directly above them. Both women looked up in unison, as the roof finally gave way. A heavy wave of snow and splintered wood crashed down, burying them both.

Their worlds went black.

***

Sarah's eyes fluttered open, her world gradually coming back into light. The room around her was a blur, slowly coming into focus like a Polaroid developing.

The ceiling above her was unfamiliar – just white and sterile. She blinked again, vision gradually clearing. Through the window beside her was the clear night sky, filled with stars and a fat, full moon.

She looked down at herself – the white hospital gown, the IV snaking into her arm, and the Pulse Oximeter clipped to her finger.

At the foot of the bed stood a petite red-headed nurse, with a big smile on her face. "Hey there, you're awake," she said, her voice warm and tinged with a Southern drawl that reminded Sarah of home. "How're you feeling?"

Sarah inhaled slowly. Her throat burned. Her mind raced, searching for answers. How had she ended up in a hospital? Who found them? Was Mya okay?

She opened her mouth to speak, but her throat felt like sandpaper. Hand shaking, she reached for the glass of water on the bedside table, but the nurse was already there, helping her take slow sips.

"Easy now," the nurse said, her touch gentle. "Just small ones."

The water was cold and gave her throat some welcome relief.

"Where am I?" Sarah rasped, her dry voice sounding huskier than ever.

"You're at St. Michael's," the nurse answered, as she checked over Sarah's vitals.

Well, I know where I am at least, the thought little more than mild comfort.

"You're lucky they found you when they did," the nurse said, her tone light, but her words heavy. "A couple more hours and you'd have frozen to death. I swear, when you came in, you were colder than the ice in my whisky, and bluer than a robin's egg."

Sarah blinked hard, still trying to clear the fog in her mind. That didn't sound right. Who found her? Who's *they?*

"Mya? Where's Mya?" Sarah asked, her voice rising, words escaping more desperate than she intended.

The nurse's eyebrow arched, and her eyes swept the room as if they were searching for the answer. "I'm sure I don't know who Mya is. You were alone. Huddled up in a cabin, shivering halfway to heaven."

Sarah's chest tightened. *No.* That wasn't how it happened. They were together. "No, we went out yesterday. The storm hit us early. but we made it to the cabin." She tried to sit up, but the sudden movement spun her vision and sent a wave of dizziness crashing over her.

The nurse moved to steady Sarah. Her warm smile now sympathetic, the kind you give when you're not sure whether to comfort or call security. "Oh sweetheart," she said gently. "Yesterday? What day do you think it is?"

Sarah's eyes darted around the room, as she racked her brain, clawing at vague fragments in her foggy memory. "December 4th, 5th maybe," she ventured, knowing they'd left on the 3rd.

The nurse's pause stretched out. She looked down at her chart, then back at Sarah. "Oh no, honey, it's the 12th. You've been missing over a week now. A touch of shock ain't no surprise after what you've been through. But the rescuers were out looking for you for days. All I know's what they told me; you went off hiking, got your poor self lost and holed yourself up in some old cabin for dang near a week."

"That don't make sense," Sarah muttered, thinking aloud more than responding to the nurse. She turned to the window, hoping the stars might provide her some clarity. But instead, the glass offered back only her own reflection.

Skeletal, almost emaciated. Gaunt, ashen skin stretched tight over her cheekbones. Her eyes, now glowing snow-white orbs, were set deep in hollow sockets.

And then she smiled. Her razor-sharp teeth glinted in the moonlight.

She closed her eyes tight and sank back onto the pillow with a sigh. A familiar feeling took over her, pushing all other thoughts aside.

"I'm hungry."

The Bonny Swan

Colin Adams-Toomey

I thought I was the craftsman; I thought I shaped the piece and shaped the story. I know better now.

Things were not always the way they are now. I wager everyone says that; everyone who suffers hard days. We remember a different time, even if it wasn't so rosy as we think. But there was a time where some things were better. I know that. Those things are gone now.

The sickness came to our village; despite all we did to stop it. It carried away the best part of all of our children, and the old. Young it took, mostly. Young girls.

I used to make fine things. I was a luthier once and made sweet fiddles. I tempted the wood into perfect shapes, and made it sing, sweeter than a nightingale. Working a fiddle, a good one, is like birthing a babe. Choosing the right wood, that's a joy. What is the grain, can it sing right, will it look beautiful once it's oiled and finished? You are proud, and know that it goes out into the world, away from you. I'm lucky now if they want a nice piece of furniture.

Mostly, these days, I make coffins.

They aren't difficult. The angles to cut are always the same. And there's no need to choose lovely wood for the working, not like before. Bleeding pine is fine enough when you go in the ground. The worms don't mind. All that matters, really, is getting the measurements off the corpse.

Tom is the undertaker now, since Jenson died, and he calls at the shop more than anyone. We had a young man from the village next who was rolled over by logs while cutting timber. I saw the result, and I didn't need Tom to tell me that his mother wouldn't like to see him that way. I measured him up as best I could and sealed him in a box that was made of the same wood he died to get.

Tom never looks me in the eye when we do our work, not when we get right down to it. I think he still remembers Lucy, and how we nailed her up. But Lucy's in the ground, sleeping now.

When a body has to go back outside our village, I go too. Like or no, I've undertaken the business of the dead, same as Tom. We see the coffin where it has to go. And we always take the lych-way, the corpse-road.

That's how I first found her.

Tom and I rode the wagon with the corpse in back, as we always do. The lych-way is out on the moors, and we had to start early, before the sun was up. It isn't nice, traveling that way: the dead in the back, the road a dark nothing ahead beyond the lantern light. There are noises in the dark, before people awake. We huddled close in the wagon, raised the lanterns high as we could, and spurred the mule on faster. It started when we came to the miller's dam.

The miller's son came and caught us as we passed. He was pale, looked sick. He's only young, after all.

"We thought it was a swan at first," is what he said.

We raised a lantern over the black water, and I could see her. She was pale, trapped against the dam, and she floated lovely. She'd hardly been in the water all that long. Her arms moved gently with the current. We fished her out together.

Laid out on the bank, she was such a small thing. She had long dark hair, and her skin was blue. She didn't look a thing like Lucy. Tom wouldn't catch my eye, at any rate.

I started measuring her out. The miller asked what we could do to find her out, who she belonged to. But that isn't our place. Tom was sharp about that. We don't question the ones we find like this. The dead is the dead, and the living is the living, and we keep to our own company. We pay them the kindness of passage, and the respects of the wood, the coffin that takes them to sleep.

Except, I couldn't quite.

I did my duty and took down the measurements. I ignored the miller and his son, wringing their hands at what their dam had caught. But as I did, I felt her wrist. Such delicate bones. Such strong dark hair. The sun was rising at this point. Pink light on the pale flesh.

I had it on me, the way I used to when they gave me a fine piece of rosewood to work with. Tone-wood, that is. It sings with the player, if you make it into a fiddle. Sometimes, when you find the right piece of wood, you can hear it singing already.

I maybe heard her singing to me then.

Maybe that's why I did what I did. I'm not proud of what came next, though I know what I do now. I told Tom:

"Can you give her to me? I need to work her into the coffin."

I had no right to say so, and Tom knew it. We'd done this maybe thirty times already. I needed only moments with the body, just to take the long and short of it, as it were. Occasionally I'd needed more time with a body; if it was larger or smaller than usual would be a reason. But we'd undertaken young girls before, a dozen or more.

That's not why I wanted her. Tom gave me the eye, but his job was over when we knew she was dead. He nodded, and they loaded her onto the cart, and we took her back.

Maybe we don't know why we do the worst things. I laid her out on my bench, pale and cold and small. Maybe we want to see how far we can come to the edge of the cliff. Maybe we want to see what happens when we fall over.

To work with wood takes skill, but there are other materials.

Lucy was this age when she passed. She who drowned, who took all that was good with her, into the stream. The little ones have no voice. They get lost so easily. No one ever hears them.

But not this one. I could give her a voice. I heard that thought as though it had been whispered in my ear; it was that clear to me. When that is the command, it isn't so hard, after all.

The first is paring the flesh away, and if you have the right knife, that works a treat.

We look for the largest bones, for they are the easiest to work with. A good knife with a curved edge will take off most of the fat and gristle. This was the hardest part, if I were to be honest. A body has blood, if it has been dead for a while or not. I felt sick.

But I heard that voice, which told me it was right. I choked my sick, and I kept the butchery. I covered her face. Not seeing the face made it easier. The white cloth over her eyes went red eventually.

The meat was rotten; she was bloated. That small cold voice was what guided me, to the last. She was not Lucy. She was not.

Next was the salt pack, to draw out moisture, and to deal with the marrow. Rot would set in otherwise. Bone works like wood, almost. But I had to make it supple first, the old way. Leach out the bad, what would decay. The right herbs, and brain too. Her brain was enough, as it happened. They say the creature has enough brain to tan itself.

As I worked, I hummed a song. I didn't know what it was, but it came into my mind. It was the right song for the work. I was grimed to the elbow, and I didn't much like to look at what I was doing, but the song helped.

I didn't just make fiddles, in the old days. I played a little too. I never played well, but songs would come into my head, sometimes.

I slept after the work stopped. And then I dreamed. I dreamed about a little girl, drowned in the water. Hands held her down, held me down. I woke choking, with the taste of water and slime in my throat. And the song ringing in my ears.

Sometimes, I dreamed of Lucy. Her dark hair, her laugh. Sometimes in the dream, she was drowning all over again. Sometimes, she drowned me.

I feared I was losing my mind. But I hadn't worked on something so beautiful in such a long time. For once, it wasn't a coffin. For once, I was giving something life again. That's what I told myself. That's what something told me.

Steam-bending bone is not for the novice. Bone does not have all the same properties as wood. Giving the wood fibers a good steam will make them supple, bendable, easy. You can form it around a mold, make a curved chair back, whatever you'd like. Not so with bone. A little, and the bone will give well. Too much, the bone goes brittle and snaps.

I hummed and slowly bent the bone. I talked to it a little too, if I'm honest. Talked about what I was doing, even asked permission. Not so strange. Considering what I was doing. Little by little, it gave, yielded to the molds, and began to take shape. I felt good, felt pure. Something smiled on me, cajoled me forward.

All I did was work and make and dream about it. The song was stronger and stronger and wove through the dreams. I saw the girl, saw Lucy, saw the shape on my workbench.

I almost heard words to the song now. Not quite: it was like words to a song you knew once, and can almost taste them on your tongue. Just a little more thinking would bring them back. Just a little more.

I was thinking about tone now, how to capture that song. Breastbone, shoulder blades, those wide flat surfaces. Bone is good for sound. Many have made flutes out of it. It could sing. She could sing, as she wanted to.

I used her guts for the strings. That was hard. I didn't like it, but nothing works better. The fibers need to be stretched, and boiled, and stretched again. After a while, they don't look like the thing they once were. Then, it's easier to work them. The shop smelled bad, but I paid no mind. She told me what to do, told me to keep going. We were almost done now. She was over my shoulder the whole time.

The bow was carved carefully from her thigh and strung with that strong dark hair. I kept it, touched it many times. It wasn't Lucy. But it helped to touch it. I felt small hands holding mine as I did.

I went out in the moonlit night, into the forest. She guided me to the best trees to gather pitch, those same pines I harvested for coffins. They gave me their blood to make rosin for the bow. When I cut the trees to make them bleed, it was like cutting the body. But she was there, whispering, guiding my hand.

Tom came to visit.

We hadn't seen each other in some time. I knew he would come along. I hurried to cover the things in my shop, to hide my work. I thought, for the first time in a long time, about what it was that I was doing. I felt the hot flush of guilt, and shame, and worry.

He came in and wrinkled his nose at the smell. "How are you, Sean?" he asked. "It's been a long while. I've had no one to share the wagon."

"Aye," I replied, "and I'm sorry for that. I've been… well, I've been busy."

"Busy with what?"

I could see his concern; I'm no fool. He helped with all the burials, and they take a toll. He knew they took a toll on me.

"I've been looking to make some fine things again. I've not made a fine piece of work since..." I did not have to finish. Tom knew the last time I had put my hand to luthier's work. She had taken that desire with her into the stream, too.

Tom glanced quickly away from me and walked around the shop. "Times have been hard. We shouldn't have had to work together as we do," he said. "I take them under the ground. You make good things. You should, at least." He smiled a sad smile at me. "We should not ride in the same wagon."

"We do what we must," I replied, and I edged back toward my workbench. I did not wish Tom to know, to pity me, to stop me from my work. He did not understand. He had not heard her song. "To serve the dead is a noble thing," I said.

"Aye," he replied. He glanced around. "What have you been making?" he asked.

"A fiddle."

I looked at Tom, and he looked at me. I saw the pity in his eyes. He was there that day, when we fished Lucy out. She had been in the drink long enough that she barely held together. The thing we pulled from the water was so far away from the girl I knew, the girl that was left to me after

Jane died. Lucy was a force to be reckoned with, and many had chided me for how I raised her, how I let her run wild. But what was I to do? How could I hold a spirit like that? She ran me ragged; I loved every day with her in it. I was teaching her to turn a good wooden bowl when she died. She was better at it than me.

I looked Tom's pity in the face. I heard the whisper in my ear, too. I had once helped to make the best thing in the world, far finer than any wooden treasure. Far better than me; should have far outlived me. She died and the world died with her, but I had something different now.

"I came to tell you…" He hesitated. "I came to tell you that I was engaged. I hoped that you could be in the wedding."

I looked at him as a stranger. How could he, my companion in the dead and gray, find happiness?

Then I forced a smile and gave him all the blessings. I agreed to whatever he would want. He knew I could play and asked for music. I agreed. I had a fiddle to play, after all.

He told me about his young wife Ella, and how they met. I forced my voice high and cheery, and opened an old bottle of cider to toast the happy couple.

As he left, he said, "You should not shun the light, Sean. Our business is grim, to be sure. But it is business, and nothing more. You should have happiness."

I thanked him. He did not know what I'd found already. The song on my lips, *our* lips.

There came a night where the fiddle was ready. There is a quiet joy that no one shares except the craftsman. All the work, all the blood and dust and sweat, it comes together to arrive as a new and beautiful thing in the world. I oiled it with the same lard from the body. I could hardly think of it as a body anymore; she was new-born again, and the fiddle shined. It caught the moonlight through the window, in the depth of the bone. She was as pale as the moon itself. And as cold, and as beautiful.

Holding her to the light, I could see. I'm not a vain man, but I could see it was the finest fiddle I'd ever wrought.

The second finest thing I'd ever made.

She smiled at me, as I turned her this way and that. I was tired; so tired. I could have dropped there on the floor of my shop.

But she told me to pick up the bow. I agreed: an instrument like this needs to be played. I set bow to string, and her small fingers grasped it with me. I sighed and relaxed into her arms. And she sang.

She sang the story she'd been waiting to sing. The song I'd hummed, the song that had no words, until now. It came together, the way the whole thing had come together. I pulled back in horror, and she seized my arm. She would have her say; they all would. I could not stop. I could not stop hearing the music, the screams. Heartbroken, sweat and tears pouring down, I understood.

Tom's wedding came soon.

The village came out for it. It had been some time since we had had something to celebrate. Some time since the bells rang for new life, rather than the ending of it. The young girls picked flowers, and the men went into the woods to cut strong, green limbs for the bower. All the village cooked and cleaned, for the happy bride and groom.

I prepared too.

I walked along the main road into the village. The candles were lit along the sides and cast pretty flashing shadows up into the trees. I could smell the woodsmoke and roasting meat. I could hear music from Tom's house, even from out here in the dark.

I came on from out of the dark. We came together.

I pushed open the door to dancing and song. The table groaned under the weight of the food, and everything was strewn with garlands of white. The music flowed golden over all, mixed with the warm light of the candles. Tom and Ella, his young bride, sat flushed and pink at the top table. When I came in, the candles flickered. A cold breath licked the dancers.

Tom saw me, and his face told of the wine he had already drunk. "Come in, Sean!" he roared. He had his hand clutched around his bride; I could see where her arm was white where he gripped. "Play us a tune!"

I took her out. The body I'd wrought. When they saw her, I think they knew this was different. The fiddle was so pale, so cold. No wood looked like that. I could see the change on Tom's face, on Ella's, on everyone's.

But there was no stopping now. I thought I was the craftsman; thought I was the player. I wasn't. *I* was the instrument. She'd worked me all along, and she'd play me now. I saw that it was so from the start.

I tuned the pegs, made of her finger-bones. I felt her small hands close around mine and felt the comfort of that. I lifted the fiddle to my chin, rested my cheek against it. Felt her rest her head against mine. I closed my eyes and smiled.

I lifted the bow to the strings, and she sang.

She sang of lazy days in the hot sun by the banks of the river, gathering flowers, running wild in the trees. She sang of her mother. Sang of how the plague changed all that. I could feel it, see it through her eyes. From the tears on the cheeks of the guests, I knew that they could see it too.

She sang of how there was no one, not once her mother died, how she lived like a cat in the streets. Though there was one kind man, who gave her food, offered her comfort. He took her down to the river, promised all good things. When a hand extends like that, you take it. When you're young and know no better.

She sang of unspeakable things, of rough and panting cruelty. Screams lost to the forest where no one heard. She sang of strong hands grasping, dragging to the water. How cold the water was, as it lapped over legs, then chest. Of strong hands gripping the throat, forcing the head beneath. Of his face, twisted and empty of all things human, wavering through a watery film. As life dimmed, and sight.

His face twisted now, snarling and fearful. His bride flinched away, seeing under the surface for the first time.

They all began to join in. All of them. The young girls, so easy to hide in these plague-ridden times. When so many young are taken by sickness, how can you tell which have washed up for some other reason?

All of them. The O'Neil girl. The blacksmith's daughter.

Lucy, of course.

I think maybe I knew; in some way I couldn't admit. He never caught my eye. Not when we buried the young girls. Not when we buried Lucy. He never would bring her up to me, since we buried her. Never spoke of her. And he was especially kind, offering me the coffin-making work when any fool could make a coffin. I never allowed myself to question that kindness.

He looked me in the eye now, though. His lips pulled back from his teeth, his eyes an animal mix of rage and fear. Same as she saw, who sang now. Same as Lucy saw.

Same as they all saw. The chaos broke then, the screams and anger. Candles were overturned, food splattered on the floor. Fire started and roared up the walls. Some lunged for Tom, who had Ella in front of him, hands around her throat, coward animal to the last. Some sought to flee, to hear the song no more. They pulled at the doors.

And there they were. Come out of the dark to join the festivities.

The lost girls, all of them, a dozen or more. Waterlogged and pale, small points of fury in the moonlit night. I had played their tune, and they answered it now.

I could not stop. Would not. She would have her say. They all would.

They walked across the floor as the fires blazed, and people screamed and burned. They paid no heed; they had come to visit the groom. Tom had relaxed his grip in panic and fear, and Ella fled, lucky girl that she was. Who knows what it could have been for her otherwise, alone with him at night?

They came on. All the lost girls.

I'd once seen a rat trapped by a hound, in the corner of a barn. It scrabbled in panic at the walls, looking for escape when there was none. It bared its teeth in one final hopeless show, before the end came.

It was much like this for Tom. They circled, and pressed in. He ran to the back wall, but there was nowhere to go. He lashed at the girls, but they were dead, beyond the fear of pain and flesh. They were pale and relentless. Their milky eyes were fixed on him. Before they came, Tom caught my eye. I thought of all the dark lonely rides we'd shared with a corpse in the back of the wagon, huddled together against the night. One time, Lucy was in the back, though he had said nothing, huddled against me all the same.

What did he expect from me, looking at me so pitifully? I was the instrument, and the girls would have their say.

They closed in, and his screams were high and painful. Those screams sang perfect with the tune she and I were playing. At a wedding, the groom is expected to give of himself in thanks for his good fortune. He had had so many brides, over the years. They each took a piece with them.

I lowered the fiddle. She had sung her song. The house blazed, Tom's blood boiling where the fire licked the pool of it. I looked around, suddenly unsure. I had played, and what was I now to do?

She knew. The girl I'd found. The swan, trapped by the miller's dam. I had been her instrument, and a good one. She smiled and took my hand. She led me from the inferno of Tom's burning house. I went with her down the path, away from the village. I knew where we were going.

I knew her before we got close. I knew her height; didn't I measure it for the coffin? I knew the tilt of her head, the smile on her face.

My Lucy.

I could see her beyond the pale, wet skin. Beyond the cloudy eyes and lank hair. I saw her different. I saw the dark hair in bouncy curls, the little force that would never stop moving. I saw her lively face, the eyes that read you in moments, the clever hands that would learn far more than mine would ever do.

The swan-girl put my hand in hers. In Lucy's. Cold it was, but it gripped me with the same force as it ever did. My tears ran into my smile, and I could hardly see, but I knew it was right.

Lucy led me to the river. As she'd been led. The river where I'd found the swan. Where they'd found Lucy. She pulled me, and there'd been no home since she'd gone. I'd had nothing and nowhere since she'd gone down there.

We were going home together now.

Shhh

Veronica Falk

Leaves brush the side of the house in a chorus of hushed songs. The branches of the apple tree Casey's father planted are in tangled webs from years of neglect. It's the very thing that inspired my husband to plant an orchard.

I sigh.

Loneliness settles deep in my marrow, even though my children are nearby getting settled in their rooms. I glance out the window at brambles, bushes, and a few scraggly trees that we will eventually clear away. In the distance, an ancient, abandoned church sits atop of a small hill. A looming cross upon its steeple shoots its shadow out like a dagger as the sun sets behind it—it's getting closer. The image unnerves me as a chill pricks at my skin. I think it'll take some time to get used to the stillness of nature.

I shudder, heeding the urge to turn away. Sweat gathers on my brow despite the cold creeping in. I head to the sink to splash water on my face. Metal squeals in protest when I turn the knob, and bright red liquid bursts out like blood gushing from a wound. A scream catches in my throat. The pipes rattle and the crimson color turns muddy. It's just rust; I tell myself. I turn the knob off, yet a faucet of splattering rusted water still hisses out.

Shhh.

"There's a spider in my room," my four-year-old, Sara, huffs and stomps into the kitchen. She frowns and glares up at me, waiting for me to handle her unwanted guest. I turn towards the sink, but the faucet sits idle. A shiver of anxiety simmers in my belly, but I shake it off and follow Sara. The aged wooden house has no neighbors for miles. It is not huge, but it's bigger than our apartment in the city. It's not the type of house I would have chosen. Looking around, only moving boxes and sparse second-hand furniture decorate the area.

In Sara's room, a brown spider sits in an intricate web between the dresser and the bed. Just a creature trying to survive—like me. A few buzzing flies have taken up residence in the house, and I think having a spider around might help our situation, but I know Sara won't stand for it to live in her room.

"Lucas!" I call down the hall. I hear a familiar groan, and a sulking teen almost as tall as me emerges with his head buried in a hoodie and music escaping headphones. One of his fingers twirls a golden ringlet of hair.

"Why don't we find this spider a home outside?" I ask, pointing to the web. He walks over, his eyes tracing the lines of the web for a moment. A loud bang startles me. Dismembered parts lay smashed on the floor, under his boot. My apprehensive muscles tense when that temper flares—the same as his fathers.

"What did you do that for?" I yell, as Sara cries. Lucas ignores me and hurries back to his room. Sara looks up at me, tears still streaming from her sky-blue eyes.

"She didn't like that," she says. The words send a chill up my spine.

"Who?" I ask, but Sara has gone back to quietly playing with her favorite stuffed doll, brushing its hair. The comb's teeth sweep through the yarn, tightening a knot in my gut as it sings,

Shhh.

***

The time for bed has come and gone, leaving me exhausted but still unable to sleep. Casey snores beside me. He had come home just in time to go to bed. He got to have dinner with his crew while I wrestled with Sara in the neighborhood grocery store and then cooked while she was constantly underfoot. An ugly pit of resentment grows in the spot where love used to shine. Casey's pale skin glistens in the dim morning rays and, for a moment, I see the handsome man I married. I wish I could sleep so soundly, but the quietness of this place is unnerving. I get up and wander around; not really sure what to do. Internet service hasn't been installed out this far, and even our phone connection can be spotty. Not that I'd call anyone at this hour. Even the time of day is different here.

I wander to the kitchen window and glance outside. It's dawn and the tips of the sun are just peeking over the horizon. Our large plot of land sprawls before me, acres of nothing at all — except that church. Chills pimple my arms as I wrap them around me. My eyes linger on the church as more light illuminates its dusty exterior. It's two stories tall and looks more like a house or a school than a church, but that white cross on top is clear as the daylight now shining on it. A shadow moves in one of its windows. Surely a bird or some other animal taking up residence there. Then an unmistakable human silhouette stands in the window, its outline dark and deep as an abyss. Yet, I can feel its eyes staring at me—through me. Wind whistles through the gnarled trees.

Shhh.

"Mommy." I jump, letting out a little squeak when Sara's cold hand touches mine.
"Your hands are freezing," I comment.
"No, yours are."

***

"It's demolition day," Casey proclaims excitedly as soon as everyone is awake for the day. I had heard the engines of bulldozers and wrecking balls traveling this way hours ago.
"Can we watch?" Sara asks, while reaching a chubby hand up towards her father.
"From a good distance away; I wouldn't want you to get hurt, sugarplum," he says as he lifts our child and kisses her on her cherub cheeks. She squeals with delight. Lucas hasn't looked up from his computer, though I think I hear him complain about the lack of internet for the millionth time.
"I'll pack some snacks, and we can sit under Grandpa's apple tree. Let's get dressed," I tell Sara, who excitedly rushes off to throw on some clothes. Casey flashes me a smile. Once that smile had swept me off my feet, now the fine lines and creases around it remind me of the troubled roads we've had to endure to get here. I sigh and smile back

as he rushes off to work. The orchard to come has no idea of the heavy burden it bears, save a family, a marriage, and be the answer to our prayers.

I grab Sara's brush and call her over. She has thrown on a mismatched shirt and skirt, but I decide not to fight her this morning. I brush her silky locks while she hums and plays with her favorite doll.

"Mommy, can you braid my hair?" she asks, her expression serious.

I can only think of a few times I have braided her hair before, but she has never once asked for it.

"Sure, how come?"

"So I can look like her," Sara says, while looking down at her doll. The stuffed dolls' yellow yarn hair swings loosely, or at least it did. Now black marker sloppily colors the yarn hair. Pieces of yarn split down the back into braids that hang where its ears might be if it had any. There is no way my four-year-old, who can't tie her shoes or hold a fork right, did this so perfectly. Sara strokes the doll's head. I point at the doll's braids with one hand and parting my daughter's hair with the other. "I think you did a great job."

"No, she!" Sara huffs, placing the doll on its butt. The soft fabric should have crumpled the doll, yet it sits erect, staring with black, unblinking button eyes. Times have been tough for us all. We're so isolated, I think maybe she has developed an imaginary friend. "Past, present, future," Sara sings each word while tracing each braid. My finger tangles in her hair, a knot formed within her braid.

"Who taught you that, sweetie?" I don't want her to think she's in trouble, but my cheery tone wavers.

Her eyes blink up at me, a darkness like a storm over the ocean passes in her eyes.

"She did."

"Who is she, baby?" Unease grasps my mind like a vise.

Sara tilts her head, then brings a finger up to her lips.

"Shhh."

***

I lay out a picnic blanket and basket, far enough away from the church and machines to be safe, but close enough to feel like part of the action. Casey waves at us. The excitement radiates off him. I wish I could feel the same. Instead, a sense of dread has buried itself deep in the pit of my stomach and is quickly sprouting. Lucas plays with an old radio I salvaged from a garage of vintage junk. Mostly oldies and static blare over the speakers. His fingers pause on the dial when the sound of rhythmic drums comes in crisp and clear. It's not like any song I've ever heard, but something about it is powerful. Voices call out; it sounds like children all singing then crying at once. A melodic cry calls out, then it's cut short with a static white noise of

Shhh.

"This is dumb," Lucas complains, flipping the radio off.

"Look mommy, a flower!" Sara exclaims, twirling a dandelion in her fingers. I feign interest in it as I hear the countdown begin. At "one," the wrecking ball releases and crashes into the church. Sara squeals, and even Lucas pulls down his hood for a clear view.

"Wow!" Sara proclaims in delight, as cement crumbles to the ground. The ball crashes repeatedly, slowly chipping away at the once looming building. There's a part of me that feels bad for it. I know it's silly. It's just an old church no longer visited or kept up. Yet it's like an elderly neighbor, withered with age, each crack a story that we will never hear, each crevice a secret forever kept, and here we are eating grapes and delighting in its death.

After a while, the fascination of destruction wanes and both my children wander off into the surrounding acres. I trust Lucas to not get lost and opt to follow Sara. With wonder, I watch as she finds fascinating rocks and interesting sticks. I search my memories, hoping to remember a time when I experienced pleasure from something as simple as a rock or stick, but I find nothing.

A gust of wind tickles my neck, and I turn to look back at the construction site. The bulldozer pushes away large debris as Casey watches proudly. He finds happiness so effortlessly, while I struggle to remember what it looks like.

I hear the men yell, and the machines stop for a moment. I glance over to make sure Sara is still playing with her rocks and then turn my gaze back to the men. My husband's crew huddle around something, gesturing and pointing. Casey joins them and bends over to see what they've found. I see him brush away some dirt, and then freeze, a whole-body stiffness that makes my blood run cold. Ten years married to this man, five years dating before that, and not once have I ever seen him truly afraid. But now, even from my distance, I can almost feel the fear permeating off him. There is something in the soil, silver, or maybe white. I strain to see then the wind blows hard against my backs. It's a warning, a whisper,

Shhh.

***

Once night falls, Casey is quick to go to bed, but by the way he tosses and turns, I can tell it's not a peaceful rest. I can't sleep either, so I get up and make my way to the phone on the wall in the kitchen. A few flies buzz annoyingly in my face. I need to talk to someone, anyone at all, that isn't here in this house. I pick up the phone and dial a number I know by heart, my best friend since high school, Ann.

"Hello?" she answers, her voice teetering between polite and annoyed. I realize she doesn't recognize this number.

"It's Sam." I reply.

"Oh my gosh, how are you? How's the new house? I miss you!" Her words run together as she talks. The familiar chipper tone in her voice is like a warm blanket wrapping me in its embrace. I fill her in on everything of importance until I get to what happened today.

"Something happened at the church today while they were clearing the rubble. Casey said they hit a water main they didn't know was there, but I don't know. The way he reacted was weird," I whisper, glancing towards the bedroom to make sure no one is stirring.

"Well, I'm sure it's stressful; he's putting everything into that orchard and I'm sure one little hiccup might not seem like a big deal but when you're there, seeing something threatening your dreams…" She trails off as a bit of static crinkles in the line and I nod. It's just what I needed to hear. I'm sure I'm overreacting."

"You're right," I agree.

'He lied,' The words come garbled, sounding faraway.

"What?" I ask, not sure I heard her right.

"I said I miss you. Sunday brunch isn't the same without you."

I laugh and let the tension slide from my shoulders. It was just static. She tells me about her last three days, but static interferes. "And you'll never believe… then we saw them!"

"Ann, you're breaking up. I think our connection is bad." I reply with a frown.

"He lied." This time her words are clear as day. "Ask him, tell him to do the right thing!" She sounds angry, and my brow crumples. My heart squeezes in my chest. Ann is having a full-on conversation without me. Static blares, then clear as a bell, she says, "Go there, see for yourself."

I immediately know she means the church. She couldn't mean the church, yet I know it's true. My hands feel clammy against the receiver of the phone.

"What will I find when I get there?" I ask. The static commands

Shhh

The dial tone squeals in monotone as the line goes dead.

***

Nightmares stalk me. Someone is starving me, someone is screaming at me, someone is burying me alive. I toss and turn. A boy's scream rips through the silence of the house.

"Lucas?!" I jump out of bed and sprint toward his room. I push open his door and see him sitting up in bed. His green eyes are filled with tears. In his hands lays a chunk of curls from his golden blond hair. His lip trembles and I don't know what to do or say. It's been so long since I've seen any emotion except indifference plastered on his teenage face, but now, at this moment, he isn't a moody teen. He's my baby boy who used to throw his arms around me and unabashedly proclaim he loved me.

"Oh, sweetie." I rush over and pull his head into my chest.

"What's going on?" Casey tentatively asks. I gently grasp up the hair from Lucas' hands and hold it up.

"Sara, you have some explaining to do," I growl at my little girl peeking her head in the room. She rushes off toward the kitchen, with Casey stalking behind her.

"It wasn't me!" Sara cries. I stroke what's left of Lucas's long curls for a moment more before he pulls away. Lucas picks up a book and murmurs about being left alone. With grief laden steps, I go to place the lock of curls on the kitchen counter.

"The hair didn't cut itself," Casey states, his mouth twisting in a scowl, and a few fresh tears fall from Sara's face.

"It was her. She wants to rest. You aren't letting her rest!" Sara wails and puts her head in her hands.

"What's she talking about?" Casey asks.

"She's got some new imaginary friend, I think." I shrug. Casey's eyes shift to the window, eying the rising sun.

"I have to get ready for work, but we're not done with this conversation, young lady," Casey says before leaving.

My fingers caress Lucas's severed curls. The edges are blunt but slightly frayed, as if cut by rusty scissors. I open every drawer, search the closet, and rifle through moving boxes, looking for the culprit. Twenty minutes later, I came up empty. I go back to the kitchen, where Sara is still pouting.

"Where are the scissors?" I ask.

"I don't have any," she whines.

"Yes, you do. Where are they?"

"I didn't do it! She did. She's mad. Her and her brothers and sisters are all mad!"

"Go to your room," I sigh, and she stomps off.

Sara's door slams and I melt into a dining room chair. My gaze goes up to the hill where I notice no machines or people are working. A notification dings on my phone and I check it. The bank is alerting me about a large withdrawal. I panic and hurriedly open my bank app. Sure enough, the pile of savings for this new life is almost down to nothing. The alert tells me of a withdrawal of ten thousand dollars. It might be his inheritance, but it still stings that he didn't even ask or tell me. I grasp my phone so tight my fingers turn white.

"What the hell is going on?"

***

I wait around all day to confront my husband, but by the time night falls and I've sent the kids to bed, my anger has slipped into apathy.

"Damnit!" Casey releases a few obscenities not so under his breath when he walks through the door. I peek at the entryway and see several dirt caked footprints leading into the house. "These are new work boots," he complains, shrugging them off. I grab a broom and pan, then head back to the mess. Among the dirt lay shreds of apple peels, crimson and bright. The treads of his boots are caked in the substance, like dried blood. I sweep up the earth and rind with a *Shhh Shhh Shhh*.

I join Casey as he sits at the table to drink a nightcap.

"What's going on at the church? No one was out there working," I ask.

"I told you; there was a water main issue. I had to make some calls today. It's going to cost a little more to get everything back on track." Part of what he's saying sounds like the truth, but the way his eyes dart away hints that he is hiding something from me.

"Ten thousand is more than a little," I snap. He smacks the table and I startle. Under his hand is the smear of a fly. He wipes the remnants on a napkin with disgust. His eyes squint at me as if he is biting back his reply.

"I'm going to bed" is the good night I get. I bury my objections and arguments next to the dreams I once held.

Persistent pests buzz around my head and land on the floor and kitchen table. For every one I kill, two more seem to take its place. I've wiped the kitchen and thrown out old food, but the insects remain, seeming to be drawn to something unseen. My eyes go out the window to the remains of the old church. A fly sits on the window, covering the image of the rubble. With a paper towel roll, I smack the fly on the window and a smudge of insect guts and blood smears over the image of the church remains.

Dark dreams of a heavy and foreboding cross with viscera smearing down it play on repeat every time I close my eyes until they snap open. I turn over and notice Casey's spot lies empty. I tentatively get up and make my way through the house. The creaking of wood under my feet reverberates through the quiet. I stop in front of the kitchen; the eerie sensation that someone is there clenches in my gut. I glance over, but the kitchen sits empty except for a lone fly buzzing at the window. The insect's fat body smacks into the window, startling me with a thwack. It lies stunned, then repeats the action. Curiously, I find myself drawn to it. Thwack. The fly doesn't get back up this time, and my gaze drifts out the window where I see the back of a familiar figure under the apple tree. Fear slithers up my spine as I rush to the door. Immediately, frosty night air claws and bites at me like a starved animal.

"Casey!" I call out, but he doesn't respond. His gaze fixates on the remains of the church. Rotten apples squish in between my toes as I scramble over them. So much decomposing fruit has piled up overnight. "Casey?" His name trembles over my lips. Buzzing of a thousand flies is all that replies. My throat constricts as his face comes into view.

Flies clamber at his eyes, which remain fixed in an unblinking stare. Bile retches up my throat as one winged bug crawls out of his mouth, which hangs open in a frozen scream. A single tear slides down his cheek. I shake his shoulder, and his body finally breaks free of its trance.

***

As soon as the sun is up, Casey offers to take Lucas to a local salon. Seems like a convenient excuse to leave this place, if only for an hour. I could unpack or explore but only one thing is on my mind. The church calls to me like a siren song and I can't help but go towards it.

"Sara and I will go rock hunting and maybe find some to paint," the lie eases off my tongue as Casey and Lucas are about to head out the door.

"Make sure to stay away from the work site," Casey warns, adding a slightly concerned "it's dangerous."

I ruffle Lucas' hair as he walks out the door, calling after him, "I love you!"

I wait a good ten minutes before I take Sara out. We make a beeline for the construction site, though I distract her with a pile of nice pebbles just outside the ring of debris. My heart pounds in my chest. I'm not sure what I'll find, but a feeling in my very core is telling me something is here, and it's important.

I balance carefully, climbing down to the spot I had seen Casey digging in yesterday. A bulldozer stands still, frozen in time. Crushed concrete and bits of wood lay scattered on the ground. I grab a nearby shovel and push aside the debris right under the bulldozer. An old, rusted pipe is underneath. A water main, just like Casey said. I chuckle at myself. I don't know what I thought I'd find. Clouds float over the sun and the sky dims for a moment.

"You found her!" Sara squeals with delight. I gasp, looking over at my daughter pointing to the pipe.

"You shouldn't be here!" I reprimand Sara, but her smile doesn't falter.

"I knew you would. I wasn't lying. You found her, you found them all."

"What?" I ask, utterly confused. I glance down at the water pipe, then back at my daughter. Her finger points just below the pipe, so I step closer and scrape a shovel across the earth.

Shhh.

The familiar noise tenses my entire body. The hairs on the back of my neck stand on edge.

Shhh.

I dig again, my teeth grinding together and my heart pounding in my ears. Then I see it. It looks a bit like a rock at first. Pale and round.

It's not a rock — I feel it in the ice in my veins. I drop to my knees and move the dirt from around it. Dirt pours from eye sockets, then a nose cavity. Tiny teeth and a broken jaw reveal themselves. It's a skull. I pull it from the ground, and it fits in the palm of my hand.

"Isn't she beautiful? They cut her hair, so she cut Lucas's," Sara says from behind me, but I can't tear my eyes away from the tragedy before me.

I realize now the shush noise wasn't just one sound but many I've heard over the last few days. Some were quiet; whispers of forbidden words, muted voices, and muffled screams. Others were louder, the sound of scissors chopping off hair and shovels digging unmarked graves.

I turn around and hold up the skull next to my daughter's head. Sara smiles as if posing for a picture, and I compare the sizes. They are the same. Sobs erupt violently from my throat. Turning back, I place the skull gently down. I dig with my bare hands, throwing loose rubble aside. I dig until my fingertips and knuckles are bleeding and I find another skull, then another and another.

Sara calls out that "Daddy is back" but it barely registers over my sobs. I hold a thick long bone in one hand and a small fragile one in the other. My lungs constrict and heave.

"Sam? Sweetie, I can explain." Casey's voice is behind me, but I don't turn to look at him.

"You knew." I spit out between sobs.

"What can I do? They are already dead. This is our dream," he tries to explain. I spin around, glaring at him through tears.

"Did you know they are children? Just babies! What kind of church was this?"

"It was a residential school," Casey replies, his eyes not meeting mine.

"A school?" My mind reels. What kind of school would do this to children?

"For the Indians." He spits the last word like it tastes vile on his tongue.

"The extra money is so the men don't say anything. We bury them deeper, plant the trees over. No one has to know."

Who is this man? He is certainly not the man I fell in love with. That man has been gone for a while now.

"I know." I wipe my tears on my long sleeves. Lucas is walking toward me, taking in the scene before him. "Our children know."

"Don't you be like that, Sam. Not now. Everything we have, everything we've worked for, is in this orchard. No one is going to want to eat apples they know grew on graves!" He's sweating now, and the creases on his face seem to deepen before my eyes.

"They want to go home." Sara's small voice pulls both our attention. I nod in agreement.

"Damnit!" Casey curses and screams nonsense. The sky darkens as storm clouds brew above us. Casey balls his hands into fists so tight I think his palms might be bleeding. "You can't do this! This is my chance to finally get ahead. This is our chance." He corrects himself at the end, but he's shown his hand. It's always been about him and his need to prove his worth. A crack of thunder makes me jump, the lightning illuminating the sky and my mind. A few raindrops fall onto my face.

"It's time they went home," I say as I carefully put the bones back and rise to my feet.

Sara slides down the rubble to me. Casey holds out his hands to her.

"Come on sweetie pie, no one has to know. We can just pretend. Right?" Casey begs, then pulls at his hair. He's unraveling before my eyes and there is nothing I can do to save him. I don't think I want to save him. On shaky legs I step up, sending bones and rubble slipping below me. I hold out my hand and Sara takes it. Casey grabs her other hand.

"Please? Be a good little girl for daddy? Please? Sara?" Sara blinks up at us both, for a moment unsure what to do, then Lucas is by my side, and we both reach out for her. Rain releases from the clouds in sheets as Sara's small fingers slide from Casey's grasp.

"No! Stay! Help me! No one can know. Sam!" Casey frantically tries to hide the bones, but the mud and rain work together to unearth them. I hold my children tight as we hike upwards.

The rain runs in rivers, exposing more skulls, rib cages, and hands. They glisten white now, washed free from their dirt graves. I glance behind me and notice the area where we are standing is a pit. Water rushes by us. It sends debris slipping and sliding, washing their way around us and filling the hole like a shallow grave...

Shhh.

Casey kicks at the dirt and curses the hallowed ground, not realizing his worsening situation. Bones outnumber debris and Casey is up to his knees now. Lucas' lips tremble and I grab his arm tighter. He blinks in understanding and together we look away. We step up and out of the earthy maw, bones jutting out like teeth chewing at my hysterical husband. I grasp Sara against my chest and grip Lucas' hand as if our lives depend on it.

"Sara!" he pleads,(formatting issue here)

"Lucas!" he wails.

"Samantha!" He lets my full name drag out, a last desperate lifeline. He hasn't said that name since our wedding vows. For a moment, I pause, the sentimental memories nudging me to go back. But the man I married is dead, buried along with this secret he tried to hide. Gripping my children, I walk, then run as fast and far as we can. Casey's visceral scream rips into the air. No one looks back.

One last prayer, apology, and promise tears up from my soul and breathes past my lips. It sounds like...

"Shhh."

Slaughter Patch

Spencer W Church

Jenkins' Pick-a-Pumpkin Patch was the biggest in the tri-state area. While primarily known for the expansive patch, its 2000 acres also offer long hayrides, corn mazes, and numerous other family-friendly activities. Event-wise, the farm has always done well throughout the year, but its best business has historically been during the Autumn months. This is why the locals have found it peculiar and inconvenient that the farm shuts down every year during the week of Halloween. But to their dismay, that's how it's always been.

Isabella could vividly recall when she, a hot-headed six-year-old at the time, threw a temper tantrum in front of the main gate because she wanted to go into the pumpkin patch so badly. The irony was not lost on her that now, ten years later, she would do just about anything to stop from entering the farm. Though she still loved visiting the old pumpkin patch during the day—she'd made a lot of good memories there over the years, after all—this time would be different.

"Oh, come on. It won't be that bad," Sophia said.

"As if," Isabella snapped back. "You get to cuddle up with your boyfriend all night while I deal with those grody twins."

"Whatever."

As the two girls passed the town welcome sign, they continued walking down the lonesome road toward the farm. Its hazy image grew clearer beneath the falling sun as they neared the entrance. With the twilight hour at hand, their breath bloomed crisp and white.

Isabella hugged herself with her hands tucked inside her long flannel sleeves. "If I knew your sister was going to bail on us, I would've worn a coat," she said. "And my feet are killing me. I feel like we've walked 50 miles already."

"Yeah, I know it's my job to dress you. Not!" Sophia glanced down at Isabella's flat-bottomed shoes and smirked. "Anyway, it's only been ten minutes, and the farm is right there." She pointed ahead. "Please, just try to have a good time. For me."

"Fine."

Fear of becoming an outcast can make someone do things they may not be comfortable with, like sneaking into a closed farm on Halloween night. Recently, Isabella found herself in many such situations. Certainly, more frequently than she would prefer.

Tagging along with her best friend, Sophia, she'd been interacting with a different friend group as of late; a group Isabella was not 100% sure she wanted to be a part of. Tonight was no exception.

This new friend group included some of the wildest boys from school. Unfortunately, Sophia was dating one of those wild boys. Not wanting to be a killjoy, Isabella reluctantly agreed to join Sophia and her new ragtag crew for a midnight pumpkin patch party. If for no other reason than to minimize any mischief that might arise.

"Oh my God!" Sophia suddenly blurted. "Something smells totally rank."

Isabella scrunched up her nose. "Eww." She looked around. The dwindling sunlight did little to illuminate the darkening dirt road. "What is that?"

"Smells like roadkill."

"I don't see anything."

As they neared the farm's entrance, the pungently sweet scent of decay overpowered them.

"I'm gonna hurl." Sophia cupped her hand over her mouth and nose.

Isabella gagged and held her breath.

"Thank God," Sophia said through her fingers. "There they are."

At the farm's unlit entrance, Ben stood next to Bryce and Mike—the Beaver twins—at the gate waiting for their arrival.

"Benny," Sophia squealed as she ran over and planted a kiss on him so hard their teeth practically cracked. "Is this everyone?"

"We're still waiting on Andrew." Ben smiled. "He has the better pot."

****

Standing outside of Jenkins' farm with her new friend group, nervous cramps set in Isabella's lower intestine, ruling out any chance of relaxing during the chilly fall night.

"That walk sucked so hard," Sophia said to the three guys. "My stupid sister was supposed to give us a ride, but she totally bailed on us."

Ben pulled her in for another warm embrace. "I'm sorry. I would've met you at your house and walked with you two, but I had to get Dingus and Mingus here." He pointed his thumb back to the odd-looking twins standing behind him. "Their mom wouldn't let them walk alone."

Isabella looked at the twins and immediately wished she hadn't. Their off-putting gaze seemed wrong.

"Ben, has anyone ever told you that you're too nice?" Sophia joked, punctuating her faux compliment with a kiss on his cheek.

"You're the first one today," he said, winking.

With a brisk Autumn wind mussing Isabella's hair and the dark farm looming in the background, she regretted her earlier suggestion of visiting the pumpkin patch when it reopened. Though she meant they should visit during the day, she wasn't surprised when things got misconstrued and the rowdy boys decided to go at night. These supposed misunderstandings happened often when she decided on an activity for the group.

There was a time when Sophia would put up a fight for her friend's sake before succumbing to peer pressure. It didn't help that the misfits' ringleader was the guy she had puppy dog eyes for. When it came to Ben, it never took much to convince Sophia to go along with whatever dim-witted scheme he cooked up.

Isabella couldn't understand why her friend was so enamored with him. He wasn't traditionally good-looking; it appeared as if the sides of his head had been slightly pinched together; his patchy beard grew more on his neck than on his pasty cheeks; and his long, greasy hair hid half of his features. Isabella desperately hoped Ben would grow out the rest of his hair and completely cover that fug-mug he called a face. Though maybe that was a bit too harsh. After all, he'd always been nice to her. She just wished Sophia would stop talking about him all the damn time.

For some reason, everyone in the friend group looked up to Ben, treating him as their leader. They would follow him anywhere: skipping class, staying out past their parents' curfew, or sneaking out after pretending to go to bed. Everyone liked him, which was exactly why Isabella was so leery of him.

They all waited another ten minutes, annoyed that they had to listen to Sophia and Ben's lips smacking. Right as their makeout session looked like it might move beyond PG-13, Andrew showed up. Out of the entire group, he was the only one Isabella could halfway stand being around.

"Took you long enough, fuckhead," Ben said, in between rounds of lip wrestling.

Andrew chuckled smugly as he hit the stop button on his Walkman and removed the headphones. "It looks like you've kept yourself busy."

"I try."

"Damn, did somebody shit their pants?" Andrew said accusingly out of the blue, looking straight at the twins.

"Right!" Sophia answered. "We smelled that on the way here. Must be a dead deer or something."

"Gnarly."

Ben nodded his head. "Come on, let's get the hell out of here."

With everyone now together, they passed the gate and walked along the fence surrounding the farm.

After searching for a few minutes, Ben whispered to the others, "Found it."

Having spotted a secret opening in the fence, he didn't hesitate to crawl through; Sophia followed close behind. The twins were next to enter, and then Andrew, leaving Isabella alone. With one final look around, she reluctantly entered, too.

As the distant darkness enveloped the group, fat, green-bellied flies swarmed out of a hole bored into the swollen carcass of a dead coyote near the fence line. The high grass concealed its rotting remains, but the odor drifted long and far.

****

The group continued walking until Ben found a spot he liked. A nice little clearing next to one of the many cornfields. Having settled in, one of the Beaver twins reached into the other's backpack, retrieving a fifth of Jim Beam they had stolen from their parents' liquor cabinet. They snickered in unison as they broke the seal.

There was something off about the twins, like they always knew what the other one was thinking. They rarely spoke with the others and always seemed to be in the middle of a private conversation. A conversation that didn't need words. With their petite frames and quiet demeanor, they were mostly harmless. Still, Isabella felt uneasy around them. It probably had something to do with their odd expressions and that constant look of vacant wonderment in their eyes, as if they were always staring into your soul.

As the Jim Beam started to make the rounds, Ben asked Sophia to reach into his back pocket. With a shy smile, she did as he asked. Her smile widened as she unrolled a plastic baggie half full of pot.

Once open, a skunky scent wafted from the bag and permeated throughout their little spot. Isabella watched Ben pinch some green, sprinkle it liberally onto a flattened paper, and try to roll a proper joint. While she watched, she felt a tap on her shoulder and glanced over to Andrew, who had the bottle of Jim Beam in his hand.

"Looks like you could use a shot."

"I think I'll pass, thanks," Isabella said curtly.

"Everyone's having a good time." Andrew took a swig from the bottle. As he attempted to stifle a grimace, he offered the bourbon. "Why come if you don't want to have a good time too?" he asked with a sly grin.

"Someone needs to make sure you guys don't do anything too stupid."

"But stupid's where the fun's at." With a shit-eating grin, Andrew held the bottle out again. "Come on."

Rolling her eyes, Isabella grabbed the bottle, half-expecting to find something floating inside. After a moment of hesitation, she put it to her lips and threw back a quick gulp. The burning alcohol coursed down her throat, ending with a sharp gasp escaping her mouth. Fighting an embarrassed smile, Isabella handed back the Jim Beam.

With a prideful smirk, Andrew plucked the bottle from her delicate hand. "See, that wasn't too bad, was it?" He pursed his lips and took another drink. "Woo! That's strong stuff. Want some more?" He offered the bottle neck toward her.

Before Isabella could respond, a fit of obscene coughing snatched her attention. Ben's shoddily rolled joint was lit; smoke drifted from the cherry into the night sky. Suppressing another bout of coughs, Ben passed the joint to Sophia. Its glow illuminated her face as she took a hit. Inhaling, the smoke filled her lungs, cutting off airflow and causing her to cough violently. Struggling to control herself, she passed the joint back to Ben.

"Who's next?" Ben asked.

"Here, I'll trade you." Andrew walked over with the whiskey bottle.

By herself, Isabella noticed the twins leering at her as they stood shoulder to shoulder. Sharing the same blank expression, their eyes followed her as she walked over to the hay bales where Ben, Sophia, and Andrew were. The twins' heads moved owl-like to keep Isabella in their line of sight as she passed by. Doing her best to ignore the identical dimwits, she turned her back to them and tried to focus on the conversation at hand.

"Damn, Ben," Andrew took another drag before passing the joint, "where did you get this shit? It's better than what I brought."

"What can I say? I know a guy." Ben inhaled deeply, gathering as much smoke as possible. After holding it for as long as he could, Ben blew the smoke into Sophia's face. The cloud engulfed her from the shoulders up. When the smoky haze dissipated, it revealed a grin that the Grinch would've been envious of.

"Yeah, but your shit normally isn't this good," Andrew laughed.

"I wanted to make sure we have a good time tonight, and that means getting the good shit."

Isabella waved off the joint when it came her way. She didn't mind a shot every once in a while, but she knew if she mixed pot with alcohol, she would spend the night throwing up in one of the pumpkin patches. However, Andrew exhaled in her direction every time he took a hit. Before she realized it, Isabella's contact high was in full effect.

Even in her increasingly inebriated state, she still felt like the twins were staring at her. Taking a peek over her shoulder, she was startled to see the two looking directly at her. They alternated when they would blink, so she'd never leave their collective sight. A chill ran up her spine so cold that she asked for another nip from the bottle to help warm herself. It did little good.

"Hey, Ben, think you can tell your set of weirdos to quit staring at me? They're giving me the creeps."

Stubbing out what was left of the joint, Ben got off the short-square hay bale he was sitting on. "Hey, how about you two find some pumpkins for us to smash?"

The twins shared a glance, and then without saying a word, they turned and ran off into the dark.

"Happy?" Ben asked, as he sat back on the bale.

"Very. Thanks."

What was left of the Jim Beam worked around the remaining four while Ben began rolling another joint. As they enjoyed the festivities, the twins ventured out in search of pumpkins. It wasn't long before they found one of the smaller patches where toddler-aged kids picked their pumpkins for carving.

Bryce picked up the first pumpkin he saw. Lifting it over his head, he slammed it down, exploding it on the ground. What followed was a melee of carnage as the brothers unleashed themselves on the small patch.

Channeling his inner Godzilla, Mike stomped and kicked his way through the patch. On the other end, Bryce found a large stick and used it to lay waste to the remaining patch.

Mike's shoes squished as he walked. Covered in pumpkin guts, wet footprints follow in his wake.

"I got seeds in my shoes." Mike lifted and shook his foot. "Mom's going to kill me."

"That's what you get for being stupid. You should've used a weapon, like me," Bryce gloated, holding up his stick; the tip darkened from the pumpkin slurry.

"Well, it looks like you missed one." Mike pointed to a nearby fence.

A jack-o'-lantern sat on top of one of the posts. The pumpkin had a jagged scowl and sad eyes carved into it. For some unknown reason, the bizarre jack-o-lantern amused Bryce. A grin stretched from ear to ear as he walked toward his next victim.

Picking up the helpless fruit, Bryce walked back to Mike and laid the jack-o-lantern in the pulpy massacre of its brethren.

Bryce raised his stick above his head but hesitated. "On second thought." He lowered the weapon and handed it to his brother.

"Really," Mike said, wide-eyed. "I get to do it?"

"Yeah, sure. Why not? Now get on with it."

Tightening his grip, Mike prepared to swing. Arching the stick above his head, he brought it down with all his might. The strike was off-center and grazed the jack-o-lantern, caving in its left side. Unimpressed with the damage from his brother's swing, Bryce decided to take matters into his own hands.

"Hey, bro, you might want to look away," Bryce said, unzipping his fly.

Unceremoniously, he freed himself, and his urine steamed in the cold fall night, drenching the pumpkin in warm liquid. When he finished, he zipped up and laughed manically as he chased after his brother with piss-moistened hands. The two ran back into the darkness toward the party.

****

Isabella's focus kept shifting to Andrew. She knew the alcohol played heavily in this, but she couldn't help herself; her eyes were drawn to him. When he caught her looking, her cheeks flushed red. She wondered if he would believe her if she said it was just from the alcohol.

The returning twins interrupted Isabella's thoughts. Their obnoxious laughter rang out as they entered the makeshift site. A headache started to form behind her eyes as their incessant chortling jackhammered its way into her ears. It finally died down to a low rumbling of giggles as the twins approached the group.

"I thought I told you guys to find some pumpkins," Ben said.

The twins looked at each other briefly and then burst into another round of annoying laughter. Fortunately, their high-pitched squeals were short-lived.

Wiping tears away, Bryce answered, "We found a whole bunch." He held his hands out to his sides to accentuate the point.

"Okay, where are they then?" Ben asked.

"We busted them all up!" Bryce yelled.

When the others didn't share in their excitement, the twins grew quiet and kept their eyes on the ground. An awkward silence fell over the group.

Bryce looked up from his shoes. "There's more," he said meekly. "We can get them and bring them back."

"We won't bust them this time," Mike added.

"It's alright, don't worry about it," Ben said dismissively. "Maybe we'll do it later." He handed what was left of the pot to Sophia. "For now, just relax."

Everyone sat in a circle as Sophia took a turn rolling a joint. It came out okay but wasn't as big as the one Ben had rolled. Still, it wasn't bad for her first time.

Ben looked it over. After a brief examination, he deemed it smokable with an approving nod. Everyone agreed that it was a fine joint—except Isabella, who looked like she would rather be anywhere else.

All the Jim Beam was gone. Isabella's headache worsened, and her churning stomach threatened to empty. "I hate to be a party pooper, but can we call it soon? I'm not feeling so hot."

Disapproving murmurs spread throughout the group, a sound Isabella was all too familiar with as the self-designated wet blanket. Normally, the disapproval would eat away at her, kicking her anxiety into overdrive. But now her body was too busy fighting to purge the alcohol in her system to care about anyone else's opinion.

"How about this? After we're done smoking, we get out of here?" Ben offered.

This time, an approving murmur ran through the friend circle. With that taken care of, Sophia lit her joint.

****

Pumpkin juice sluiced over the grass blades, coalescing with the piss-soaked dirt, allowing something sinister to take root in the rich, fertile soil. With a subterranean quake, moving mounds wormed tunnel-like to the surface. The ground groaned in agony beneath the ruined patch.

****

The joint made three rotations before someone stubbed it out. Wisps of smoke swirled skyward, and the smell of burnt pot permeated the area. Desperate for one final hit, Andrew relit the remaining roach, but the hot cherry burned the tip of his fingers. "Shit," he snapped, tossing the roach into the dark cornfield.

Only the twins saw the ember sail into the night and stop mid-air. Tilting their heads, Bryce and Mike stared awestruck at the floating flare.

"What's that?" they asked simultaneously, pointing at the glowing flicker.

Isabella, tired of the twin's nonsense, prepared to yell at the moronic twosome when she saw the light.

The small flame expanded ever so slightly. Bobbing left to right, it inched forward and separated into three distinct orbs. Each one grew brighter as it neared the end of the cornfield. The fireballs assembled into a busted smile with crooked eyes; the twins exchanged a look of disbelief.

Frozen with fear, the group watched the uncanny entity for what felt like an eternity. Transfixed by its unearthly face, no one dared to move.

Sweat trickled down Isabella's back despite the chilly air. Without warning, a sound like a snapping bullwhip cracked the eerie silence that had set in.

A vine shot out of the darkness with the speed of a streaking spear, cutting through the air before anyone could react. The vine punctured Bryce's abdomen and exploded through his back. His body dropped and hung limp as his brother clawed in a futile attempt to free him.

An immense bulk emerged from the black cornfield and lifted Bryce's corpse into the air. Mike clung desperately to his brother before his grip failed; he severely fractured his ankle upon landing. The injury left him immobile and crying out for help, but the others ran away screaming.

Atop a heap of thick-corded intertwining vines that formed the body, sat a deformed jack-o-lantern with its left side caved in. The jack-o-lantern looked like worn-out, sun-bleached leather. Beneath its grotesque head, other pumpkin chunks covered part of its chest, stomach, shoulders, and back to construct a type of armor.

The creature grew in size as it approached Mike, dangling his brother's corpse above him. The jack-o-lantern whipped the end of its vine down, shattering many of his bones like matchsticks.

Lying in a pool of blood, he could only watch as the vine rose high above him. His brother's mutilated body danced marionette-like overhead, before the next strike came and turned Mike's world dark.

The pumpkin-headed behemoth dumped Bryce's flaccid body on top of Mike and lashed both repeatedly until the brothers merged into a single mass of dismembered bits. Stomping on what was left of the Beaver twins, their spongy entrails squashed under the creature's rugged foot as it hunted for its next victim.

Andrew had the bad luck of being next in the creature's path. He avoided the first few stabs of capture, but eventually, one of the creature's vines harpooned through the meat of his left calf. He screamed out in anguish as he fought to unsnare himself. No matter how hard he tried, he couldn't remove the vine from his muscle tissue. As a last-ditch effort, he reached into his pocket and pulled out his lighter.

Struggling to get it to work, the vine began dragging him across the abrasive ground. Andrew thought his time was up, but then Ben snuck behind the creature and struck it with a two-by-four he had found leaning against one of the fences. The plank broke across its back.

The attack provided Andrew enough time for one more chance with the lighter. He placed his thumb on the wheel for a final turn. To his relief, it sparked to life. Before the flame could go out, he plunged the lighter into the vine's husk.

The creature unleashed a horrid shriek and released Andrew from its grasp. Gingerly getting to his feet, he had just enough time to wonder how something with hardly a head could make such a shrill noise.

The creature flailed about, trying to extinguish the flame that had worked its way up its vine-arm. Andrew saw that Ben had rejoined the girls, hiding behind a hay bale, but the creature thrashed so violently that Andrew didn't think he could get around it unscathed, with his injured leg hindering him.

"Guys, get the fuck out of here," he shouted.

The three nodded remorsefully. Unable to help, they retreated in the direction of the nearby woods.

After watching his friends escape, he staggered away in the opposite direction. The creature still shrieked and thrashed behind him but didn't pursue. Blood trailed Andrew toward the corn maze.

****

Sophia was the first to stop running. Bent over, steam billowed from her mouth with each gasp. Ben jogged back to the tree she was leaning on and grabbed her by the arm, trying to get her moving again. "Come on, babe, we need to keep going," Ben said with labored breaths. "That thing could be anywhere."

"Sorry… I can't … It feels like my lungs … on fire … need a break."

Isabella, who'd run farther ahead, doubled back to where they were. "Hey," she said to the weary couple. "I think I might have an idea where we can go." They looked at her curiously. "Jenkins' house shouldn't be too far from here. Maybe someone there can help us."

It was a long shot, but with no one else coming up with a better idea, they started heading to where they thought Jenkins' house might be. Hoping to remain hidden from the creature, they crept silently through the wooded area adjacent to a cornfield.

Out front and leading the way, fear of being lost set in like the cold had set in Isabella's bones. They'd been walking longer than she thought it should take to get to the house.

Booze sloshed around inside her gut as she walked; it made her hungry and sick all at once. Fighting back the urge to vomit, she focused on the throbbing pain in her feet until the feeling passed.

Glancing back over her shoulder, Isabella noticed Ben and Sophia had fallen behind again, so she stopped. It was her idea to go looking for the house. What if it was her fault they froze to death wandering the farm? Or even worse, she could be leading them to the thing that killed the twins. These worries only scratched the surface of negative thoughts whirling through her mind as she waited for her friends to catch up.

After a few cold moments, Ben and Sophia arrived at the fallen tree Isabella was using as a seat.

"How much farther, you think?" Ben asked, wrapping Sophia in his arms. Even with their combined body heat, they struggled to stay warm.

Standing up, Isabella wanted to put on a brave face for her friends, but she was too cold and tired. "I'm not sure." She avoided making eye contact with them. "I think we might be lost."

Before anyone could speak, a blood-curdling scream shook the still night, and then all went quiet again.

"What the hell was that?" Ben whispered.

A deathly howl answered him from across the farm as it cut through the frigid air like a hot knife.

"Jesus," Sophia cried. "We gotta go."

The three rushed through the scant woods until they reached a clearing. With her head down, Isabella had been hurrying behind the others and nearly crashed into Ben's back when he suddenly stopped.

"Hey, is that it?" he said, pointing ahead of them.

A two-story house stood alone in the clearing. Some distance behind it, a large red barn loomed in the darkness.

With hope finally in sight, Isabella whispered, "Yes."

***

Andrew hobbled along, desperate to find somewhere to hide and regroup. He entered the corn maze, and once inside the labyrinth, he trudged around the corners until his foot caught a root, upending him. Landing face-first in the dirt, he rolled onto his back. Staring up at the stars, he did his best to slow his breathing until the rise and fall of his chest relaxed.

Weary, Andrew stood unsteadily and brushed the dirt off himself. His ringing ears made it difficult to think. A bout of dizziness washed over him, almost putting him on his ass again. He looked around, trying to ascertain which way he had come from, when he saw the red blood streak he'd left behind. As the world around him came back into focus, something rustled deep from within the corn.

At first, it sounded far away. Then it rapidly closed the distance, like a bat shooting out of Hell toward him. A vine cut through the corn, slicing a hole through his shirt. It barely missed slashing his belly open.

With his one good leg, he hopped out of the way. The cornstalks rustled once more as more vines shot out. Ducking, they were like razor blades whizzing past his head.

Not wanting to stick around for the next barrage, Andrew limped on. Hoping the maze's odd angles would make him a more difficult target to hit, he covered as much ground as possible. He protected his head and kept moving as best he could without slowing down.

One after another, vines shredded the corn in pursuit. Snapping stalks were the only warning of their incoming strikes. Each one whistled with every near miss, leaving him with tiny lacerations over his face and neck. Dollops of blood leaked from the numerous papercut-like nicks as he blindly stumbled forward.

As he wondered how long he could evade the lashing vines, one swung in from the right. It sliced through the corn scythe-like, shearing a swath of stalks. He raised his arms right in time to block the blow, but the impact slammed him onto the ground with a sickening thud. Ruined corn silks rained down on top of his broken body.

Sprawled out on his back, Andrew couldn't move his destroyed arms. Splintered bone protruded through the skin like rebar from concrete. A numb sensation set in and spread throughout his body. Unable to lift his head, he was left staring at the moon.

The clouds parted. He couldn't remember the last time he saw such a full moon. Then the creature leaped high into the air, and all he could see was what was left of its hideous face as it descended upon him. While the dirt greedily soaked up his blood, everything began to go dark. In his final miserable moments of life, a terrible scream echoed in his ears. He didn't know whether it was his or the creature's.

****

The little hope that ignited when they found the house was quickly extinguished when no one answered Isabella's repeated rapping on the worn-out front door. Not surprising, considering the inside of the house was as dark as the woods they'd just walked out of. Trying to stay calm, Isabella slowed her breathing; panicking now wouldn't do them any good.

Once composed, she walked down the steps and around the side of the house without saying a word. Exchanging a bewildered look, Sophia and Ben followed after her.

"Hey, where are you going?" Ben asked, as they quickened their pace.

As they made it around the house, the couple saw Isabella enter the barn. Graduating to a full sprint, they reached the open door before they lost Isabella in the barn's deep shadows.

Hardly any light reached inside, plunging them into intense darkness as they stepped through the threshold. Glancing back at the open door, a thin sliver of moonlight cut through the otherwise pit of black.

"What are we doing inside of this shit shack?" Sophia asked, stepping farther inside.

"Hold on a second." Isabella disappeared into the shadows. Sophia and Ben heard rummaging throughout the barn and did their best to follow Isabella in the dark, but it wasn't long before they lost her. Staring into the barn's shadowy abyss, their eyes began to adapt to the darkness. Like the dark, hidden shapes became clear as a bright flame sparked to life.

Gasping, Ben stepped in front of Sophia, knowing it wouldn't do much to protect her. After cowering, they realized they weren't being torn to pieces and looked up.

Isabella stood there holding an old lantern by its handle. The flame revealed a fair amount of the barn, including an old red tractor. A medium-sized flatbed used for hauling kids around the hayride was attached to the tractor's rear.

"I think I can drive it if we can get it started," Isabella said, patting the tractor's dust-coated tire.

"Sounds great, but how are we going to do that?" Ben asked, still embarrassed from getting scared by the lantern flame.

"I kind of remember how to drive it from when I was a kid. The hayride was always my favorite, and Mr. Jenkins showed me how it worked once. We just need to find the key."

"Maybe it's hidden somewhere in here," Sophia offered, stepping into the light.

"You two look for the key and anything else we can use." She set the lantern on the ground. "I'll see if I can remember anything about running this thing."

Sophia and Ben explored the barn while Isabella studied the tractor. It had been a few years since her last hayride. It seemed everything was in order. There was gas in the tank, and the tractor looked in working condition. Climbing inside the cab, Isabella flipped down the visor, sending a key falling onto her lap.

With the key in hand, she jumped out of the cab. "Hey guys, I found it," Isabella said, walking to Sophia and Ben. They were huddled in the corner. "What are you doing?"

Ben was flipping through a small, black leather-bound book. The pages were yellowed and worn as if they could fall out at the slightest touch. Without saying a word, Ben handed over the book. The leather was cold to the touch.

"What is it?" Isabella asked. She didn't like how the book felt in her hands.

"It was wrapped in some old rags in a crate," Ben answered.

"Did you read any of it?"

"Just skimmed a couple of pages. It was hard to make most of it out. There are a lot of scribbles and weird drawings."

Using one hand, Isabella opened the journal to a crude portrayal of the creature that killed the twins. Bile rose to the back of her throat at the sight of the drawing. She was about to shut the book when Ben stopped her.

"You'll want to check this out." He flipped a few pages.

Isabella read aloud, "*No matter what I do, the thing comes back. Year after year, the horror never stops. When I was a small child, I heard awful sounds from the woods, and I thought it was coyotes or the sort. It wasn't till Pa's death that I inherited the farm and found out the truth.*"

She skipped the next couple of pages filled with unsettling drawings. "*The first Halloween after Pa died, I witnessed the thing lurking on the property. It was Halloween Eve, and I had just finished setting up for the big fall festival. The first without Pa, and I wanted to make him proud.*

"*Walking from the barn to the house, I heard whimpering. I followed it down the path, ending in a clearing where I found the body, or what was left of it.*

"*Everything from the chest down had been torn off, the arms were stuck, frozen and reaching for help that never came. I was in such shock; I didn't think to look for whatever could have done it.*

"As it turns out, I didn't need to look far. No more than 20 feet away stood a monster that looked to be made of thick, twisted vines.

"I thought I was dead as a doornail. But the thing only looked at me before lumbering off into the woods. I dared not follow.

"Once I got my breath back, I returned home and waited for dawn to cancel the festival."

Closing the book, Isabella looked at her friends. "So, Mr. Jenkins has known about that thing the whole time?"

"It looks like it," Ben answered. "It would explain why he always closes the place during Halloween."

"But why wouldn't he tell anyone?" Sophia asked.

"Who would believe there was a monst—"

Isabella stopped talking and looked at the entrance of the barn. Holding a finger to her lips, she crept to the slightly open door.

The moonlight shone on the creature like a spotlight. It had shrunk to a more normal size, slightly bigger than an average man. It stood there, unmoving, like it was made of stone. Slowly backing away from the door, Isabella motioned for the others to meet her by the tractor.

"What's out there?" Sophia whispered.

With only a look, the others knew what was waiting for them outside. Just as Isabella was about to tell them her plan, a predatory shriek cut her off and rocked the barn. Not knowing if her friends could hear her, Isabella motioned for them to get onto the flatbed.

Climbing into the tractor's cab, Isabella inserted the key into the ignition. Frantically, hoping she remembered how to start the tractor, she followed the steps Mr. Jenkins showed her all those years ago: she depressed the clutch, disengaged the parking brake, and then turned the key and released the clutch slowly. To her relief, the engine sputtered to life. She stomped the accelerator, and the tractor lurched forward.

A dark shape fell over the barn's entrance. Before she could build up speed, they met the creature at the threshold, crashing into it. Isabella thrashed about inside the cab. Using all her weight, she practically stood on the pedal, but the creature had extended its vines into the barn door's framework, creating a standstill. Looking up from the steering wheel, what she saw almost knocked her back into the tractor seat.

Set atop the wretched jumble of vines was Andrew's severed head. His eyes had been removed, leaving dry, hollow pits in their place. Cracking had started at the mouth and ran up his cheeks, forming a wicked smile with darkening skin that had turned a deep orange.

Struggling to break through the obstruction, the tractor squealed against the creature's vinyweb. Sophia jumped off the flatbed and raced to the glass lantern they had left on the floor. In one swift motion, she picked the lantern up by its handle and flung it with all her might. Glass exploded across the thing's back. Fire engulfed the viny mass and spread to the barn door within seconds. The growing flames freed the creature's grip on the building, allowing the tractor the leverage to overtake it. The tires rolled up and over the thing's bulk, and its vines snapped under the pressure.

As the tractor gained momentum, Sophia rushed back to the flatbed. Ben was hanging onto the edge, waiting with an extended hand. The tractor cleared the burning barn door, but the flatbed remained inside.

At the last possible second, Sophia leapt toward Ben. He caught her mid-air and pulled her onto the flatbed; the heat from the flames kissed their skin as they fell into each other's arms.

The tractor and its bed cleared the barn by about 20 feet before stalling. When Isabella tried restarting it, she realized the temperature gauge had spiked into the red. She poked her head out the window, looking back at the flaming structure and then at Ben and Sophia.

"What are you doing?" Ben shouted.

Sophia raised her head from Ben's chest. "Why aren't we moving? We need to get out of here."

"The engine overheated," Isabella hollered. "It needs to cool down before it'll run again."

"Fuck it," Ben readied himself, "let's just run for it."

Before they could move, a scorched vine shot out from the flames and wrapped around Sophia's ankle. She cried out in pain as the hot vine singed her soft skin and ripped her away from Ben. With a skull-splitting ting, her head bounced off the flatbed's metal gate as the thing yanked her toward the barn. Ben dove desperately for Sophia's hand. He managed to take hold of her fingertips, but the creature pulled her from his grasp.

Rapidly, the vine snatched Sophia's lax body back into the blazing fire. Without thinking, Ben charged after her.

"Ben!" Isabella screamed from the cab. "Stop!" Tears flooded her eyes. "There's nothing we can do!"

Ben stopped and looked back a final time. "I have to try."

As if entering through the gates of Hell, he put his head down and braved the inferno. The barn roof groaned as flames licked the rafters. Weakened beams popped and began to give way. Billowing clouds of black smoke and fiery ash swallowed Ben's silhouette as he disappeared inside the collapsing barn.

Several anxious moments passed while shadows danced beyond the barn's fiery veil with no sign of Ben or Sophia. With each passing second, it looked less likely that they would emerge. Though it would kill her to do so, Isabella didn't see any other option but to leave her friends behind.

The tractor's temp gauge dropped to the safe operating range, but before Isabella restarted it, she heard a sudden hiss from the flatbed tires. Looking back, she realized the fire had melted the rubber, and all the tires on one side were deflating. She would have to unhook it or take her chances escaping on foot. The idea of outrunning the creature terrified her, so she hopped out of the cab to unhook the flatbed.

It took some time, but she was able to free the tractor. By now, the barn was fully engulfed, and there was no chance of her friends' survival. Doing her best to hold it together, Isabella climbed back into the tractor cab and started the engine. In the rearview mirror, she saw the barn roof collapse. With the steady rumble beneath her feet, Isabella put the tractor in gear and headed for the distant entrance.

Without the added weight from the flatbed, it took little time to cross the farm. As she neared the closed entrance gate, she kept driving steadily until she crashed into the gate and burst through to the other side. Turning onto the main road, she stopped the tractor and finally looked back.

The dark outlines of the Jenkins' Farm sign lay splayed out along the asphalt. An orange haze settled in the distance as black ash floated down and began to cover the sign. In that moment, Isabella had a crazy thought. She probably just gave the last hayride at Jenkins' Pick-a-Pumpkin Patch.

Without meaning to, Isabella chuckled. And then laughed. And then laughed harder. Before long, she was in full-on hysterics.

Ash continued to fall, mixing with her tears, streaking her cheeks with black lines. The tractor vibrated noisily. The dark road stretched ahead, ending in the soft glow of the town. Still laugh-crying, Isabella put the tractor in gear. Its wheels moved slowly over the smooth concrete.

****

A crow's caw echoed through the early morning. Inside the barn's smoldering remains, the debris shifted. Burnt support beams fell away, revealing Ben's soot-covered face. Slowly, coddled by charred vines, it rose above the dwindling embers. Swaying, the vines spread over the detached head before submerging back into the rubble.

LYLAS

Lisa Battiston

"You were invited," Fran told Sybil, "Because the sisters pick one Senior for a visit to the fourth floor at the end of every school year. For an end-of-year treat." Her inflection was faux-demure, her pinky raised as she held her water bottle to her lips. "It's like an old-fashioned teatime with scones and cakes and little cucumber sandwiches. Very adult."

"*Really.*" Sybil smirked across the lunch table. "It sounds more like an indoctrination." Her mom had given her the message last night – Sister Ruth, the school principal, had called with a request for Sybil to join the sisters after class this Friday. It was an invitation to the fourth floor.

Sybil's eyes met Fran's, both of them pursing their lips and raising their eyebrows before a silence emerged between them – again.

Fran cast her eyes down at the table as she poked a fork at the twice-baked potato on her lunch tray. She shook her head, cleared her throat, said, "Anyway, they know they're dying off, so I bet they're trying to get you to join them. Like a cult or something."

Sybil smiled and nodded. "Exactly. Like Manson family nuns." She brought her soda can to her lips.

"Or Mormons."

Sybil nearly spit out her Coke as they both laughed at Fran's joke, the weirdness between them momentarily paused.

"Well, all of the girls who've been invited become big shots after they graduate," Fran told her. "Kennedy Stout's sister was invited a few years ago – she's the one who ran in the Olympics last summer? I heard last year's pick is some breakout New York City chef or whatever. And Zoe's mom was invited up when she went here, and she's a state senator."

Sybil raised an eyebrow and crossed her arms on the lunch table. "So why would they pick me?"

She saw the split-second shift in Fran's demeanor, her cocked head and narrowed eyes as Fran responded coldly. "Honestly? No idea."

Sybil winced.

"Anyway," Fran said, clearing her throat. "You're definitely going, right?"

"I don't know, man. It's a little weird?"

"Oh, it's very weird." Fran smiled. "But that's exactly why you should go. Why you *need* to go. No one gets to go to the fourth floor – you're gonna get an eyeful."

"Maybe," Sybil said. "We'll see."

The bell rang over the PA, signaling the end of lunch period. Together and without a word, they gathered their trays and headed out of the cafeteria toward their neighboring first-floor lockers to gather their afternoon books. Sybil topped her armful with the journal she carried everywhere, filled with half-finished poems and drawings and short stories. She grabbed a ballpoint from her backpack, shoving it through the messy bun on top of her head before shutting her locker door with a bang, realizing… She was alone. Fran was already halfway down the hall, strutting toward class without her. Without having said goodbye. Without having said anything at all.

At the end of the day, she found Fran at the school entrance, the two friends joining the sea of loud girls in gray uniform skirts exiting Saint Mary's Most Holy Eye of Assumption School for Young Women, heading toward their respective secondhand cars parked side by side in the school's lot.

"Coffee?" Fran asked as they walked.

Sybil grinned, tightening the grip on her backpack straps. "For sure," she said. It had been weeks since they'd met up after school at their regular spot.

"Cool." Fran smiled back, plopping into her driver's seat. "See you over there."

***

Sybil and Francine had met after being involuntarily partnered on an assignment in their freshman Music of the World class. Fran had invited Sybil to her house that weekend to work on their joint essay, something about Beethoven's impact on the modern world, saying they could hang out too, it would be fun, that she'd give Sybil a makeover.

"You're already pretty," Fran had said with a smile as she leaned next to Sybil's locker between classes, giving her a once over. "You just, you know. Need a new coat of paint."

Sybil's face flushed and she'd raised an eyebrow. "Right, thanks."

"Come on!" Fran had laughed. "It'll be fun!"

Something clicked between them that Saturday. They fell into an easy rhythm, were somehow already finishing each other's sentences, sharing Fran's mascara, erupting into giggles at the inside jokes they would make reference to for the rest of high school. After they'd officially forgotten Beethoven and settled on Sybil's look – a pair of Fran's baggy hip-huggers and a black babydoll tee, black eyeliner raccooning her lids, Sybil's long auburn hair gathered on top of her head in a strategically messy bun – Fran spent a good part of the afternoon teaching Sybil "The Strut."

The Strut, Fran had explained, was the only way to enter a room. It was confidence. Independence.

And it was boys.

"I don't know any boys," Sybil had said.

"Oh, we'll change that." Fran smirked. "You know you've mastered it when it looks easy," she'd said as she thudded toward the full-length mirror positioned by her bedroom door, performing an exaggerated heel-toe-heel-toe clomp, her face something like an expressive fish. It was an homage to a seasoned runway model's swagger, hands clutching her hips, eyes somewhere between a glaze and a glare, mouth a properly puckered pout.

She stopped in front of her own image, her long brown hair cascading down her back, her blue eyes adorned with drugstore falsies, lips shiny with gloss. She crossed her arms decisively and regarded herself, nodding with approval as she did an about-face, strutting back toward Sybil, twirling a lock of her long hair between her fingers, grinning.

Every weekend over the next quarter, Fran brought Sybil to meet the friends and boys she'd gone to public school with before St. Mary's. With every backyard pool party, basement movie night, and Saturday afternoon at the mall food court, Fran and Sybil would enter the scene with their elbows hooked, performing Their Strut, peacocking their way to the middle of whatever gathering had assembled. Boys buzzed around them like horse flies – loud, distracting, attempting to land on their necks. Sybil and Fran pretended to be annoyed and aloof, pretended to swat them away. The boys all thought one was prettier than the other, but no one could agree which one.

After school at Fran's while they pretended to do homework, they watched a weathered *Empire Records* DVD on repeat, having serious discussions about which of them was a Gina and which was a Corey, and when they called each other Categorically A Bigger Banana Head, they loved that no one else was in on their joke.

The two were considered an indissoluble item – where one went, the other could soon be found. They were BFFs 4eva, signing the notes they left in each other's lockers with LYLAS and meaning it. They were so thoroughly conjoined that they were referred to as one word by most adults and teachers – FranandSybil, SybilandFran.

They were inseparable.

****

Saint Mary's chapel was at the top of the stairwell at the back of the school building on the fourth floor. It was the only part of the fourth floor where the girls were permitted, even encouraged. All other fourth floor areas, however, were strictly prohibited.

Musty with stale incense and dust, the room was brown – coffee-colored carpet, wooden pews, and a podium at the front made of sturdy, polished oak. Father Tim, the priest who lived in an apartment off-site, drove to Saint Mary's every morning in a rusty Toyota Camry that the girls called the Holy Roller to deliver the same sermon to each grade level once a day, every single week.

There were no crucifixes hanging at the front of the chapel, no statues of martyrs or saints. Hung high above the podium from the ceiling instead was a large stained glass art piece. A mosaic. In many thousands of shards of colored glass held together with the thinnest gold metal striping was an almond-shaped oval. Massive at nearly ten feet across and six feet high, the mosaic's glass pieces were set in a deliberate and careful pattern.

It was one giant eye.

The innermost circle of the eye was outfitted in inky dark navy glass for the pupil, the iris shaded in shards of tan and yellow and brown, and the whites in clear, textured glass. Each piece was held in place with polished gold metal. There was no light directed at the glass, but the entire piece somehow managed to shine brightly at all times of day.

The eye was beautiful.

***

Sybil couldn't believe Fran's joke had been right. So far, it was all tea and cucumber sandwiches.

Fran had surprised Sybil at her locker at the end of the day on Friday and wished her luck, telling her to get ready for all the snacks and indoctrination. Sybil had laughed as she loaded her books into her backpack, told her she was considering just skipping it, but figured her mom would be miffed. Maybe they could get together later, Sybil said as she closed her locker, assuming Fran had no plans?

"Girl, of course I'll see you later," Fran said, opening her arms for a hug. "It's Friday – we'll have a killer night."

After Fran and the rest of the girls had filtered out, Sybil ascended the stairs at the end of the hall, the school quiet, devoid of chatter and whoops and hollers. After she'd rapped her knuckles twice on the door opposite the chapel at the top of the stairs, the door had swung open, the fourth floor emerging.

The room was essentially one large classroom, but instead of desks, there were overstuffed loveseats, recliners, sofas and end tables flanking the seating. Sybil quickly realized the nuns lived up here, that she'd just passed through the front door of their home, that this was their living room. She felt a little silly that that hadn't occurred to her before.

Sister Monica Marie, the lunch lady, appeared in front of her, presenting Sybil with a plate of fresh-baked oatmeal chip cookies in one hand, her other gesturing to the inside of the space.

"Welcome, dear," Sister Monica had said. "Please, leave your bag at the door and come in."

Sister Monica placed the plate of cookies on a coffee table and gestured for Sybil to take a seat. As she perched on one of the largest sofas and Sister Monica settled into a recliner, the rest of the sisters filed in one at a time as if on cue, each of them bearing more plates of food – tiny sandwiches and cream cheese rolled in salami and mini spinach quiches. Hermana Rachel brought a plate of empanadas con frijoles, Sister Dianne held miniature pigs in a blanket, Sister Justina plugged in a crockpot full of meatballs in barbecue sauce, and on it went until all of the sisters were seated around her.

Sister Ruth was the last to file in, holding an oversized teapot beneath a crocheted warmer and two mismatched mugs – one for her, one for Sybil.

The coffee table was full of food, each sister watching Sybil expectantly. They had each made what they brought and hoped she liked the spread, Sister Ruth explained as she sat next to the girl and filled her mug with tea.

Sister Ruth sat so close that her knees brushed Sybil's. She smiled at her, handed her the mug, said, "Why don't you tell us about your future plans?"

The sisters all looked expectantly at her, on the edge of their collective seats, ankles crossed, hands in their laps. They gazed at her with rapt attention. None of them ate their snacks.

Sybil was going out of state to UMaine, she told them as she took a gulp of the warm tea, something herbal and licorice-tasting, and popped a stuffed mushroom into her mouth. She'd gotten a scholarship, she said between bites and gulps, and wanted to major in creative writing. She'd been taking AP English this year, studying the Transcendentalists and writing her final on *Walden*, but her personal tastes gravitated more toward Zadie Smith and Carmen Maria Machado. The things they don't teach you in high school, she'd told the sisters, who chuckled, their eyes on her as she spoke. She wanted to write like Lorrie Moore someday, and she was hoping college somewhere new and different could help her do that, could help her figure herself out.

For perhaps the first time, no one asked, "What about Fran?" Sybil was privately relieved.

She didn't want to lie to them if they had asked. To say Fran was staying in town to go to Framingham State. It was cheaper and she'd gotten a scholarship, and it was fine, it was a great decision for her, they would stay best friends and visit on weekends and talk all the time, and it was fine. It was fine. All of it was fine.

Because it hadn't been fine.

Sybil had confessed to Fran six weeks ago that she wasn't planning to go to FSU, that she hadn't even applied there, that she needed to get out of here and try something else. They were at their regular coffee shop, sipping iced coffees, Fran debating the color scheme of the matching duvet covers they should get for their dorm bunks when Sybil blurted it out.

"I'm leaving," she had said. "On my own."

Sybil remembered the look on Fran's face, the way her eyes had instantly become glossy, pink, wet. A look of disbelief as she processed what Sybil had said. Sybil reached for her friend's hand and Fran wrenched it back sharply, narrowing her eyes.

"Miss Self-Righteous," Fran had whispered, quoting their favorite DVD. She pushed away from the table, threw her bag over her shoulder, and left the shop, leaving her half empty iced coffee on the table. Sybil recognized her doing The Strut as she left, not looking back when she called out to her.

Fran ignored Sybil's emails and texts that weekend. She didn't know what to expect at school that Monday, but when they saw each other, it was as if nothing had happened. It was a big blank, an omission. Sybil didn't say anything and neither did Fran. Things were normal, Fran was normal, Sybil was normal. They were fine. LYLAS still. BFFs.

But Sybil didn't say this on the fourth floor as she ate her fifth mini quiche and took another gulp of the tea.

Instead, she told the nuns she was excited to take college courses, that she thought she might study abroad, that she wanted to write for the school newspaper. There were possibilities ahead. Clubs to join. Friends to make.

Sister Ruth smiled at Sybil as she spoke, let out a tiny laugh. Sybil realized she was the only one drinking the tea. The other mug was empty.

"You're not going to do any of that," Sister Ruth said.

Sybil nearly choked, dropping her half-eaten mini quiche. "Sorry, what?"

Sister Ruth leaned in closer, her knee digging harder into Sybil's leg. "Sybil, my dear. *You* are not going to do any of that."

Sybil could feel someone looming behind her, the hair on the back of her neck raised, and as she glanced backwards, her eyes met Sister Monica Marie's, saw her lips curl back on her yellowing teeth, grinning, the gums exposed, all of it a little too clown-wide, all of the nuns' smiles seeming to be bigger than their faces.

Their grins were the last thing she saw before her vision blurred and tumbled, before it all went black, her mouth still full of half-chewed egg and crust.

***

Sybil woke slowly, her focus hazy around the edges, her mouth chalk dry. Her head throbbed as she tried to shake the fog from her mind. As her eyes refocused, she glanced around the room and knew exactly where she was – the front row pew of St. Mary's chapel, seated below the altar, the giant glass eye beaming down at her.

Her heart began to thunder in her chest, fear settling in her stomach. Her eyes welled. On the altar among many dripping candles, she saw dozens of glass jars of varying sizes overtaking its surface – they looked like leftover food jars that had had their labels rubbed off. Pickle jars, olive jars, jelly jars, all different shapes and sizes filling the altar's top and the floor beneath, piled high. The jars were filled with a clear liquid, their caps on tight. Their contents hit her with a jolt, what floated there in the liquid.

Eyes.

Perfectly preserved, she could see suspended in the liquid soft, round pairs, the balls of them looking like cloudy milk, the irises of varying color, the optic nerve waggling behind some, others with the nerve missing.

A wave of nausea settled in her mouth and she tried not to vomit.

The air in the room seemed active, warm, and buzzing. Like hot static. There was a low hum, something guttural and constant, and Sybil realized she wasn't alone. Turning her head to glance behind her, she could see them – the sisters. They were all here, all of them packed into the pews behind her, and they all hummed. She saw their lips clasped tight in concentration, their eyes closed, each of them slowly rocking back and forth, the sound a low, steady octave reverberating from deep in their throats.

Each of the sisters wore thin, white, cotton smocks, and she could see the outline of their bodies, their flat, hanging breasts and heavy hips silhouetted beneath the thin fabric. She saw their hair free of their veils, oily and stringy and long, varying shades of greasy gray against the white smock. She could smell them too, all of their hair emitting an unclean combination of body odor and earthy slow rot.

She saw that she matched them, wearing the same long, white smock, naked beneath it, her feet bare, her hair loose. She couldn't contain it anymore – she vomited, trying as best she could to avoid herself, all of the treats they'd fed her a wet, chunky pile next to her on the pew. She continued the spew until her stomach lurched into dry heaves, the vomit replaced with acidic bile that burned her throat, the orange mess coming in choking coughs, the smell of it making her heave again.

When she finished, her stomach now empty, she felt better, more alert, and she wiped her mouth with the back of her wrist, realizing for the first time that she wasn't restrained. Her eyes widened – *Get up!* she thought, *Run! Scream!* – but she couldn't. Her bottom was glued to the seat by some heavy unseen weight, her body paralyzed. When she opened her mouth to yell, her vocal cords were still. No sound came. She looked up at the chapel's stained-glass eye above the altar and knew the weight she felt, the stillness, was coming from there. It seemed to bear down, and she stayed put.

Sister Ruth appeared at the front of the altar – had she been there the entire time? Sybil blinked repeatedly, the edges of her vision still fuzzy, watched as Sister Ruth extended her arms, seemed to get taller, to hover, her bare toes dragging against the floor. Her greasy, unwashed silver-blonde hair was parted down the middle, hanging long over her shoulders, and Sybil saw the silhouette of her skinny body reflected beneath the white smock, saw the deep lines around her mouth moving as she whispered silently, imperceptibly.

"It is time," Sister Ruth said aloud to the room. The sisters' hums quieted, their eyes staring ahead as Sister Ruth made eye contact with each of them.

As if on cue, the room broke out in applause and hoots, Sybil flinching at the sudden noise. Sister Ruth raised her arms in triumph, trumpeting the moment, turned to meet the gaze of the eye, and bowed.

The glass pupil seemed to widen in acknowledgement toward Sister Ruth, the almond shape flexing. The eyes in the jars seemed to swim.

Sister Ruth looked down at Sybil and smiled. "Each year, we choose one." She stepped down from the altar and placed her hand on Sybil's shoulder. Cold sweat dripped down Sybil's back as her heart continued to pound. Her body seemed to move without her, her legs rising to a stand as she followed Sister Ruth to the front of the chapel, turning toward the congregation.

"Each year," said Sister Ruth as she stood beside Sybil, her gaze down the center aisle of the chapel, "We ask one."

Sybil followed Sister Ruth's stare as they looked beyond the crowd of sisters, her recognition turning again to fear.

At the back of the room stood Fran.

Sybil's eyes widened as she watched Fran glide down the chapel's center aisle to Sister Ruth, her eyes vacant. She wore another long smock, hers a deep brown maroon, like autumn leaves or dried blood, and Sybil watched as Sister Ruth gathered Fran in her arms in an embrace. Fran's eyes never moved, never blinked, and Sybil wondered what kind of tea would make her look like that – empty, a void. She silently willed her body to move, the need to get up and fight feeling much more urgent. She needed to grab Fran's hand, to get them both out of here.

Fran and Sybil stood side by side in front of the altar, the white of Sybil's smock and the maroon of Fran's a treacherous pairing. Sister Ruth stood behind Fran, caressing her hair, and gestured for the girls to face one another.

"Each year," Sister Ruth smiled to her crowd. "We offer one."

The sisters began to hum again, the noise slowly growing in volume, the collective hum rising to a moderate chant, then a raucous and incessant cry before the sisters started outright screaming, their voices cracking as they ran out of breath.

Sybil felt dampness on her cheeks as she began to cry.

The sisters' shrieks came to an abrupt and immediate halt. Sister Ruth extended her hands toward the girls, an object in each of her fists, each object sparkling in the candlelight.

In one hand, a hammer. Silver, shimmering, shined to a bright sheen, larger than any hammer Sybil had seen before, nearly 18 inches long, the square head looking like a meat tenderizer, each side made of tiny points.

In the other, a metal soup spoon. It was one of the same spoons from the cafeteria that Sybil had eaten dozens of yogurts and tomato soups with. Sybil glanced at the jarred eyes and felt her mouth water again.

Sybil looked toward Fran, still unblinking. Even with Sybil directly in front of her, it seemed as if Fran looked through or beyond her. She couldn't seem to get through.

"Fran," Sybil said, surprising herself with her own voice. "Fran!" she said louder. "Fran, please!" She looked at Sister Ruth with wild eyes.

"We know accepting the offer can be difficult," Sister Ruth said, extending the tools in front of her. Horrified, Sybil realized what was being asked of her.

"Stop talking like some fucking video game," Sybil growled. "Just let us go. I could never hurt Fran."

"I disagree."

It was Fran who had spoken, smirking again at her friend. Her eyes saw the disbelief in Sybil's as her friend turned back toward her, saw the recognition of a betrayal, the mounting fear, and she was pleased. Satisfied.

Fran plucked the hammer and spoon from Sister Ruth's hands, gripping them tight as Sybil's heart dropped into her stomach. The sisters' hum began again, Sister Ruth's voice joining them as she held a clean, empty jar in her hands.

"Listen, Banana Head," Fran said as she gave Sybil a tight smile, tucking a lock of hair behind her ear. "By the time I use the spoon, I doubt you'll even be able to feel it."

Sybil's eyes grew wide as she watched Fran raise the hammer high above her head.

***

Saint Mary's Most Holy Eye of the Assumption Quarterly Alumni Newsletter

Happy New Year, alums! The sisters hope this newsletter finds you well and that your Christmas celebrations were full of cheer. During this winter's break, the sisters have been taking a well-deserved rest between semesters before preparing for the spring – check the photos at the back of this issue of Sister Ruth keeping warm with a kettle of tea in the sitting room on the fourth floor!

We're excited to bring you news and photos of your classmates' accomplishments. Remember to bring your alumni newsletter on your travels – snap a photo and mail it to us for a chance to appear in a future issue! We're especially pleased to bring you photos of Jennifer Baker ('06) holding her Saint Mary's newsletter while visiting the Elizabeth Montgomery statue in Salem, Massachusetts!

This season's feature is an alum we're very excited to highlight. Graduating in last year's class, Francine Reeve's recently published novella *Lucas in Atlantic City* recently topped the *New York Times* Bestseller list, making her one of the youngest of the list's authors. Compared to the work of Lorrie Moore with its clever tongue-in-cheek descriptions, the novella is an American post-modern exploration of the power of friendship. Below is a photo of Fran at her most recent sold-out reading – holding a Saint Mary's alumni newsletter of course! Pick up *Lucas in Atlantic City* at your local bookstore, ladies!

Read on for more news about your accomplished classmates. We sisters are proud of your achievements and remember – Her Most Holy Eye always watches over you.

Bone Stew

Damon Nomad

Rachel saw the opening a short distance ahead of them along the narrow foot path. "Just about there. First segment complete. Good job, Cliff."

They were approaching a small village after four days backpacking one of the country's most remote and challenging long-distance hikes, known as Bone Eaters' Trail. A name harkening back to a legend associated with the next portion of the trek.

Cliff answered, "You sound surprised. You didn't think I could hack it?" His voice had a hint of protest. She couldn't see his face, as he was trailing behind her a few paces.

"I didn't say that." She wondered more about how the two of them would fare together. She did wonder a bit about Cliff; he was in great physical shape but had never been a hiker or backpacker. Rachel had been on the trails since middle school. The two of them had done some day hikes and car camping since they started dating a little more than a year ago. This was their first extended trip together, and it had gone quite well, so far. No quarrels, and Cliff had no trouble carrying the heavier pack.

Cliff mumbled something she couldn't make out as they came out from the thick forest and into a small park on the edge of town. Rachel turned and kissed him on the cheek. "One night in a hostel, hot showers, and sleep in a bed." That's what they had agreed on.

Cliff nodded his agreement. "Sounds good." He smirked, "You could use a shower."

***

Early the next morning, Rachel sat across from Cliff in a booth at a cozy cafe. A large map lay on the table between them. She sipped her coffee as he traced his finger along the route they would be starting on today. Cliff looked up from the map. "Thirty-two miles until the next town. No road crossings; nothing."

"Yeah, and no mobile phone reception for most of the way. True wilderness. We will stock up with enough food for five days; we can easily make it in four. There are plenty of fresh water sources near the trail."

The waitress came by and refilled their coffee cups. "You going north into that stretch? You know what people say, don't you?" The young woman stared with a frown.

Rachel answered, "You are talking about this bone-eater myth?" She knew there was some folklore about some monster, but she didn't know what it was about and wasn't worried about such nonsense.

"I ain't talking about no crazy story. I been living here three years, and there have been three people gone missing in that stretch of backcountry since I've been here."

Cliff responded, "Well, people go missing in the wilderness. Not so strange. Were there searches?"

"Yeah, the sheriff and forest service didn't find nothing. Not a trace. Like three people just disappeared." She paused. "It's a serial killer, that's what I think. Other people, who've been here longer, say the same thing. The crazy ones talk about this bone-eater thing." She asked, "You need anything else?"

Rachel answered, "We're good, just the check."

***

A few hours later, they were deep in the back country. Warm days and chilly nights made for perfect weather in midsummer. Rachel smiled as she took in the view from the ridgeline they were on, just above the tree line. "This is beautiful. What a wonderful morning."

She was happy to be with Cliff, and they were lucky to have this extended time off. She was a post-doctoral researcher, and he was an associate professor at the same university. They had the entire month off together, and it was turning out to be a great trip.

"Yeah, it's amazing. Look at those glaciers across the valley." He paused and said, "What the waitress said, about a serial killer. That worry you any? We don't have a gun."

"No. I'm sure there are a lot more killers back home than out here. Even though we live in decent neighborhoods."

"Yeah, I know. Just feel more exposed out here."

Rachel did as well, and the story did bother her just a bit. She also had a strange sensation ever since they got up on this ridge, like someone was watching them. She felt a bit of a shiver but shook it off. "Trail heads down into the valley just ahead. A couple more hours and we will make camp well before sunset."

Cliff was leading the way along the valley floor. They should be at the spot for the next campsite in about fifteen minutes. Rachel suddenly came to a stop. "Did you hear that?" She went quiet and thought she saw movement from the corner of her eye.

Cliff turned around. "What? I didn't hear anything."

She pointed off to the left. "Something, over there. Maybe twenty yards away." Her eyes scanned for something, but she didn't see anything, and the woods were thick. The light was getting dimmer as the sun started to slip below the ridgeline.

Cliff moved closer to Rachel. "I don't see anything. Maybe a deer?"

"Yeah, probably." She had goose bumps, and the sense that someone was watching them was stronger. But she didn't want to seem like the panicky sort. She didn't say anything about it. "Let's get going and set up camp."

They huddled around a stone fire ring a few hours later. The warm blaze broke the evening chill and gave them some light. They had finished dinner, and things were cleaned up and stowed away to keep away the bears and critters.

Cliff poured them each a hot cup of tea as they sat on a bench improvised from a flat stone. The fire ring and two stone benches had been here from previous campers. There were two other spots nearby with similar setups. It was a prime spot for a campsite near a fresh spring.

Rachel's dull sense of anxiety had passed. She wrapped her hands around the warm mug. "I'm going to sleep well tonight."

Cliff stood up. "Did you hear that?"

"Ha. Ha. Very funny." She bolted up when she heard the sound of something moving through the woods.

Cliff turned on the gas lantern and turned up the intensity. He gestured with a wave. "Somebody coming along the trail." He crept a few steps in that direction. "Maybe we should have brought a gun." Rachel was sure he didn't even own one.

Rachel followed beside him, and then she saw the outline of someone coming toward their camp, and they were wearing a headlamp. Cliff was a pretty big guy, just over six feet, and had played rugby in college. Whoever this was looked like they were just about the same size.

"Hi, there." A man came into the light. "Hope I didn't startle you." He was about the same size as Cliff, a bit thinner and older, maybe in his mid-forties with a well-trimmed beard.

Cliff answered, "No problem. Why you moving at night?"

"Well, I was pushing for this spot myself and put in a long day. Twelve miles."

Rachel gasped quietly. "That is a lot of ground to cover in this wilderness while carrying a heavy pack."

He turned off the head lamp and took it off. "I'm doing at least ten miles a day. I've done this trail twice before; it's a kind of training route for me."

Cliff asked, "Training? For what?"

"Annapurna Range in the Himalaya next year." He paused. "You mind if I take a break by your fire and get a drink of water?"

Rachel scratched her nose; the warning about a serial killer came back to mind. The guy didn't seem like a killer, but she heard that a lot of psychopaths seem normal. There was a kind of code in the back country of offering hospitality to fellow travelers. "Sure. We have some warm tea."

She gestured at the other fire rings. "You can take one of the other spots if you're ready to call it a day." *Better to have him where we can keep an eye on him.* She thought to herself.

She glanced at Cliff. He nodded his head in agreement and added, "Yeah, plenty of room in this spot."

"That sounds good, thanks. I'm Ray."

After introductions, the three of them gathered around the fire. They listened as Ray told them about some of his adventures. He said he sold his software business thirteen years ago. He had spent more than a decade taking on some of the world's most difficult mountains and wilderness areas. He didn't sound like he was making it up, and Rachel knew enough to probe him with a few questions to satisfy herself that he was legitimate. She was feeling a little better about offering him a spot at their site.

Cliff asked Ray,"What's the deal with that knife? Doesn't look like it's metal."

Ray pulled the dark-bladed knife from a scabbard hanging from his belt. "A flint blade and deer bone handle, made for me for this trail."

Rachel asked, "What do you mean? Made for this trail."

He rubbed his chin. "Hmm . . . well . . . You might think I'm a bit crazy. You got to be careful, especially when traveling alone here." He went quiet.

Rachel probed for more. "What are you talking about? The serial killer that supposedly hunts here?"

"Not him." Ray shrugged, "You know about the legend? Why its called Bone Eaters' Trail?"

Rachel glanced at Cliff and then back to Ray. "Not really. We know there is a folk tale. Is it something you believe in?" Seemed strange that this guy might believe in some sort of boogie man.

Cliff prodded, "Come on, tell us. No judgment."

"Okay, I guess I should explain something as background. I had never been one to believe in the supernatural or cryptozoology tales. In my first three years of exploration, I spent most of my time in the Nepal Himalaya. I developed a close bond with two lead sherpas that I met the first year. We became friends."

He took a sip of tea. "They are both fearless in the mountains. Careful, but not timid. Not well educated, but they are smart and practical." He paused. "The third year, we got in an argument when they met me in Kathmandu. They didn't want any part of the route that I was proposing. They finally admitted it was fear of the Yeti."

Ray smiled. "I finally won them over with a bonus." The smile evaporated, and he spoke in a somber tone. "A few hours after sunset on the third night, we were camped just above the tree line. Three of us relaxing around a campfire, much like we are right now." He continued with a minute-by-minute explanation of what he had seen, heard, and experienced that night.

He finished, "It wasn't a bear, and it wasn't human. It broke my friend's arm when he kept it from attacking me. I think about these kinds of things differently, ever since." He went quiet.

None of them spoke for several minutes. Cliff broke the silence. "Keep going. Tell us about the knife and this area." He got up and refilled everyone's cup with hot tea and tossed another log on the fire. He sat back down next to Rachel.

Rachel scooted closer to Cliff. "Yeah, keep going."

Ray held his hands up to the fire and then started again. "First time I came here was five years ago. An old man, a native American, told me the tale of the myth and how to protect yourself from the creature. He said they have been in these mountains for thousands of years. Very few are left."

He gave a detailed account of what the old medicine man told him and then paused to take a few sips of tea.

Cliff commented, "So, to kill it, you've got to stab it with a flint blade. Made by a medicine man." He chuckled. "Kind of sounds like a monster movie." He shrugged. "Sorry, didn't mean to make a joke of it."

Ray smiled with a shrug, "That's okay. Anyway, the second time I came here was three years ago. Something happened that put a scare into me. I can't say for sure it was the creature, but what I found the next morning made me think I might have been lucky to escape harm."

He told them a story of what he encountered on the trail along this portion of the route. He finished up, "It was gone the next morning. I found a spot about fifty feet from the campsite. I was looking for a place to dig a small latrine. There was a large fire ring, with a big pot sitting on a bed of old coals. There were bones, long bones, sticking out of the pot. I moved closer to get a look."

He exhaled slowly. "I could see that there was a human skull inside. The pot and coals weren't warm, but it had been used since the last rain. Maybe a week or two."

He continued, "I contacted the police on my mobile as soon as I had a signal and told them where the spot was. I heard later that someone had been reported missing, but they never found that pot or the bones." He finished, "I sure as heck didn't imagine it."

They all went quiet, and Rachel stared at the fire, watching the flames dance about. Ray didn't seem like the type to just lie. *Maybe it's true. Still could be a lunatic serial killer. Not a monster that the old Indian told him about.* She took Cliff's hand and squeezed it.

Cliff and Rachel had just climbed into their sleeping bags, and Ray was still setting up his tent. He said he didn't need any help; he was used to going solo. She whispered, "What do you think about him?"

"Pretty cool dude. Great stories about his adventures. Monster thing is kind of strange."

"Yeah." There was something about him that bothered her, she couldn't put her finger on what it was. She pushed it aside and drifted off to sleep.

***

Ray was already up when Rachel and Cliff got out of their tent the next morning. His gear was packed up and he was ready to hit the trail. "Thanks for the hospitality and conversation."

He held out his hand. "This is a smaller flint blade I got last time I was here. A sort of backup." He paused. "You should be safe traveling together. Better safe than sorry."

Cliff reached out and grabbed the knife that was inside a leather sheath. "Thanks. No harm in being careful."

Rachel didn't see any reason to turn the gift down; it would make for an interesting keepsake. "Safe journey. I don't think we will see you again at the pace you're moving at." Maybe they were lucky to have crossed paths.

They watched as Ray headed down the trail. Rachel headed for the camp stove. "Let's have some breakfast and get moving."

An hour later, they had everything packed up. Rachel took a look around and picked up her pack. "You ready?"

Cliff took the flint blade, still inside its sheath, from his pants pocket and slipped it into an outside compartment of his backpack. "Yep."

Rachel took the lead as they headed down the footpath.

***

Mid-afternoon the next day, Cliff gestured at something. "Somebody camping there?" He stopped and turned around. "Is there water close to here?"

Rachel stopped beside Cliff. "Yeah, I think so. A hundred yards down that culvert." She looked ahead at the tent. "Not the best place to camp." The spot they had picked out was another two hours ahead, with more shelter from the wind, and a closer water supply.

Rachel spotted the guy as they got closer. She spoke in a hushed voice. "Not your typical solo backcountry type." She waved at the man. "Hello."

The guy looked to be mid-thirties, about their age. He was a bit overweight, not obese; husky was a nice way of putting it. He was sitting on a stone bench, leaning back against a big tree, with his stocking feet propped up on a foot stool fashioned from large stones. He was reading a thick paperback book.

He laid the book down on the foot stool as he stumbled out of his seat. "Howdy." He slipped his feet into his boots but didn't lace them up. He shuffled towards them with a slight limp. "Lovely day."

Cliff asked, "You okay? Looks like you're limping."

"Yes, I'm fine." His voice had a slight tremble. "Honestly, I'm struggling just a bit. Twisted my ankle near here early yesterday and have been here since." He gestured at his foot. "I will be ready for the trail tomorrow."

Rachel asked, "You see a guy, beard, mid-forties come through?"

"Ray!" The man smiled. "Yes. He stopped for a while. Did a water run for me and sat with me a while this morning. My name is Bernard; well Bernie."

Bernie poured them some warm tea after introductions and some small talk. "I have some cookies. A nice little snack." He headed for his backpack next to his tent.

Cliff whispered, "You think we should camp here for the night? Help him out."

Rachel nodded in agreement. "I was thinking the same thing."

A few hours later, Cliff finished cooking dinner on their camp stove. "You aren't going to eat? You've got to keep up the calories on the trail."

"Massive breakfast and lunch. I simply cannot." Bernie said with a chuckle.

Rachel finished the last bit of pasta in her bowl. "Midday tomorrow, we should have a mobile signal." They kept them turned off to conserve battery power. They would check tomorrow to see if they had a signal.

Cliff turned the control on their lantern to give them more light. "That's right." The fire was dying down, and they didn't have much more firewood.

Bernie asked with a puzzled look, "What are you talking about?"

Cliff answered, "Mobile phone signal. Surely you have your mobile with you out here on a solo trip."

"Ahh, yes. Of course. Of course." He paused. "Mobile phone signal, tomorrow."

Rachel asked, "What is the book you are reading?"

He handed it to her. "Have you heard of it?"

Rachel thought he was joking, but he seemed serious. "Yeah. I think everyone has heard of it." It was a heavily worn paperback copy of To Kill a Mockingbird. She looked inside and saw it was printed in 1981, nearly fifty years ago. Seemed peculiar; he must have picked it up at a yard sale or second-hand shop. She handed the book back.

Bernie suddenly jumped out of his seat. "What's that?"

Cliff was holding the knife that Ray had given him. "It's just a flint knife. Ray gave it to us." He gestured for Bernie to calm down. "I just wanted to get a look at it."

Bernie gasped, "What a peculiar weapon. Do you mind putting it away? I don't like weapons of any sort."

Cliff got up and put it back into his pack. "Sure, no problem." He sat back down. "Ray didn't tell you the story that gives this trail its name?"

Bernie sat back down with a look of an interested child. "No, tell me."

Cliff gave a recounting of Ray's tale. He finished up, "Ray seemed sincere, and he gave us the knife so we could protect ourselves."

Bernie frowned. "Why would someone want to kill an ancient creature like that? We all have to survive in this world."

Rachel answered, "He doesn't hunt them down. Just for self-defense." She thought Bernie's response was peculiar. He seemed to be a bit of an oddball. She added, "Not that I believe his story."

There was a sound of someone or something moving in the darkness. Something big. Rachel glanced at Cliff; he nodded his head. "Yeah, I heard it." He pointed toward the spot. "Over there, maybe twenty or thirty feet in the trees."

Rachel looked at Bernie. His eyes were closed and his head was cocked back. It looked like he was sniffing the air, like a wolf or dog might do. His nose twitched, and he opened his eyes.

He saw she was watching him. "Just focusing my hearing. A critter foraging about."

Cliff stood up and moved towards the spot. "Sounded like footsteps to me. Human footsteps." He paused. "I might be wrong. I don't hear a thing, now."

They all went quiet, but the sound was gone. Rachel got up. "I'm ready to bed down."

They had been in their sleeping bags for maybe twenty minutes, and Bernie was in his tent. Rachel whispered, "Bernie is a bit odd. Don't you think?"

"What do you mean?"

"His speech is kind of formal. Uses a lot of old phrases." She paused. "He wasn't sure if I had heard of To Kill a Mockingbird. What he said about killing the creatures that Ray talked about." She paused. "He did something strange when we heard something near the camp." She explained that it looked like he was sniffing the air.

Cliff was quiet for several moments. "There was something else. I might have imagined it. It probably was just my imagination. You remember what Ray told us about the creatures, even in a disguised form. Their eyes can reflect light like animals. For just a moment, I thought I saw the fire reflect like that from his eyes."

Rachel gasped, "Cliff!" She lowered her voice. "I was thinking about the kind of guy who might be a weird serial killer. Not a shape-shifting monster."

Cliff sighed. "Like I said, I probably imagined it." He paused. "I think we are both letting this place get to us. Let's get some sleep."

***

Cliff shouted as he climbed out of the tent the next morning. "He's gone!"

"What?" Rachel slipped on her boots and got out of the tent. Bernie's tent, backpack, and gear were all gone. "Didn't even say goodbye. Like I said, he's a bit weird."

"He can't be moving too fast. We will catch up with him on the trail. You want to do breakfast or start packing up the gear?"

"I'll do breakfast and coffee."

A few hours later, Cliff stopped on the trail a few yards in front of Rachel. "I need to take a piss." He pulled off his backpack and laid it on the ground. "Can't believe we haven't caught up with Bernie. Unless maybe we passed him and he was on a toilet break."

Rachel took off her pack and used it for a seat as Cliff disappeared into the trees. Moments later, she heard a noise; it sounded like Cliff calling out. "Cliff!" She shouted louder, "Cliff! You, okay?"

Snake bite, bear, broke his ankle, fell and hit his head. A jumble of thoughts raced through her mind. Not one to panic, but she knew there were ways to get hurt in the wilderness. To make things worse, they weren't near mobile phone range yet.

She leaned her backpack and Cliff's up against a tree and moved slowly in the direction Cliff had been going. She knew to be deliberate. "Cliff!" She shouted and listened about every ten feet.

She saw a small clearing up ahead and instinctively moved faster. Her pulse pounded in her ears. Cliff was lying motionless on the ground, about twenty feet from her. She heard something; it sounded like fire. She turned and saw a large pot sitting inside a stone fire ring.

A guttural voice came from behind her. "More bones for the stew." Everything went dark.

"Rachel. Rachel." She recognized Cliff's voice. Her eyes fluttered open. She was sitting on the ground, with a rope securing her to a tree. Cliff was next to her, tied to another tree. "He hit you on the back of the head. You, okay?"

She answered, "My head's throbbing. Am I bleeding?"

"No, I don't think he drew blood from me either." Cliff paused. "It's just like Ray said. It's Bernie. The face looks a little like Bernie, and it sounds a little bit like him. Kind of a neanderthal version and wearing the same clothes."

Rachel watched as someone came walking out of the woods, carrying their backpacks.

The face and especially the eyes looked something like Bernie. His forehead and jaws were heavier; his chubby and flabby body had transformed into a lean and muscular structure. It tossed the packs to the ground, reached into Cliff's side pocket and pulled out the flint knife. He turned toward them. "You'd kill me with this!"

He moved a few steps closer. "I've the right to survive same as you."

The voice was rougher and deeper. But Rachel knew Cliff was right; it was Bernie. "Like I said before, only for self-defense."

The creature began to quiver, and it doubled over, grunting and moaning. It happened quickly, not a drawn-out process. He looked the same as Bernie from yesterday as he stood back up. He smirked as he gestured with a wave. "Bernie's back, for a little while."

He walked over to his backpack, near the large fire ring. He pulled out a hatchet and laid the flint knife on one of the big stones. He used the opposite end of the hatchet blade, a sort of hammer, to smash the flint knife to bits. "You won't be needing this."

He looked at them. "Bone eaters? That's not correct. It's a stew with flesh on the bones." He chuckled. "Bone Stew Trail would be more accurate."

He shuffled slowly towards Rachel and Cliff. "The kettle is just about ready." He held up the hatchet. "I don't need both of you for my stew. You look absolutely delicious, Rachel."

He looked at Cliff and said, "I'll have to bring my inner being back and hack you up. Carry you out into the woods and spread you out for the critters."

Bernie bent over, the same as when he transformed before.

A man bolted out of the woods moments later. Ray had his flint dagger in his right hand. He lunged and stuck it into Bernie's lower back.

Bernie was mostly the monster as he stood up and screeched in pain. He swung the hatchet wildly at Ray but missed. "I'm stronger than you like this."

He moved toward Ray and drew the hatchet back. He paused, his eyes widening, and he fell to the ground. His body began to smoke as if it were on fire, but there were no flames. The smoke got thicker, then dissipated without leaving a trace of anything on the ground.

Ray bent over to catch his breath. Rachel and Cliff excitedly thanked him. He stood up and gestured with a wave. "It was nothing." Rachel asked him, a"That was you last night near our camp. Right?"

"Yeah, I was suspicious when I came across him on the trail. They only know as much about our world as any trips they make in human form. He had this old copy of To Kill a Mockingbird. That seemed like a peculiar choice to haul around on the trail. Several of his comments seemed dated."

He reached into his pocket and pulled out a pack of cigarettes and a lighter. "I don't smoke." He flicked the lighter. "It makes for a good test of the eyes if you get close enough. I was sure when I saw the reflection in his eyes."

Ray stuffed them back into his pocket, and he bent down and picked up the hatchet that Bernie was going to use on Rachel and Cliff.

Cliff glanced at Rachel. "You thought I was crazy about his eyes." He struggled against the ropes. "Can you untie us, Ray?"

Ray headed toward Cliff. "That looks like it's tied pretty tight. I can cut you lose." Ray cocked the sharp hatchet back and savagely and deliberately struck Cliff in the head. Cliff went limp without uttering a word.

Rachel instinctively turned away and was speechless. Her thoughts were confused as she struggled to process what had just happened. After a few moments, she managed to speak in a whisper and could only utter a single word as she focused her glare on Ray. "Why?"

Ray had a wild look in his eyes as he crept closer. "There is a serial killer who visits this trail. Many other places as well. A different kind of monster." He paused. "Bernie was right. You will make a delicious stew."

His lips curled into a crooked smile. "I couldn't bear the thought of letting that creature have you for himself."

There was nothing she could do as he crept toward her. She closed her eyes and silently recited a childhood prayer, and then everything went black.

Raptured

Nolan Krypt

1

It was my first camping trip as an adult. I hadn't been in years, not since I was a kid, when my dad took me and my brother up into the Smoky Mountains one early spring day. I don't remember much of that trip, a whole two decades later. Just impressions. I didn't like it much–the humidity (God, the humidity!) and how the salty sweat pooled in the creases of our armpits, asscracks, hairline; the musty scent of the forest, how it clung with invisible weight to the trees, whose canopy made me feel smothered, buried, like I was underground, not up top beneath an open blue sky; the way my father treated me, calling me a wuss for whining about the bugs or my sweat-soaked clothes. Toxic masculinity caked every word. My brother had soaked it all up, only to shit it back out at his own sons. I pitied those kids.

So, needless to say, I didn't relish the idea of wandering into nature's torture chamber, where the wildlife wanted us dead, even as we defied it with nylon backpacks and half-baked wilderness knowledge from cash-grabbing influencers on the internet. Along with its boring aspirations, it struck me as needlessly discomforting. In the age of AC, modern showers, and grocery stores, why anyone would risk losing that for a few days, stripped of such luxuries, in the hopes of rekindling the survival instincts of our ancestors, was beyond me.

But Willo wanted to go.

Ever since we'd moved to Asheville, he'd set to the self-burdened task of making friends. As I unpacked our boxed belongings and made our new home comfy, he'd galavanted off in his filthy coupe (the car he refused to wash or have cleaned) to make new friends. Willo, the same guy who had panic attacks at the mere thought of a social gathering, was out there striking up conversations with complete strangers he'd met via chat apps. It was absurd. But he'd made up for it in his own way. His leftover free time was spent helping me or taking care of our two dogs. So, I couldn't exactly hold it against him. As it was, he was sweet; thoughtful. He checked in with me every day to make sure I wasn't turning resentful of him for his spontaneous streak of extroversion.

Which is why, in the end, I agreed to go camping. I wanted to meet this new couple he'd been texting for a while; the trio had actually met up last week for the first time. I had to stay home with the dogs and ensure they got their evening walk. Willo had fussed over this decision, pestering me with sincere inquiries such as 'Are you sure you still want me to go?' and 'Is this because they're gay? Are you worried they'll flirt with me?,' all of which I swatted away like a pesky fly. I wasn't jealous, wasn't upset. Honestly, I just wanted to rest. To be at peace in my new home that we'd fought so hard to get amidst a floundering market. If he wanted to be a social butterfly, he could have at it. Perfect chance for me to catch up on some reading.

A part of me did wonder, though, what this couple's motives were. This wasn't my first time around the block. Gay men are notoriously salacious, which wasn't exactly a bad thing, just somewhat troublesome. As a member of that same community, I knew it came with the territory. Perhaps these new acquaintances wanted nothing more than to engage in platonic pastimes with us. But one never knew. The camping trip would allow me the chance to gauge their personalities. Lure out their private motivations. If they wanted sex with us, or even just Willo, so be it. But it wouldn't be at my expense or humiliation. I'd be in the know, goddamn it.

So, with my own ulterior motives, we found ourselves packing my four-wheel-drive truck. Sleeping bags, a cooler full of alcoholic drinks (and some water bottles), clothes fit for chilly October, and other camping essentials. I watched Willo expertly strap down the bulky items in the bed of the truck under a web of bungee cords.

"So, what are these guys' names again?" I asked.

"Sebastian and Wayne."

"Remind me who they are again. You've mentioned so many new chat buddies. It's been hard to keep them all separate in my head."

"These are the guys that both grew up here in the mountains. Sebastian comes from an ultra-conservative family, didn't receive a warm welcome from his coming out, went to Appalachian State. He smokes *a lot* of weed. What else… oh, he's six years older than Wayne. Sebastian is thirty-eight, Wayne is thirty-two. Wayne's from Boone, but he left the state to go to Cal Tech. He's a little odd."

"How so?"

"He's just…" Willo trailed off, even stopped what he was doing to squint in thought. His eyes snapped over to mine. "You ever met an engineer? They're a peculiar bunch. Their brains just work differently from the rest of us. Smart, very smart, but the smart ones are always a little off."

"Off. As in he's gonna murder us in the middle of the night, off?"

Willo snorted as he stretched the final bungee cord. His masterpiece would have made any spider proud. "Odd in the sense that I doubt we could ever get lost or starve to death with him around. I'd bet you fifty bucks that he's gonna have a compass, survival gear, whatever the hell one could think of for a trip to the forest for an entire month."

"Month? I thought we were only–"

"It was a joke. We're only camping for the week, babe."

"He sounds useful."

"Keep that in mind when you get stranded alone with the guy. He's not exactly a conversationalist."

"Then why are we hanging out with them?"

Willo sighed. "Because we need friends, Trent, and we aren't gonna make them staying at home with the dogs. Speaking of which, you let Melissa know we were leaving this morning, right? She's gonna come feed them this evening, tomorrow, and Sunday?"

I nodded, but I was unwilling to go off topic. "So, we're about to go hang out with a social weirdo and his partner? I'm assuming Sebastian is a better companion?"

"They're both great, Trent. Stop overthinking this. Wayne is just quiet, prepared, smart. Sebastian is a really nice guy. You'll get along great with him. Wayne might need to warm up to you–me–us."

Thus began my first regrets about agreeing to this trip.

"Besides, Queenie is gonna be there."

The only saving grace to this whole ordeal. In fact, it might have been the thing that hooked me like a fish to the bait. I adored Willo's sister. Only a few years younger than my partner, she could transform an otherwise boring evening into one of the most enjoyable nights of my entire life. Just by showing up with her gregarious personality and one of her common tokens: a bottle of merlot, a bag of edibles, or if she really wanted a crazy night, both.

If all else failed, I would just chill with Queenie. Let Willo socialize until this strange flare of extroversion sputtered out. I was beginning to miss the old Willo, the hermit and shut-in who hated guests and social obligations. Hopefully that version would return soon.

Because I wasn't going on any more camping trips after this.

2

The Blue Ridge Mountains are hard to miss, but they aren't what most people envision with the term 'mountain.' There are no snow-capped peaks. No steep pinnacles. More like giant rolling hills. At certain angles, at particular times of the day, and with the right weather, they appear wreathed in bluish haze. To me, they looked like massive waves frozen in place, doomed to collapse someday. And we were tiny fish, weaving between these hibernating leviathans.

Queenie stirred me from these sentiments.

"Me and my girls held a seance last weekend. During the Blue Moon. You should have been there. It was magical. Haunting, even."

Queenie's psychic abilities weren't anything new to us. She had a harmless habit of slipping it into conversation. During the course of our friendship, she had claimed to see people's auras, absorb energy from crystals, talk to spirits, see ghosts. Willo confided in me once that those were just the tip of the iceberg. That there were countless other 'talents' his sister 'exhibited.' He'd said this with a smirk, of course. Despite his upbringing. Despite the diet of hippie mumbo jumbo his parents had raised him and his sister on. No sirree; he didn't buy any of it.

Queenie, on the other hand, believed all of it.

I found it amusing. It wasn't really hurting anyone, unlike certain religions. I kept my reactions balanced: respect with a pinch of friendly teasing. Queenie knew I jested in good fun, not mockery. Still, she never backed down from her convictions.

So, when I cocked an eyebrow and grinned at Willo, she punched my arm and feigned offense even as she smiled back at me. "You smile all you want, Trent, but Willo knows all about my seance superpowers. Ain't that right, Willo?"

Willo didn't say anything. Kept his eyes glued to the road. Almost like he didn't want to be wrapped up in her antics. I risked his frustration and entertained the question. "What's this she's talking about?"

"Just something stupid we did as kids," he murmured, throwing daggers at his sister in the rearview mirror.

But Queenie was already leaning forward over the middle console. "Let's see," she began. "It was the fourth grade. Our grandfather had just passed a few days prior. Mommy dearest had explained to us how grandpa's spirit had been released from his body to go join the celestial–"

"Yada, yada, yada," Willo interjected, his next words directed to me. "You know our parents were kooks. Wannabe spirit gurus."

"Be nice," said Queenie. "I'm just setting the stage. We were young. Impressionable. It was our first funeral, and we hadn't really been exposed to death all that much. Not like that. Grandpa was someone we knew. Someone we'd interacted with, broke bread with. Now he was gone. It naturally led to us asking some pretty serious questions about life. Well, I got in my head to try and communicate with ol' gramps, ask him about the afterlife. I can't remember exactly how I came up with a seance. Where the hell did I pick that up? Probably some friends at school putting weird ideas in my head. But anyways, that night, Willo and I lit some candles, sat in the dark, and called on Grandpa." She said these last few words with a mixture of awe and emphasized dramatics, like a storyteller regaling a captivated audience. I sneaked a grin at Willo, who rolled his eyes.

"So did it work?" I asked.

"Why don't you ask your loverboy here?" she taunted.

"Nothing happened," said Willow.

"Nothing?" Queenie challenged. "I got fucking possessed. At four years old."

"Possessed?" My gaze darted between the two, trying to decipher the joke, the punchline. Willo was acting skittish, ducking behind curt responses, while Queenie had made it her mission to drag this out and… what? Humiliate her brother? Make him relive something embarrassing?

"She acted all weird," he said, sounding unimpressed. "Started babbling in another language. She refused to tell me how she managed to roll her eyes into the back of her head, but however she did it, it made her puke all over the place, including my lap."

"I don't remember any of that," said Queenie, leaning back into her seat. "I blacked out, then came to and found this one flailing his arms like a sissy. He was squealing about the vomit. Tiny splotch on his shirt. Didn't even touch his skin."

"Yes, it did," said Willo. "And it wasn't regular vomit. I don't know what the hell kind of stomach bug you'd picked up, but what you puked out was all white and clumpy."

"White and clumpy," Queenie snorted. "Sounds like something my gay brother would be all about." I didn't say anything. All this talk of vomit had me feeling a bit queasy, especially with these winding roads, back and forth, back and forth… "Well, I got over it, whatever it was. I've had a ton of seances since, and I don't ever get sick. Just bad timing back then, I guess."

I looked at Willo. "So, that was your only seance, huh?"

"One too many, for my books."

"Yeah, he got spooked or grossed out, or both," said Queenie. "The beginning of his fall from grace in the eyes of my family. Kept on a steady path away from all things spiritual after that."

"It was more than just that," said Willo. "It was… a lot of things."

I kept with the teasing. "Maybe we should reel him into one more for old times' sake."

Queenie's face flashed between our seats. "Yes! Yes! Yes!"

"NO!"

The car fell silent. Queenie slunk back into her seat, muttering something about 'can't take a joke' and 'buzzkill.' I studied Willo's face. He looked tense. A bit wild eyed. I racked my brain–had we ever discussed this event before? This botched childhood seance with his sister? I didn't think so. If I'd known this was a sensitive subject, I would, of course, not have jested so lightly about it.

I took his right hand off the wheel and squeezed it in mine. His face softened.

Ten minutes later, Queenie cracked a joke about dildos, and the car was energized again.

***

Willo was right. Wayne was an odd one.

Sebastian was gregarious, bubbly. Came right up to me and gave me a hug. Nothing overly intimate, but I still wasn't expecting it. He stepped back, beaming, and turned his attention to Willo. I watched his eyes. Yup. He wanted my husband. Go figure. It didn't bother me. Everyone wanted to get in Willo's pants, me included. But for once, it would've been nice to be the desired one. Or at least hold my own in Willo's company. Guess that wasn't going to be the case.

My gaze drifted past them. There was another man hovering around an all-terrain SUV. Hadn't even looked our way, intent on a backpack sitting on the open trunk. Unlike the rest of us, he'd dressed in frumpy, practical clothes. Fisherman overalls seemed a strange choice for a hike. A swamp green bucket hat completed the look.

For some reason, I made my way over to him. Maybe I didn't want to engage the sexual tension between Willo and Sebastian (which Queenie was eating up; she kept trying to get my attention for a reaction). I introduced myself to the man, who was obviously Wayne, but got no response. Well, I think he may have grunted. I sort of missed it because Queenie let out a squeal at something one of the other boys had said. But I think it was a grunt of acknowledgment. Or maybe he was just clearing his throat.

"You must be Wayne," I said. "I hear you're the survival expert."

He cocked an eyebrow. "I've learned that if I don't prep, I'll be screwed when the guy next to me doesn't either. Someone's gotta do it. Might as well be me."

"Surely you've rubbed off on Sebastian," I teased. His pursed lips told me that wasn't the case. "Well, I'm glad you're the guy. This group needs one."

He finally disengaged from the backpack, looked at me briefly, then slid his gaze to the others. He put his hands on his hips and sighed. "I don't like being up here."

This caught me off guard. "You worried about the weather or something? It's supposed to be–"

"You grow up anywhere near the mountains?"

I shook my head. Rude fucker.

"Being up here is a bad idea right now. Something's in the air."

Yup. Wayne. Weird guy. I glanced over at Willo, hoping he'd notice my distress. No such luck.

"Do me a favor, will ya." His stern eyes finally graced me. "If I say we need to turn around and go back, head home, at any point this weekend, you back me up. From one survival guy to another."

"Dude, you're kinda freakin me out," I said.

His expression faltered. "Sorry. Jitters, is all. Look, just… take me seriously if it gets to that point. If I say it's time to turn around… it's time to turn around."

He eyed me expectantly. I gave a nod, if only to end this conversation. Not that it mattered, because here came the other three, right on cue. Sebastian saddled up next to Wayne, gave him a flirty slap on the ass. He beamed at me, all smile. "Trading spooky stories over here, gents?"

"No…" I said. "Should we be?"

"Well, it *is* October," Queenie reminded me.

"I'm not in the habit of introducing myself with ghost stories," I said.

"Wayne's got plenty of 'em," said Sebastian as he rubbed Wayne's chest. So, they're big on PDA. Fun. "He grew up here in the Apps. Had some weird experiences growing up." Wayne mumbled something about 'not ghost stories, but I didn't quite catch it.

"Sounds like good campfire material," said Queenie.

Willo didn't look amused. He was wearing his signature forced grin whenever he was in a social situation not to his liking. What was his deal today? I'd never known him to act so tense about stuff like this. Was it Queenie's story from earlier? I made a mental note to ask him about it in private.

"If we're going, we should start now," said Wayne. "Best to make it to our campsite before dark."

Assent sounded from the others, save for me. Wayne's attitude rubbed me wrong. So did our conversation before the others had interrupted.

Such odd things to say to someone you'd just met.

***

The next days went as expected. We hiked, we ate, we hiked some more, we ate again, then we slept. Rinse, repeat. Queenie and Sebastian hit it off, no surprise there. Predictably, Sebastian teased Willo with conversational innuendos and playful body contact. Willo wasn't oblivious; he knew the other man's game. Just as predictable, my partner basked in the attention. To his credit, he checked in with me after every flirtation. Make sure I wasn't getting jealous. I did find some anxiety in the anticipation. It was only a matter of time before Willo snuck off to do the deed. Just do it already. Get it over with.

Hmm. Maybe I *was* jealous.

Wayne remained stoic; gloomy. Originally, I thought he and Queenie might find some common ground, what with her occult tendencies and his mysterious past. Sebastian had made it sound like Wayne had similar tastes. But the opposite occurred. Queenie's woo-woo talk made him even more tense. Every time she so much as mentioned something supernatural, he'd shut the conversation down. Queenie found his intimidation off-putting, and their dynamic added a sour note to the excursion.

Sebastian took it as his personal mission to fix this. One evening, as we huddled around the campfire, he encouraged Queenie's spirit talk. She eagerly took the bait, yapping about this spirit and that spirit, haunted locations she'd visited, how she'd been followed by a bad spirit one time. Wayne looked visibly angry. He kept flashing Sebastian horrible looks, gritting his teeth as Queenie kept at it. Just as I braced for Wayne to lose his cool, Sebastian dragged him into the conversation.

"Sounds like some of your stories, babe."

Wayne grimaced.

"What? No giant spiders? No lecture on forest etiquette?" Sebastian grinned at us. "Can't whistle at night. And don't look in the trees."

"What's that mean?" asked Willo.

"Don't mock me." Wayne poked a stick in the fire, sending embers flying.

"I'm not mocking you," said Sebastian. "But stop acting like an outcast and join in. This bunch might actually enjoy some of your superstitions."

We waited. I didn't expect much. Wayne didn't strike me as someone who liked being thrust into the spotlight. To my surprise, his expression seemed to soften. But maybe that was just the flames dancing between us.

"These mountains are old," he said, staring into the fire. "Very old. Sometimes they feel like home. Sometimes… like this weekend…" He paused. "We're strangers here. I just don't want her *talk* to upset… anything."

Queenie's face scrunched up, like she was smelling something bad. "Are you talking about me?"

Sebastian: "Wayne…"

"I didn't mean offense. I'm just saying, don't talk about spirits unless you want their attention."

"I do," said Queenie.

"Not the ones up here."

That was the end of that. Awkward silence followed. Eventually we all slipped away to our tents.

I dreamed of the mountains at night. Massive mounds, blotting out the horizon, hiding the stars. And a red light, a beam, sweeping over their slumber. It lit up the trees in a dreadful fashion. Shadows grew and bumbled together, away from the red. It seemed violating. Forcing the forest to give up its secrets.

I did my best to avoid it.

It kept finding me.

3

The next day was different.

Everyone seemed grumpy, even Sebastian. He wasn't nearly as flirtatious with Willo. Queenie wasn't bouncing around like a caffeine addict. The whole vibe had me wanting to turn around. We'd made it far enough. Was fun for a while, now it was time to go home.

But Willo, bless his heart, wanted to hike some more. Insisted we could find a better campsite near the river. A few of us protested (me), but in the end, he got his way. We packed up and set a course for…

A trap.

We didn't notice it at first. The scenery transitioned with an insidious slothfulness. By the time we took note of it, we were already in the thick of it. Trees looked barren. A cemetery of leafless bark. Beneath our boots, the ground was all dirt and half-buried stone, naked and dry. Heavy air choked us of moisture. My tongue felt papery. Thirst set in quickly, and we all downed our canteens without much thought. But this provided only short relief. Whatever sorcery was at play soon had our throats parched again. I surveyed our surroundings. Grey, smoky haze engulfed us, but I could still spot the perimeter of this dead zone off in the distance, where greenery returned.

How had we marched so far into this desert?

It was quiet. In our vicinity, there were no signs of life. I heard birds chittering somewhere far off, which led to me looking up…

More bizarre details. Nearly every branch clawed upward towards the sky. There was no typical wandering and twisting to these appendages, no wasted time in chasing the sun. No twigs, either. Almost like a powerful wind tunnel had rushed out of the ground, charging towards the heavens, taking with it anything too weak to resist its pull.

"We should go back," said Wayne. He glanced my way with a knowing look.

"Why? It's just a dead patch," said Sebastian. "Probably from a fire or something. The green comes back up ahead, less than a mile."

Queenie, I noticed, appeared shaken. She kept glancing about, almost jumpy.

"You ok?" I asked.

"I think he's right," she said in a soft voice. "We should go back." She said something else, but she murmured it. Something about 'bad energy,' I think.

"There's something over there."

We followed Willo's gaze, which was directed up ahead. I couldn't make out anything, too distracted by Queenie's twitchy vibe.

"Something, as in alive?" I asked. "Like an animal?"

"No," said Wayne. He'd come up beside Willo, stared off in the same direction. "Looks… structural."

"Like a house?" I asked.

No answer.

"Well, let's go find out." Sebastian headed off with Willo on his heels. Wayne held back. He had the same look as Queenie. Wary. Dazed.

"You ok?" I asked him. "What's wrong?"

He peeled his gaze off whatever he'd been staring at and turned to me. I couldn't read him. Was he scared? Dehydrated?

"The mountains are seeping out more spirits than usual…"

"What was that?"

He didn't repeat himself. After a few blinks, it's like he came to, fixing me with a sober, intense expression. "We need to go back. Now."

"Then go get the others," I said, a bit irritated at the whole mess.

Wayne left me alone with Queenie, who'd gone through a dizzy spell already and was now sitting on one of the rocks jutting from the ground. I consoled her, kept checking in with her every few seconds to make sure she wasn't about to faint on me. She remained quiet.

Footsteps approached. I stood from my crouch, turned to see Wayne back with us, but that sober look in his eyes had solidified into something else now. Something I immediately didn't like. Before I could speak, he took me by the arm, led me away from Queenie.

"Don't let her go over there."

"Why?"

"There's a body."

I couldn't comprehend what he'd said, so I just stared at him.

"It's a weird scene."

More gibberish. More staring.

He sighed. "Not a fresh one. It's been here awhile."

"What the fuck are you–"

"Shh!" He tightened his grip on my arm. "I don't want her to hear about this–"

"About what?" I still couldn't wrap my head around this conversation. Something in me refused to register it.

"The fucking body I just told you about."

"Is Willo ok?" It started setting in, what he was telling me. I tried to yank my arm free but failed.

"He's fine, he's fine. Willo and Sebastian are fine. They're just taking pictures."

"Doing what?"

"For proof. None of us have signal, so we can't call the cops right now."

I checked my phone with my free hand. He was right. No goddamn signal.

"Is it another camper?" I asked.

Wayne hesitated.

"Fuck."

"I don't know," he quickly admitted. "It's a weird scene."

"You keep saying that."

"Because it is."

Willo and Sebastian came trotting back then. I studied their faces, saw suppressed emotion there. Disgust, or maybe inklings of horror. The unease leaked through, enough that Queenie asked them if they were feeling alright.

"It's time to go back," Wayne reiterated.

This time, no one protested.

***

Twilight played tricks on us.

The forest line of healthy foliage we'd seen just moments earlier now eluded us. Dead trees leapt up at every turn. The panic amongst us became prickly and tense. Emotions ran high. Bickering ensued, and all progress came to a screeching halt as night invaded the heavens. Spotty signal prevented any communication to emergency services. We were too remote. The best we could do was mark on our physical map an approximation to our current location. That way, we could point them to the… scene… once we were able.

Wayne made the decision to camp for the night. He pointed out that wandering in the dark wasn't wise. Didn't bode well for survival. Queenie was vehemently against this. She argued with him for a good while, making it known just how unsettled she found our circumstances, peppering her argument with superstitious claims like 'cursed land' and 'tormented souls.' Her temper tantrum didn't win her any favors. In the end, it was Willo who had to calm her down. He assured her that come morning, everything would be different. There'd be enough light to find our way out of the dead patch. We'd make it back to cell coverage. Everything would work out. Queenie looked skeptical, but she relented. She wasn't going to brave a trek in the dark alone. At least, we all hoped she wouldn't be that stupid.

We erected our tents. Wayne took on the task of constructing a meager campfire. The smoke spoiled the air with a putrid smell. We rushed to eat, lest it make our stomachs too queasy. I couldn't help but notice how the trees looked even worse in the dark. Stiff tentacles, or fingers barbed with unfiled nails, scratching at the black canvas. The air grew cold, and I shivered. Gooseflesh infected me.

Just as Wayne was dousing the flames, Willo hopped up from his seat and hollered, frantically pointing. We all saw it: red beams streaking from the sky. They swayed like searchlights; the kind associated with an old-timey circus. But their source point came from the air, not the ground, as if they were attached to aircraft. The valley below us cowered under their judgment.

Queenie was shrieking. "What are those things? *What are they?*"

No one answered.

Because none of us *had* an answer.

I was hypnotized, even as one of the beams came sweeping up from the valley at us. Noise came with it, the sound of a million wasps. But then it doubled back, sparing our campsite. Like deer in headlights, we stood there frozen. Watched the restless beams. Then one of them stilled. I noticed nothing special about its focus–just more trees amongst endless woodland. But there came an ear-splitting shriek in the valley. Dozens of logs and branches skyrocketed upward. Something smaller, too. It stood out from the other debris. Looked… not like a tree. It careened wildly into the thinning scope of light.

It reached the pinprick of the light's genesis.

Then it was lost. The shrieking abruptly ended.

Hell broke loose. Queenie began hyperventilating and bolted for her tent. Willo rushed after her, but she zipped herself in. He stood outside, shouting at her. I had turned to watch them, so I missed the sudden vanishing of the light beams. Sebastian and Wayne hollered when it happened, drawing back my attention. Nothing but darkness around us now. The buzzing faded gradually until it was quiet.

Very, very quiet. No crickets. No croaking frogs.

Quiet.

"What was that?" one of us asked, though I can't recall which of us it was. Regardless, none of us were quick to theorize. A tense silence bewitched us, aside from Willo, who was still trying to coerce Queenie to respond.

"Maybe… maybe it was a rescue." Sebastian said this slowly, but the rest of this theory came out in a torrent, as if a quick answer would put this all to rest. "Yeah, yeah, like, those lights were coming from helicopters. Someone must have gotten lost out there. Turned around. Maybe somebody called them in as missing. They were probably hurt. That's why they screamed."

"I didn't see a line," said Wayne.

"A line?"

"Rope. Cord. If that was a rescue, and the thing flying in the air was a person, there should've been a line connecting the copter to the gurney."

"Oh." Sebastian grew quiet, but not for long. "It's dark out. We probably just couldn't see it. I bet if that had happened during the day, we wouldn't be so confused by it."

Wayne didn't argue the point. Neither did I. Maybe Sebastian was right. It just didn't seem like a rescue. The scream wasn't right. Not of pain, or the kind a lost man might make when salvation finally arrived. That was a scream of fear.

Fear and surprise.

And the log–person–whatever it was, had spiraled wrong. Not like a gurney should have. It'd gone head over heels, over and over and over again. And what about all that tree debris rising upward too?

But I didn't voice these discrepancies. Sebastian had to be right.

It'd been a rescue.

***

I joined Willo in our tent. He relayed that he'd finally forced his way into Queenie's tent, and found her sitting in the far corner with her knees drawn up to her chest and arms wrapped around her legs, rocking a bit like a scared child. He'd talked her down; told her the lights were gone. She'd laid down after that, not saying much of consequence. A flashlight lit the interior of our tent, and I watched him strip off his boots and socks.

"What do you think that was?" I asked him, keeping my voice a whisper. Didn't want Queenie getting all worked up again.

Willo sighed, shook his head. "Not sure. I didn't like it though."

"Sebastian thinks it was a rescue. He said maybe someone got lost, and those were helicopters pulling the person up."

Willo's eyes met mine. I knew he was thinking the same as me.

Bullshit.

But we didn't have a better explanation.

"Wayne told me about the body."

Willo looked away. Resumed his descent into his sleeping bag. Ignored me.

"Willo."

"I don't want to talk about that."

"I'm your partner. I deserve to know."

"It's not about that. It'll upset you."

"Oh, so you can handle it, but I can't?"

"Enough."

He sounded frustrated. I dropped it. We were all a bit frayed by the day's (and night's) events. But my mind churned as it digested the mystery. Kept me awake longer than Willo. Eventually, I heard snoring. I maneuvered quietly, carefully, despite my beating heart. I knew this was wrong. A violation of trust.

But I deserved to know what he knew.

I retrieved his phone. Tapped my finger on the number grid. Same password as last time. Easy peasy. My hands shook. I managed to open the Photos app.

Jackpot.

There were over a dozen pics from the day. I started with the earliest, worked my way through them chronologically. Flipped through until I got to the dead tree scenery. I hovered over the first. It was hard to make out what I was looking at. An irregular form lying on the ground, several yards away from the photographer (Willo). It blended too much with the ghastly palette around it.

I swiped to the next pic.

Closer now. Only a yard or so away. My skin ran cold. Definitely a skeleton. Prostrate on the ground, no flesh left on its bones. Caked in a crusty layer of dirt. There were odd, curving lines near the feet.

Swipe.

Very close now, right up on it. Could make out the tattered ropes around its ankles. They trailed off-screen, so I swiped again. The camera angle lifted, the skeletal feet still in the lower right corner, but the rope was the focus. It trailed to two small boulders, to which it had been wrapped around and knotted. It took me a minute to tease out the implication.

Anchors.

Maybe it was my exhaustion, but I couldn't make sense of this.

Swipe.

Back to the skeleton, tighter on its upper region. The arms were stretched out. I saw something jutting from the palms. Zoomed in.

Metal stakes.

My stomach twisted.

The fuck.

That was the last pic. I ran through them again, and then again, and yet again. I wasn't an expert, had no idea how to date the remains. If all the flesh was gone, it'd been awhile, right? But animals might have sped up that process. No blood on the scene either. This bothered me, along with something else I couldn't put my finger on. It wasn't until I'd exited the app, locked the phone, placed it back near Willo, and laid my head on the pillow that it hit me.

No clothes. Not one tattered piece, not even a shoe.

This person had died in the nude.

4

I woke up to the sound of a pig.

My body locked up.

A boar?

I listened. Blind inside a dark tent.

More grunts. My skin crawled. I had visions of a snarling beast, tusks drooling with snot. That clogged noise, the snot shriveling back up like worms every time it inhaled. If not a boar, then a person choking, gagging, struggling to breathe.

Wait.

I rolled over, gently tapped the space where Willo should be. A part of me expected empty space. The snorts were him and Sebastian. Finally hooking up.

But my fingers brushed skin, and I realized (much to my relief, I will confess) that I wasn't alone in the tent. I waited for Willo to wake, but he didn't. The snorts, the grunts, grew louder. Despite my better judgement, I emerged from my cocoon, unzipped the tent, and peeked out. Pointless. It was still night. Deep night. The creature might be mere feet away and I wouldn't see it.

Another drawn-out snort. I whipped my gaze to the other tents. Maybe it was just an ugly snore from one of them. But the noises kept coming, garbled and inconsistent. Closer to Queenie's tent, past Wayne and Sebastian's. If it *was* a boar…

I mustered weak courage after flipping my phone's light on, shined it first at the tents, then everywhere else I could manage to cast it. Stiff tongues of bark everywhere. No signs of life. I thought of going back to bed. But I worried over Queenie. So, I ducked out of the tent, hobbled over to hers. Pebbles, twigs, all manner of sharp things punctured my socks during the short trek. I caught whiffs of a strong, herby smell as I passed the boy's tent. Marijuana. Maybe that was why Willo was sleeping so deeply. He and Sebastian had probably shared a few puffs.

Standing just outside Queenie's tent, I heard the noises again, clearly originating from within. My worry thickened. I unzipped the tent, hissed her name, shoved my phone's light past the flaps–

Something between a gasp and a yelp escaped me.

No, no, no, no–what the fuck–

Thick globs of–

what? Mucus? Ropes of snot? Worms? –

drooled out of Queenie's nose and mouth. Just floated there above her, collecting and growing like a white tumor.

Queenie writhed in her sleeping bag. The streams of snot garbled her voice. It was her I'd been hearing: those awful pig snorts. I'd barely arrived at this realization when she grew stiff, arched her back, croaked like a swamp frog. Other weird noises came from her, a stream of them. Wait… words? She was speaking? That couldn't be her voice; she didn't sound like that, this was deep, this was guttural and thick and toxic. The language wasn't even English. Nothing I'd ever heard. It was different, wrong, old, cursed. A draconic tongue that rasped against the throat, harsh enough that I feared for Queenie, that she might incur injury.

Yet her lips never moved. Sludge continued to spool out of her orifices.

I lunged for her. Had to wake her.

She responded by digging her nails into my skin and thrashing against my grip. The words raked out even faster now. They carried a kind of heat that stank. I gagged with ill timing: we tumbled into the snot orb, and it splattered on me, some on my tongue. It tasted bitter. Felt like congealed pudding against my skin.

I shouted at her, shook her hard.

That deranged voice, shrieking at me continued.

Then it was over. I was still shouting, but I could hear myself again. Queenie was coughing, sputtering, choking, spitting out that gunk. Followed by whimpers. Followed by reality setting in. She bucked, yanked free of my grip, all the while looking about frantically, not grasping who I was, why I was in her tent at this hour. It didn't help when the others arrived, pushing their faces in, shouting at us to explain. Queenie had had enough. She pushed past me, past the others outside, and bolted. Everyone had their phone lights on, and their beams followed her staggering form. She didn't go far, just to the campfire's ashes, where she bent over at the waist, hands to face.

And sobbed.

Willo rushed to her side. The rest of us stood at the tent line, bewildered. Wayne turned to me, caught in my phone's light like an angry sasquatch. "What happened?"

"I don't know," I answered. "I heard noises coming from her tent, so I went to go check on her, and I found–" My mind snagged at the rest of the memory, unwilling to process anything after opening the flaps to Queenie's tent. My mouth worked, shutting and closing, but only squeaky air came out.

"Did you hurt her?"

Was he–was he seriously suggesting–

I stared at him, daring him to repeat himself. Sebastian tried to interject, murmuring his partner's name, but Wayne ignored this and asked the question again.

"Of course I didn't hurt her."

"Then what happened?"

Sebastian repeated Wayne's name, firmer this time, but this did nothing, just like before.

"She was babbling in her sleep," I said, "and she had–mucus, slobber, whatever the fuck you wanna call it–coming out of her nose and mouth. Go see for yourself."

Wayne did just that. With him gone, I turned my attention back to Queenie and Willo and dared to approach. I wasn't allowed close. Willo shot his arm up, signaling that I keep my distance. I complied. Queenie's head was down; she was still crying. I backed away slowly, rejoined the other men. Wayne had re-emerged from Queenie's tent. He regarded me with a wary, but less accusatory look. "What is all that stuff in there?" he asked. I told him I had no idea, and he let it go.

"Maybe she ate something," said Sebastian. Another bullshit theory, like the helicopter rescue.

Willo tore himself from his sister. He looked worn out. Frayed at the edges.

"Do any of you have a signal?" he asked. I didn't dare hope for such a miracle, but we all checked our phones anyway. No such luck. No fucking signal. "I need to get her out of here. She's not… doing well."

"What does that mean?" asked Wayne. "Is she cracking?"

"She's tired and upset," said Willo. "Just like the rest of us. She didn't like the lights."

Sebastian huffed. "Well, no shit. None of us did. But we're in the middle of the woods, in the middle of the night. We can't do anything until morning."

"She needs to sleep," said Wayne. "We all do."

"I don't think she's going to sleep," said Willo. "She's…" He sighed through his nostrils. "…worked up, I guess. Convinced we're in danger."

"Danger? What kind of danger?" Sebastian asked, and I could hear the suppressed worry in his voice.

"There's no danger," Willo assured us. "She's just upset. Maybe she had a bad dream." He glanced at me when he said this. "If we can't call for help, then let's just try to go back to sleep. Tomorrow, we get the fuck out of here."

Queenie entered the coven of phone light. We said nothing, wary of spooking her. She ignored us. Before we could react, she wrestled her tent and dragged it out of sight. Willo called after her, but she didn't respond. We heard the rustling of the plastic, then the soft crunch of her boots returning. She entered the cold light again, empty-handed.

"Burn it in the morning."

***

I found the discarded tent while urinating.

Queenie hadn't taken it far, maybe twenty feet from camp. She'd dumped it haphazardly so that it sat frumpy on uneven ground. I'm not sure what possessed me to investigate further. Perhaps I expected daylight to clear up the lingering dread of the previous night. Prove to me that it hadn't been as bad as it'd seemed. I lifted the flaps, poked my head in, fully expecting to find dried vomit.

White splattered the interior. Definitely not vomit. More like bird shit flung everywhere.

A grotesque face hid under the muck. Stared back at me. I recoiled with a whimper and braced myself.

But nothing happened. I inched forward again. It was a trick of the eye. Pareidolia at its finest. I couldn't shake it, though. Every time I glanced over at that particular glob, my mind registered a face with a gaping jaw. Was it laughing or shrieking?

Queenie's instructions came back to me.

I went back to the camp to retrieve some matches and found Wayne standing with tin cup in hand. I explained my intentions. He caught my unspoken request and joined me. After we cleared the mulch around the tent, I set it ablaze. Something–the flames feasting on nylon and polyester, I suppose–emitted a shrill noise. As the flames grew, so did that whine. Sounded too much like a person screeching.

Or maybe it was just Queenie.

Because all of the sudden all of a sudden she was right there, trying to put out the fire, screaming obscenities at us, demanding why I put fire to the 'golem.' Willo and Sebastian came bounding over, groggy and pissed off. I felt a twinge of anger; subtle body language suggested they'd been engaged in something intimate. Queenie lost the fight with the fire and watched the tent's demise with a snarl on her lips. Willo approached her, but she turned on him and snapped her teeth at him, like she was a goddamn animal. She even growled at him.

Deranged banshee shit.

***

Breakfast was a depressing ordeal, full of noncommittal grunts and haggard body language, as if the lot of us were a tribal village still evolving beyond rudimentary communication. The eggs tasted sour. Just bad. And Wayne burnt the toast.

Queenie remained aloof and antisocial. Picked at her food, obsessively glancing over in the direction of her expired tent. When she wasn't doing that, she was shooting me glares, the kind that had me worrying over my safety. After a few of those, I kept my gaze averted.

Wayne started dismantling the campsite. I jumped up, eager to get the hell out of this hellscape, and set to the task of breaking down my tent.

No one saw it happen.

One moment we were moving about the camp like zombies. Then bone-chilling wails, the kind that make a man's insides curdle. I turned around and saw a walking sheet of fire. I'd never heard a living creature make that kind of sound. Nor had I ever witnessed a creature burn to death–still alive, still breathing, still capable of feeling the flames eat at their skin and elicit noises not fit for the tongue or the lungs. Endless, breathless screams.

Time slowed.

Willo and Sebastian paraded around the spectacle, shouting and panicking.

Queenie, like me, watched this unfold. But she had her arms up like a zealot churchgoer stirred by a mysterious spirit. Her expression… she looked ecstatic. Pleased and aroused. At her feet, the lighter fluid.

The scene turned a blood red. Like someone put a red filter on the sun, the shift so abrupt that we all cried out and hid our faces. Except Wayne. He was still screaming. His flames went from orange to crystal white.

The sound of a thousand wasps.

Ascent started slow. Weight abandoned us. I felt myself float off the ground, an astronaut with no gravity.

Liftoff.

The red grew brighter. Brighter.

Uprooted trees spiraled around me. I glimpsed a crisp husk at one point. Wayne wasn't screaming anymore. The others were.

Blinding bright.

Before the end, far too late, I understood–

OTHER HELLBOUND BOOKS
www.hellboundbooks.com

Anthology of Extreme Horror

If you prefer to take your horror yarns with copious amounts of spilled blood, eviscerated guts, dollops of messy gore, and dark, disturbing themes, then boy howdy, does HellBound Books have a terrifying treat in store for you!

If not, please not this book is definitely *not* for the faint of heart!

With a foreword and brand-spanking-new, never-read-before short story by the grand maestro of extreme horror himself, Matt Shaw, this collection of eighteen stomach-churning tales of terror is guaranteed to have the bile rising and heart thumping with each turn of the page.

So, buckle in, dear reader, and brace yourself for a blood-soaked ride littered with assorted body parts and particularly nasty doers of evil. And, for heaven's sakes, please don't attempt to eat while you're reading this anthology!

You have been warned…

Eighteen exceptional tales from: Matt Shaw, Taylor Z. Adams, Priyanuj Mazumdar, Gabriel Giddings, Dave Davis, Paul Lonardo, Anthony Ferguson, Keith Durocher, Ronan Grey, Galo Romero, Kira Blackwood, James Patrick Riser, Dewey L. Yeatts, Daniel Rust, Brit Jones, HellBound Books' very own James H Longmore, and British national treasure, Joe Pasquale

Anthology of Splatterpunk Volume II

splat·ter·punk
noun
informal
noun: splatterpunk
Definition: "A literary genre characterized by graphically described scenes of an extremely gory nature."

Welcome once again, fellow gore lovers, to HellBound Books' second foray into the deliciously bloody, innards-strewn world of splatterpunk!

Death, dismemberment, and destruction abound within these pages, as we bring to you nineteen perfectly ghoulish tales of terror that are definitely not to be read while eating!

Go on, we dare you!

You have short tales from: Shannon Blake Skelton, Juan Ozuna, Sarah Moon, Seaton Kay-Smith, S.C. Vincent, S. Michael Wilson, Carson Demmans, Diana Parrilla, Michael Errol Swaim, John Schlimm, P.J. Verfall, Karly Foland, W.L. Lewis, Caleb James K., Brian J. Smith, D.J. Tuskmor, Terry Grimwood, Dave Davis, and Paul Allih.

Anthology of Creature Features

Come on, admit it, we all love a gripping tale of our fellow creatures gone bad. Think *Jaws*, *The Rats*, *The Crabs*, *Pede*, *Them!* – the list is practically endless (hell, they even made a movie about killer bunny rabbits! *Night of the Lepus*, 1972, anyone?).

There's just something so inherently terrifying about the animals we see every day and take for granted are going to stay in their dens, burrows, nests, swamps, and crevices going on a murderous rampage of mayhem and outright slaughter against us poor human beings. Knowing what they are truly capable of has us keeping one wary eye on the critters, that's for sure.

And so, gathered within the pages of this skin-crawling, nerve-jangling anthology, you'll discover a collection of the most horrifying examples of Mother Nature gone psycho we could unearth. We have killer goldfish, a murderous mantis, a hellish giant arachnid, giant lizards, turtles, something altogether indescribable with tentacles, and so much more. Heck, there's even a tale of butterflies we guarantee will chill you to your very soul!

Featuring zoological tales of terror from: *Tim Newton Anderson, R. D. Tyler, Chad Barger, Seaton Kay-Smith, Milan Kovačević, Julien Jayus, Robb White, Serena Daniels, Rose Strickman, Janna Layton, J. Neira*, and the amazing *Cliff McNish.*

The Last Customer

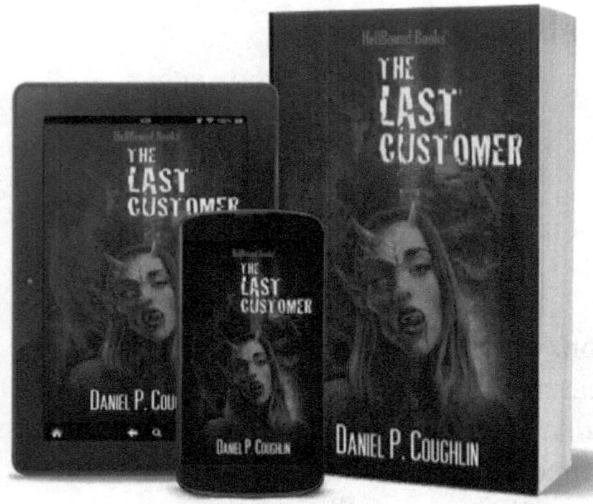

One hot August evening in the small town of Dodge Junction, Wisconsin, Win and Garth Gasper close their family-owned liquor store for the night.

When the demons Sammael and Jezebeth show up in search of Father Leslie Gardner—the priest that many years ago exorcised Sammael—the Gaspers are forced to confront the most terrifying customers they have ever experienced!

Up the hill from the liquor store, Father Gardner senses he is being challenged by the demons. Unable to ignore their foul presence, he makes his way to where the demons have kicked off their destructively sinister plans for the evening.

Now, Garth, Win, Gardner and three unexpected armed robbers must fight their way out of the liquor store where their flesh and souls are being shredded by the denizens of Hell.

Father Gardner must revisit his terrifying past and renew his faith to defeat the nastiest demon he's ever encountered and protect the lives of his neighbors against the last - and by far the worst - customer of the night.

And Then You Die

Following a drunken, hedonistic night out in New Orleans, highly successful businesswoman and sexual deviant, Claire Jepson, accidentally soils herself in her car. The resulting excrement comes to life as a sardonic fecal spirit, and not only dishes out a gruesome death to Claire's unfaithful, gold-digging fiancé, but also thwarts a kidnap/murder plot by her employees. It then introduces Claire to a world of depraved pleasures beyond her imagination.

A year later, the errant spirit has spiraled wildly out of control - its insatiable appetite for perverted sex and human flesh and has destroyed Claire's life. Then, to her horror, Claire discovers the fecal spirit must consume her unborn child to attain immortality; she must return to the seedy underbelly of the Big Easy in a heart-pounding race against time to confront the spirit's creator - a high priest of an ancient, deadly order, who is the only one who can put a stop to the spirit's murderous intentions.

A wicked, fast-paced story laced with tongue-in-cheek, dark humor, which is at the same time incredibly erotic and stomach churning. Most definitely not one to be read whilst eating!

Anthology of Bizarro

Welcome to the wonderfully horrific world of Bizarro - that dark, forbidding corner of the horror genre where absolutely anything goes and one may delve into the farthest recesses of the authors' warped imaginations.

Prepare yourself, dear reader, for a journey into the unknown reaches of terror, from which you can only hope you will return with your sanity intact...

Enjoy 16 outstanding stories from:

Scott McGregor, A.L. King, Garvan Giltinan, Keith Kennedy, Robert Prescott, T.M. Morgan, Lee Rozelle, John W. Leonard, A.L. King, Matthew McKiernan, Aron Beauregard, Ken Goldman, Victor Marrow, Ryan Woods, and Stephen Daultrey

A HellBound Books Publishing LLC Publication

www.hellboundbooks.com

9 781966 296140